Hugo Pratt

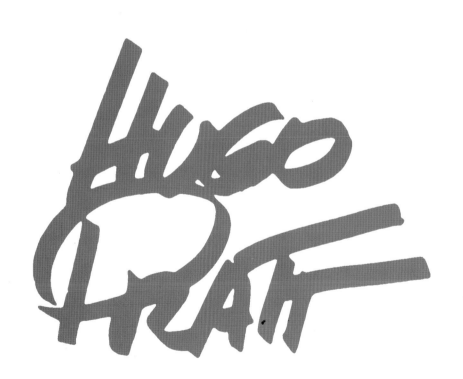

EDITED AND DESIGNED BY Dean Mullaney
ART DIRECTOR AND CO-COVER DESIGNER Lorraine Turner
CONSULTING EDITOR Patrizia Zanotti

Lettering font based on hand-lettering by Frank Engli.

EuroComics.us

EuroComics is an imprint of
IDW Publishing
a Division of Idea and Design Works, LLC
5080 Santa Fe Street
San Diego, CA 92109
www.idwpublishing.com

Distributed by Diamond Book Distributors
1-410-560-7100

ISBN: 978-1-63140-065-0
First Printing, December 2014

IDW Publishing
Ted Adams, Chief Executive Officer/Publisher
Greg Goldstein, Chief Operating Officer/President
Robbie Robbins, EVP/Sr. Graphic Artist
Chris Ryall, Chief Creative Officer/Editor-in-Chief
Matthew Ruzicka, CPA, Chief Financial Officer
Alan Payne, VP of Sales
Dirk Wood, VP of Marketing
Lorelei Bunjes, VP of Digital Services

THANKS TO:
Diana Schutz, Greg Goldstein, Dana Renga, Bob Schreck,
Scott Tipton, Justin Eisinger, and Alonzo Simon.

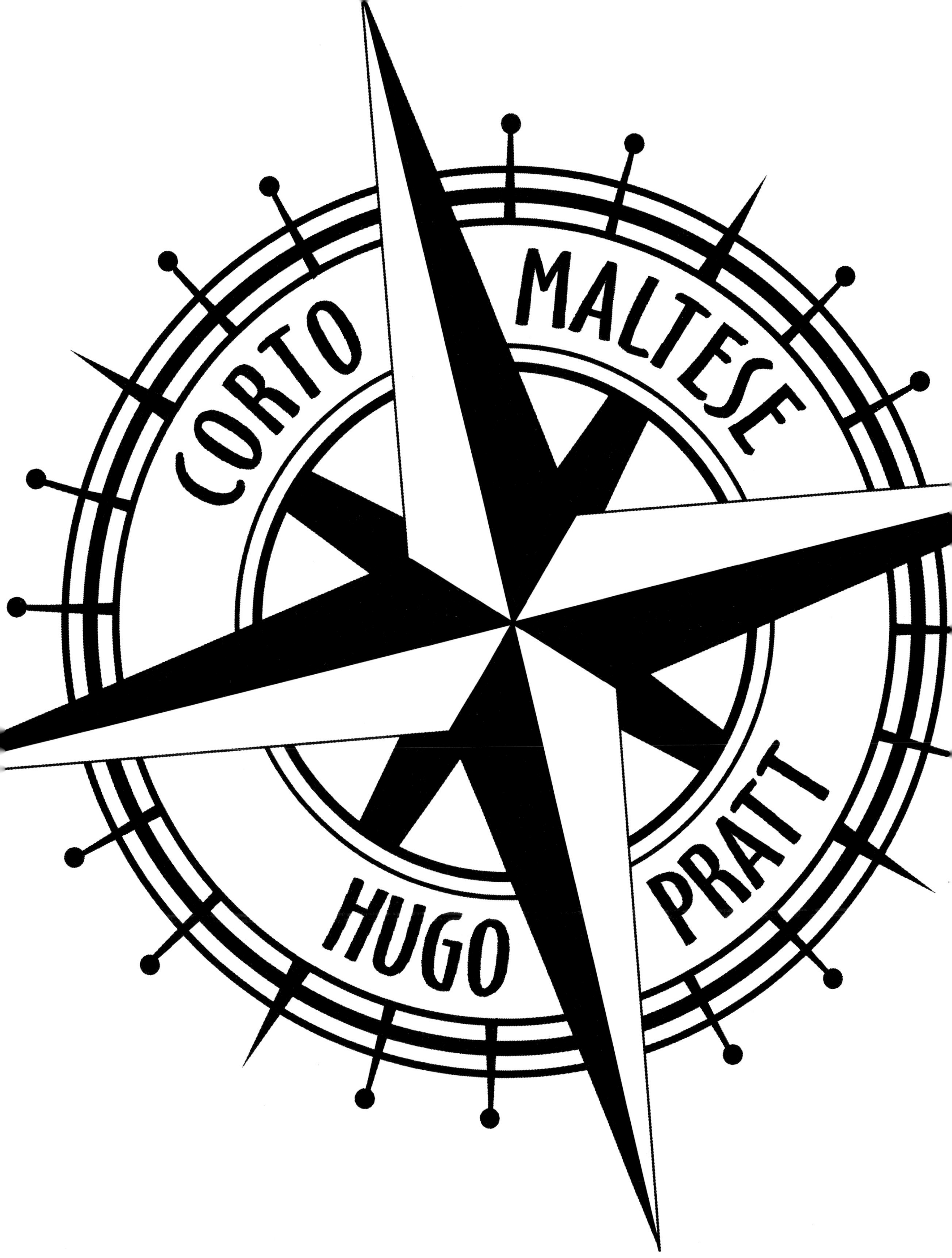
CORTO MALTESE
HUGO PRATT

UNDER THE OF

SIGN CAPRICORN

A CORTO MALTESE *Graphic Novel*

Translated by Dean Mullaney and Simone Castaldi

EURO COMICS
ENGLISH EDITION · GRAPHIC NOVELS

An imprint of IDW PUBLISHING

CHAPTER ONE:

THE SECRET OF
TRISTAN BANTAM

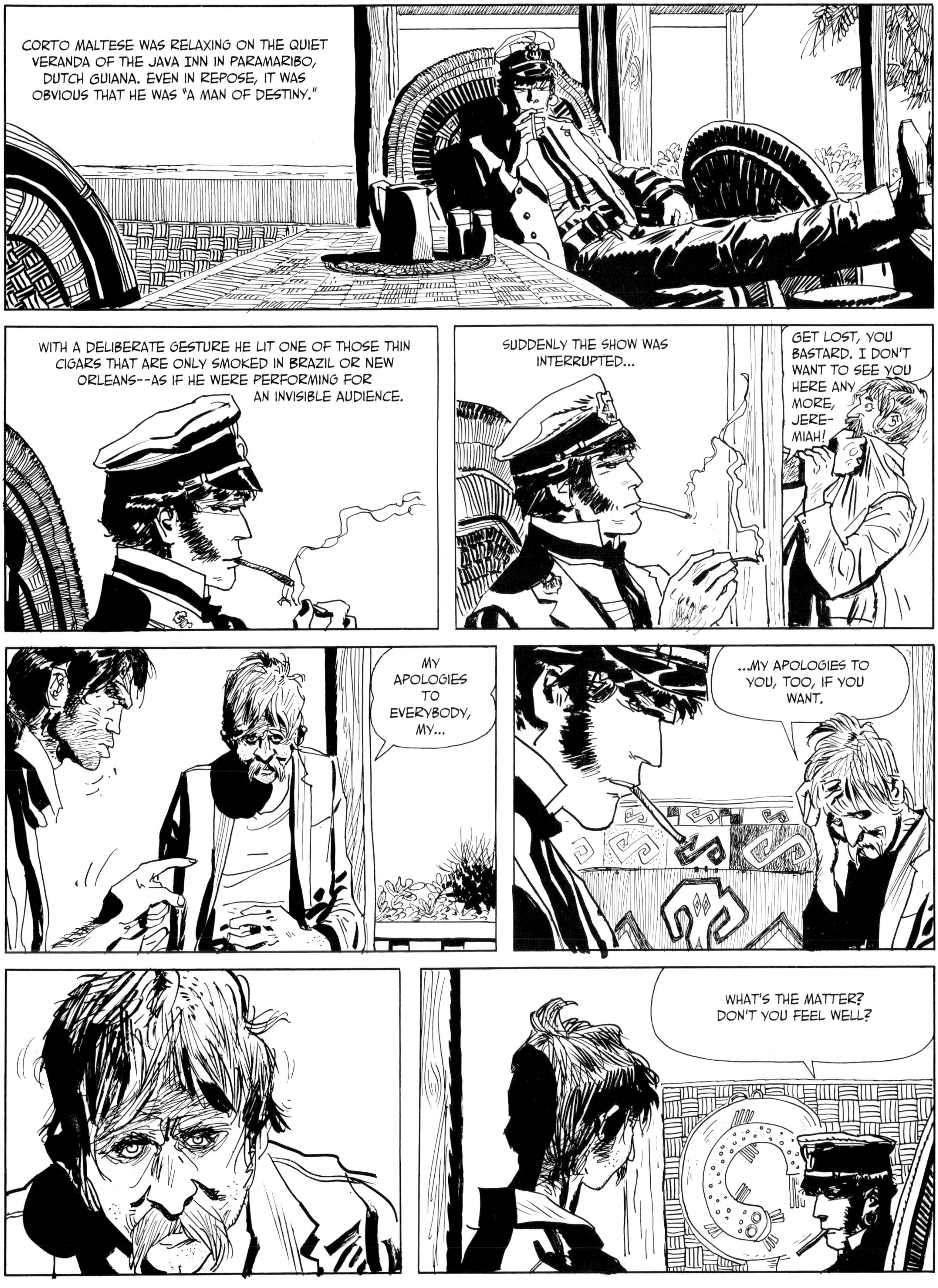
CORTO MALTESE WAS RELAXING ON THE QUIET VERANDA OF THE JAVA INN IN PARAMARIBO, DUTCH GUIANA. EVEN IN REPOSE, IT WAS OBVIOUS THAT HE WAS "A MAN OF DESTINY."
WITH A DELIBERATE GESTURE HE LIT ONE OF THOSE THIN CIGARS THAT ARE ONLY SMOKED IN BRAZIL OR NEW ORLEANS--AS IF HE WERE PERFORMING FOR AN INVISIBLE AUDIENCE.
SUDDENLY THE SHOW WAS INTERRUPTED...
GET LOST, YOU BASTARD. I DON'T WANT TO SEE YOU HERE ANY MORE, JERE-MIAH!
MY APOLOGIES TO EVERYBODY, MY...
...MY APOLOGIES TO YOU, TOO, IF YOU WANT.
WHAT'S THE MATTER? DON'T YOU FEEL WELL?

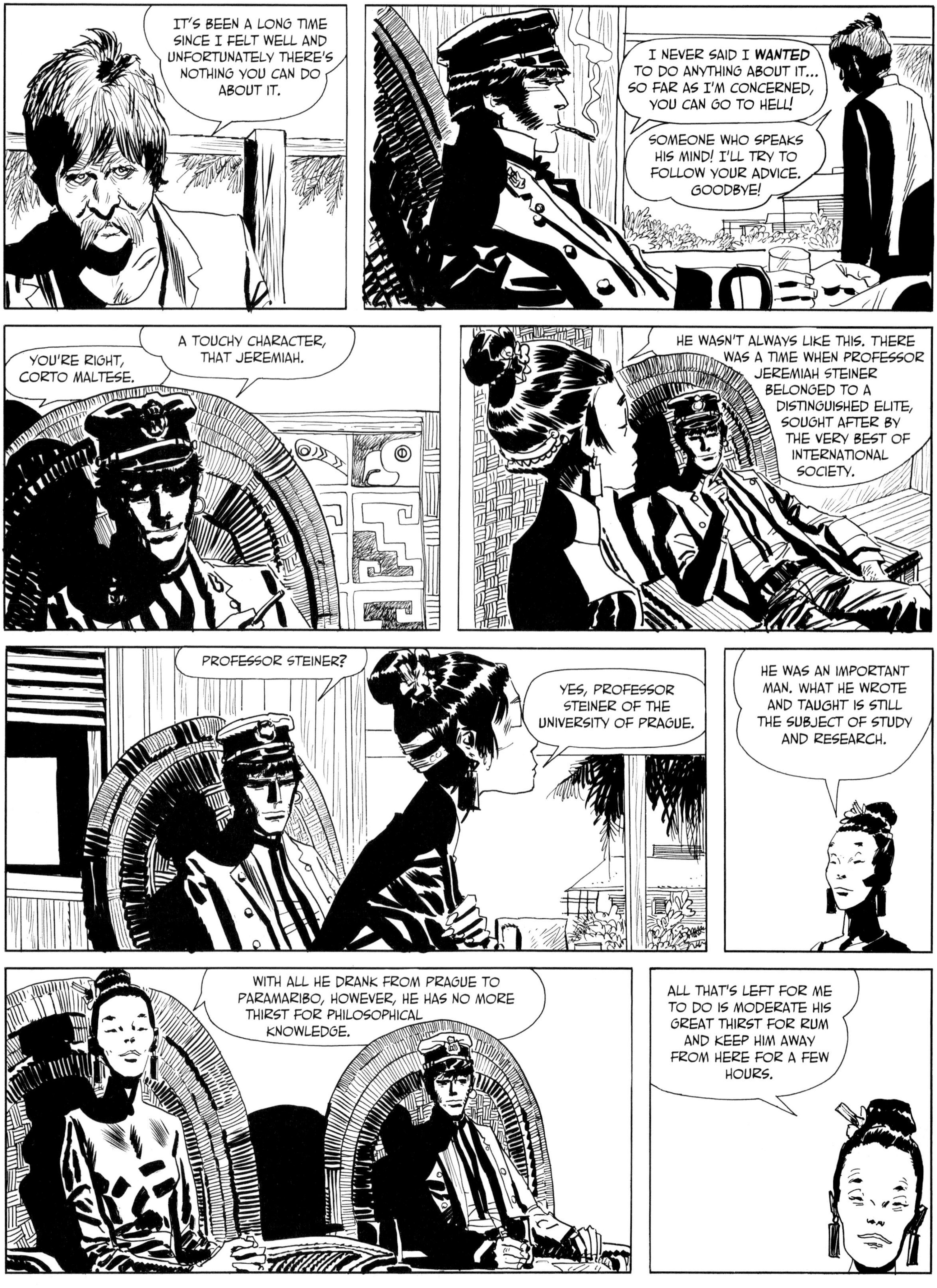
IT'S BEEN A LONG TIME SINCE I FELT WELL AND UNFORTUNATELY THERE'S NOTHING YOU CAN DO ABOUT IT.
I NEVER SAID I **WANTED** TO DO ANYTHING ABOUT IT... SO FAR AS I'M CONCERNED, YOU CAN GO TO HELL!
SOMEONE WHO SPEAKS HIS MIND! I'LL TRY TO FOLLOW YOUR ADVICE. GOODBYE!
A TOUCHY CHARACTER, THAT JEREMIAH.
YOU'RE RIGHT, CORTO MALTESE.
HE WASN'T ALWAYS LIKE THIS. THERE WAS A TIME WHEN PROFESSOR JEREMIAH STEINER BELONGED TO A DISTINGUISHED ELITE, SOUGHT AFTER BY THE VERY BEST OF INTERNATIONAL SOCIETY.
PROFESSOR STEINER?
YES, PROFESSOR STEINER OF THE UNIVERSITY OF PRAGUE.
HE WAS AN IMPORTANT MAN. WHAT HE WROTE AND TAUGHT IS STILL THE SUBJECT OF STUDY AND RESEARCH.
WITH ALL HE DRANK FROM PRAGUE TO PARAMARIBO, HOWEVER, HE HAS NO MORE THIRST FOR PHILOSOPHICAL KNOWLEDGE.
ALL THAT'S LEFT FOR ME TO DO IS MODERATE HIS GREAT THIRST FOR RUM AND KEEP HIM AWAY FROM HERE FOR A FEW HOURS.

HERE'S A NEW ASPECT OF YOUR PERSONALITY. YOU NEVER STRUCK ME AS THE CHARITABLE TYPE. DO YOU DO IT FOR HIS OWN GOOD OR BECAUSE HE DOESN'T PAY FOR WHAT HE DRINKS?

YOU JUDGE OTHERS BASED ON YOUR OWN VIEW, CORTO MALTESE. BUT THIS TIME YOU'RE WRONG. I HAVE THE HIGHEST ESTEEM FOR PROFESSOR STEINER.

GOOD DAY! IS THIS MADAME JAVA'S INN?

MY NAME IS...

I AM MADAME JAVA.

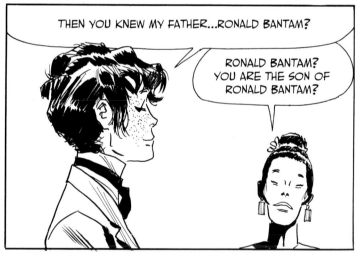

THEN YOU KNEW MY FATHER...RONALD BANTAM?

RONALD BANTAM? YOU ARE THE SON OF RONALD BANTAM?

YES, MA'AM. MY FATHER TOLD ME A LOT ABOUT YOU ...BEFORE HE DIED.

YOUR FATHER WAS A DEAR FRIEND AND HIS DEATH SADDENS ME.

AHEM! PARDON ME, "MADAME JAVA," BUT I SEE THAT YOU'RE BUSY AT THE MOMENT. I'LL GO DOWN TO THE PORT AND HAVE A LOOK AT MY BOAT.

VERY WELL. I'LL SEE YOU TONIGHT.

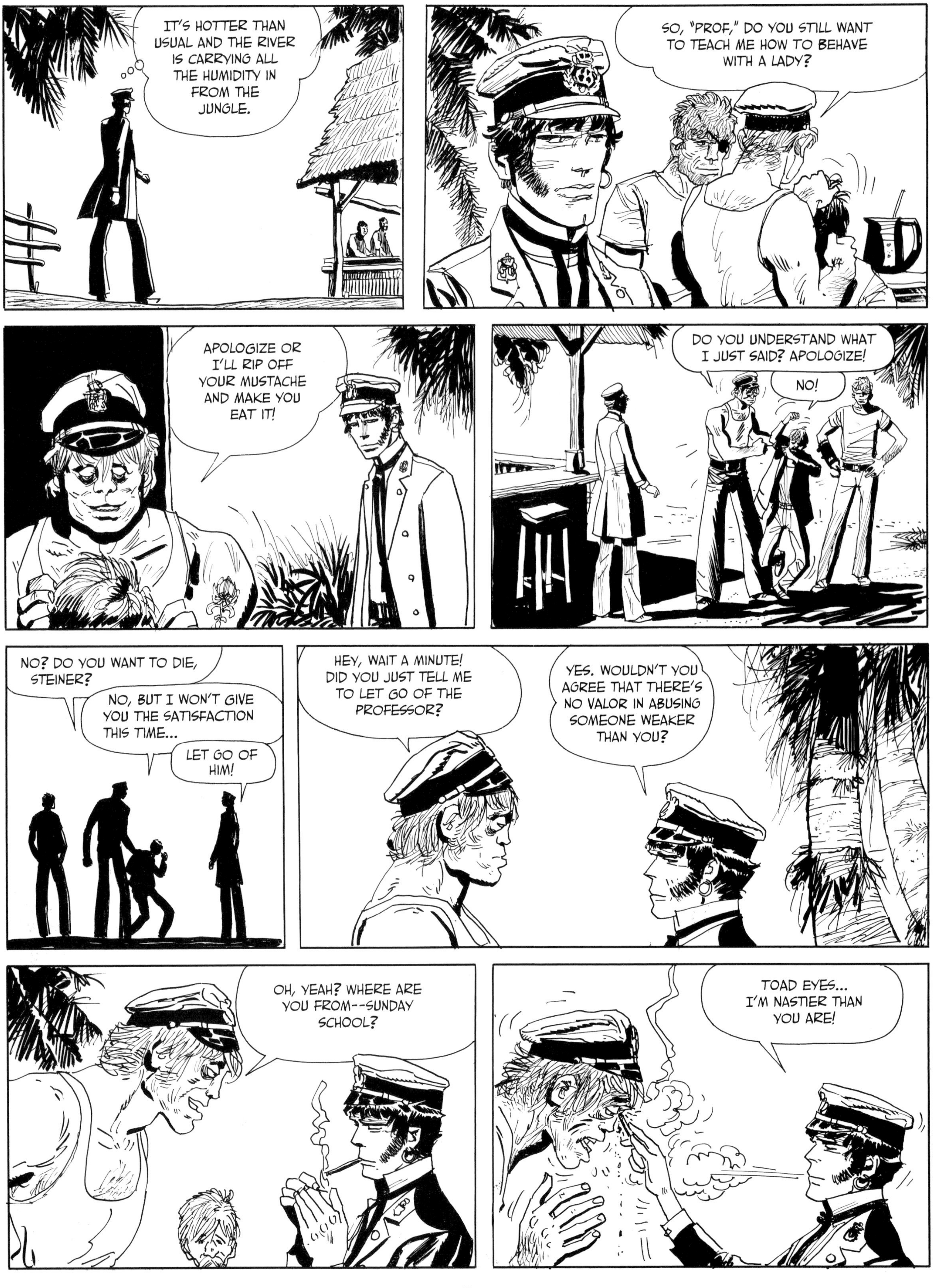
IT'S HOTTER THAN USUAL AND THE RIVER IS CARRYING ALL THE HUMIDITY IN FROM THE JUNGLE.
SO, "PROF," DO YOU STILL WANT TO TEACH ME HOW TO BEHAVE WITH A LADY?
APOLOGIZE OR I'LL RIP OFF YOUR MUSTACHE AND MAKE YOU EAT IT!
DO YOU UNDERSTAND WHAT I JUST SAID? APOLOGIZE!
NO!
NO? DO YOU WANT TO DIE, STEINER?
NO, BUT I WON'T GIVE YOU THE SATISFACTION THIS TIME...
LET GO OF HIM!
HEY, WAIT A MINUTE! DID YOU JUST TELL ME TO LET GO OF THE PROFESSOR?
YES. WOULDN'T YOU AGREE THAT THERE'S NO VALOR IN ABUSING SOMEONE WEAKER THAN YOU?
OH, YEAH? WHERE ARE YOU FROM--SUNDAY SCHOOL?
TOAD EYES... I'M NASTIER THAN YOU ARE!

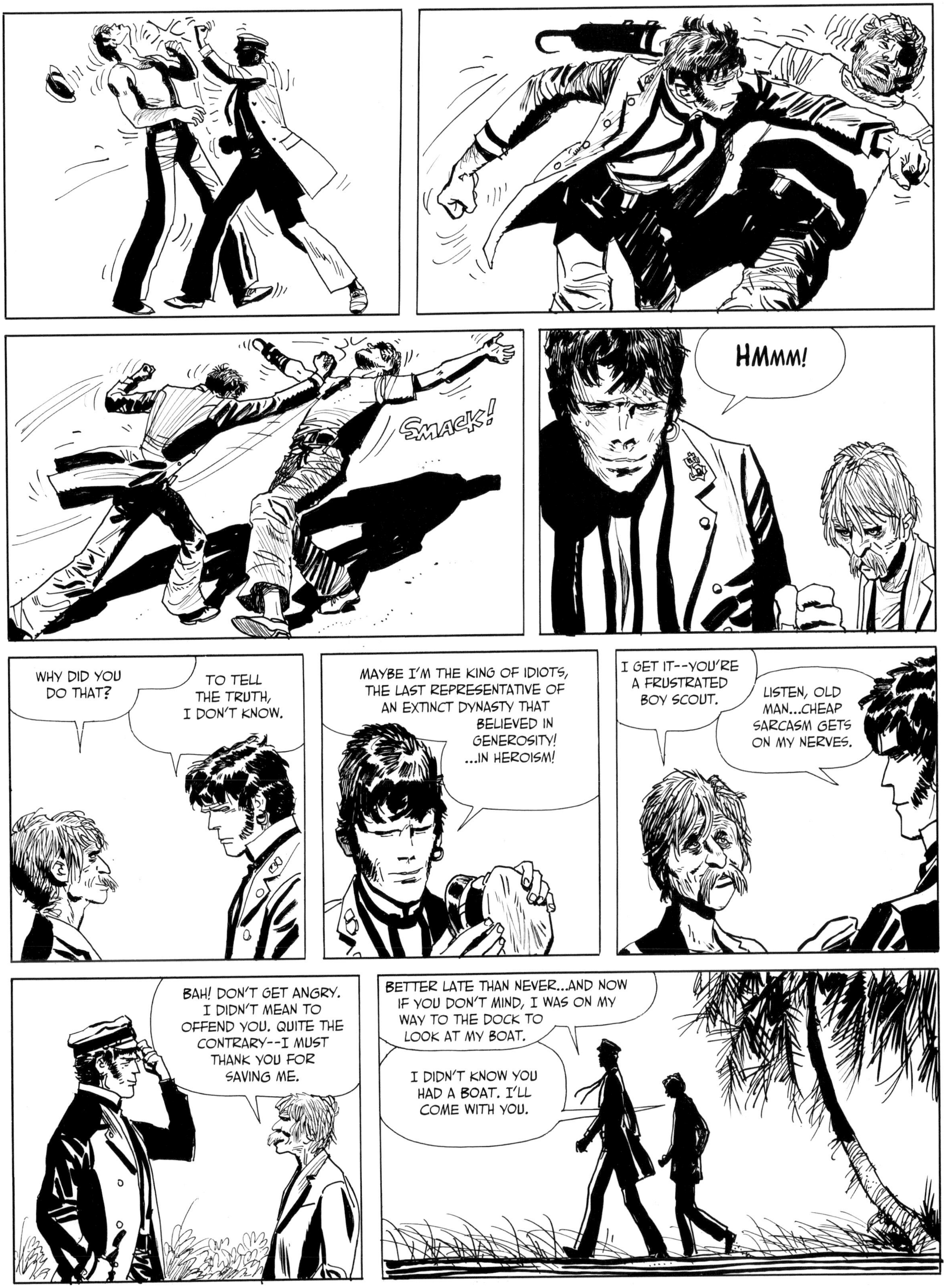
SMACK!
HMMM!
WHY DID YOU DO THAT?
TO TELL THE TRUTH, I DON'T KNOW.
MAYBE I'M THE KING OF IDIOTS, THE LAST REPRESENTATIVE OF AN EXTINCT DYNASTY THAT BELIEVED IN GENEROSITY! ...IN HEROISM!
I GET IT--YOU'RE A FRUSTRATED BOY SCOUT.
LISTEN, OLD MAN...CHEAP SARCASM GETS ON MY NERVES.
BAH! DON'T GET ANGRY. I DIDN'T MEAN TO OFFEND YOU. QUITE THE CONTRARY--I MUST THANK YOU FOR SAVING ME.
BETTER LATE THAN NEVER...AND NOW IF YOU DON'T MIND, I WAS ON MY WAY TO THE DOCK TO LOOK AT MY BOAT.
I DIDN'T KNOW YOU HAD A BOAT. I'LL COME WITH YOU.

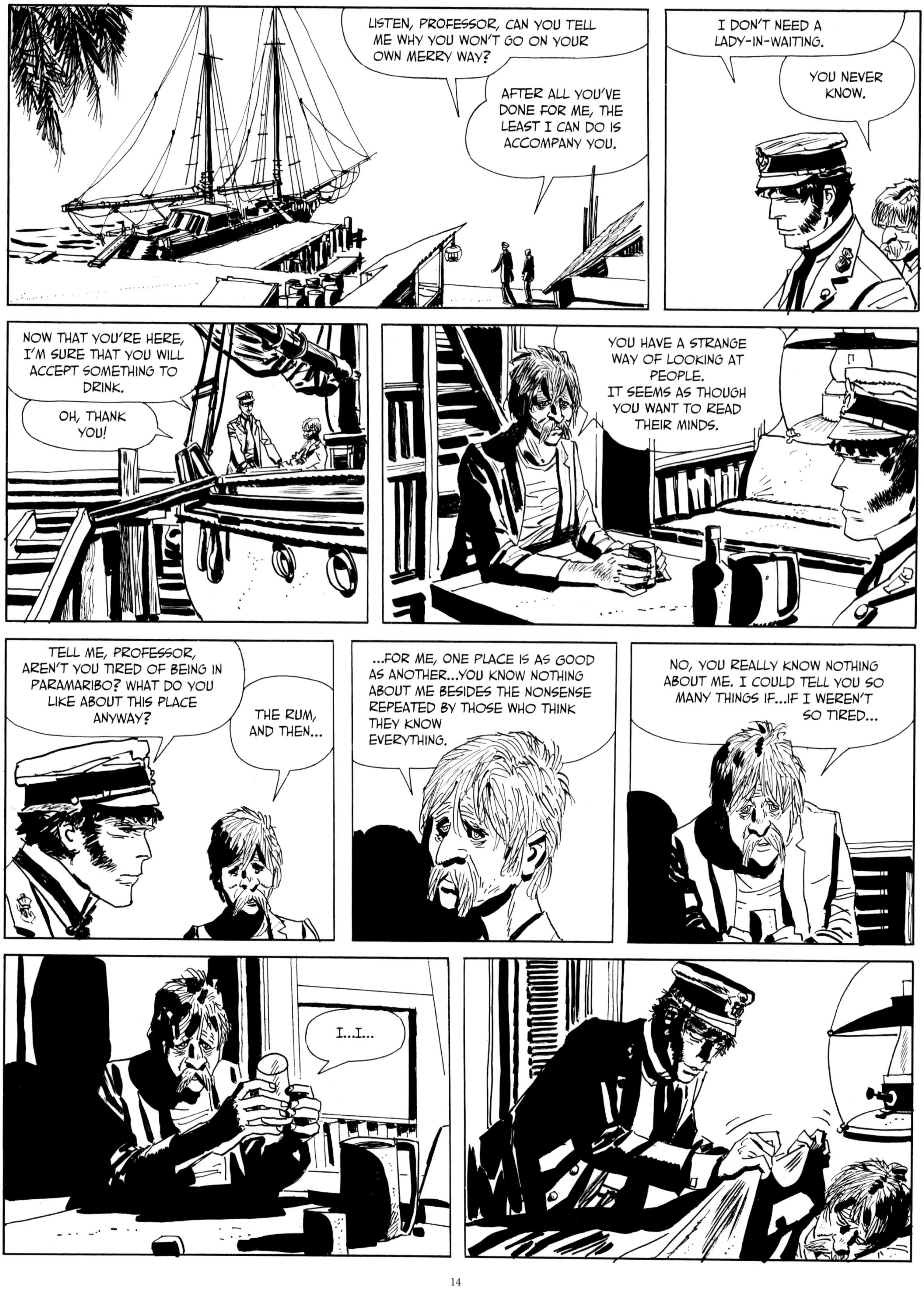

LISTEN, PROFESSOR, CAN YOU TELL ME WHY YOU WON'T GO ON YOUR OWN MERRY WAY?
AFTER ALL YOU'VE DONE FOR ME, THE LEAST I CAN DO IS ACCOMPANY YOU.
I DON'T NEED A LADY-IN-WAITING.
YOU NEVER KNOW.
NOW THAT YOU'RE HERE, I'M SURE THAT YOU WILL ACCEPT SOMETHING TO DRINK.
OH, THANK YOU!
YOU HAVE A STRANGE WAY OF LOOKING AT PEOPLE. IT SEEMS AS THOUGH YOU WANT TO READ THEIR MINDS.
TELL ME, PROFESSOR, AREN'T YOU TIRED OF BEING IN PARAMARIBO? WHAT DO YOU LIKE ABOUT THIS PLACE ANYWAY?
THE RUM, AND THEN...
...FOR ME, ONE PLACE IS AS GOOD AS ANOTHER...YOU KNOW NOTHING ABOUT ME BESIDES THE NONSENSE REPEATED BY THOSE WHO THINK THEY KNOW EVERYTHING.
NO, YOU REALLY KNOW NOTHING ABOUT ME. I COULD TELL YOU SO MANY THINGS IF...IF I WEREN'T SO TIRED...
I...I...

SO NOW I'VE BECOME A BABYSITTER! ...OH, THE LIGHTS ARE STILL ON AT THE INN.

STILL UP, "MADAME JAVA?"

YES. I WAS WAITING FOR YOU, CORTO MALTESE.

THERE'S SOMETHING THAT MIGHT INTEREST YOU--IT CONCERNS THE YOUNG BANTAM YOU MET TODAY. HE NEEDS HELP AND I TOLD HIM YOU'D LISTEN.

AH. THEN I WILL LISTEN TO HIM! WHERE IS HE?

HERE'S CAPTAIN CORTO MALTESE, TRISTAN. IF ANYONE CAN HELP YOU, HE CAN.

THANK YOU, MADAME JAVA, AND THANK YOU, CAPTAIN, FOR YOUR CONSIDERATION.

I'VE OVERCOME GREAT ADVERSITIES TO GET HERE. THANKS TO THE MONEY MY GUARDIAN GAVE ME, I WANT TO CONTINUE THE SEARCH THAT MY FATHER STARTED. I'LL SHOW YOU SOME CORRESPONDENCE AND DOCUMENTS.

HERE ARE A FEW OF THE LETTERS MY FATHER LEFT TO ME. FRANKLY, I COULDN'T UNDERSTAND MUCH. THERE ARE ALSO MAPS...I LOOKED FOR A LONG TIME IN THE ATLAS BUT WASN'T ABLE TO LOCATE ANY OF THESE PLACES.

I HAD THE DOCUMENTS EXAMINED IN LONDON... BY PEOPLE WHO SEEMED VERY INTERESTED IN THE MATTER...

...BUT THEN THINGS GOT COMPLICATED. THEY DEMANDED TOO MUCH MONEY TO HELP ME.

HOW STRANGE. THERE'S SOMETHING INTERESTING HERE...THESE SYMBOLS, THESE SIGNS, REMIND ME OF SOMETHING I ONCE SAW CARVED IN STONE ON AN ISLAND IN THE SOUTH PACIFIC.

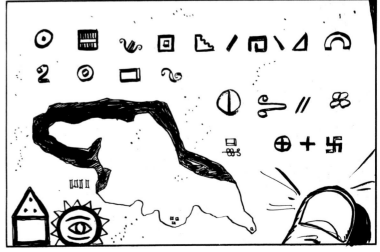

YES, WE HAD STOPPED AT PANAPE AND WHILE EXPLORING THE ISLAND'S INTERIOR I FOUND MYSELF IN FRONT OF AN ANCIENT TEMPLE HIDDEN IN THE JUNGLE. ON ITS PEDIMENT WERE INSCRIBED SYMBOLS SIMILAR TO THESE.

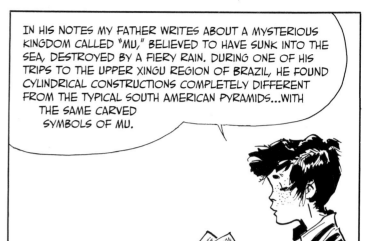

IN HIS NOTES MY FATHER WRITES ABOUT A MYSTERIOUS KINGDOM CALLED "MU," BELIEVED TO HAVE SUNK INTO THE SEA, DESTROYED BY A FIERY RAIN. DURING ONE OF HIS TRIPS TO THE UPPER XINGU REGION OF BRAZIL, HE FOUND CYLINDRICAL CONSTRUCTIONS COMPLETELY DIFFERENT FROM THE TYPICAL SOUTH AMERICAN PYRAMIDS...WITH THE SAME CARVED SYMBOLS OF MU.

HERE HE TALKS OF ANOTHER SERIES OF DOCUMENTS BELONGING TO MISS MORGANA DIAS DO SANTOS BANTAM OF SAN SALVADOR DE BAHIA. WHO IS SHE?

MY SISTER. ACTUALLY, MY HALF SISTER. I'VE NEVER MET HER. AFTER MY FATHER DIVORCED MY MOTHER, HE MARRIED AGAIN IN SOUTH AMERICA, WHERE HE LIVED FOR MANY YEARS.

WHEN MY MOTHER DIED, HE LEFT SOUTH AMERICA TO TAKE CARE OF ME, BUT SHORTLY AFTER, HE FELL SICK AND DIED, TOO.

I REMEMBER SOMETHING STRANGE HAPPENED DURING THAT PERIOD. I CAN'T EXPLAIN...IT WAS AS IF MYSTERIOUS FORCES HAD TAKEN POSSESSION OF OUR HOUSE, OUR BELONGINGS, AND OF OURSELVES...

MY FATHER WOULD OFTEN SAY THAT IT WAS A MESSAGE FROM HIS FRIENDS IN SAN SALVADOR THAT WE MUST RETURN TO HIS HOME IN SOUTH AMERICA. BUT I DIDN'T TAKE HIM SERIOUSLY. I THOUGHT HE WAS DELIRIOUS.

BUT LATER I STARTED HEARING VOICES CALLING ME. THESE VOICES WHISPERED A NAME... "OGUN FERRAILLE."

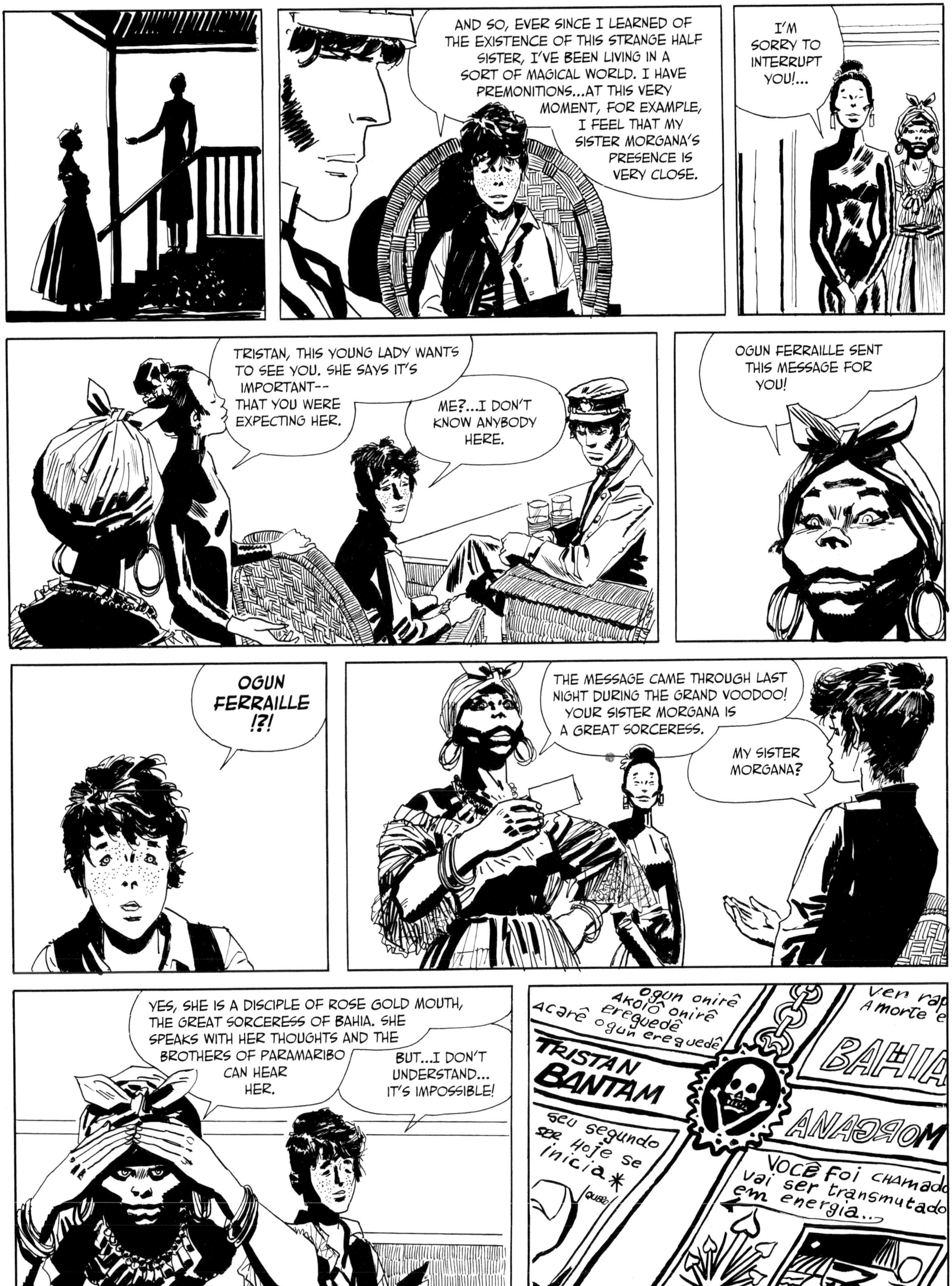

AND SO, EVER SINCE I LEARNED OF THE EXISTENCE OF THIS STRANGE HALF SISTER, I'VE BEEN LIVING IN A SORT OF MAGICAL WORLD. I HAVE PREMONITIONS...AT THIS VERY MOMENT, FOR EXAMPLE, I FEEL THAT MY SISTER MORGANA'S PRESENCE IS VERY CLOSE.
I'M SORRY TO INTERRUPT YOU!...
TRISTAN, THIS YOUNG LADY WANTS TO SEE YOU. SHE SAYS IT'S IMPORTANT-- THAT YOU WERE EXPECTING HER.
ME?...I DON'T KNOW ANYBODY HERE.
OGUN FERRAILLE SENT THIS MESSAGE FOR YOU!
OGUN FERRAILLE !?!
THE MESSAGE CAME THROUGH LAST NIGHT DURING THE GRAND VOODOO! YOUR SISTER MORGANA IS A GREAT SORCERESS.
MY SISTER MORGANA?
YES, SHE IS A DISCIPLE OF ROSE GOLD MOUTH, THE GREAT SORCERESS OF BAHIA. SHE SPEAKS WITH HER THOUGHTS AND THE BROTHERS OF PARAMARIBO CAN HEAR HER.
BUT...I DON'T UNDERSTAND... IT'S IMPOSSIBLE!
ogun onirê
akoiô onirê
ereguedê
acarê ogun ereguedê
ven rap
A morte e
TRISTAN BANTAM
BAHIA
seu segundo se hoje se inicia
VOCÊ Foi chamado vai ser transmutado em energia...

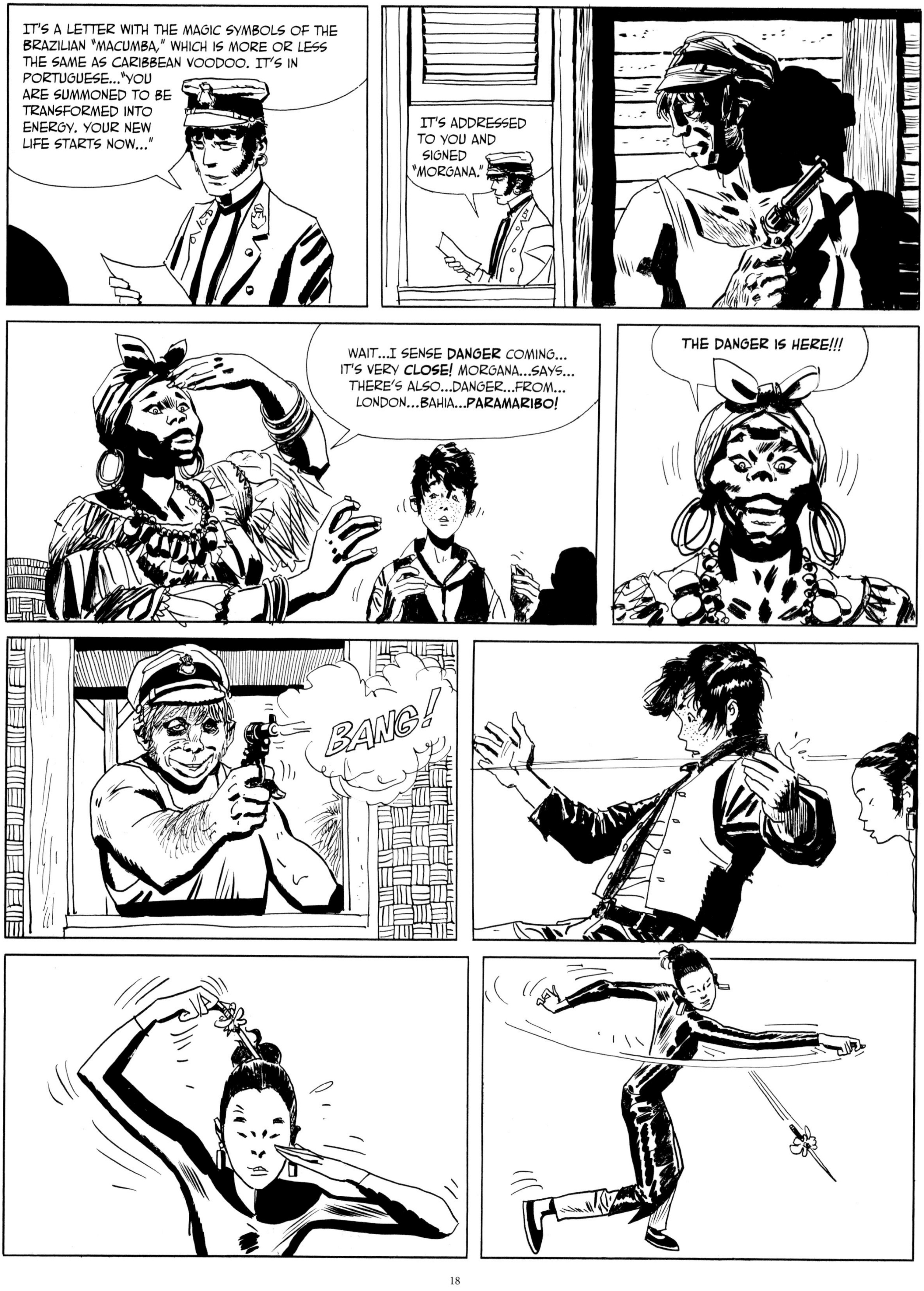
IT'S A LETTER WITH THE MAGIC SYMBOLS OF THE BRAZILIAN "MACUMBA," WHICH IS MORE OR LESS THE SAME AS CARIBBEAN VOODOO. IT'S IN PORTUGUESE..."YOU ARE SUMMONED TO BE TRANSFORMED INTO ENERGY. YOUR NEW LIFE STARTS NOW..."
IT'S ADDRESSED TO YOU AND SIGNED "MORGANA."
WAIT...I SENSE DANGER COMING... IT'S VERY CLOSE! MORGANA...SAYS... THERE'S ALSO...DANGER...FROM... LONDON...BAHIA...PARAMARIBO!
THE DANGER IS HERE!!!
BANG!

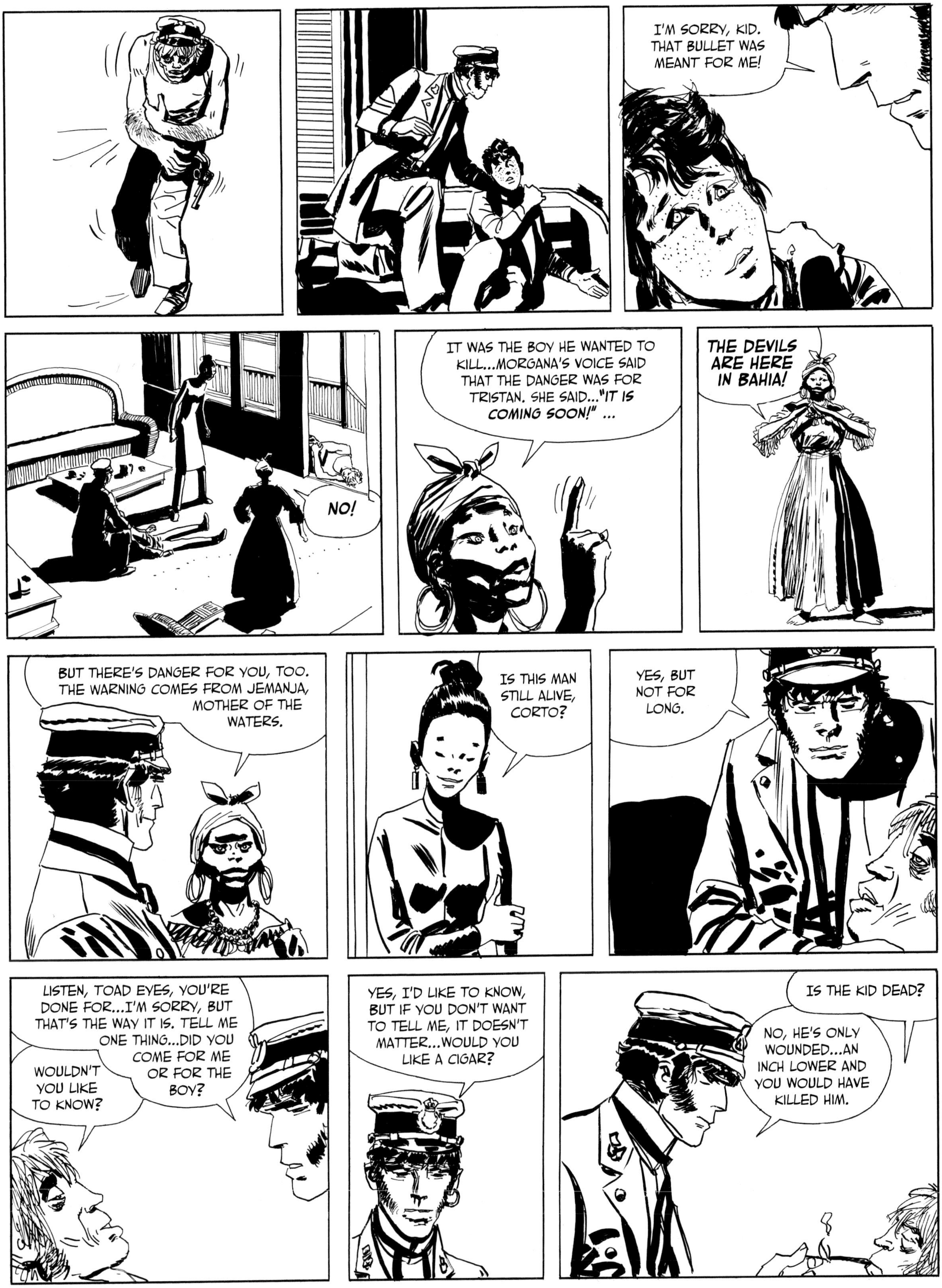
I'M SORRY, KID. THAT BULLET WAS MEANT FOR ME!
NO!
IT WAS THE BOY HE WANTED TO KILL...MORGANA'S VOICE SAID THAT THE DANGER WAS FOR TRISTAN. SHE SAID..."IT IS COMING SOON!" ...
THE DEVILS ARE HERE IN BAHIA!
BUT THERE'S DANGER FOR YOU, TOO. THE WARNING COMES FROM JEMANJA, MOTHER OF THE WATERS.
IS THIS MAN STILL ALIVE, CORTO?
YES, BUT NOT FOR LONG.
LISTEN, TOAD EYES, YOU'RE DONE FOR...I'M SORRY, BUT THAT'S THE WAY IT IS. TELL ME ONE THING...DID YOU COME FOR ME OR FOR THE BOY?
WOULDN'T YOU LIKE TO KNOW?
YES, I'D LIKE TO KNOW, BUT IF YOU DON'T WANT TO TELL ME, IT DOESN'T MATTER...WOULD YOU LIKE A CIGAR?
IS THE KID DEAD?
NO, HE'S ONLY WOUNDED...AN INCH LOWER AND YOU WOULD HAVE KILLED HIM.

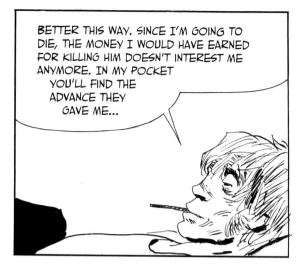

BETTER THIS WAY. SINCE I'M GOING TO DIE, THE MONEY I WOULD HAVE EARNED FOR KILLING HIM DOESN'T INTEREST ME ANYMORE. IN MY POCKET YOU'LL FIND THE ADVANCE THEY GAVE ME...

...GIVE IT TO THE PROFESSOR...SO HE CAN DRINK TO MY MEMORY... I HAD NOTHING AGAINST HIM...I WAS ONLY SORE BECAUSE I COULDN'T MAKE HIM MY FRIEND...

WHO PAID YOU?

YOU'RE SMART. FIGURE IT OUT!

HE'S DEAD.

THAT BULLET WAS REALLY FOR ME... POOR GUY... HERE'S THE MONEY.

THERE'S ALSO AN ADDRESS...ONLY THE NUMBER AND THE STREET...

19 MANGROVE STRAAT

WE NEED TO CALL A DOCTOR FOR THE BOY. YOU'RE PRETTY QUICK WITH THAT KNIFE, AREN'T YOU!

I HAD NO CHOICE.

I'LL GO TO THE POLICE AND... HEY! WHAT'S GOING ON?

HEY, CORTO MALTESE! CORTO MALTESE!

YOUR BOAT IS ON FIRE!!

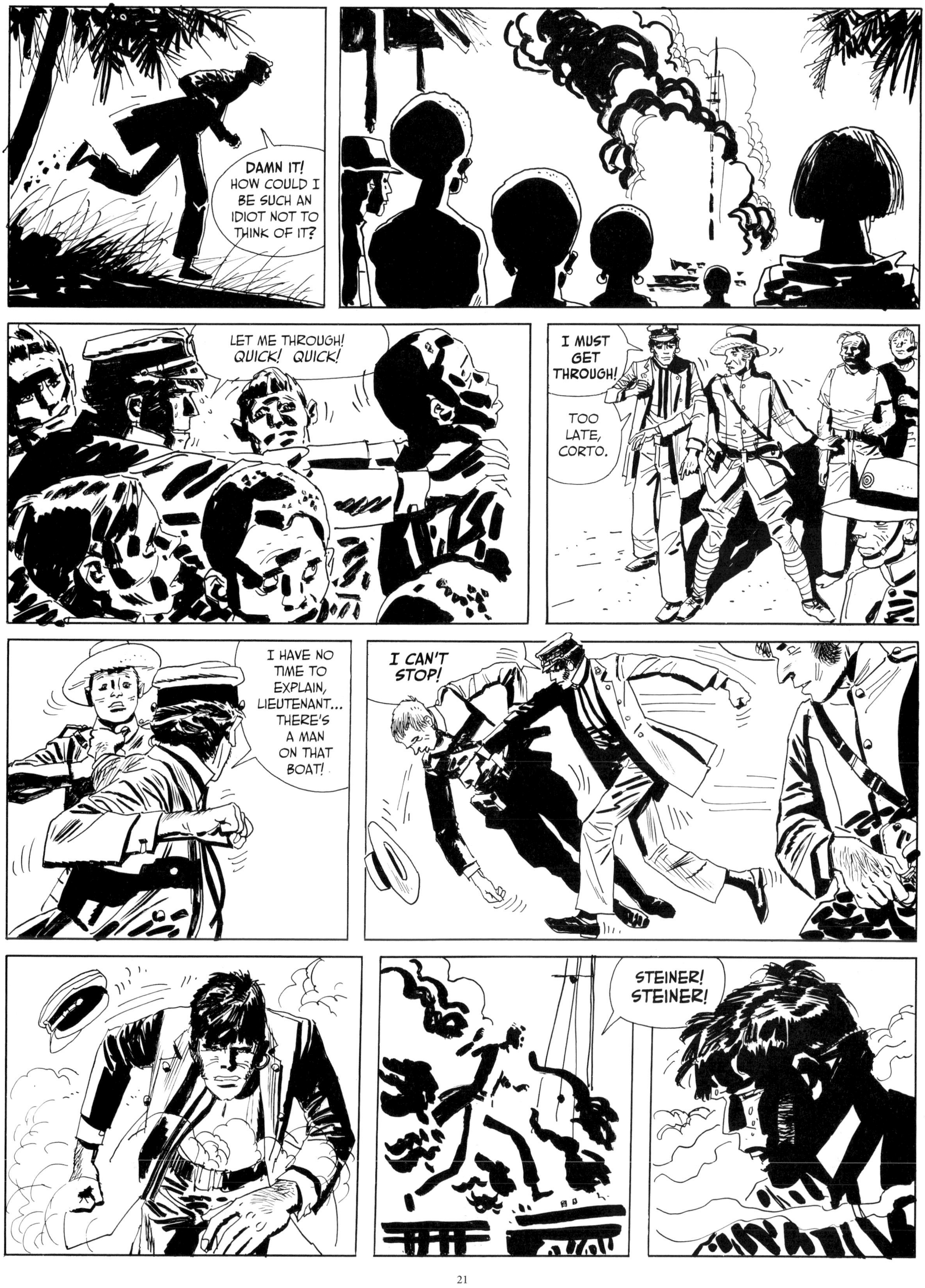
DAMN IT! HOW COULD I BE SUCH AN IDIOT NOT TO THINK OF IT?
LET ME THROUGH! QUICK! QUICK!
I MUST GET THROUGH!
TOO LATE, CORTO.
I HAVE NO TIME TO EXPLAIN, LIEUTENANT... THERE'S A MAN ON THAT BOAT!
I CAN'T STOP!
STEINER! STEINER!

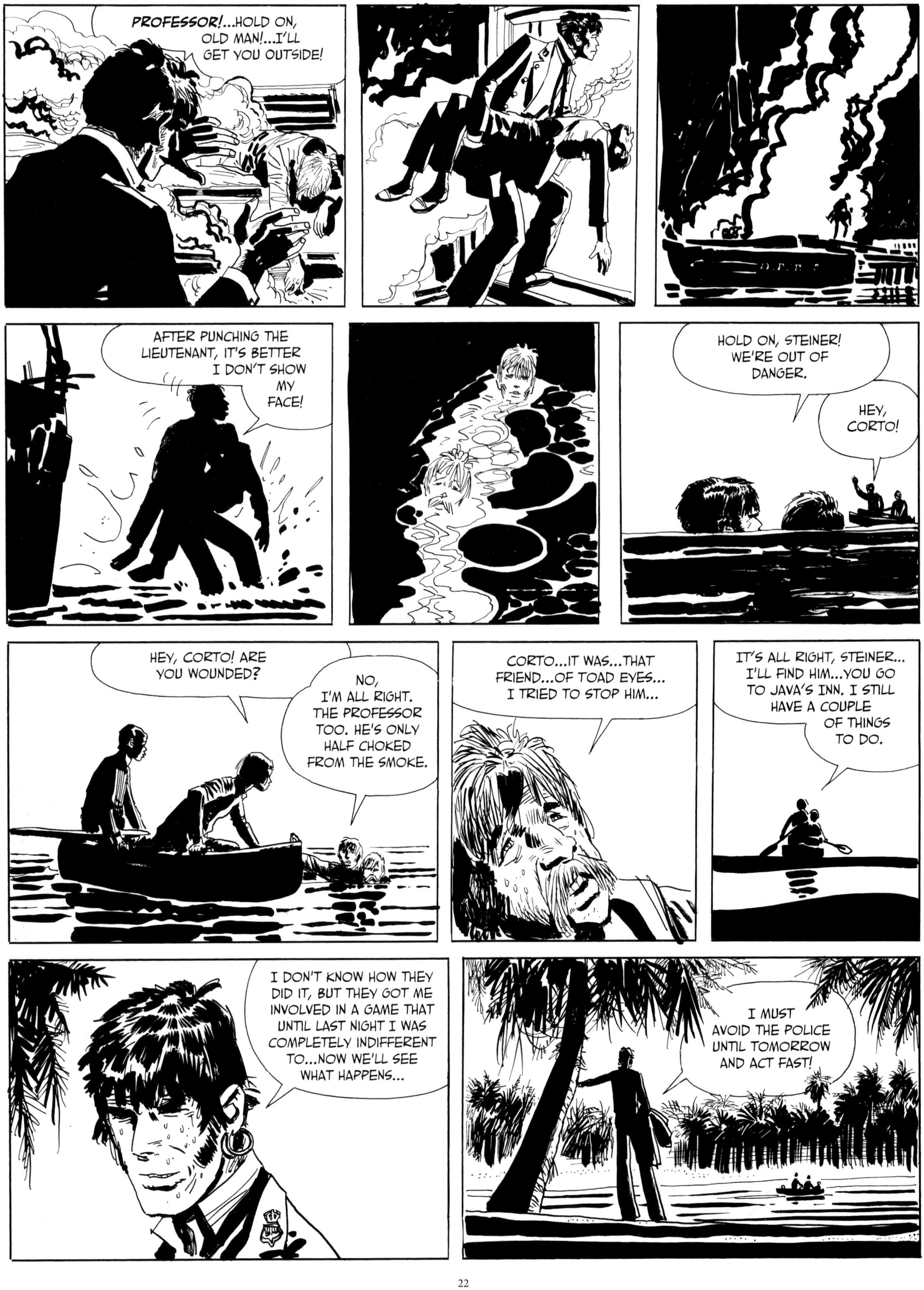
PROFESSOR!...HOLD ON, OLD MAN!...I'LL GET YOU OUTSIDE!
AFTER PUNCHING THE LIEUTENANT, IT'S BETTER I DON'T SHOW MY FACE!
HOLD ON, STEINER! WE'RE OUT OF DANGER.
HEY, CORTO!
HEY, CORTO! ARE YOU WOUNDED?
NO, I'M ALL RIGHT. THE PROFESSOR TOO. HE'S ONLY HALF CHOKED FROM THE SMOKE.
CORTO...IT WAS...THAT FRIEND...OF TOAD EYES... I TRIED TO STOP HIM...
IT'S ALL RIGHT, STEINER... I'LL FIND HIM...YOU GO TO JAVA'S INN. I STILL HAVE A COUPLE OF THINGS TO DO.
I DON'T KNOW HOW THEY DID IT, BUT THEY GOT ME INVOLVED IN A GAME THAT UNTIL LAST NIGHT I WAS COMPLETELY INDIFFERENT TO...NOW WE'LL SEE WHAT HAPPENS...
I MUST AVOID THE POLICE UNTIL TOMORROW AND ACT FAST!

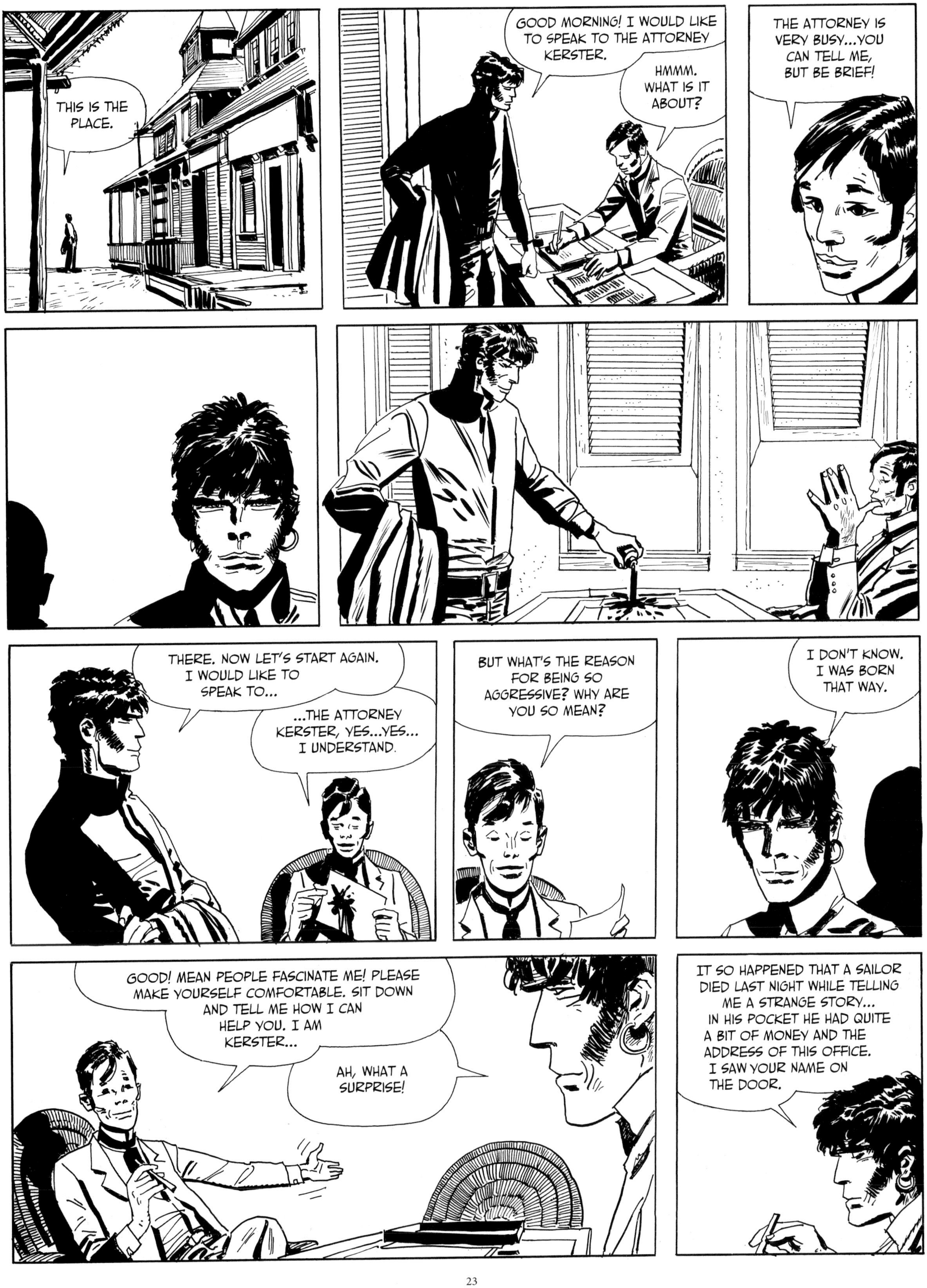

THIS IS THE PLACE.
GOOD MORNING! I WOULD LIKE TO SPEAK TO THE ATTORNEY KERSTER.
HMMM. WHAT IS IT ABOUT?
THE ATTORNEY IS VERY BUSY...YOU CAN TELL ME, BUT BE BRIEF!
THERE. NOW LET'S START AGAIN. I WOULD LIKE TO SPEAK TO...
...THE ATTORNEY KERSTER, YES...YES... I UNDERSTAND.
BUT WHAT'S THE REASON FOR BEING SO AGGRESSIVE? WHY ARE YOU SO MEAN?
I DON'T KNOW. I WAS BORN THAT WAY.
GOOD! MEAN PEOPLE FASCINATE ME! PLEASE MAKE YOURSELF COMFORTABLE. SIT DOWN AND TELL ME HOW I CAN HELP YOU. I AM KERSTER...
AH, WHAT A SURPRISE!
IT SO HAPPENED THAT A SAILOR DIED LAST NIGHT WHILE TELLING ME A STRANGE STORY... IN HIS POCKET HE HAD QUITE A BIT OF MONEY AND THE ADDRESS OF THIS OFFICE. I SAW YOUR NAME ON THE DOOR.

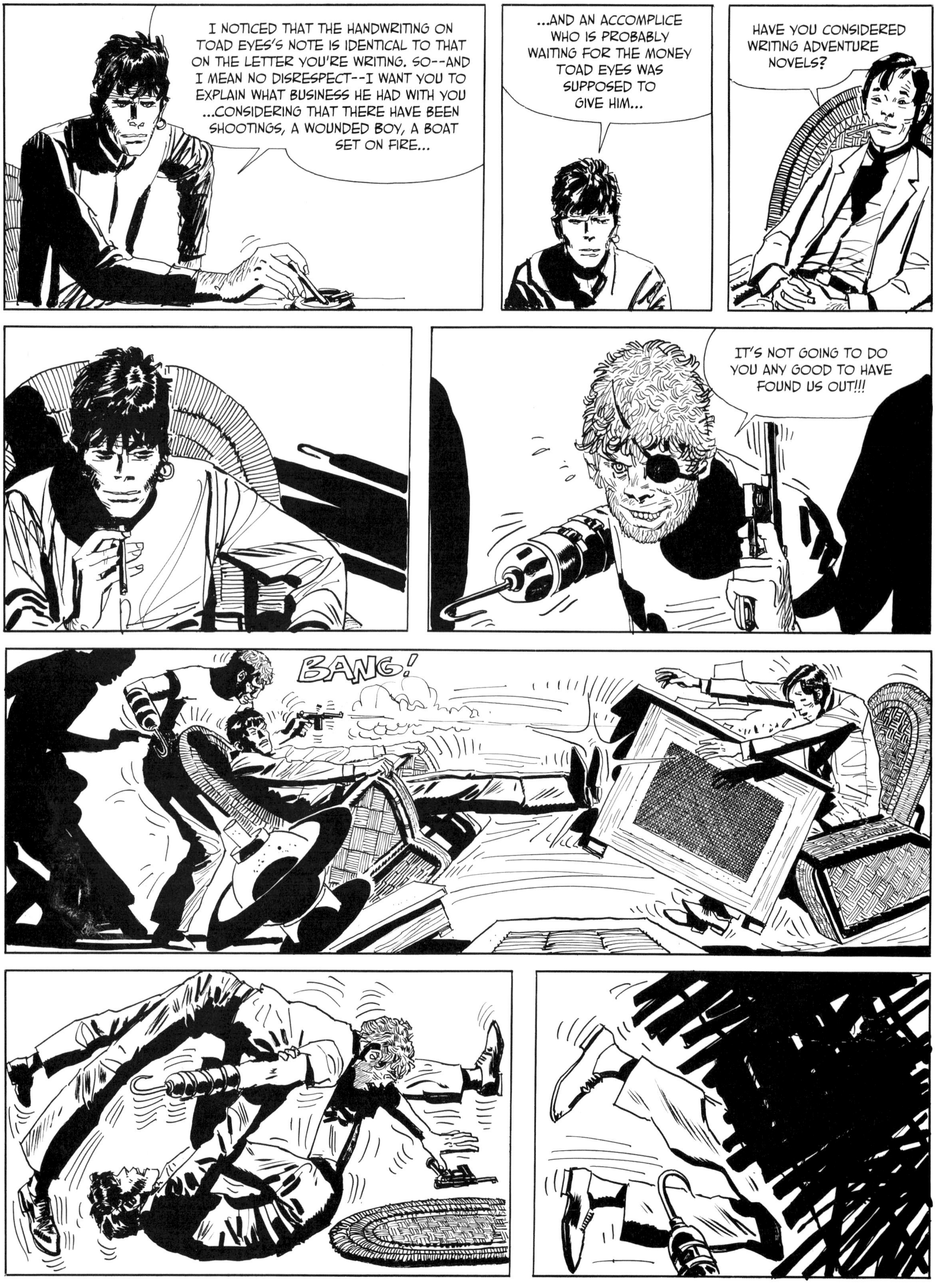

I NOTICED THAT THE HANDWRITING ON TOAD EYES'S NOTE IS IDENTICAL TO THAT ON THE LETTER YOU'RE WRITING. SO--AND I MEAN NO DISRESPECT--I WANT YOU TO EXPLAIN WHAT BUSINESS HE HAD WITH YOU ...CONSIDERING THAT THERE HAVE BEEN SHOOTINGS, A WOUNDED BOY, A BOAT SET ON FIRE...
...AND AN ACCOMPLICE WHO IS PROBABLY WAITING FOR THE MONEY TOAD EYES WAS SUPPOSED TO GIVE HIM...
HAVE YOU CONSIDERED WRITING ADVENTURE NOVELS?
IT'S NOT GOING TO DO YOU ANY GOOD TO HAVE FOUND US OUT!!!
BANG!

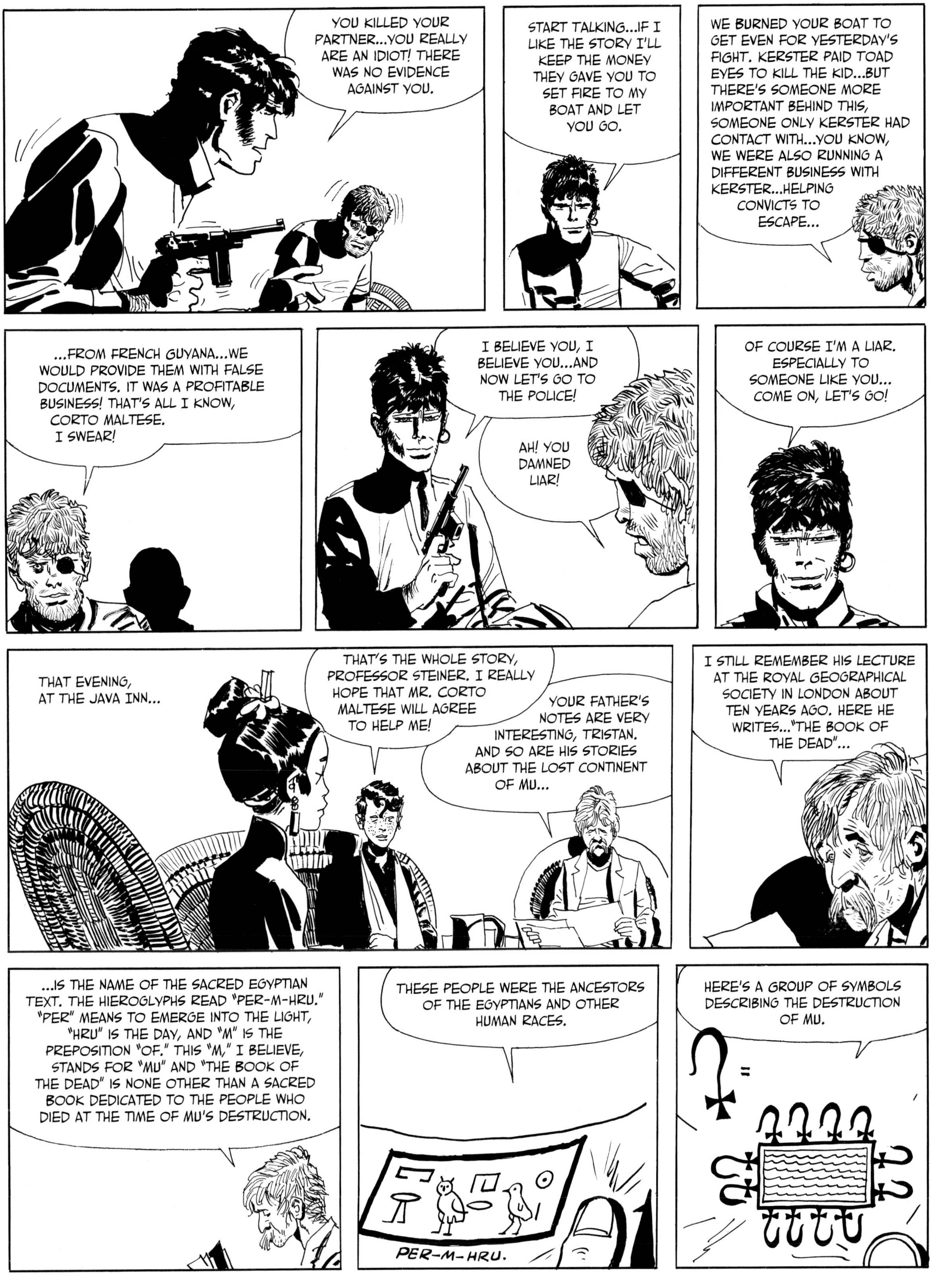

YOU KILLED YOUR PARTNER...YOU REALLY ARE AN IDIOT! THERE WAS NO EVIDENCE AGAINST YOU.
START TALKING...IF I LIKE THE STORY I'LL KEEP THE MONEY THEY GAVE YOU TO SET FIRE TO MY BOAT AND LET YOU GO.
WE BURNED YOUR BOAT TO GET EVEN FOR YESTERDAY'S FIGHT. KERSTER PAID TOAD EYES TO KILL THE KID...BUT THERE'S SOMEONE MORE IMPORTANT BEHIND THIS, SOMEONE ONLY KERSTER HAD CONTACT WITH...YOU KNOW, WE WERE ALSO RUNNING A DIFFERENT BUSINESS WITH KERSTER...HELPING CONVICTS TO ESCAPE...
...FROM FRENCH GUYANA...WE WOULD PROVIDE THEM WITH FALSE DOCUMENTS. IT WAS A PROFITABLE BUSINESS! THAT'S ALL I KNOW, CORTO MALTESE. I SWEAR!
I BELIEVE YOU, I BELIEVE YOU...AND NOW LET'S GO TO THE POLICE!
AH! YOU DAMNED LIAR!
OF COURSE I'M A LIAR. ESPECIALLY TO SOMEONE LIKE YOU... COME ON, LET'S GO!
THAT EVENING, AT THE JAVA INN...
THAT'S THE WHOLE STORY, PROFESSOR STEINER. I REALLY HOPE THAT MR. CORTO MALTESE WILL AGREE TO HELP ME!
YOUR FATHER'S NOTES ARE VERY INTERESTING, TRISTAN. AND SO ARE HIS STORIES ABOUT THE LOST CONTINENT OF MU...
I STILL REMEMBER HIS LECTURE AT THE ROYAL GEOGRAPHICAL SOCIETY IN LONDON ABOUT TEN YEARS AGO. HERE HE WRITES..."THE BOOK OF THE DEAD"...
...IS THE NAME OF THE SACRED EGYPTIAN TEXT. THE HIEROGLYPHS READ "PER-M-HRU." "PER" MEANS TO EMERGE INTO THE LIGHT, "HRU" IS THE DAY, AND "M" IS THE PREPOSITION "OF." THIS "M," I BELIEVE, STANDS FOR "MU" AND "THE BOOK OF THE DEAD" IS NONE OTHER THAN A SACRED BOOK DEDICATED TO THE PEOPLE WHO DIED AT THE TIME OF MU'S DESTRUCTION.
THESE PEOPLE WERE THE ANCESTORS OF THE EGYPTIANS AND OTHER HUMAN RACES.
PER-M-HRU.
HERE'S A GROUP OF SYMBOLS DESCRIBING THE DESTRUCTION OF MU.

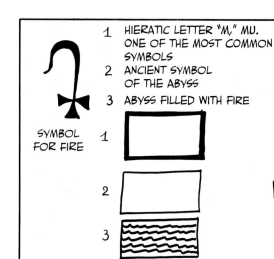

SYMBOL FOR FIRE

1 HIERATIC LETTER "M," MU. ONE OF THE MOST COMMON SYMBOLS
2 ANCIENT SYMBOL OF THE ABYSS
3 ABYSS FILLED WITH FIRE

1
2
3

SACRED LOTUS, FLORAL SYMBOL REPRESENTING MU

MU AFTER THE FLOODING

THREE, SYMBOLIC NUMBER OF MU

M = MU

EMPIRE OF THE SUN

CARA-MAYAN ALPHABET (INVADERS OF INDIA)

THE GREEK ALPHABET IS ACTUALLY AN EPIC FORMED BY CARA-MAYAN CHARACTERS, A MEMORIAL TO THEIR ANCESTORS WHO DIED IN THE DESTRUCTION OF MU. I WOULD TRANSLATE LIKE THIS: "ALPHA" CAN BE DECONSTRUCTED AS "AL," HEAVY, "PAA," BREAK, AND "HA," WATER...

"BETA" AS "BE," MOVEMENT AND "TA," PLACE, GROUND, PLAINS. "GAMMA" AS "KAM," RECEIVES AND "MA," MOTHER EARTH. "DELTA" AS "TEL," DEEP AND "TA," WHERE. "EPSILON" AS "EP," OBSTRUCTION, "ZIL," MAKE EDGES, AND "ONOM," WIND. "ETA" AS "ET," WITH, AND "HA," WATER. "ZETA" AS "ZE," DEADLY BLOW AND "TA," WHERE, PLACE...

WHAT'S THIS--A FAIRY TALE?

GOOD EVENING, CORTO. WE WERE WAITING FOR YOU.

GOOD EVENING, MR. CORTO.

SO YOU'RE INTERESTED IN STORIES OF LOST WORLDS AND HIDDEN TREASURES... I THOUGHT YOU WERE ONLY INTERESTED IN DRINKING...

DON'T BE SO CYNICAL...AT HEART YOU'D LIKE TO BELIEVE IN FAIRY TALES. OTHERWISE, WHY DO YOU ALWAYS END UP EMBROILED IN SITUATIONS THAT YOU CAN AVOID BY SIMPLY LOOKING THE OTHER WAY?

STEINER, ONE OF THESE DAYS YOU'LL MAKE ME LOSE MY PATIENCE!

DON'T GET ANGRY! YOU KNOW, WHAT I WAS READING EARLIER IS NOT INCOMPREHENSIBLE. THERE ARE MANY SOURCES THAT REFER TO...

...THE WORLD THAT DISAPPEARED 50,000 YEARS AGO. A BUDDHIST MONK ONCE TOLD ME ABOUT SOME TABLETS INSCRIBED IN NAGA-YAMA, THE LANGUAGE OF A CIVILIZATION THAT ONCE INVADED INDIA, THAT CONFIRM THE EXISTENCE OF MU.

EXCUSE ME, MR. CORTO... I BOUGHT MADAME JAVA'S YAWL SO I CAN FIND MY SISTER MORGANA IN BAHIA. IF YOU'RE INTERESTED I'D LIKE TO HIRE YOU TO CAPTAIN THE BOAT...

QUITE A JOURNEY!

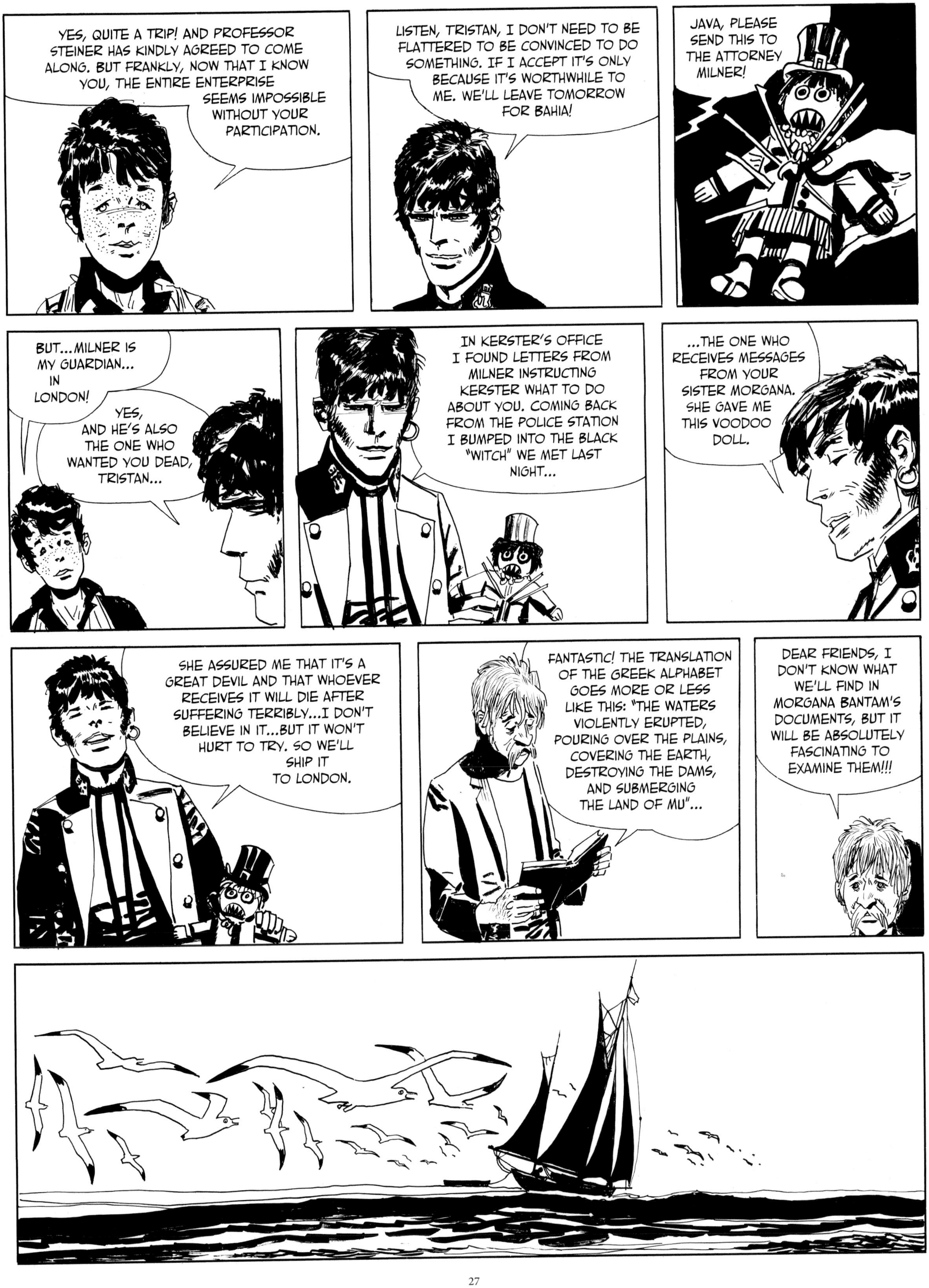
YES, QUITE A TRIP! AND PROFESSOR STEINER HAS KINDLY AGREED TO COME ALONG. BUT FRANKLY, NOW THAT I KNOW YOU, THE ENTIRE ENTERPRISE SEEMS IMPOSSIBLE WITHOUT YOUR PARTICIPATION.
LISTEN, TRISTAN, I DON'T NEED TO BE FLATTERED TO BE CONVINCED TO DO SOMETHING. IF I ACCEPT IT'S ONLY BECAUSE IT'S WORTHWHILE TO ME. WE'LL LEAVE TOMORROW FOR BAHIA!
JAVA, PLEASE SEND THIS TO THE ATTORNEY MILNER!
BUT...MILNER IS MY GUARDIAN... IN LONDON!
YES, AND HE'S ALSO THE ONE WHO WANTED YOU DEAD, TRISTAN...
IN KERSTER'S OFFICE I FOUND LETTERS FROM MILNER INSTRUCTING KERSTER WHAT TO DO ABOUT YOU. COMING BACK FROM THE POLICE STATION I BUMPED INTO THE BLACK "WITCH" WE MET LAST NIGHT...
...THE ONE WHO RECEIVES MESSAGES FROM YOUR SISTER MORGANA. SHE GAVE ME THIS VOODOO DOLL.
SHE ASSURED ME THAT IT'S A GREAT DEVIL AND THAT WHOEVER RECEIVES IT WILL DIE AFTER SUFFERING TERRIBLY...I DON'T BELIEVE IN IT...BUT IT WON'T HURT TO TRY. SO WE'LL SHIP IT TO LONDON.
FANTASTIC! THE TRANSLATION OF THE GREEK ALPHABET GOES MORE OR LESS LIKE THIS: "THE WATERS VIOLENTLY ERUPTED, POURING OVER THE PLAINS, COVERING THE EARTH, DESTROYING THE DAMS, AND SUBMERGING THE LAND OF MU"...
DEAR FRIENDS, I DON'T KNOW WHAT WE'LL FIND IN MORGANA BANTAM'S DOCUMENTS, BUT IT WILL BE ABSOLUTELY FASCINATING TO EXAMINE THEM!!!

CHAPTER TWO:
RENDEZ-VOUS
IN BAHIA

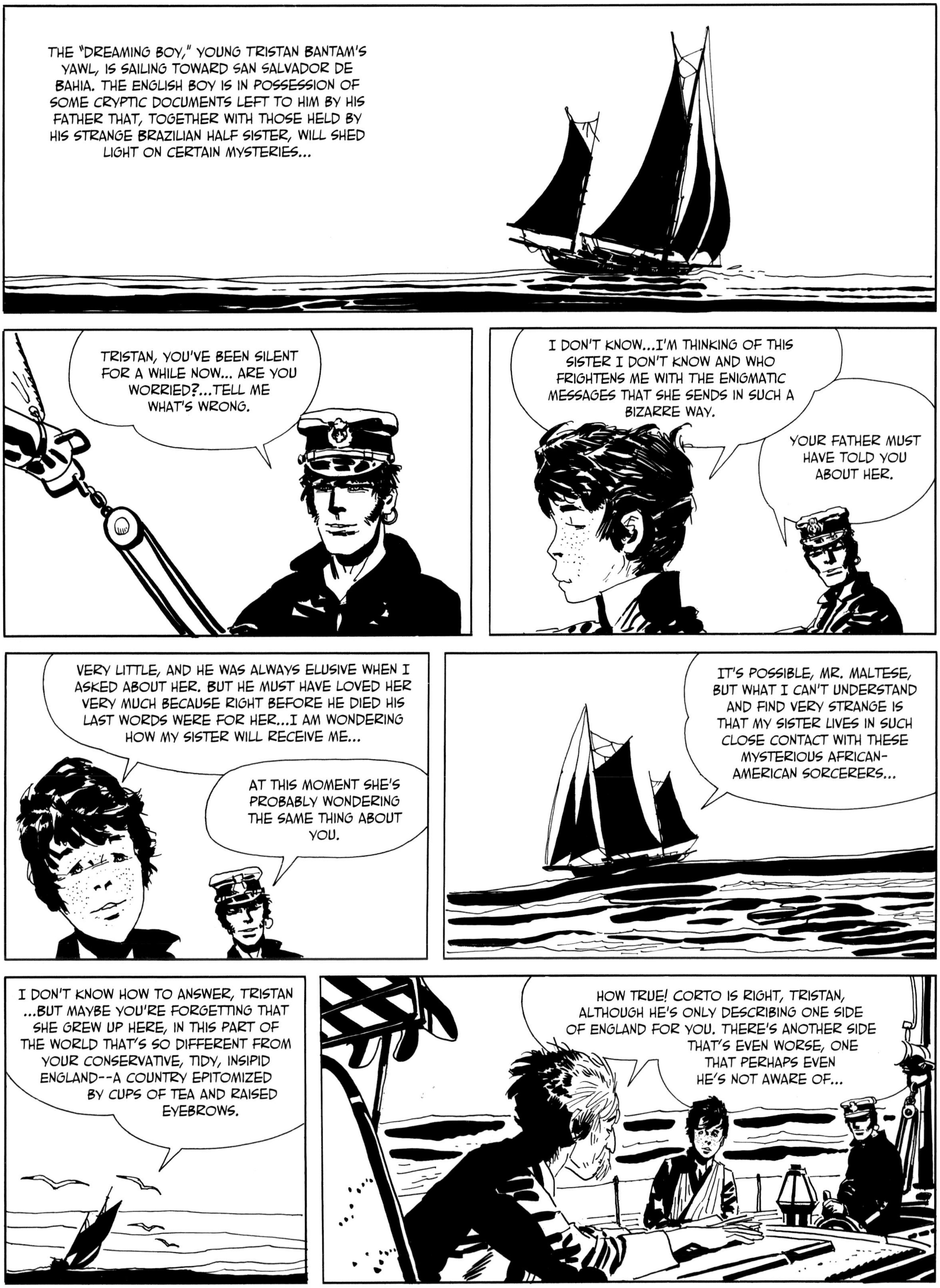

THE "DREAMING BOY," YOUNG TRISTAN BANTAM'S YAWL, IS SAILING TOWARD SAN SALVADOR DE BAHIA. THE ENGLISH BOY IS IN POSSESSION OF SOME CRYPTIC DOCUMENTS LEFT TO HIM BY HIS FATHER THAT, TOGETHER WITH THOSE HELD BY HIS STRANGE BRAZILIAN HALF SISTER, WILL SHED LIGHT ON CERTAIN MYSTERIES...
TRISTAN, YOU'VE BEEN SILENT FOR A WHILE NOW... ARE YOU WORRIED?...TELL ME WHAT'S WRONG.
I DON'T KNOW...I'M THINKING OF THIS SISTER I DON'T KNOW AND WHO FRIGHTENS ME WITH THE ENIGMATIC MESSAGES THAT SHE SENDS IN SUCH A BIZARRE WAY.
YOUR FATHER MUST HAVE TOLD YOU ABOUT HER.
VERY LITTLE, AND HE WAS ALWAYS ELUSIVE WHEN I ASKED ABOUT HER. BUT HE MUST HAVE LOVED HER VERY MUCH BECAUSE RIGHT BEFORE HE DIED HIS LAST WORDS WERE FOR HER...I AM WONDERING HOW MY SISTER WILL RECEIVE ME...
AT THIS MOMENT SHE'S PROBABLY WONDERING THE SAME THING ABOUT YOU.
IT'S POSSIBLE, MR. MALTESE, BUT WHAT I CAN'T UNDERSTAND AND FIND VERY STRANGE IS THAT MY SISTER LIVES IN SUCH CLOSE CONTACT WITH THESE MYSTERIOUS AFRICAN-AMERICAN SORCERERS...
I DON'T KNOW HOW TO ANSWER, TRISTAN ...BUT MAYBE YOU'RE FORGETTING THAT SHE GREW UP HERE, IN THIS PART OF THE WORLD THAT'S SO DIFFERENT FROM YOUR CONSERVATIVE, TIDY, INSIPID ENGLAND--A COUNTRY EPITOMIZED BY CUPS OF TEA AND RAISED EYEBROWS.
HOW TRUE! CORTO IS RIGHT, TRISTAN, ALTHOUGH HE'S ONLY DESCRIBING ONE SIDE OF ENGLAND FOR YOU. THERE'S ANOTHER SIDE THAT'S EVEN WORSE, ONE THAT PERHAPS EVEN HE'S NOT AWARE OF...

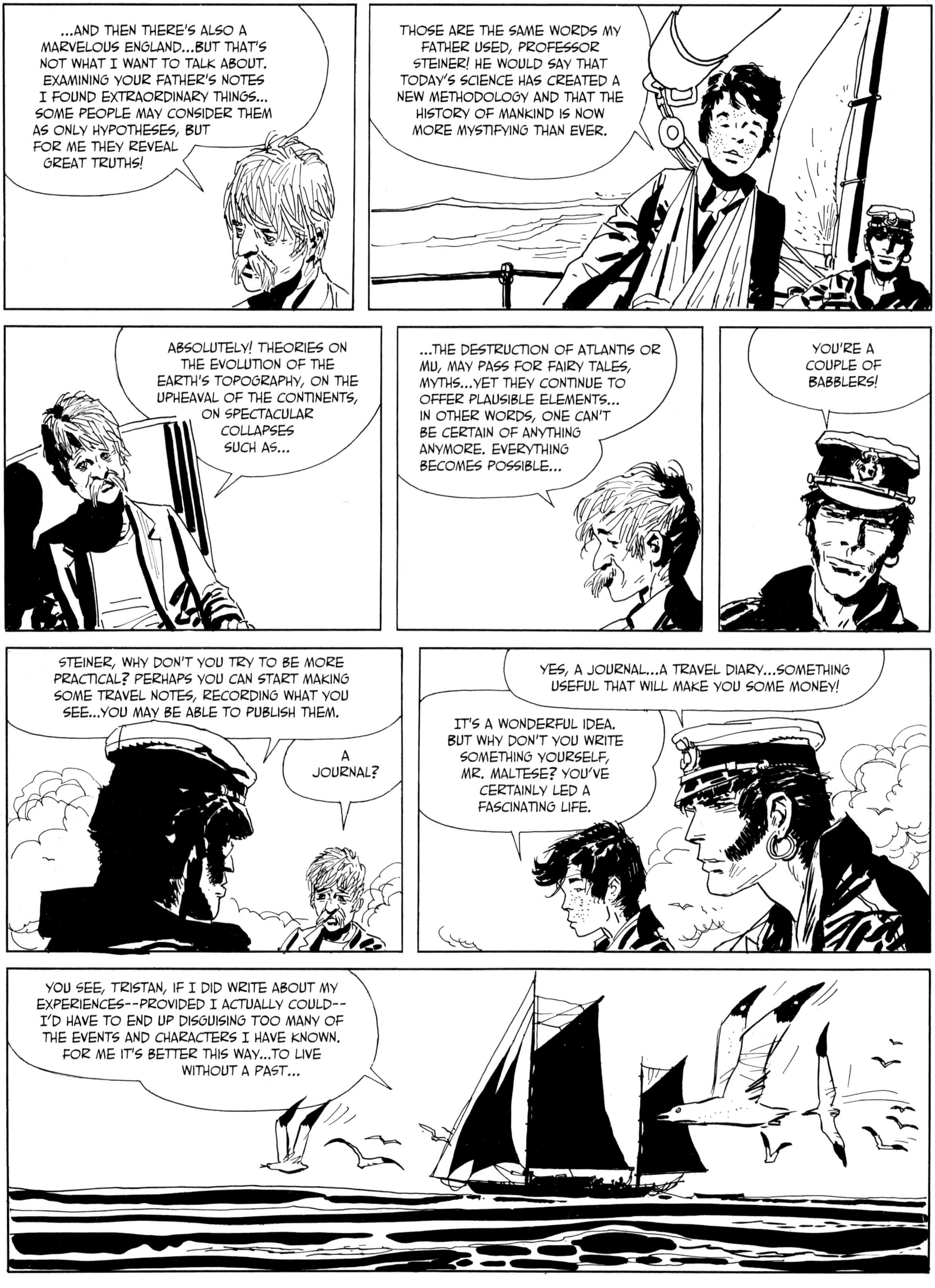
...AND THEN THERE'S ALSO A MARVELOUS ENGLAND...BUT THAT'S NOT WHAT I WANT TO TALK ABOUT. EXAMINING YOUR FATHER'S NOTES I FOUND EXTRAORDINARY THINGS... SOME PEOPLE MAY CONSIDER THEM AS ONLY HYPOTHESES, BUT FOR ME THEY REVEAL GREAT TRUTHS!
THOSE ARE THE SAME WORDS MY FATHER USED, PROFESSOR STEINER! HE WOULD SAY THAT TODAY'S SCIENCE HAS CREATED A NEW METHODOLOGY AND THAT THE HISTORY OF MANKIND IS NOW MORE MYSTIFYING THAN EVER.
ABSOLUTELY! THEORIES ON THE EVOLUTION OF THE EARTH'S TOPOGRAPHY, ON THE UPHEAVAL OF THE CONTINENTS, ON SPECTACULAR COLLAPSES SUCH AS...
...THE DESTRUCTION OF ATLANTIS OR MU, MAY PASS FOR FAIRY TALES, MYTHS...YET THEY CONTINUE TO OFFER PLAUSIBLE ELEMENTS... IN OTHER WORDS, ONE CAN'T BE CERTAIN OF ANYTHING ANYMORE. EVERYTHING BECOMES POSSIBLE...
YOU'RE A COUPLE OF BABBLERS!
STEINER, WHY DON'T YOU TRY TO BE MORE PRACTICAL? PERHAPS YOU CAN START MAKING SOME TRAVEL NOTES, RECORDING WHAT YOU SEE...YOU MAY BE ABLE TO PUBLISH THEM.
A JOURNAL?
YES, A JOURNAL...A TRAVEL DIARY...SOMETHING USEFUL THAT WILL MAKE YOU SOME MONEY!
IT'S A WONDERFUL IDEA. BUT WHY DON'T YOU WRITE SOMETHING YOURSELF, MR. MALTESE? YOU'VE CERTAINLY LED A FASCINATING LIFE.
YOU SEE, TRISTAN, IF I DID WRITE ABOUT MY EXPERIENCES--PROVIDED I ACTUALLY COULD--I'D HAVE TO END UP DISGUISING TOO MANY OF THE EVENTS AND CHARACTERS I HAVE KNOWN. FOR ME IT'S BETTER THIS WAY...TO LIVE WITHOUT A PAST...

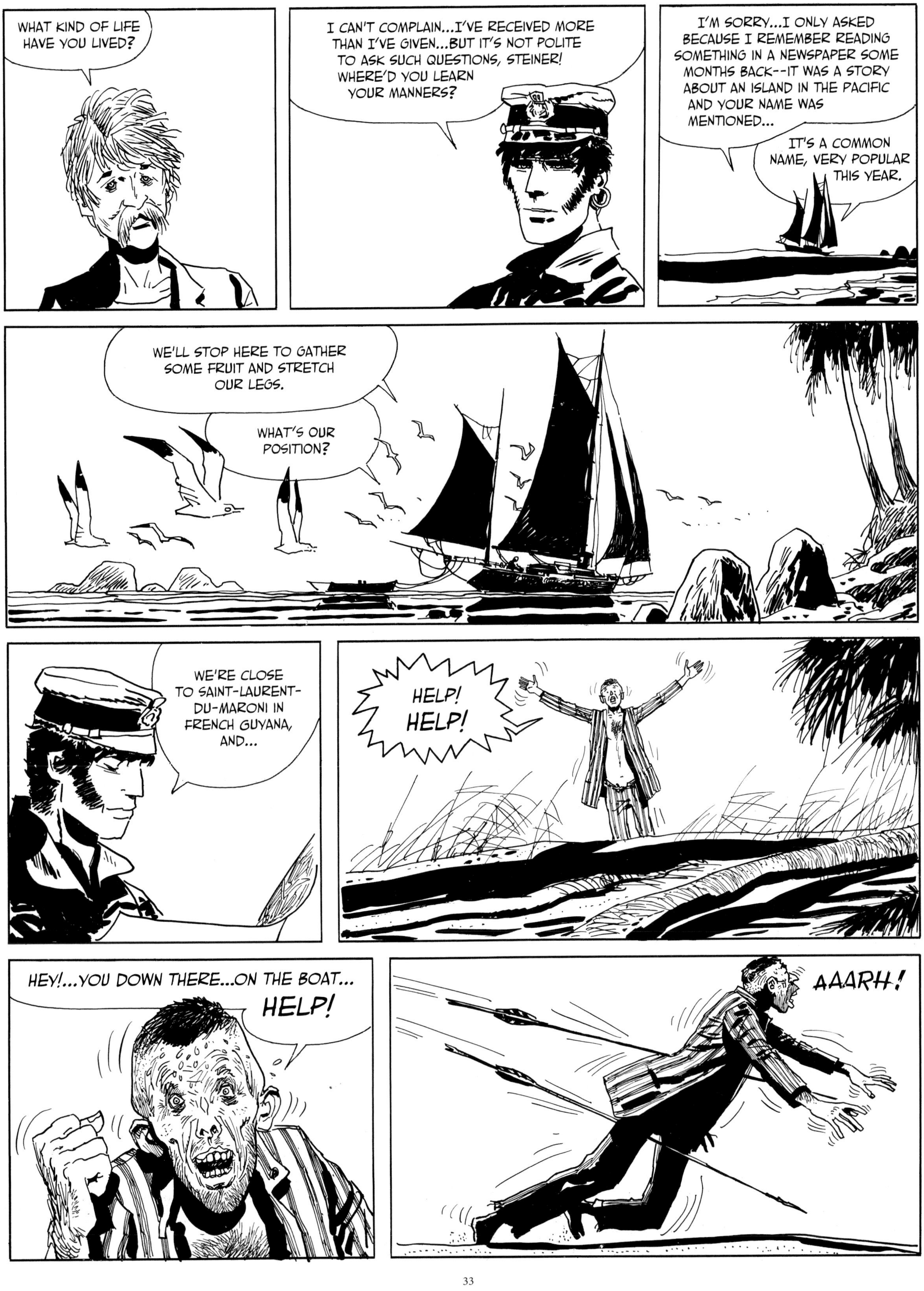

WHAT KIND OF LIFE HAVE YOU LIVED?
I CAN'T COMPLAIN...I'VE RECEIVED MORE THAN I'VE GIVEN...BUT IT'S NOT POLITE TO ASK SUCH QUESTIONS, STEINER! WHERE'D YOU LEARN YOUR MANNERS?
I'M SORRY...I ONLY ASKED BECAUSE I REMEMBER READING SOMETHING IN A NEWSPAPER SOME MONTHS BACK--IT WAS A STORY ABOUT AN ISLAND IN THE PACIFIC AND YOUR NAME WAS MENTIONED...
IT'S A COMMON NAME, VERY POPULAR THIS YEAR.
WE'LL STOP HERE TO GATHER SOME FRUIT AND STRETCH OUR LEGS.
WHAT'S OUR POSITION?
WE'RE CLOSE TO SAINT-LAURENT-DU-MARONI IN FRENCH GUYANA, AND...
HELP! HELP!
HEY!...YOU DOWN THERE...ON THE BOAT... HELP!
AAARH!

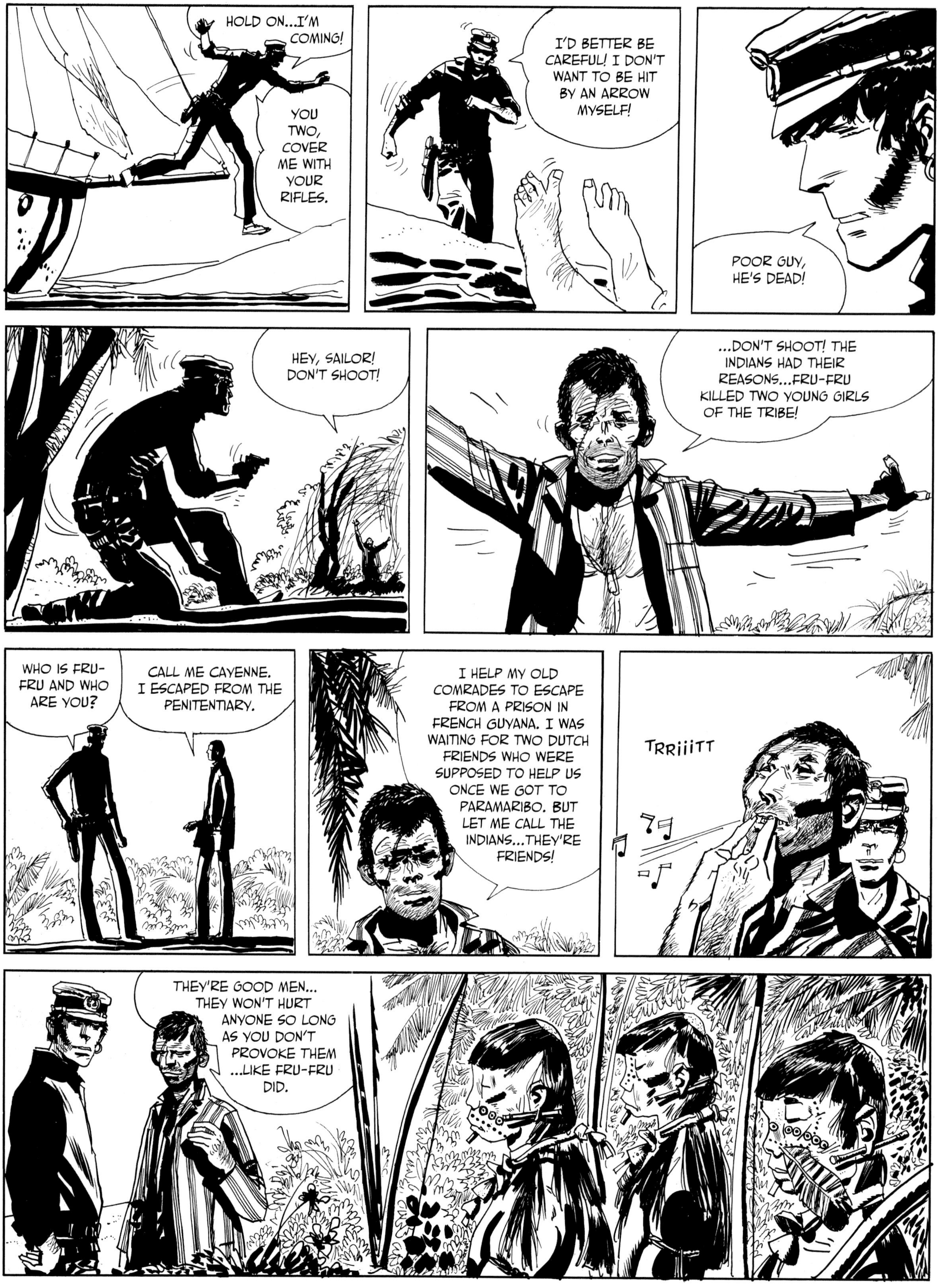
HOLD ON...I'M COMING!
YOU TWO, COVER ME WITH YOUR RIFLES.
I'D BETTER BE CAREFUL! I DON'T WANT TO BE HIT BY AN ARROW MYSELF!
POOR GUY, HE'S DEAD!
HEY, SAILOR! DON'T SHOOT!
...DON'T SHOOT! THE INDIANS HAD THEIR REASONS...FRU-FRU KILLED TWO YOUNG GIRLS OF THE TRIBE!
WHO IS FRU-FRU AND WHO ARE YOU?
CALL ME CAYENNE. I ESCAPED FROM THE PENITENTIARY.
I HELP MY OLD COMRADES TO ESCAPE FROM A PRISON IN FRENCH GUYANA. I WAS WAITING FOR TWO DUTCH FRIENDS WHO WERE SUPPOSED TO HELP US ONCE WE GOT TO PARAMARIBO. BUT LET ME CALL THE INDIANS...THEY'RE FRIENDS!
TRRiiiTT
THEY'RE GOOD MEN... THEY WON'T HURT ANYONE SO LONG AS YOU DON'T PROVOKE THEM ...LIKE FRU-FRU DID.

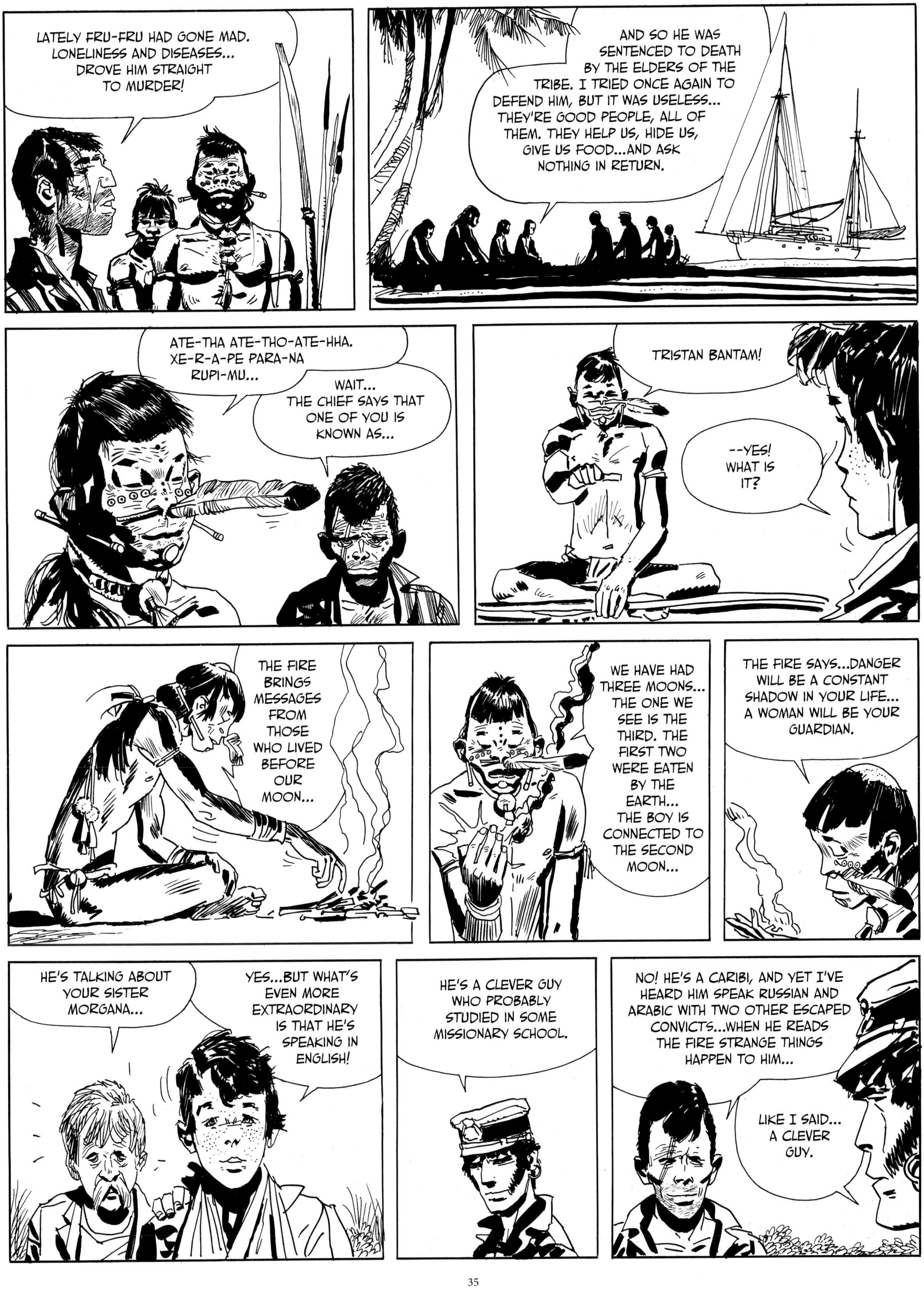
LATELY FRU-FRU HAD GONE MAD. LONELINESS AND DISEASES... DROVE HIM STRAIGHT TO MURDER!
AND SO HE WAS SENTENCED TO DEATH BY THE ELDERS OF THE TRIBE. I TRIED ONCE AGAIN TO DEFEND HIM, BUT IT WAS USELESS... THEY'RE GOOD PEOPLE, ALL OF THEM. THEY HELP US, HIDE US, GIVE US FOOD...AND ASK NOTHING IN RETURN.
ATE-THA ATE-THO-ATE-HHA. XE-R-A-PE PARA-NA RUPI-MU...
WAIT... THE CHIEF SAYS THAT ONE OF YOU IS KNOWN AS...
TRISTAN BANTAM!
--YES! WHAT IS IT?
THE FIRE BRINGS MESSAGES FROM THOSE WHO LIVED BEFORE OUR MOON...
WE HAVE HAD THREE MOONS... THE ONE WE SEE IS THE THIRD. THE FIRST TWO WERE EATEN BY THE EARTH... THE BOY IS CONNECTED TO THE SECOND MOON...
THE FIRE SAYS...DANGER WILL BE A CONSTANT SHADOW IN YOUR LIFE... A WOMAN WILL BE YOUR GUARDIAN.
HE'S TALKING ABOUT YOUR SISTER MORGANA...
YES...BUT WHAT'S EVEN MORE EXTRAORDINARY IS THAT HE'S SPEAKING IN ENGLISH!
HE'S A CLEVER GUY WHO PROBABLY STUDIED IN SOME MISSIONARY SCHOOL.
NO! HE'S A CARIBI, AND YET I'VE HEARD HIM SPEAK RUSSIAN AND ARABIC WITH TWO OTHER ESCAPED CONVICTS...WHEN HE READS THE FIRE STRANGE THINGS HAPPEN TO HIM...
LIKE I SAID... A CLEVER GUY.

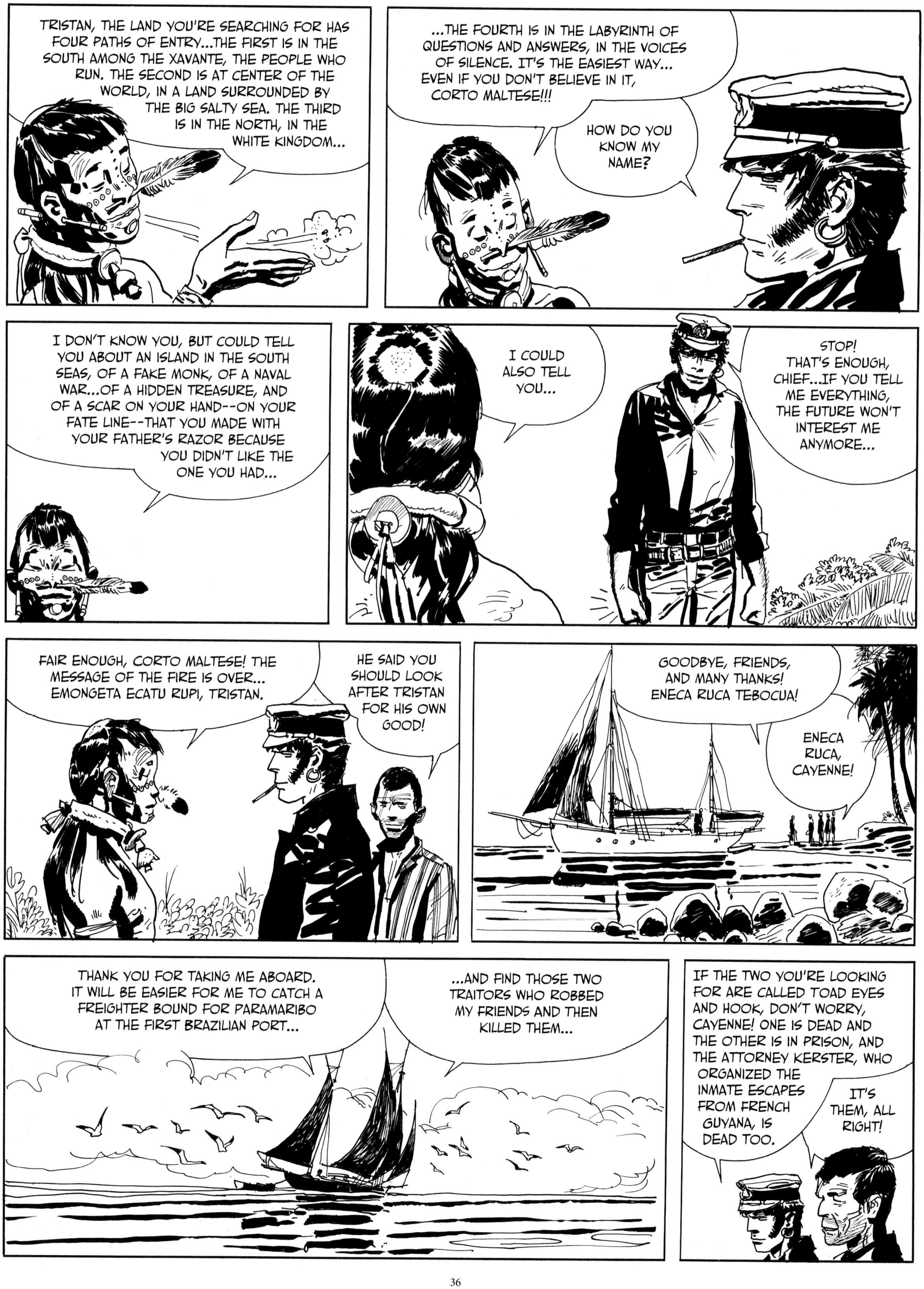
TRISTAN, THE LAND YOU'RE SEARCHING FOR HAS FOUR PATHS OF ENTRY...THE FIRST IS IN THE SOUTH AMONG THE XAVANTE, THE PEOPLE WHO RUN. THE SECOND IS AT CENTER OF THE WORLD, IN A LAND SURROUNDED BY THE BIG SALTY SEA. THE THIRD IS IN THE NORTH, IN THE WHITE KINGDOM...
...THE FOURTH IS IN THE LABYRINTH OF QUESTIONS AND ANSWERS, IN THE VOICES OF SILENCE. IT'S THE EASIEST WAY... EVEN IF YOU DON'T BELIEVE IN IT, CORTO MALTESE!!!
HOW DO YOU KNOW MY NAME?
I DON'T KNOW YOU, BUT COULD TELL YOU ABOUT AN ISLAND IN THE SOUTH SEAS, OF A FAKE MONK, OF A NAVAL WAR...OF A HIDDEN TREASURE, AND OF A SCAR ON YOUR HAND--ON YOUR FATE LINE--THAT YOU MADE WITH YOUR FATHER'S RAZOR BECAUSE YOU DIDN'T LIKE THE ONE YOU HAD...
I COULD ALSO TELL YOU...
STOP! THAT'S ENOUGH, CHIEF...IF YOU TELL ME EVERYTHING, THE FUTURE WON'T INTEREST ME ANYMORE...
FAIR ENOUGH, CORTO MALTESE! THE MESSAGE OF THE FIRE IS OVER... EMONGETA ECATU RUPI, TRISTAN.
HE SAID YOU SHOULD LOOK AFTER TRISTAN FOR HIS OWN GOOD!
GOODBYE, FRIENDS, AND MANY THANKS! ENECA RUCA TEBOCUA!
ENECA RUCA, CAYENNE!
THANK YOU FOR TAKING ME ABOARD. IT WILL BE EASIER FOR ME TO CATCH A FREIGHTER BOUND FOR PARAMARIBO AT THE FIRST BRAZILIAN PORT...
...AND FIND THOSE TWO TRAITORS WHO ROBBED MY FRIENDS AND THEN KILLED THEM...
IF THE TWO YOU'RE LOOKING FOR ARE CALLED TOAD EYES AND HOOK, DON'T WORRY, CAYENNE! ONE IS DEAD AND THE OTHER IS IN PRISON, AND THE ATTORNEY KERSTER, WHO ORGANIZED THE INMATE ESCAPES FROM FRENCH GUYANA, IS DEAD TOO.
IT'S THEM, ALL RIGHT!

YES, TWO ARE DEAD AND THE THIRD IS IN A DUTCH PRISON. BUT THERE'S A FOURTH ONE RESPONSIBLE...AN ENGLISH LAWYER WHO HIRED KERSTER TO DO HIS DIRTY WORK.

THIS MAN RUNS A NETWORK OF SHADY OPERATIONS FROM JAMAICA TO BUENOS AIRES. A SORT OF "BLACK HAND" BETWEEN THE ENGLISH COLONIES AND THE WEST INDIES.

HE IS TRYING TO KILL TRISTAN, THE BOY WHO'S WITH ME, AND I'M CERTAIN THAT THIS LAWYER WAS RESPONSIBLE FOR KILLING THE BOY'S FATHER. IT'S A MATTER OF INHERITANCE...

NOW WE'RE GOING TO BAHIA TO SEE TRISTAN'S HALF SISTER, WHO HAS SOME DOCUMENTS FOR HIM. I HAVE A FEELING THAT WHEN WE GET THERE, SOMETHING SIGNIFICANT IS GOING TO HAPPEN...

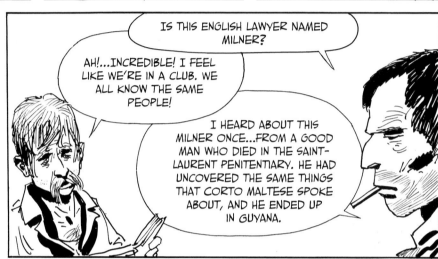

IS THIS ENGLISH LAWYER NAMED MILNER?

AH!...INCREDIBLE! I FEEL LIKE WE'RE IN A CLUB. WE ALL KNOW THE SAME PEOPLE!

I HEARD ABOUT THIS MILNER ONCE...FROM A GOOD MAN WHO DIED IN THE SAINT-LAURENT PENITENTIARY. HE HAD UNCOVERED THE SAME THINGS THAT CORTO MALTESE SPOKE ABOUT, AND HE ENDED UP IN GUYANA.

THIS MILNER MUST HAVE SOME EXQUISITE MANNERS... I HOPE TO MEET HIM SOME DAY.

HE'S BOUND TO DO SOMETHING WHEN HE LEARNS THAT HIS ACCOMPLICES IN PARAMARIBO DIDN'T MANAGE TO COMPLETE THEIR ASSIGNMENT.

HE MUST HAVE OTHER HIRED MEN AT HIS DISPOSAL, EVEN IN BAHIA... BY THE WAY, WHEN WILL WE ARRIVE?

IF IT KEEPS UP LIKE THIS, WE SHOULD GET THERE IN ABOUT TWELVE DAYS...

A FEW DAYS LATER, IN BAHIA...

AH, NO, MY DEAR! YOU CAN'T ARRANGE YOUR TAROT CARDS THAT WAY. PRACTICE AND A STRONG DESIRE ARE NOT ENOUGH TO BECOME A GOOD TAROT READER. IT TAKES A NATURAL TALENT.

I STUDIED EACH CARD IN THE MAJOR ARCANA FOR A FULL WEEK...

DURING THE LAST THREE WEEKS SCORPIO HAS APPEARED SEVEN TIMES. IT'S A WATER SIGN, UNDER THE INFLUENCE OF MARS AND PLUTO...AND IT'S ACCOMPANIED BY CANCER AND GEMINI. CAN YOU TELL ME WHY THESE THREE SIGNS ARE ALWAYS APPEARING TOGETHER?

I THINK IT HAS TO DO WITH THE PEOPLE WE'RE WAITING FOR. YOUR BROTHER'S SIGN IS AQUARIUS, YOURS IS GEMINI...SO YOU HAVE NOTHING IN COMMON...

DOES THIS MEAN THAT THERE'S ANOTHER GEMINI AMONG TRISTAN AND HIS FRIENDS?

TAKE HEART, MORGANA. NO ONE SAYS THAT GEMINIS ARE INCAPABLE OF BEING TOGETHER...ESPECIALLY FOR A BRIEF PERIOD. DID YOU KNOW THAT YOUR FATHER'S ENEMY, THE LAWYER, HAS ARRIVED IN BAHIA? HE IS LODGING AT THE "BARRA."

GOLD MOUTH TOLD ME. NO DOUBT HE'S COME TO ACQUIRE THE LETTERS YOU HAVE ATTESTING TO THE FACT THAT YOU ARE THE SOLE HEIR TO THE "ATLANTIC FINANCE COMPANY."

LET'S GO SEE HIM AND PUT AN END TO THIS NOW!

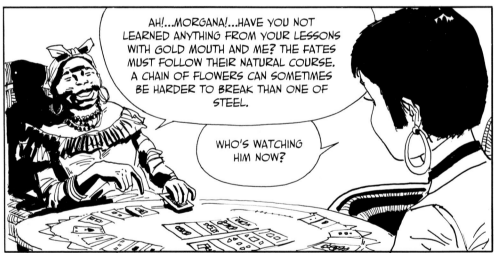

AH!...MORGANA!...HAVE YOU NOT LEARNED ANYTHING FROM YOUR LESSONS WITH GOLD MOUTH AND ME? THE FATES MUST FOLLOW THEIR NATURAL COURSE. A CHAIN OF FLOWERS CAN SOMETIMES BE HARDER TO BREAK THAN ONE OF STEEL.

WHO'S WATCHING HIM NOW?

THE "CAPOEIRA" OF CHAME CHAME... IN THE MEANTIME, YOUR BROTHER IS ARRIVING!

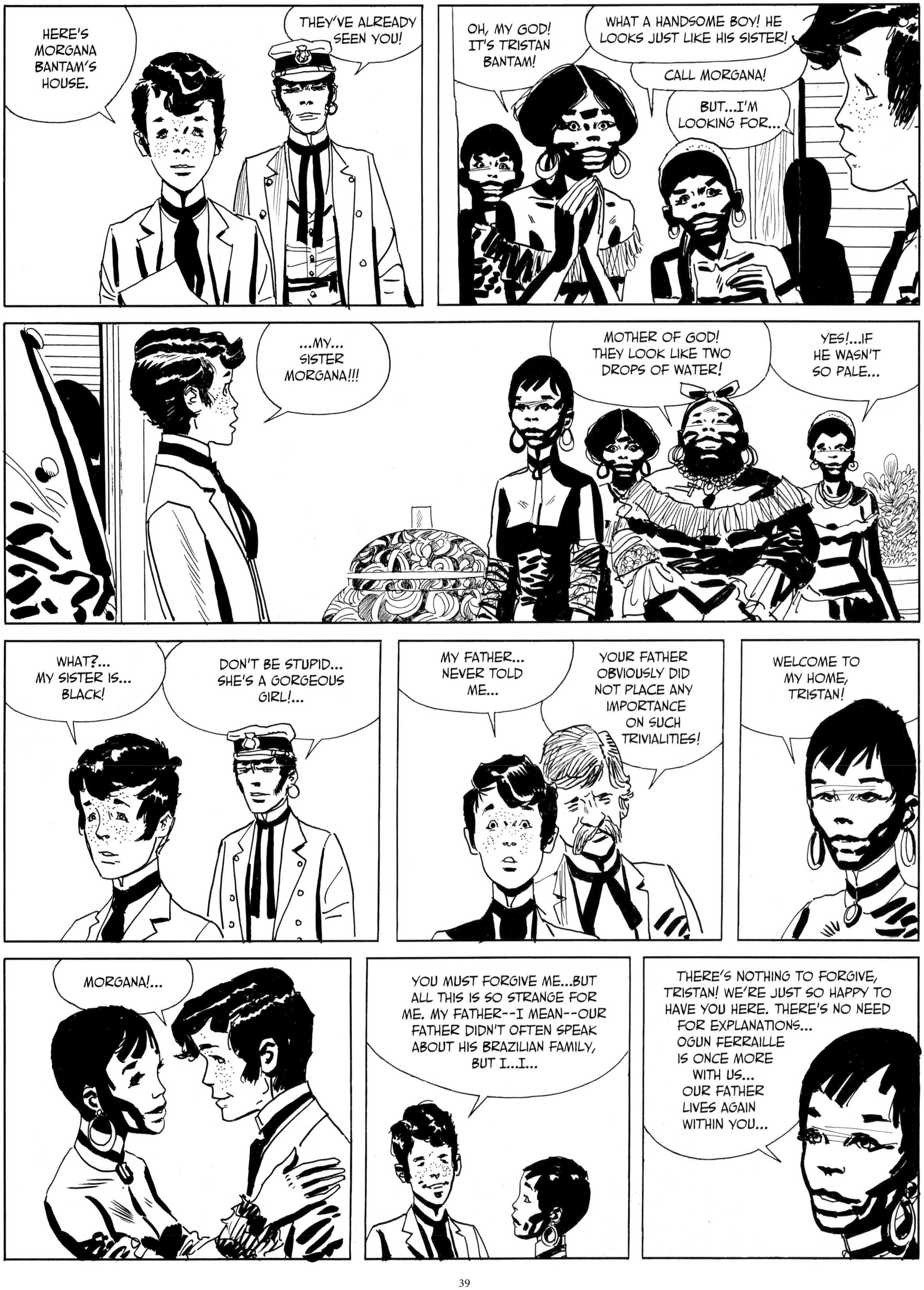
HERE'S MORGANA BANTAM'S HOUSE.
THEY'VE ALREADY SEEN YOU!
OH, MY GOD! IT'S TRISTAN BANTAM!
WHAT A HANDSOME BOY! HE LOOKS JUST LIKE HIS SISTER!
CALL MORGANA!
BUT...I'M LOOKING FOR...
...MY... SISTER MORGANA!!!
MOTHER OF GOD! THEY LOOK LIKE TWO DROPS OF WATER!
YES!...IF HE WASN'T SO PALE...
WHAT?... MY SISTER IS... BLACK!
DON'T BE STUPID... SHE'S A GORGEOUS GIRL!...
MY FATHER... NEVER TOLD ME...
YOUR FATHER OBVIOUSLY DID NOT PLACE ANY IMPORTANCE ON SUCH TRIVIALITIES!
WELCOME TO MY HOME, TRISTAN!
MORGANA!...
YOU MUST FORGIVE ME...BUT ALL THIS IS SO STRANGE FOR ME. MY FATHER--I MEAN--OUR FATHER DIDN'T OFTEN SPEAK ABOUT HIS BRAZILIAN FAMILY, BUT I...I...
THERE'S NOTHING TO FORGIVE, TRISTAN! WE'RE JUST SO HAPPY TO HAVE YOU HERE. THERE'S NO NEED FOR EXPLANATIONS... OGUN FERRAILLE IS ONCE MORE WITH US... OUR FATHER LIVES AGAIN WITHIN YOU...

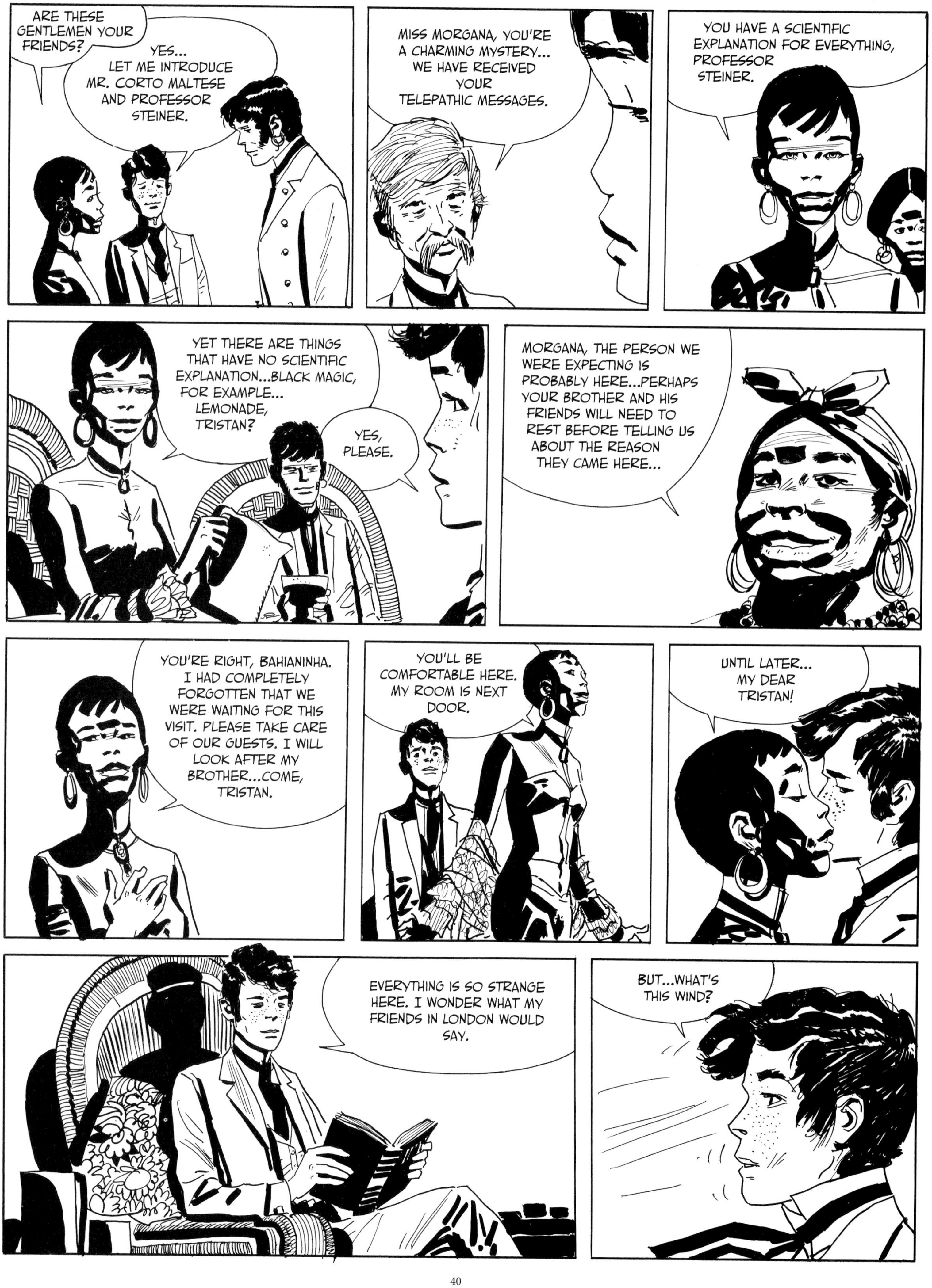
ARE THESE GENTLEMEN YOUR FRIENDS?
YES... LET ME INTRODUCE MR. CORTO MALTESE AND PROFESSOR STEINER.
MISS MORGANA, YOU'RE A CHARMING MYSTERY... WE HAVE RECEIVED YOUR TELEPATHIC MESSAGES.
YOU HAVE A SCIENTIFIC EXPLANATION FOR EVERYTHING, PROFESSOR STEINER.
YET THERE ARE THINGS THAT HAVE NO SCIENTIFIC EXPLANATION...BLACK MAGIC, FOR EXAMPLE... LEMONADE, TRISTAN?
YES, PLEASE.
MORGANA, THE PERSON WE WERE EXPECTING IS PROBABLY HERE...PERHAPS YOUR BROTHER AND HIS FRIENDS WILL NEED TO REST BEFORE TELLING US ABOUT THE REASON THEY CAME HERE...
YOU'RE RIGHT, BAHIANINHA. I HAD COMPLETELY FORGOTTEN THAT WE WERE WAITING FOR THIS VISIT. PLEASE TAKE CARE OF OUR GUESTS. I WILL LOOK AFTER MY BROTHER...COME, TRISTAN.
YOU'LL BE COMFORTABLE HERE. MY ROOM IS NEXT DOOR.
UNTIL LATER... MY DEAR TRISTAN!
EVERYTHING IS SO STRANGE HERE. I WONDER WHAT MY FRIENDS IN LONDON WOULD SAY.
BUT...WHAT'S THIS WIND?

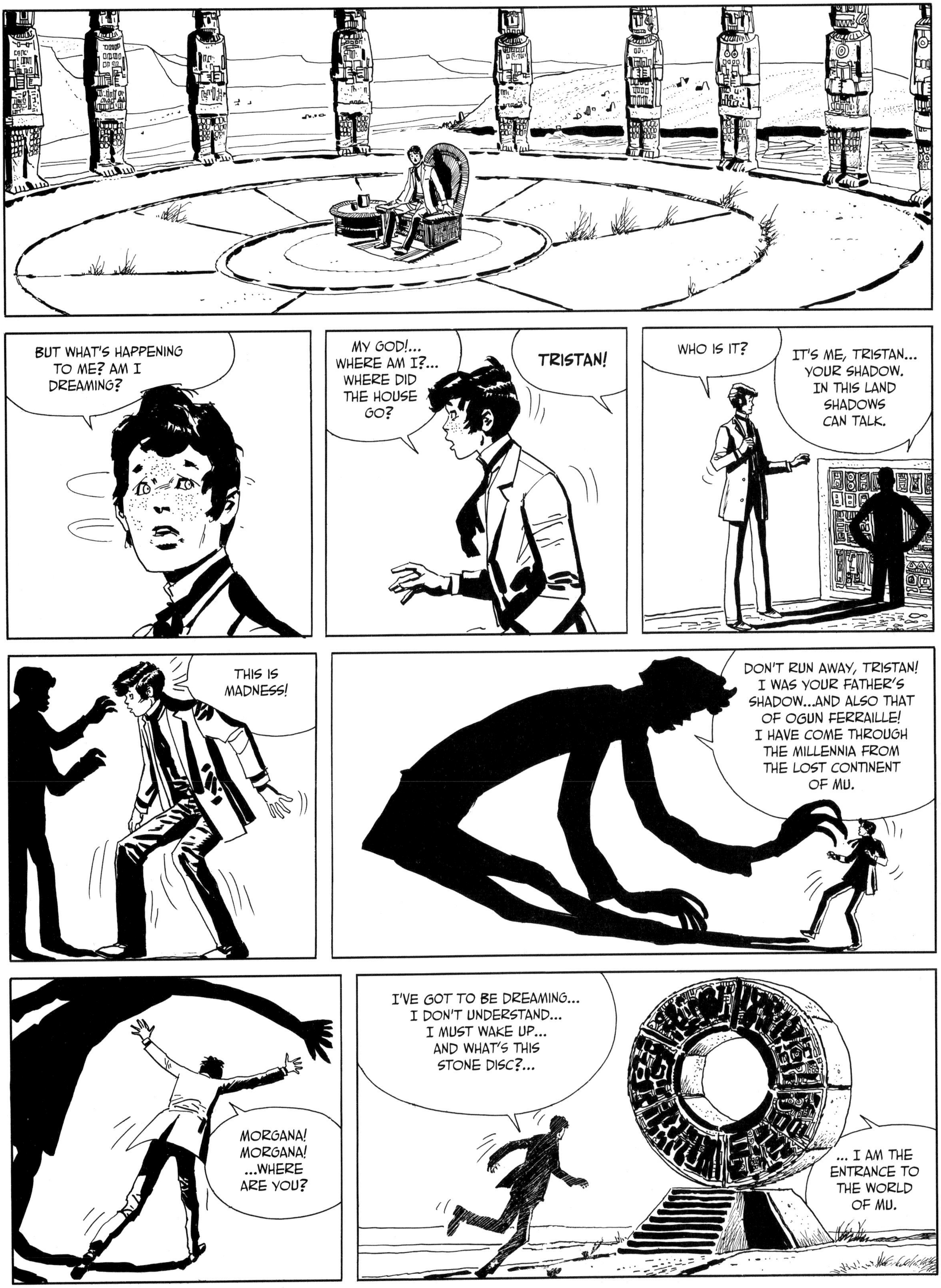

BUT WHAT'S HAPPENING TO ME? AM I DREAMING?
TRISTAN!
MY GOD!... WHERE AM I?... WHERE DID THE HOUSE GO?
WHO IS IT?
IT'S ME, TRISTAN... YOUR SHADOW. IN THIS LAND SHADOWS CAN TALK.
THIS IS MADNESS!
DON'T RUN AWAY, TRISTAN! I WAS YOUR FATHER'S SHADOW...AND ALSO THAT OF OGUN FERRAILLE! I HAVE COME THROUGH THE MILLENNIA FROM THE LOST CONTINENT OF MU.
MORGANA! MORGANA! ...WHERE ARE YOU?
I'VE GOT TO BE DREAMING... I DON'T UNDERSTAND... I MUST WAKE UP... AND WHAT'S THIS STONE DISC?...
... I AM THE ENTRANCE TO THE WORLD OF MU.

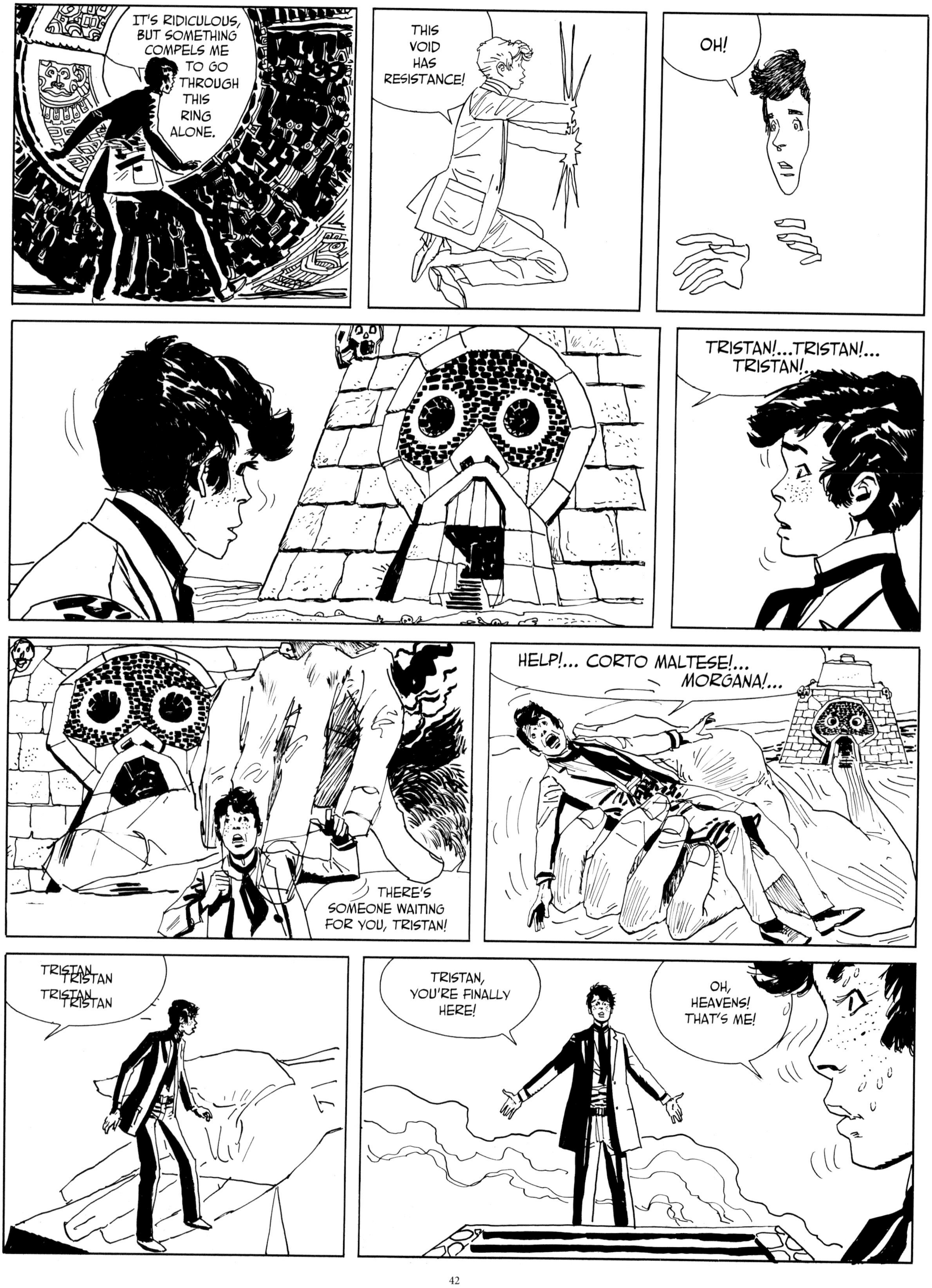
IT'S RIDICULOUS, BUT SOMETHING COMPELS ME TO GO THROUGH THIS RING ALONE.
THIS VOID HAS RESISTANCE!
OH!
TRISTAN!...TRISTAN!... TRISTAN!...
THERE'S SOMEONE WAITING FOR YOU, TRISTAN!
HELP!... CORTO MALTESE!... MORGANA!...
TRISTAN TRISTAN TRISTAN TRISTAN
TRISTAN, YOU'RE FINALLY HERE!
OH, HEAVENS! THAT'S ME!

 ...BUT YOU'RE NOT JUST "ONE"... YOU ARE ALSO THOSE WHO HAVE LIVED IN PREVIOUS LIVES... AND YOU ARE ALSO THOSE WHO WILL LIVE IN THE FUTURE...

BUT WHO ARE YOU?

 WHO AM I?...WHO AM I?...WHAT DOES IT MATTER IF YOU KNOW THAT I AM YOU, YOUR PROJECTION MATERIALIZED FROM THE PAST...OR INTO THE FUTURE?...DO YOU UNDERSTAND?

NO!

BUT...YES, TRISTAN! YOU'RE SEARCHING FOR A DISTANT WORLD... THE BEST WAY TO FIND IT IS TO RELIVE ALL YOUR PAST LIVES. HERE YOU ARE IN THE KINGDOM OF MU.

YOU ARE THOUSAND TIMES A THOUSAND LIVES OF YOUR RACE. YOURS IS THE FIFTH RACE SINCE THE BEGINNING. MU IS THE FOURTH, THE "RACE OF ATLANTIS." THE FLYING MEN, HAILING FROM ANOTHER PLANET, WILL SOON DESTROY THIS EMPIRE. BUT IF YOU WANT, YOU CAN BRING BACK TO YOUR WORLD OF THE FIFTH RACE... THE SKULL OF THE GOD TEZCATLIPOCA!

 THERE IS NO TREASURE ANYWHERE ON EARTH THAT COMPARES TO THIS RELIC. IF YOU POSSESS IT, YOU WILL BE THE MASTER OF YOUR DESTINY!

 LOOK, TRISTAN! HERE'S QUETZALCOATL!

WHO?

 TRISTAN!...SOON MU WILL DISAPPEAR FROM MOTHER EARTH IN A SEA OF FIRE!

BUT...I REALLY DON'T UNDER-STAND ANY OF THIS!

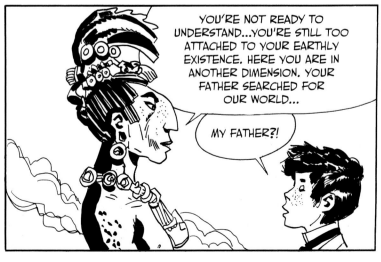 YOU'RE NOT READY TO UNDERSTAND...YOU'RE STILL TOO ATTACHED TO YOUR EARTHLY EXISTENCE. HERE YOU ARE IN ANOTHER DIMENSION. YOUR FATHER SEARCHED FOR OUR WORLD...

MY FATHER?!

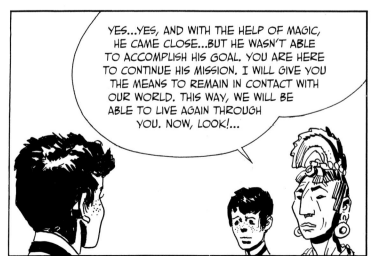 YES...YES, AND WITH THE HELP OF MAGIC, HE CAME CLOSE...BUT HE WASN'T ABLE TO ACCOMPLISH HIS GOAL. YOU ARE HERE TO CONTINUE HIS MISSION. I WILL GIVE YOU THE MEANS TO REMAIN IN CONTACT WITH OUR WORLD. THIS WAY, WE WILL BE ABLE TO LIVE AGAIN THROUGH YOU. NOW, LOOK!...

TEZCATLIPOCA! OUR BROTHER, ACCOMPANY TRISTAN BANTAM ON HIS RETURN VOYAGE...

YOU HAVE BEEN CHOSEN TO MAINTAIN CONTACT BETWEEN OUR DIMENSION AND THE FUTURE.

BROTHER FEATHERED SNAKE, FOR HIM TO RETURN TO HIS WORLD TRISTAN BANTAM MUST BE SACRIFICED!

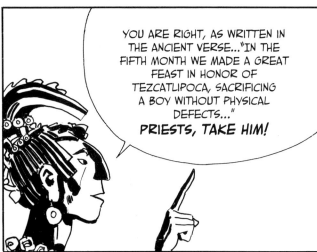

YOU ARE RIGHT, AS WRITTEN IN THE ANCIENT VERSE..."IN THE FIFTH MONTH WE MADE A GREAT FEAST IN HONOR OF TEZCATLIPOCA, SACRIFICING A BOY WITHOUT PHYSICAL DEFECTS..." **PRIESTS, TAKE HIM!**

I DON'T WANT TO DIE... I DON'T WANT TO...NO...NO... MY GOD! EVEN THE ATTORNEY MILNER IS HERE!

YOU'RE AWAKE NOW, TRISTAN...YOU HAD A NIGHTMARE!

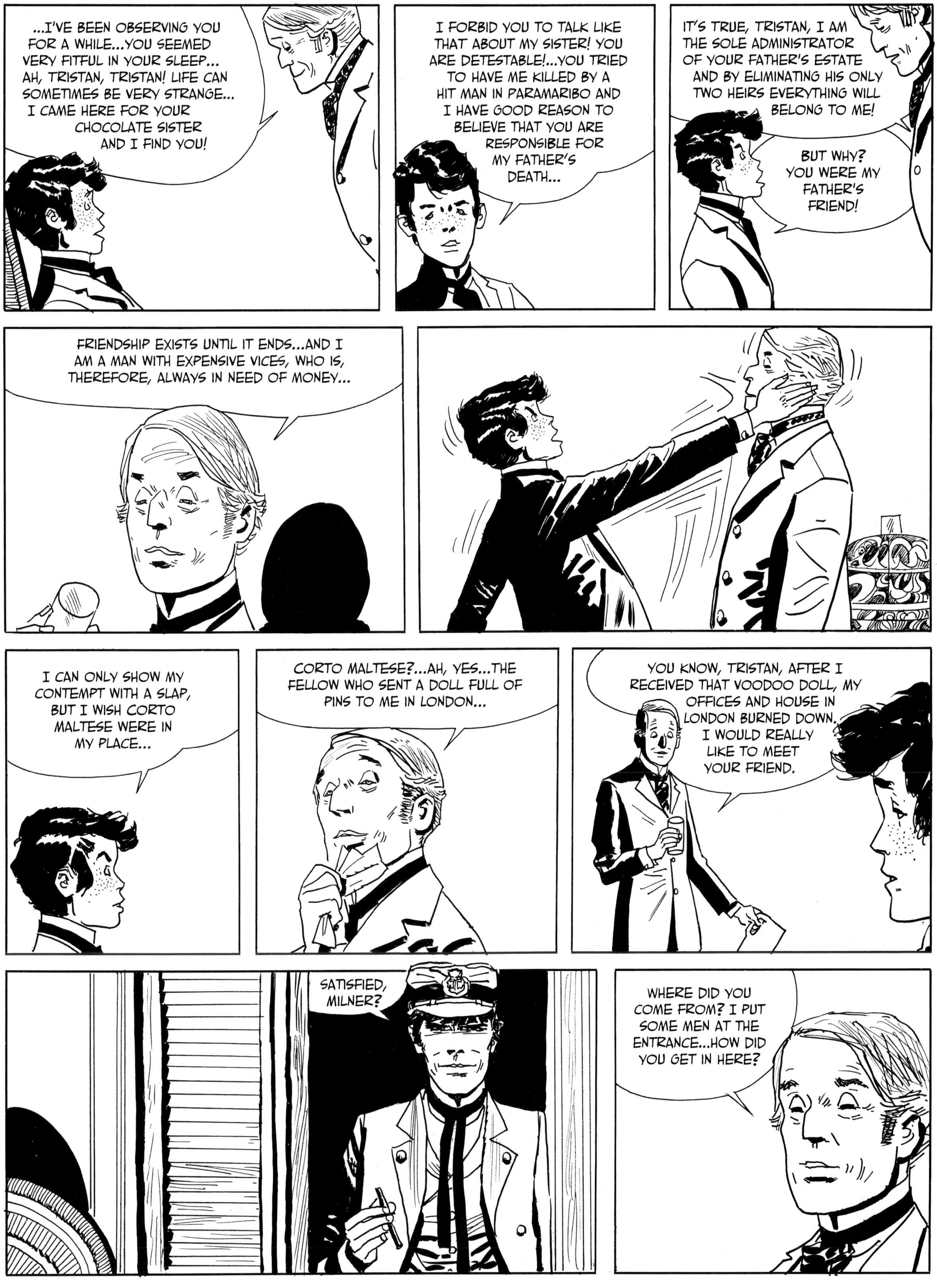
...I'VE BEEN OBSERVING YOU FOR A WHILE...YOU SEEMED VERY FITFUL IN YOUR SLEEP... AH, TRISTAN, TRISTAN! LIFE CAN SOMETIMES BE VERY STRANGE... I CAME HERE FOR YOUR CHOCOLATE SISTER AND I FIND YOU!
I FORBID YOU TO TALK LIKE THAT ABOUT MY SISTER! YOU ARE DETESTABLE!...YOU TRIED TO HAVE ME KILLED BY A HIT MAN IN PARAMARIBO AND I HAVE GOOD REASON TO BELIEVE THAT YOU ARE RESPONSIBLE FOR MY FATHER'S DEATH...
IT'S TRUE, TRISTAN, I AM THE SOLE ADMINISTRATOR OF YOUR FATHER'S ESTATE AND BY ELIMINATING HIS ONLY TWO HEIRS EVERYTHING WILL BELONG TO ME!
BUT WHY? YOU WERE MY FATHER'S FRIEND!
FRIENDSHIP EXISTS UNTIL IT ENDS...AND I AM A MAN WITH EXPENSIVE VICES, WHO IS, THEREFORE, ALWAYS IN NEED OF MONEY...
I CAN ONLY SHOW MY CONTEMPT WITH A SLAP, BUT I WISH CORTO MALTESE WERE IN MY PLACE...
CORTO MALTESE?...AH, YES...THE FELLOW WHO SENT A DOLL FULL OF PINS TO ME IN LONDON...
YOU KNOW, TRISTAN, AFTER I RECEIVED THAT VOODOO DOLL, MY OFFICES AND HOUSE IN LONDON BURNED DOWN. I WOULD REALLY LIKE TO MEET YOUR FRIEND.
SATISFIED, MILNER?
WHERE DID YOU COME FROM? I PUT SOME MEN AT THE ENTRANCE...HOW DID YOU GET IN HERE?

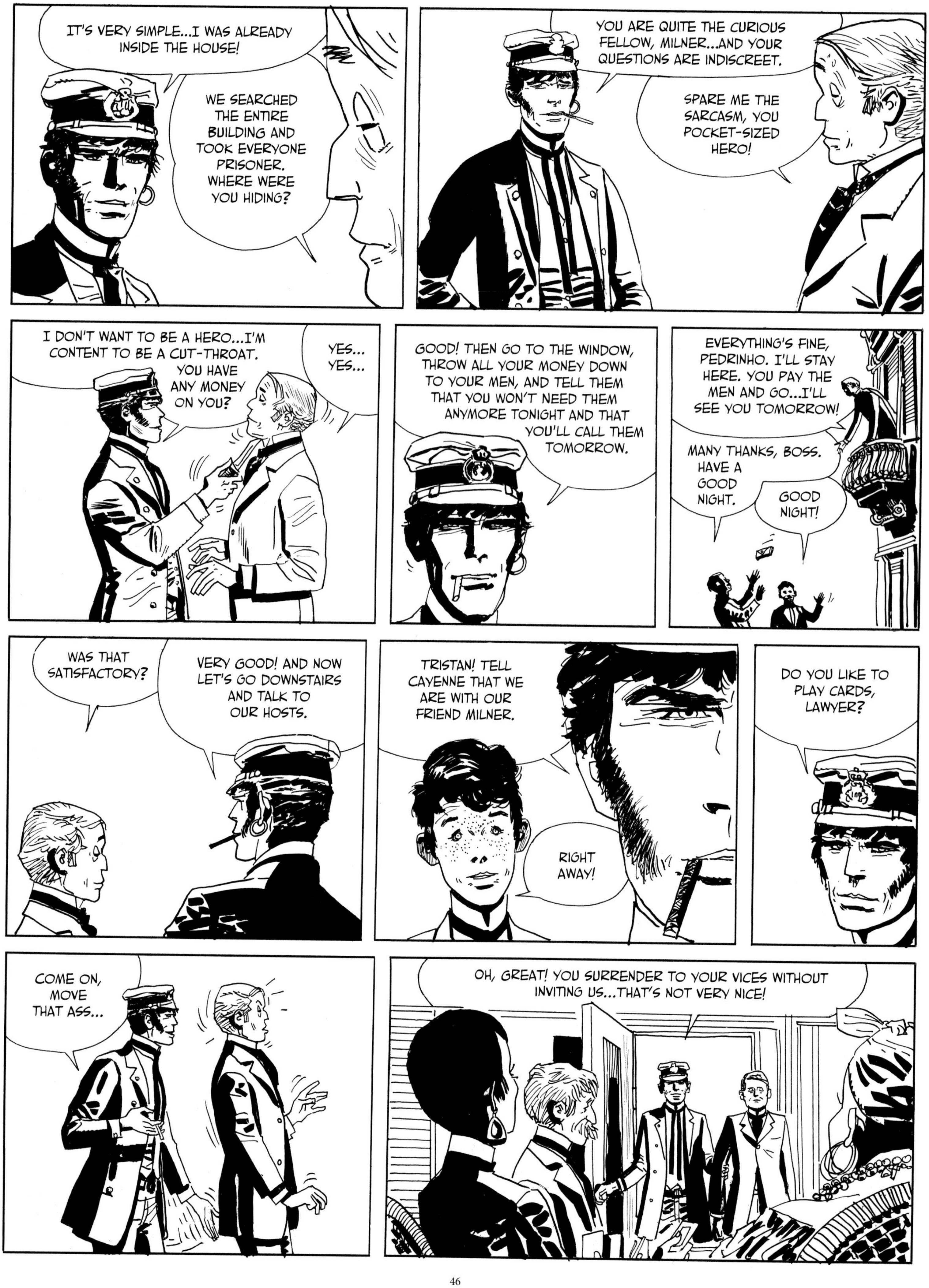
IT'S VERY SIMPLE...I WAS ALREADY INSIDE THE HOUSE!
WE SEARCHED THE ENTIRE BUILDING AND TOOK EVERYONE PRISONER. WHERE WERE YOU HIDING?
YOU ARE QUITE THE CURIOUS FELLOW, MILNER...AND YOUR QUESTIONS ARE INDISCREET.
SPARE ME THE SARCASM, YOU POCKET-SIZED HERO!
I DON'T WANT TO BE A HERO...I'M CONTENT TO BE A CUT-THROAT.
YOU HAVE ANY MONEY ON YOU?
YES... YES...
GOOD! THEN GO TO THE WINDOW, THROW ALL YOUR MONEY DOWN TO YOUR MEN, AND TELL THEM THAT YOU WON'T NEED THEM ANYMORE TONIGHT AND THAT YOU'LL CALL THEM TOMORROW.
EVERYTHING'S FINE, PEDRINHO. I'LL STAY HERE. YOU PAY THE MEN AND GO...I'LL SEE YOU TOMORROW!
MANY THANKS, BOSS. HAVE A GOOD NIGHT.
GOOD NIGHT!
WAS THAT SATISFACTORY?
VERY GOOD! AND NOW LET'S GO DOWNSTAIRS AND TALK TO OUR HOSTS.
TRISTAN! TELL CAYENNE THAT WE ARE WITH OUR FRIEND MILNER.
RIGHT AWAY!
DO YOU LIKE TO PLAY CARDS, LAWYER?
COME ON, MOVE THAT ASS...
OH, GREAT! YOU SURRENDER TO YOUR VICES WITHOUT INVITING US...THAT'S NOT VERY NICE!

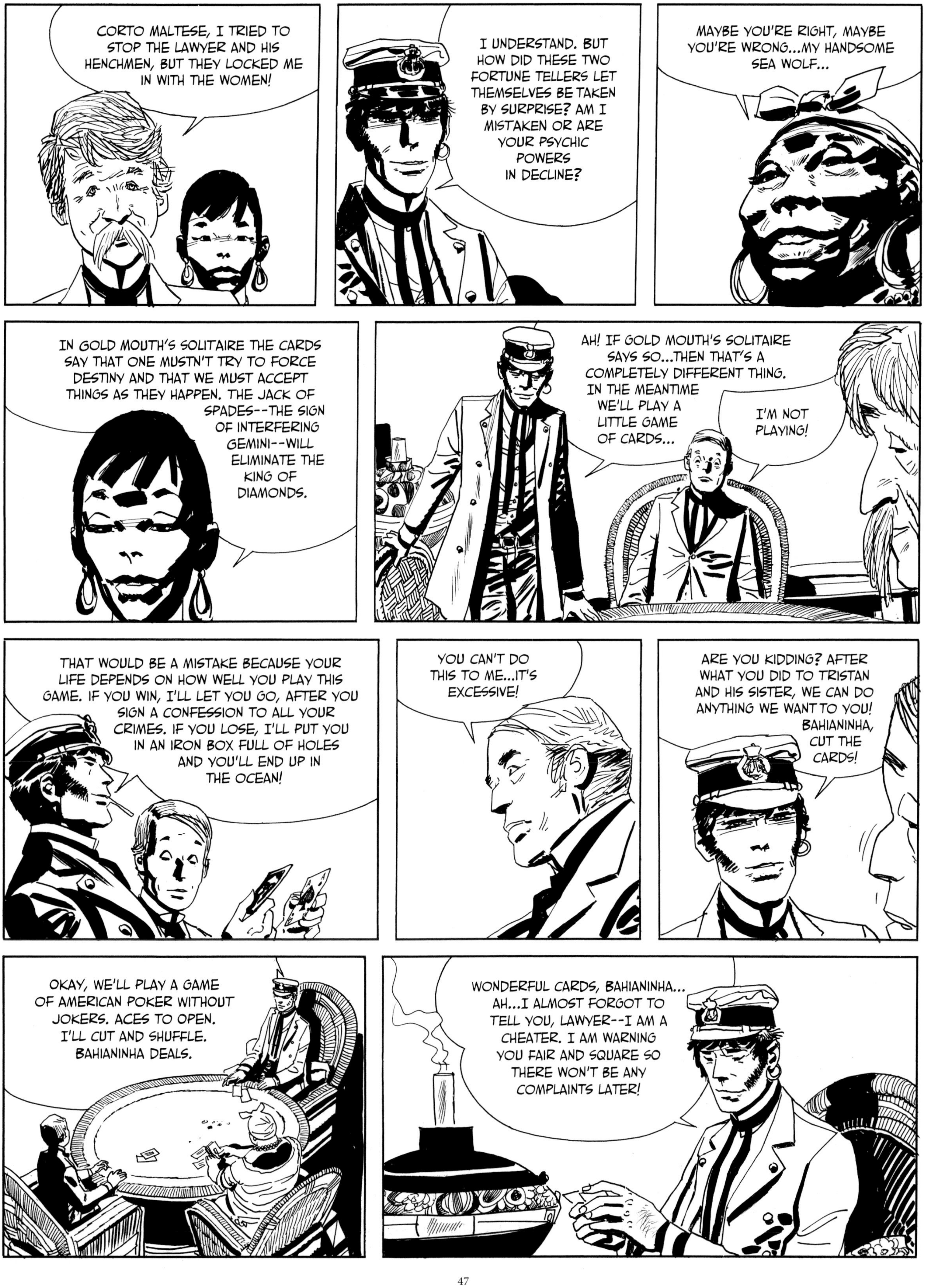
CORTO MALTESE, I TRIED TO STOP THE LAWYER AND HIS HENCHMEN, BUT THEY LOCKED ME IN WITH THE WOMEN!
I UNDERSTAND. BUT HOW DID THESE TWO FORTUNE TELLERS LET THEMSELVES BE TAKEN BY SURPRISE? AM I MISTAKEN OR ARE YOUR PSYCHIC POWERS IN DECLINE?
MAYBE YOU'RE RIGHT, MAYBE YOU'RE WRONG...MY HANDSOME SEA WOLF...
IN GOLD MOUTH'S SOLITAIRE THE CARDS SAY THAT ONE MUSTN'T TRY TO FORCE DESTINY AND THAT WE MUST ACCEPT THINGS AS THEY HAPPEN. THE JACK OF SPADES--THE SIGN OF INTERFERING GEMINI--WILL ELIMINATE THE KING OF DIAMONDS.
AH! IF GOLD MOUTH'S SOLITAIRE SAYS SO...THEN THAT'S A COMPLETELY DIFFERENT THING. IN THE MEANTIME WE'LL PLAY A LITTLE GAME OF CARDS...
I'M NOT PLAYING!
THAT WOULD BE A MISTAKE BECAUSE YOUR LIFE DEPENDS ON HOW WELL YOU PLAY THIS GAME. IF YOU WIN, I'LL LET YOU GO, AFTER YOU SIGN A CONFESSION TO ALL YOUR CRIMES. IF YOU LOSE, I'LL PUT YOU IN AN IRON BOX FULL OF HOLES AND YOU'LL END UP IN THE OCEAN!
YOU CAN'T DO THIS TO ME...IT'S EXCESSIVE!
ARE YOU KIDDING? AFTER WHAT YOU DID TO TRISTAN AND HIS SISTER, WE CAN DO ANYTHING WE WANT TO YOU! BAHIANINHA, CUT THE CARDS!
OKAY, WE'LL PLAY A GAME OF AMERICAN POKER WITHOUT JOKERS. ACES TO OPEN. I'LL CUT AND SHUFFLE. BAHIANINHA DEALS.
WONDERFUL CARDS, BAHIANINHA... AH...I ALMOST FORGOT TO TELL YOU, LAWYER--I AM A CHEATER. I AM WARNING YOU FAIR AND SQUARE SO THERE WON'T BE ANY COMPLAINTS LATER!

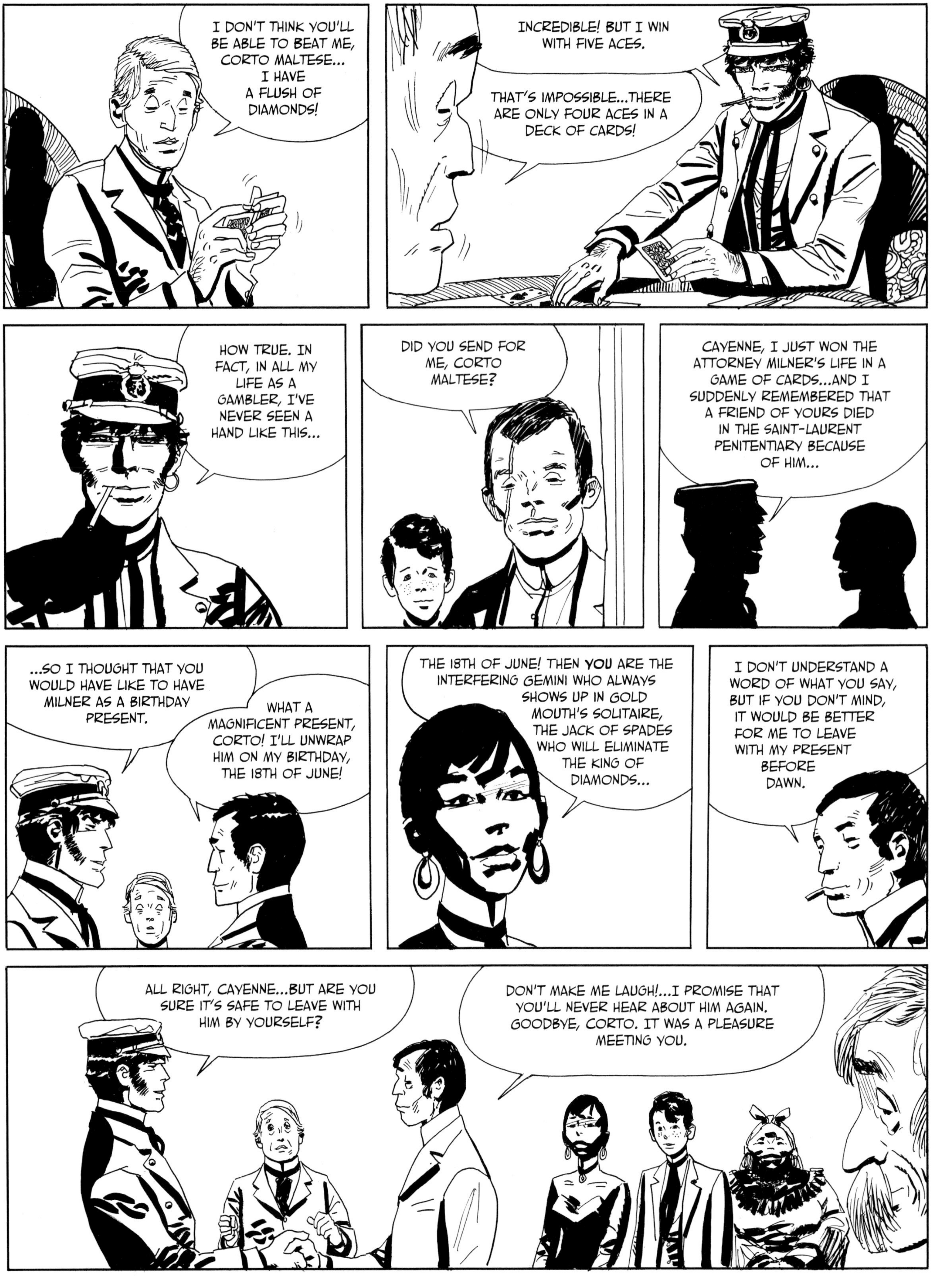
I DON'T THINK YOU'LL BE ABLE TO BEAT ME, CORTO MALTESE... I HAVE A FLUSH OF DIAMONDS!
INCREDIBLE! BUT I WIN WITH FIVE ACES.
THAT'S IMPOSSIBLE...THERE ARE ONLY FOUR ACES IN A DECK OF CARDS!
HOW TRUE. IN FACT, IN ALL MY LIFE AS A GAMBLER, I'VE NEVER SEEN A HAND LIKE THIS...
DID YOU SEND FOR ME, CORTO MALTESE?
CAYENNE, I JUST WON THE ATTORNEY MILNER'S LIFE IN A GAME OF CARDS...AND I SUDDENLY REMEMBERED THAT A FRIEND OF YOURS DIED IN THE SAINT-LAURENT PENITENTIARY BECAUSE OF HIM...
...SO I THOUGHT THAT YOU WOULD HAVE LIKE TO HAVE MILNER AS A BIRTHDAY PRESENT.
WHAT A MAGNIFICENT PRESENT, CORTO! I'LL UNWRAP HIM ON MY BIRTHDAY, THE 18TH OF JUNE!
THE 18TH OF JUNE! THEN **YOU** ARE THE INTERFERING GEMINI WHO ALWAYS SHOWS UP IN GOLD MOUTH'S SOLITAIRE, THE JACK OF SPADES WHO WILL ELIMINATE THE KING OF DIAMONDS...
I DON'T UNDERSTAND A WORD OF WHAT YOU SAY, BUT IF YOU DON'T MIND, IT WOULD BE BETTER FOR ME TO LEAVE WITH MY PRESENT BEFORE DAWN.
ALL RIGHT, CAYENNE...BUT ARE YOU SURE IT'S SAFE TO LEAVE WITH HIM BY YOURSELF?
DON'T MAKE ME LAUGH!...I PROMISE THAT YOU'LL NEVER HEAR ABOUT HIM AGAIN. GOODBYE, CORTO. IT WAS A PLEASURE MEETING YOU.

I'M SORRY TO SEE CAYENNE GO... BUT I'M SURE WE'LL SEE HIM AGAIN SOME DAY...

THESE ARE THE DOCUMENTS THAT OUR FATHER ENTRUSTED TO ME BEFORE GOING BACK TO LONDON...HE HAD DISCOVERED THE RUINS OF A VERY ANCIENT CIVILIZATION IN THE UPPER XINGU REGION OF BRAZIL...

...AND HERE HE GIVES DIRECTIONS TO GET THERE. HE WAS SURE THAT THESE RUINS WERE CONNECTED TO THE LOST CONTINENTS OF MU AND ATLANTIS.

HERE HE WRITES THAT FOR MANY NIGHTS HE FELT THE PRESENCE OF ANCIENT COSMIC FORCES AND THAT FOR A MOMENT HE THOUGHT HE HAD FINALLY ARRIVED AT THE SOLUTION TO THE ENIGMA OF THE MYTH OF MU.

PERHAPS THEY WERE THE SAME DREAMS I HAD LAST NIGHT...AS SOON AS I SAT IN MY ROOM, I FELL INTO A DEEP DREAM... I HAD A NIGHTMARE...I WAS EVEN GIVEN THE SKULL OF TEZCATLIPOCA! WHEN I WOKE UP THE SKULL WAS NOT THERE BUT THE ATTORNEY MILNER WAS SITTING IN FRONT OF ME.

TOCK! TOCK! TOCK!

NO ONE'S THERE.

THERE WAS ONLY THIS LEATHER BAG.

LISTEN... THE WIND SAYS THAT IT'S FOR TRISTAN!

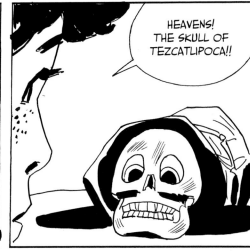

HEAVENS! THE SKULL OF TEZCATLIPOCA!!

BUT THEN, WHAT'S HAPPENING TO ME? AM I STILL DREAMING...?

MAYBE YOU WERE NOT DREAMING YESTERDAY...THIS RELIC COMES FROM ANOTHER WORLD!

IT'S AN INCREDIBLE STORY... IT'S NOT POSSIBLE!

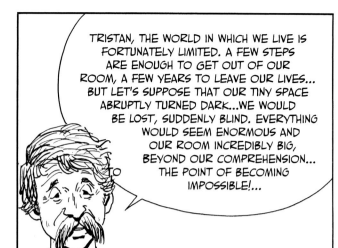

TRISTAN, THE WORLD IN WHICH WE LIVE IS FORTUNATELY LIMITED. A FEW STEPS ARE ENOUGH TO GET OUT OF OUR ROOM, A FEW YEARS TO LEAVE OUR LIVES... BUT LET'S SUPPOSE THAT OUR TINY SPACE ABRUPTLY TURNED DARK...WE WOULD BE LOST, SUDDENLY BLIND. EVERYTHING WOULD SEEM ENORMOUS AND OUR ROOM INCREDIBLY BIG, BEYOND OUR COMPREHENSION... THE POINT OF BECOMING IMPOSSIBLE!...

IMPOSSIBLE!...AND ALL THE SAME, ONE ANSWER CAN EXPLAIN EVERYTHING. BUT THEN YOU'LL ASK A HUNDRED MORE QUESTIONS AND THERE WILL BE A HUNDRED OTHER ANSWERS... YOU'LL SEE THAT THE ABSOLUTE DOESN'T EXIST IN ONE SENSE OR THE OTHER...THAT EVERYTHING IS POSSIBLE!!!

THIS ADVENTURE IS OUTSIDE MY DIMENSION... I SUGGEST WE TAKE A BOAT RIDE.

LET'S HEAD TOWARD ITAPOA, WHERE WE'LL FIND GOLD MOUTH, THE WOMAN WHO TAUGHT MAGIC TO MORGANA.

SINCE WE'LL BE IN THAT PART OF BRAZIL, I'D LIKE TO SPEND TIME WITH MY FRIENDS IN AREIA BRANCA.

THE WEATHER'S NICE TODAY AND I'M HAPPY.

MY DEAR STEINER, HAVE I EVER TOLD YOU ABOUT THE GALLEON LOADED WITH GOLD THAT SANK OFF THE NORTHERN COAST OF BRAZIL, CLOSE TO BELEM...

A GALLEON LOADED WITH GOLD... SHIPWRECKED?!

YES, IT WENT DOWN ON THE REEF NEAR THE ISLAND OF MARACÀ IN BRAZILIAN GUYANA.

HOW DID YOU LEARN ABOUT IT, CORTO?

WELL, THE DAY BEFORE YESTERDAY I MET CLEOPATRA'S MUMMY AT A CAFÉ AND I HAD A CHAT WITH HER-- SHE TOLD ME ABOUT THE GALLEON...

YOU'RE PULLING OUR LEGS.

AH, NO, MY FRIENDS! YOU ARE THE ONES WHO STARTED TELLING STORIES ABOUT GHOSTS, DEAD PEOPLE, AND THE LIKE...DON'T I ALSO HAVE THE RIGHT TO SPIN MY OWN TALES OF THE DEAD? SO, AS I WAS SAYING, I WAS SITTING THERE WITH CLEOPATRA AND SHE...

CHAPTER THREE:

SURESHOT
SAMBA

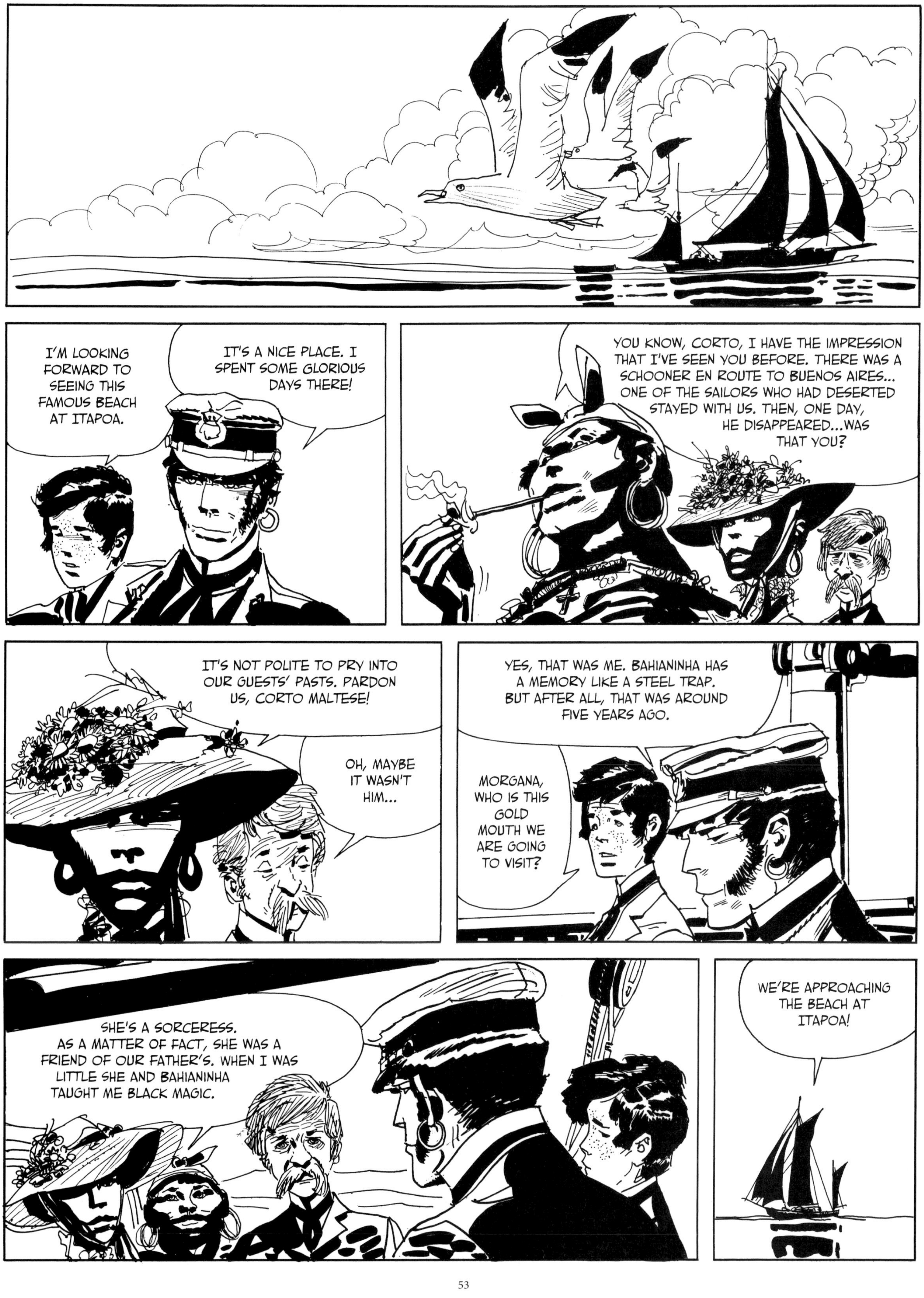
I'M LOOKING FORWARD TO SEEING THIS FAMOUS BEACH AT ITAPOA.
IT'S A NICE PLACE. I SPENT SOME GLORIOUS DAYS THERE!
YOU KNOW, CORTO, I HAVE THE IMPRESSION THAT I'VE SEEN YOU BEFORE. THERE WAS A SCHOONER EN ROUTE TO BUENOS AIRES... ONE OF THE SAILORS WHO HAD DESERTED STAYED WITH US. THEN, ONE DAY, HE DISAPPEARED...WAS THAT YOU?
IT'S NOT POLITE TO PRY INTO OUR GUESTS' PASTS. PARDON US, CORTO MALTESE!
OH, MAYBE IT WASN'T HIM...
YES, THAT WAS ME. BAHIANINHA HAS A MEMORY LIKE A STEEL TRAP. BUT AFTER ALL, THAT WAS AROUND FIVE YEARS AGO.
MORGANA, WHO IS THIS GOLD MOUTH WE ARE GOING TO VISIT?
SHE'S A SORCERESS. AS A MATTER OF FACT, SHE WAS A FRIEND OF OUR FATHER'S. WHEN I WAS LITTLE SHE AND BAHIANINHA TAUGHT ME BLACK MAGIC.
WE'RE APPROACHING THE BEACH AT ITAPOA!

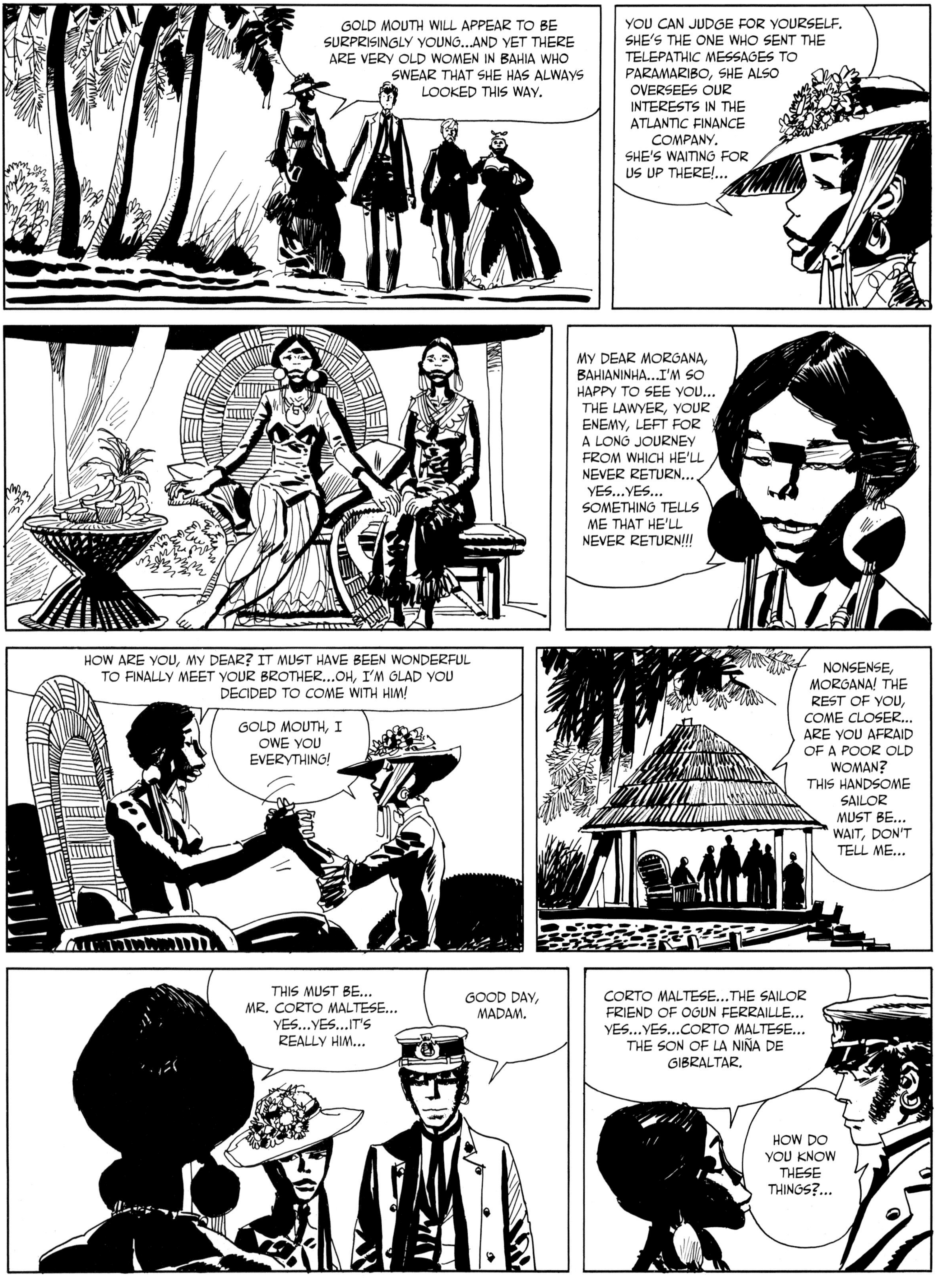
GOLD MOUTH WILL APPEAR TO BE SURPRISINGLY YOUNG...AND YET THERE ARE VERY OLD WOMEN IN BAHIA WHO SWEAR THAT SHE HAS ALWAYS LOOKED THIS WAY.
YOU CAN JUDGE FOR YOURSELF. SHE'S THE ONE WHO SENT THE TELEPATHIC MESSAGES TO PARAMARIBO, SHE ALSO OVERSEES OUR INTERESTS IN THE ATLANTIC FINANCE COMPANY. SHE'S WAITING FOR US UP THERE!...
MY DEAR MORGANA, BAHIANINHA...I'M SO HAPPY TO SEE YOU... THE LAWYER, YOUR ENEMY, LEFT FOR A LONG JOURNEY FROM WHICH HE'LL NEVER RETURN... YES...YES... SOMETHING TELLS ME THAT HE'LL NEVER RETURN!!!
HOW ARE YOU, MY DEAR? IT MUST HAVE BEEN WONDERFUL TO FINALLY MEET YOUR BROTHER...OH, I'M GLAD YOU DECIDED TO COME WITH HIM!
GOLD MOUTH, I OWE YOU EVERYTHING!
NONSENSE, MORGANA! THE REST OF YOU, COME CLOSER... ARE YOU AFRAID OF A POOR OLD WOMAN? THIS HANDSOME SAILOR MUST BE... WAIT, DON'T TELL ME...
THIS MUST BE... MR. CORTO MALTESE... YES...YES...IT'S REALLY HIM...
GOOD DAY, MADAM.
CORTO MALTESE...THE SAILOR FRIEND OF OGUN FERRAILLE... YES...YES...CORTO MALTESE... THE SON OF LA NIÑA DE GIBRALTAR.
HOW DO YOU KNOW THESE THINGS?...

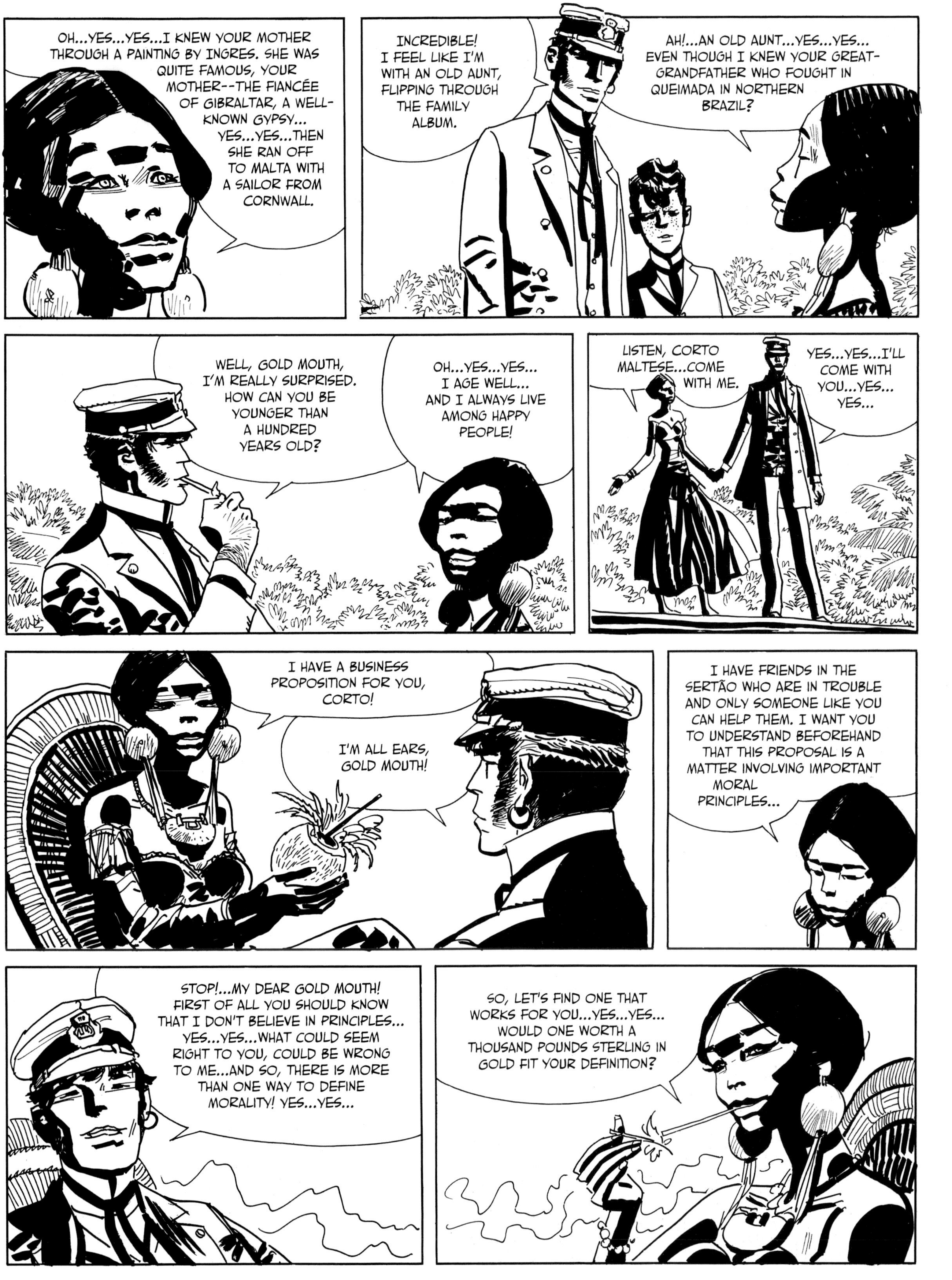
OH...YES...YES...I KNEW YOUR MOTHER THROUGH A PAINTING BY INGRES. SHE WAS QUITE FAMOUS, YOUR MOTHER--THE FIANCÉE OF GIBRALTAR, A WELL-KNOWN GYPSY... YES...YES...THEN SHE RAN OFF TO MALTA WITH A SAILOR FROM CORNWALL.
INCREDIBLE! I FEEL LIKE I'M WITH AN OLD AUNT, FLIPPING THROUGH THE FAMILY ALBUM.
AH!...AN OLD AUNT...YES...YES... EVEN THOUGH I KNEW YOUR GREAT-GRANDFATHER WHO FOUGHT IN QUEIMADA IN NORTHERN BRAZIL?
WELL, GOLD MOUTH, I'M REALLY SURPRISED. HOW CAN YOU BE YOUNGER THAN A HUNDRED YEARS OLD?
OH...YES...YES... I AGE WELL... AND I ALWAYS LIVE AMONG HAPPY PEOPLE!
LISTEN, CORTO MALTESE...COME WITH ME.
YES...YES...I'LL COME WITH YOU...YES... YES...
I HAVE A BUSINESS PROPOSITION FOR YOU, CORTO!
I'M ALL EARS, GOLD MOUTH!
I HAVE FRIENDS IN THE SERTÃO WHO ARE IN TROUBLE AND ONLY SOMEONE LIKE YOU CAN HELP THEM. I WANT YOU TO UNDERSTAND BEFOREHAND THAT THIS PROPOSAL IS A MATTER INVOLVING IMPORTANT MORAL PRINCIPLES...
STOP!...MY DEAR GOLD MOUTH! FIRST OF ALL YOU SHOULD KNOW THAT I DON'T BELIEVE IN PRINCIPLES... YES...YES...WHAT COULD SEEM RIGHT TO YOU, COULD BE WRONG TO ME...AND SO, THERE IS MORE THAN ONE WAY TO DEFINE MORALITY! YES...YES...
SO, LET'S FIND ONE THAT WORKS FOR YOU...YES...YES... WOULD ONE WORTH A THOUSAND POUNDS STERLING IN GOLD FIT YOUR DEFINITION?

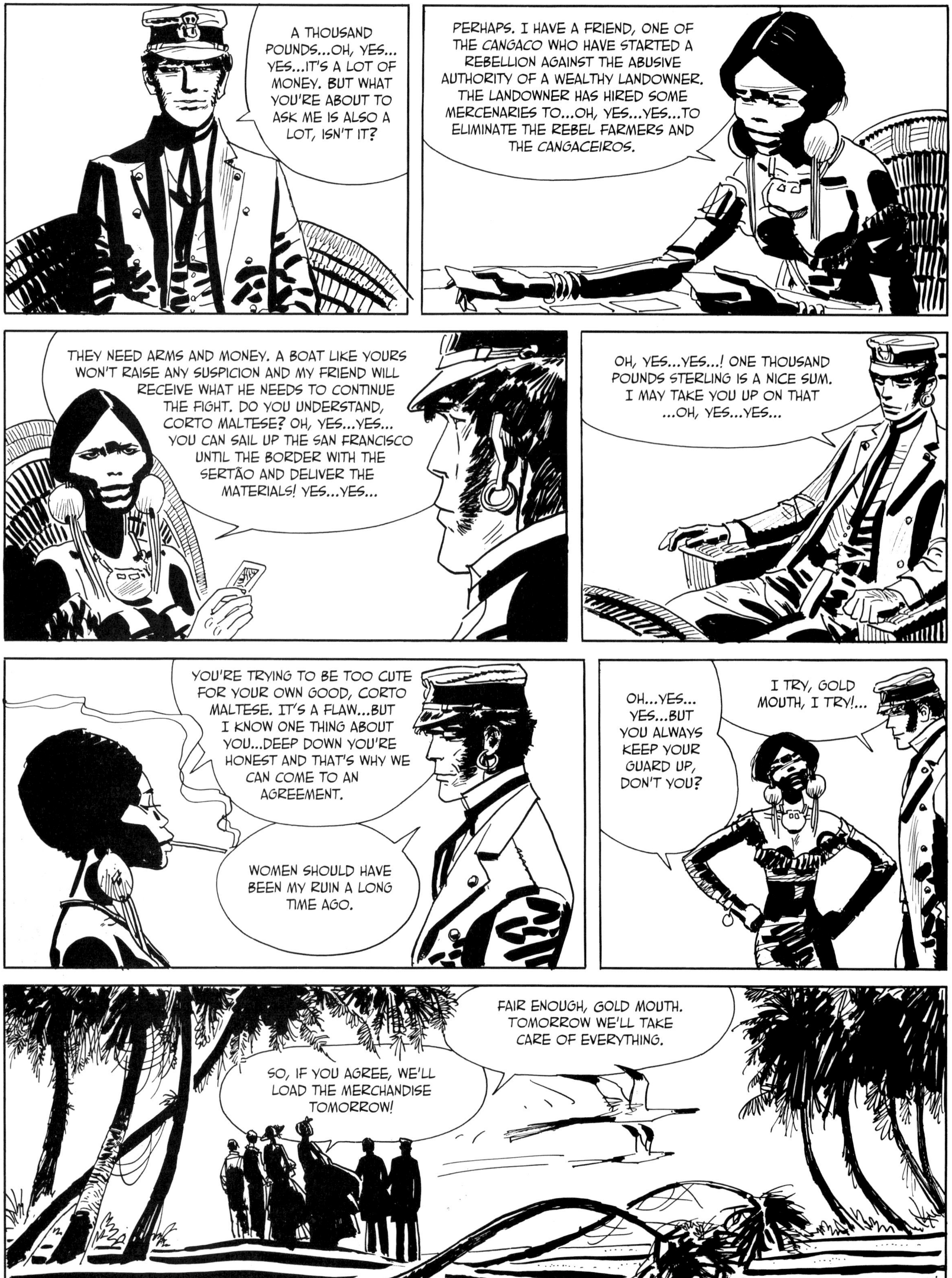

A THOUSAND POUNDS...OH, YES... YES...IT'S A LOT OF MONEY. BUT WHAT YOU'RE ABOUT TO ASK ME IS ALSO A LOT, ISN'T IT?
PERHAPS. I HAVE A FRIEND, ONE OF THE *CANGACO* WHO HAVE STARTED A REBELLION AGAINST THE ABUSIVE AUTHORITY OF A WEALTHY LANDOWNER. THE LANDOWNER HAS HIRED SOME MERCENARIES TO...OH, YES...YES...TO ELIMINATE THE REBEL FARMERS AND THE *CANGACEIROS*.
THEY NEED ARMS AND MONEY. A BOAT LIKE YOURS WON'T RAISE ANY SUSPICION AND MY FRIEND WILL RECEIVE WHAT HE NEEDS TO CONTINUE THE FIGHT. DO YOU UNDERSTAND, CORTO MALTESE? OH, YES...YES... YOU CAN SAIL UP THE SAN FRANCISCO UNTIL THE BORDER WITH THE SERTÃO AND DELIVER THE MATERIALS! YES...YES...
OH, YES...YES...! ONE THOUSAND POUNDS STERLING IS A NICE SUM. I MAY TAKE YOU UP ON THAT ...OH, YES...YES...
YOU'RE TRYING TO BE TOO CUTE FOR YOUR OWN GOOD, CORTO MALTESE. IT'S A FLAW...BUT I KNOW ONE THING ABOUT YOU...DEEP DOWN YOU'RE HONEST AND THAT'S WHY WE CAN COME TO AN AGREEMENT.
WOMEN SHOULD HAVE BEEN MY RUIN A LONG TIME AGO.
OH...YES... YES...BUT YOU ALWAYS KEEP YOUR GUARD UP, DON'T YOU?
I TRY, GOLD MOUTH, I TRY!...
SO, IF YOU AGREE, WE'LL LOAD THE MERCHANDISE TOMORROW!
FAIR ENOUGH, GOLD MOUTH. TOMORROW WE'LL TAKE CARE OF EVERYTHING.

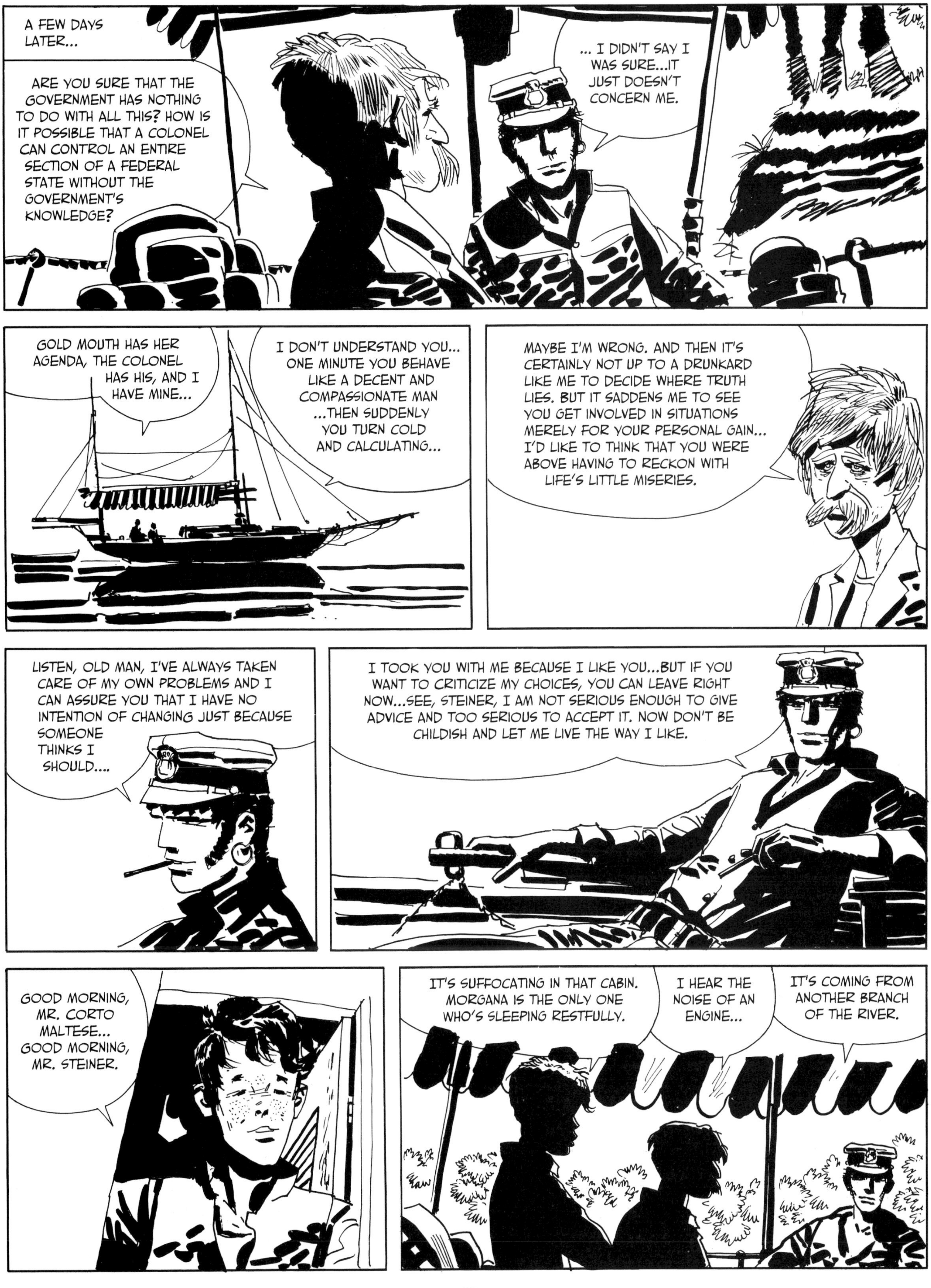
A FEW DAYS LATER...
ARE YOU SURE THAT THE GOVERNMENT HAS NOTHING TO DO WITH ALL THIS? HOW IS IT POSSIBLE THAT A COLONEL CAN CONTROL AN ENTIRE SECTION OF A FEDERAL STATE WITHOUT THE GOVERNMENT'S KNOWLEDGE?
... I DIDN'T SAY I WAS SURE...IT JUST DOESN'T CONCERN ME.
GOLD MOUTH HAS HER AGENDA, THE COLONEL HAS HIS, AND I HAVE MINE...
I DON'T UNDERSTAND YOU... ONE MINUTE YOU BEHAVE LIKE A DECENT AND COMPASSIONATE MAN ...THEN SUDDENLY YOU TURN COLD AND CALCULATING...
MAYBE I'M WRONG. AND THEN IT'S CERTAINLY NOT UP TO A DRUNKARD LIKE ME TO DECIDE WHERE TRUTH LIES. BUT IT SADDENS ME TO SEE YOU GET INVOLVED IN SITUATIONS MERELY FOR YOUR PERSONAL GAIN... I'D LIKE TO THINK THAT YOU WERE ABOVE HAVING TO RECKON WITH LIFE'S LITTLE MISERIES.
LISTEN, OLD MAN, I'VE ALWAYS TAKEN CARE OF MY OWN PROBLEMS AND I CAN ASSURE YOU THAT I HAVE NO INTENTION OF CHANGING JUST BECAUSE SOMEONE THINKS I SHOULD....
I TOOK YOU WITH ME BECAUSE I LIKE YOU...BUT IF YOU WANT TO CRITICIZE MY CHOICES, YOU CAN LEAVE RIGHT NOW...SEE, STEINER, I AM NOT SERIOUS ENOUGH TO GIVE ADVICE AND TOO SERIOUS TO ACCEPT IT. NOW DON'T BE CHILDISH AND LET ME LIVE THE WAY I LIKE.
GOOD MORNING, MR. CORTO MALTESE... GOOD MORNING, MR. STEINER.
IT'S SUFFOCATING IN THAT CABIN. MORGANA IS THE ONLY ONE WHO'S SLEEPING RESTFULLY.
I HEAR THE NOISE OF AN ENGINE...
IT'S COMING FROM ANOTHER BRANCH OF THE RIVER.

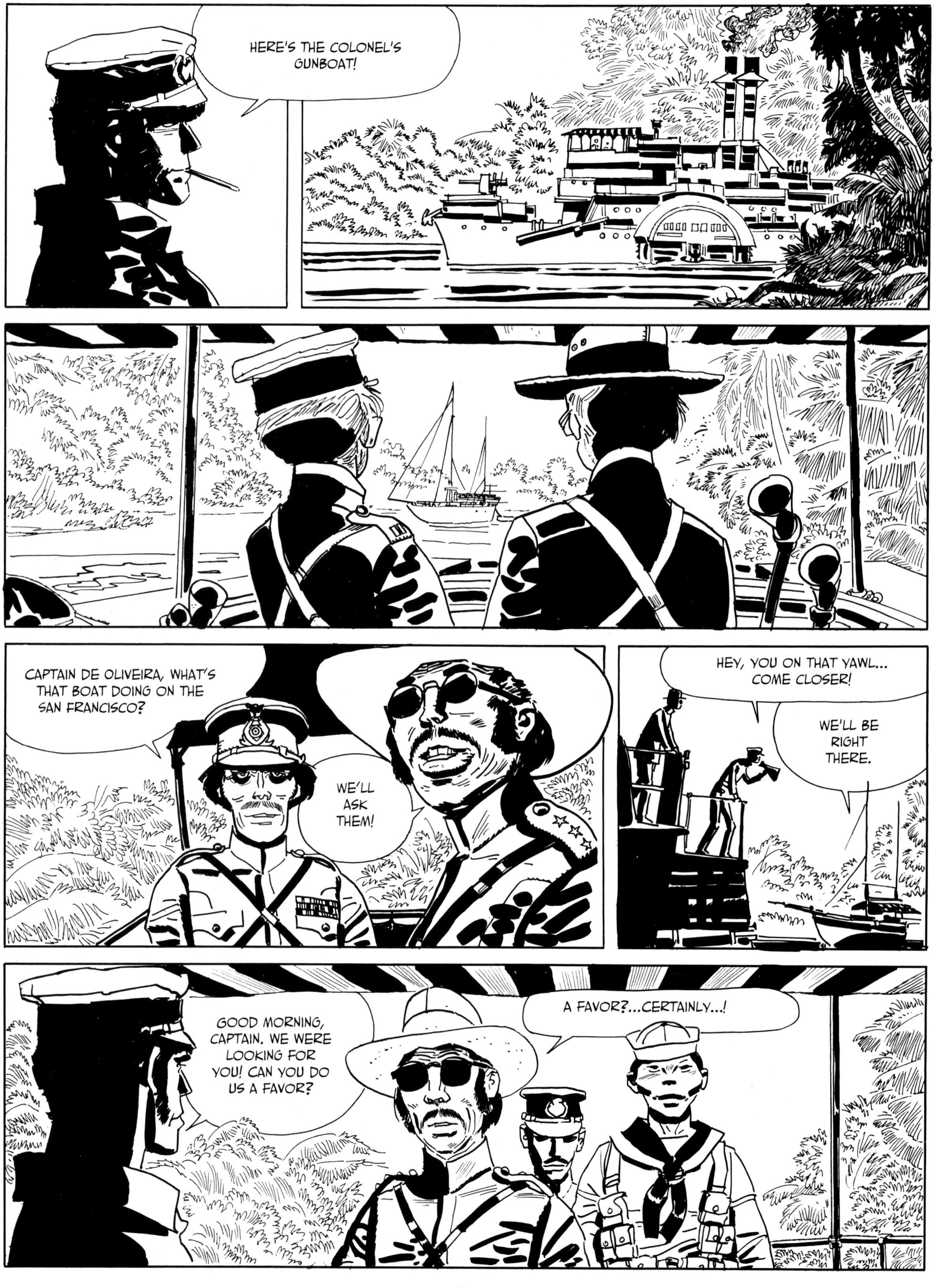
HERE'S THE COLONEL'S GUNBOAT!
CAPTAIN DE OLIVEIRA, WHAT'S THAT BOAT DOING ON THE SAN FRANCISCO?
WE'LL ASK THEM!
HEY, YOU ON THAT YAWL... COME CLOSER!
WE'LL BE RIGHT THERE.
GOOD MORNING, CAPTAIN. WE WERE LOOKING FOR YOU! CAN YOU DO US A FAVOR?
A FAVOR?...CERTAINLY...!

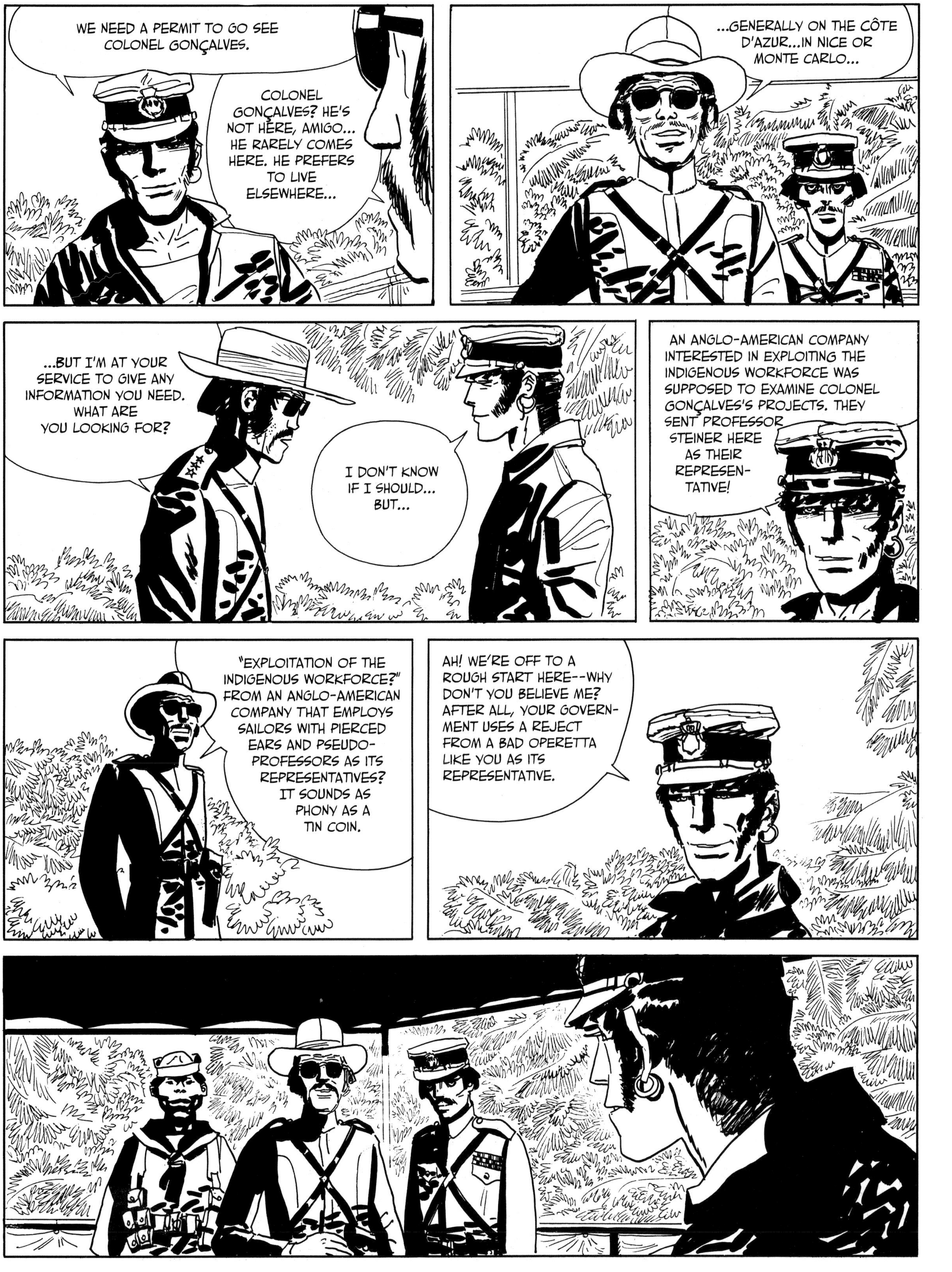
WE NEED A PERMIT TO GO SEE COLONEL GONÇALVES.
COLONEL GONÇALVES? HE'S NOT HERE, AMIGO... HE RARELY COMES HERE. HE PREFERS TO LIVE ELSEWHERE...
...GENERALLY ON THE CÔTE D'AZUR...IN NICE OR MONTE CARLO...
...BUT I'M AT YOUR SERVICE TO GIVE ANY INFORMATION YOU NEED. WHAT ARE YOU LOOKING FOR?
I DON'T KNOW IF I SHOULD... BUT...
AN ANGLO-AMERICAN COMPANY INTERESTED IN EXPLOITING THE INDIGENOUS WORKFORCE WAS SUPPOSED TO EXAMINE COLONEL GONÇALVES'S PROJECTS. THEY SENT PROFESSOR STEINER HERE AS THEIR REPRESEN-TATIVE!
"EXPLOITATION OF THE INDIGENOUS WORKFORCE?" FROM AN ANGLO-AMERICAN COMPANY THAT EMPLOYS SAILORS WITH PIERCED EARS AND PSEUDO-PROFESSORS AS ITS REPRESENTATIVES? IT SOUNDS AS PHONY AS A TIN COIN.
AH! WE'RE OFF TO A ROUGH START HERE--WHY DON'T YOU BELIEVE ME? AFTER ALL, YOUR GOVERN-MENT USES A REJECT FROM A BAD OPERETTA LIKE YOU AS ITS REPRESENTATIVE.

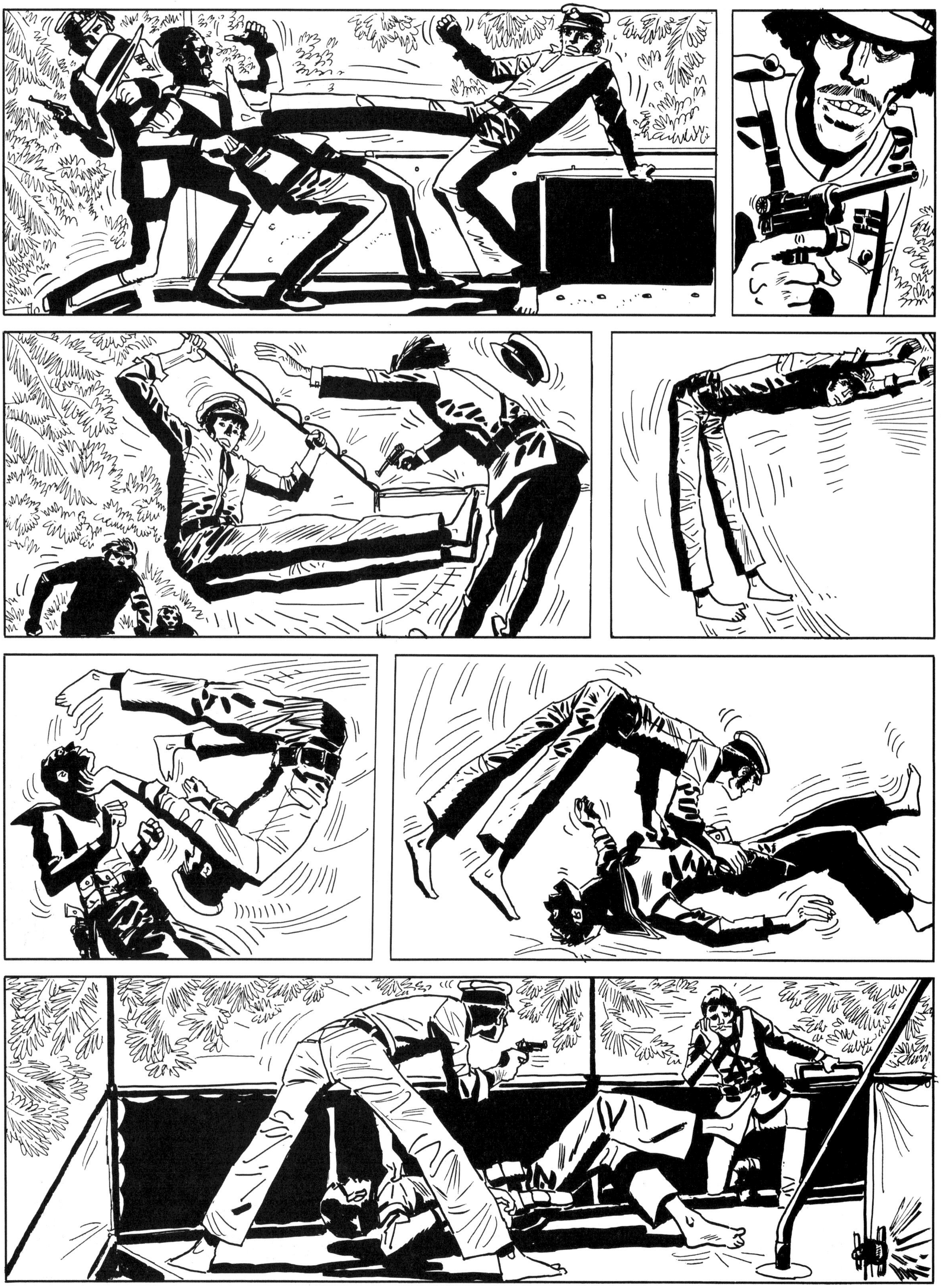

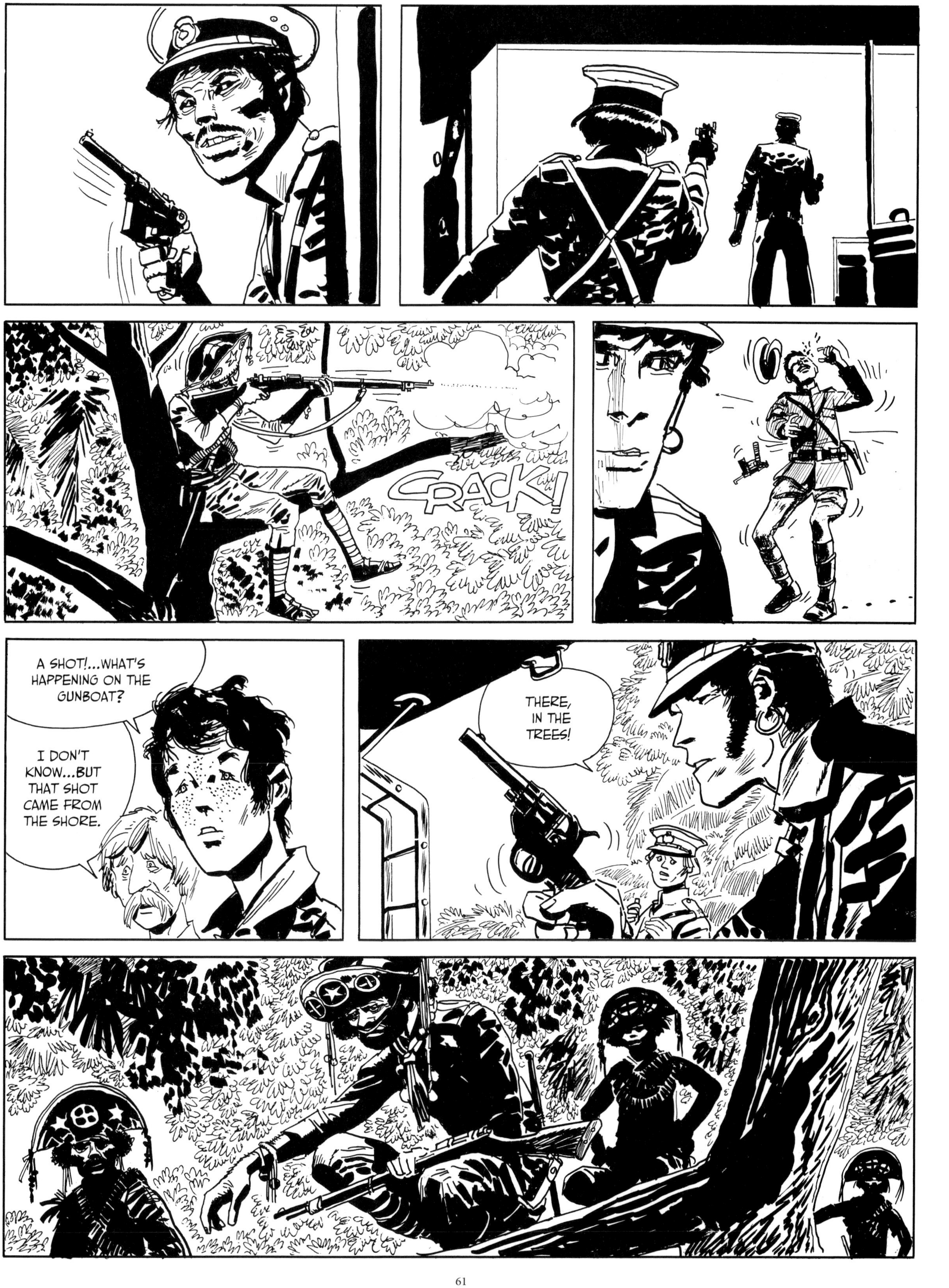
CRACK!
A SHOT!...WHAT'S HAPPENING ON THE GUNBOAT?
I DON'T KNOW...BUT THAT SHOT CAME FROM THE SHORE.
THERE, IN THE TREES!

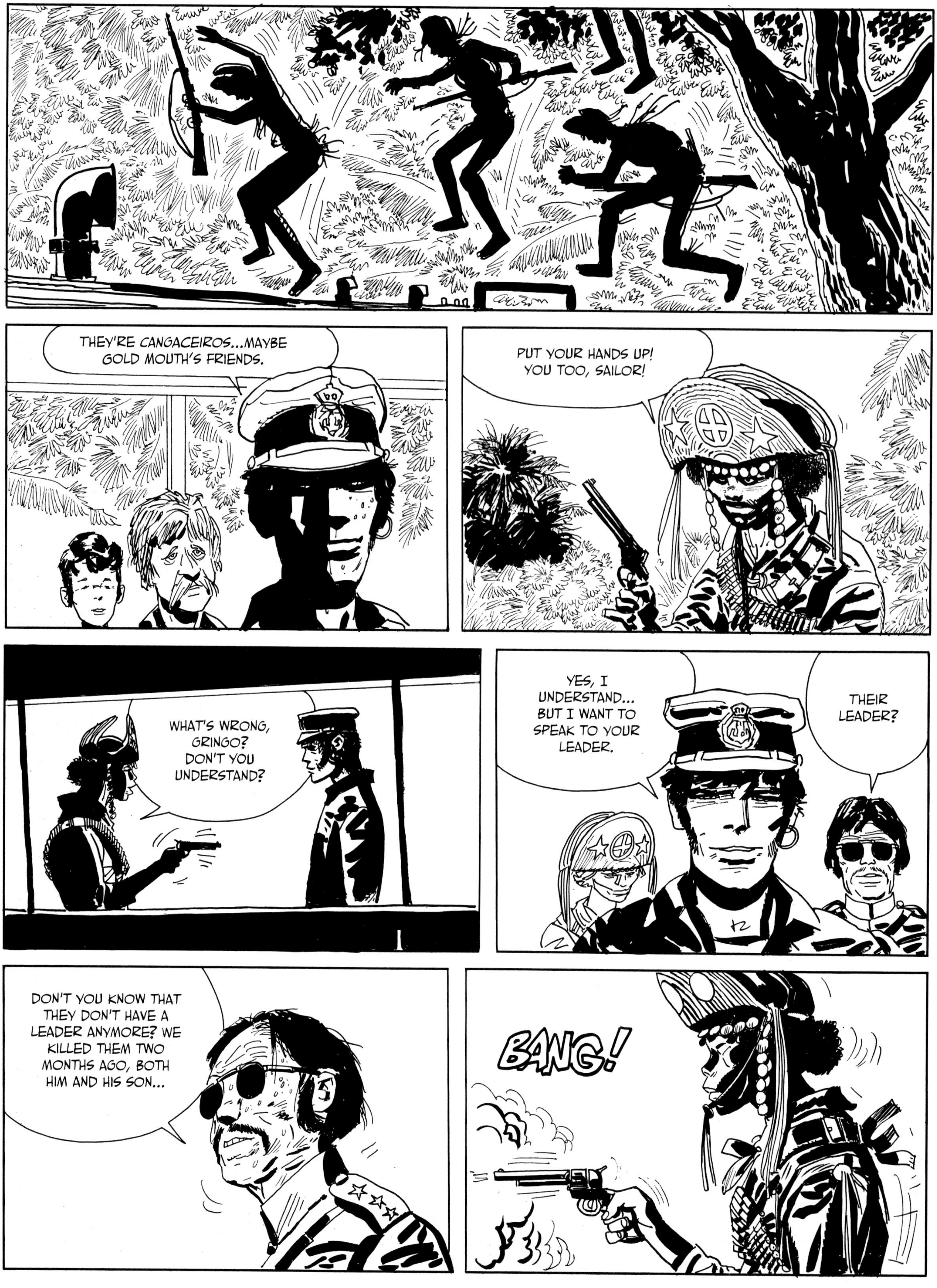
THEY'RE CANGACEIROS...MAYBE GOLD MOUTH'S FRIENDS.
PUT YOUR HANDS UP! YOU TOO, SAILOR!
WHAT'S WRONG, GRINGO? DON'T YOU UNDERSTAND?
YES, I UNDERSTAND... BUT I WANT TO SPEAK TO YOUR LEADER.
THEIR LEADER?
DON'T YOU KNOW THAT THEY DON'T HAVE A LEADER ANYMORE? WE KILLED THEM TWO MONTHS AGO, BOTH HIM AND HIS SON...
BANG!

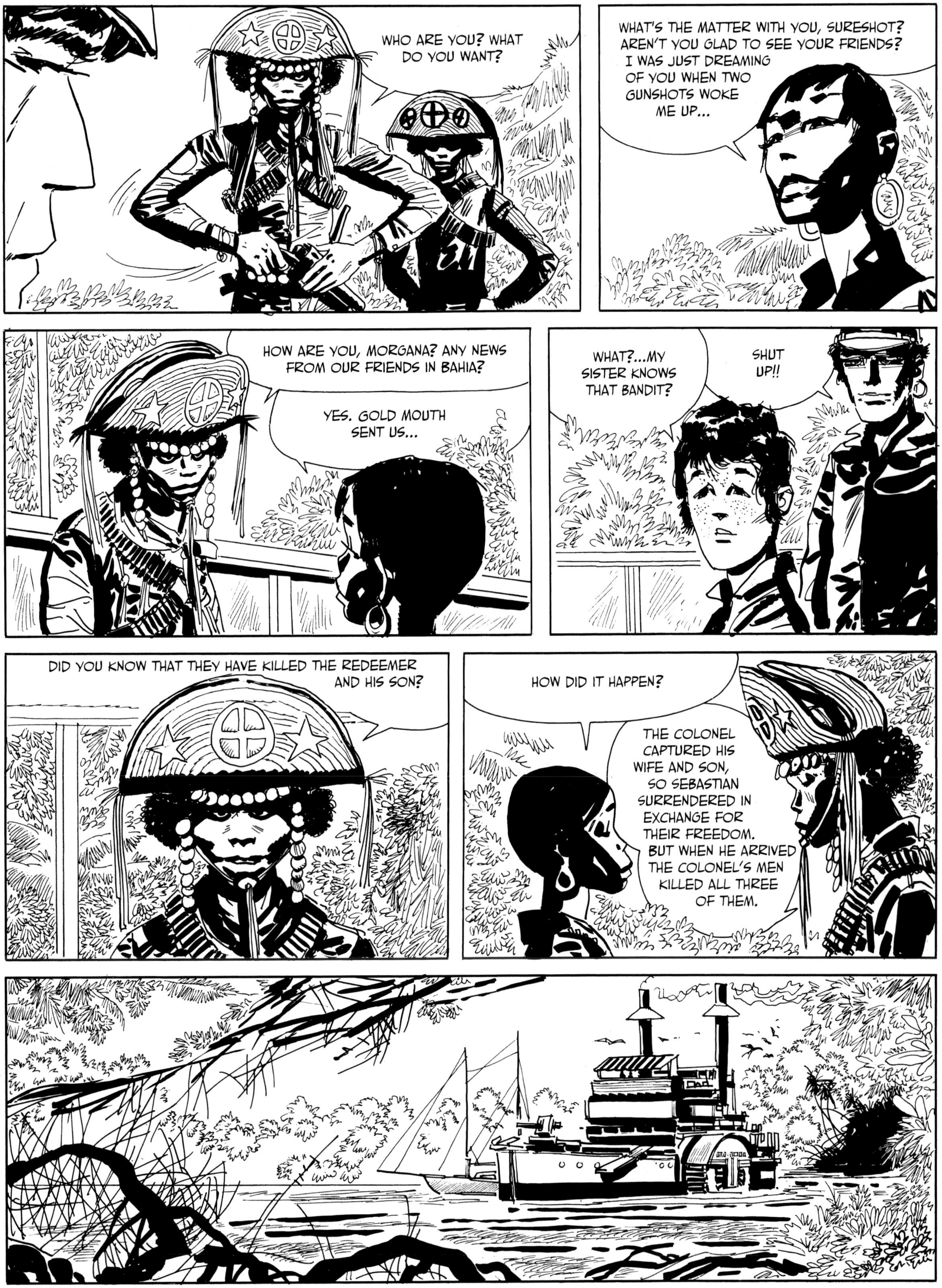

WHO ARE YOU? WHAT DO YOU WANT?
WHAT'S THE MATTER WITH YOU, SURESHOT? AREN'T YOU GLAD TO SEE YOUR FRIENDS? I WAS JUST DREAMING OF YOU WHEN TWO GUNSHOTS WOKE ME UP...
HOW ARE YOU, MORGANA? ANY NEWS FROM OUR FRIENDS IN BAHIA?
YES. GOLD MOUTH SENT US...
WHAT?...MY SISTER KNOWS THAT BANDIT?
SHUT UP!!
DID YOU KNOW THAT THEY HAVE KILLED THE REDEEMER AND HIS SON?
HOW DID IT HAPPEN?
THE COLONEL CAPTURED HIS WIFE AND SON, SO SEBASTIAN SURRENDERED IN EXCHANGE FOR THEIR FREEDOM. BUT WHEN HE ARRIVED THE COLONEL'S MEN KILLED ALL THREE OF THEM.

WELL, THAT'S THAT, SURESHOT. I DID WHAT I WAS SUPPOSED TO DO. IF YOUR LEADER IS DEAD, THERE'S NOTHING I CAN DO ABOUT IT. THE ARMS AND MONEY SENT BY GOLD MOUTH ARE IN THE YAWL.

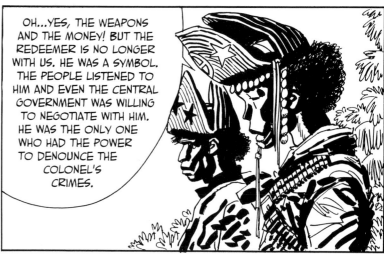

OH...YES, THE WEAPONS AND THE MONEY! BUT THE REDEEMER IS NO LONGER WITH US. HE WAS A SYMBOL. THE PEOPLE LISTENED TO HIM AND EVEN THE CENTRAL GOVERNMENT WAS WILLING TO NEGOTIATE WITH HIM. HE WAS THE ONLY ONE WHO HAD THE POWER TO DENOUNCE THE COLONEL'S CRIMES.

OKAY, MAYBE YOU LOST A GREAT MAN, BUT AFTER ALL, A LEADER WHO LEAVES HIS PEOPLE WITHOUT A PLAN AND LETS HIMSELF BE CAPTURED LIKE A CHILD IN ORDER TO SOLVE WHAT WAS A PERSONAL MATTER DOESN'T SEEM VERY COMPETENT TO ME.

LISTEN, GRINGO, DON'T SPEAK LIKE THAT ABOUT THE REDEEMER OR I'LL KILL YOU. YOU CAN'T UNDERSTAND WHAT HE REPRESENTED TO US. WITHOUT HIM IT'S ALL OVER! THE PEOPLE ARE LETTING THEMSELVES BE HUMILIATED BY THESE RUTHLESS OPPRESSORS.

ACTIONS ARE MORE IMPORTANT THAN WORDS!

THE ASSAULT ON THE GUNBOAT WAS A BOLD ACT OF COURAGE...WHY DID YOU DO IT?

I KILLED CAPTAIN DE OLIVEIRA TO AVENGE THE DEATH OF THE REDEEMER!

WELL, NOW IT'S DONE...YOU KILLED THE EXECUTIONER. BUT WHAT ABOUT THE ONE WHO'S TRULY RESPONSIBLE? WHAT ABOUT THE COLONEL WHO, UNBEKNOWNST TO THE CENTRAL GOVERNMENT, SURVIVES OFF OF HIS ABUSE AND CRIMES? WILL HE CONTINUE TO TERRORIZE YOU WITH HIS PISTOLEROS?

WHAT CAN I DO?

TAKE THE REDEEMER'S PLACE!

AH!... GRINGO, I AM A BANDIT!

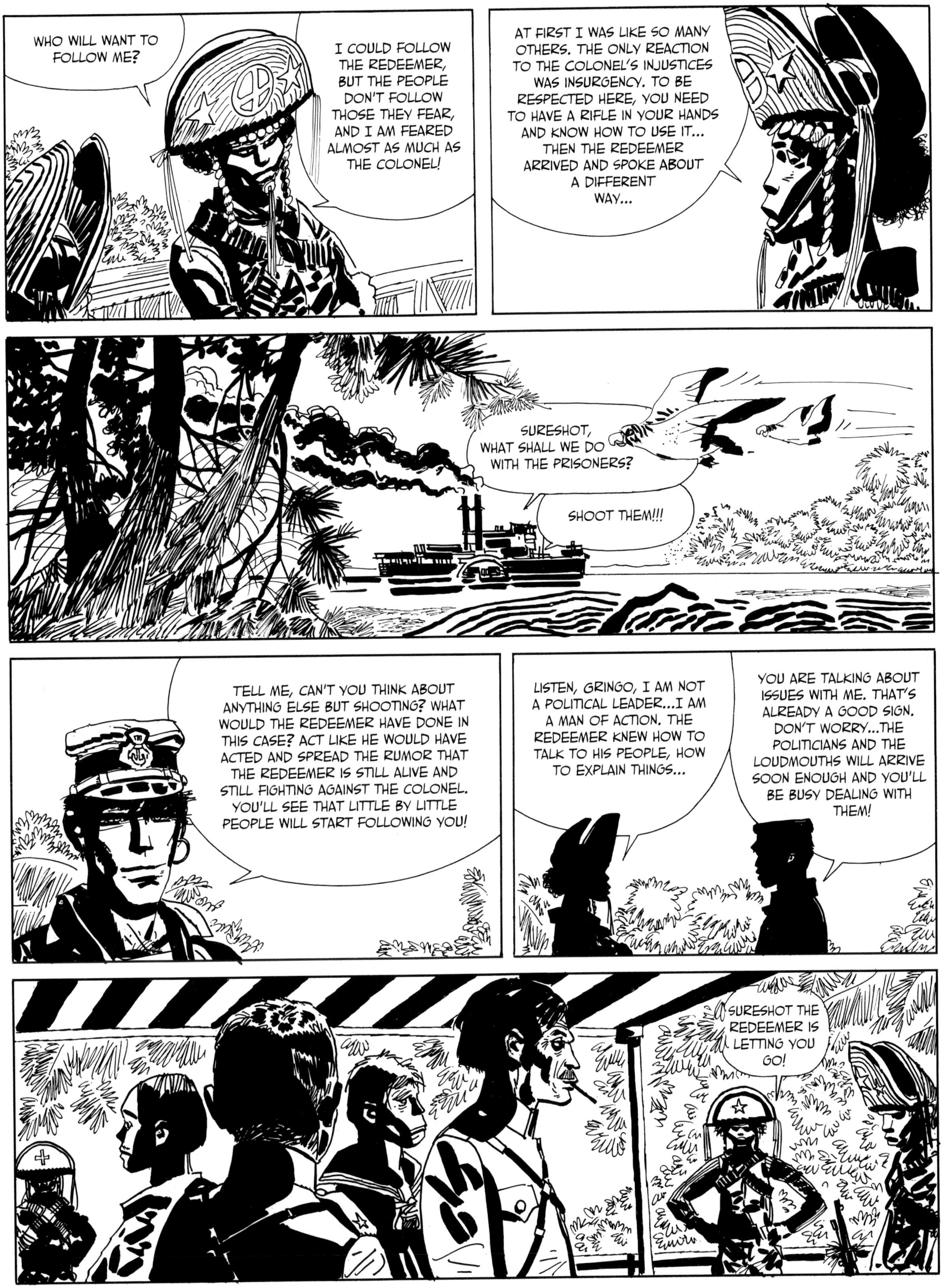
WHO WILL WANT TO FOLLOW ME?
I COULD FOLLOW THE REDEEMER, BUT THE PEOPLE DON'T FOLLOW THOSE THEY FEAR, AND I AM FEARED ALMOST AS MUCH AS THE COLONEL!
AT FIRST I WAS LIKE SO MANY OTHERS. THE ONLY REACTION TO THE COLONEL'S INJUSTICES WAS INSURGENCY. TO BE RESPECTED HERE, YOU NEED TO HAVE A RIFLE IN YOUR HANDS AND KNOW HOW TO USE IT... THEN THE REDEEMER ARRIVED AND SPOKE ABOUT A DIFFERENT WAY...
SURESHOT, WHAT SHALL WE DO WITH THE PRISONERS?
SHOOT THEM!!!
TELL ME, CAN'T YOU THINK ABOUT ANYTHING ELSE BUT SHOOTING? WHAT WOULD THE REDEEMER HAVE DONE IN THIS CASE? ACT LIKE HE WOULD HAVE ACTED AND SPREAD THE RUMOR THAT THE REDEEMER IS STILL ALIVE AND STILL FIGHTING AGAINST THE COLONEL. YOU'LL SEE THAT LITTLE BY LITTLE PEOPLE WILL START FOLLOWING YOU!
LISTEN, GRINGO, I AM NOT A POLITICAL LEADER...I AM A MAN OF ACTION. THE REDEEMER KNEW HOW TO TALK TO HIS PEOPLE, HOW TO EXPLAIN THINGS...
YOU ARE TALKING ABOUT ISSUES WITH ME. THAT'S ALREADY A GOOD SIGN. DON'T WORRY...THE POLITICIANS AND THE LOUDMOUTHS WILL ARRIVE SOON ENOUGH AND YOU'LL BE BUSY DEALING WITH THEM!
SURESHOT THE REDEEMER IS LETTING YOU GO!

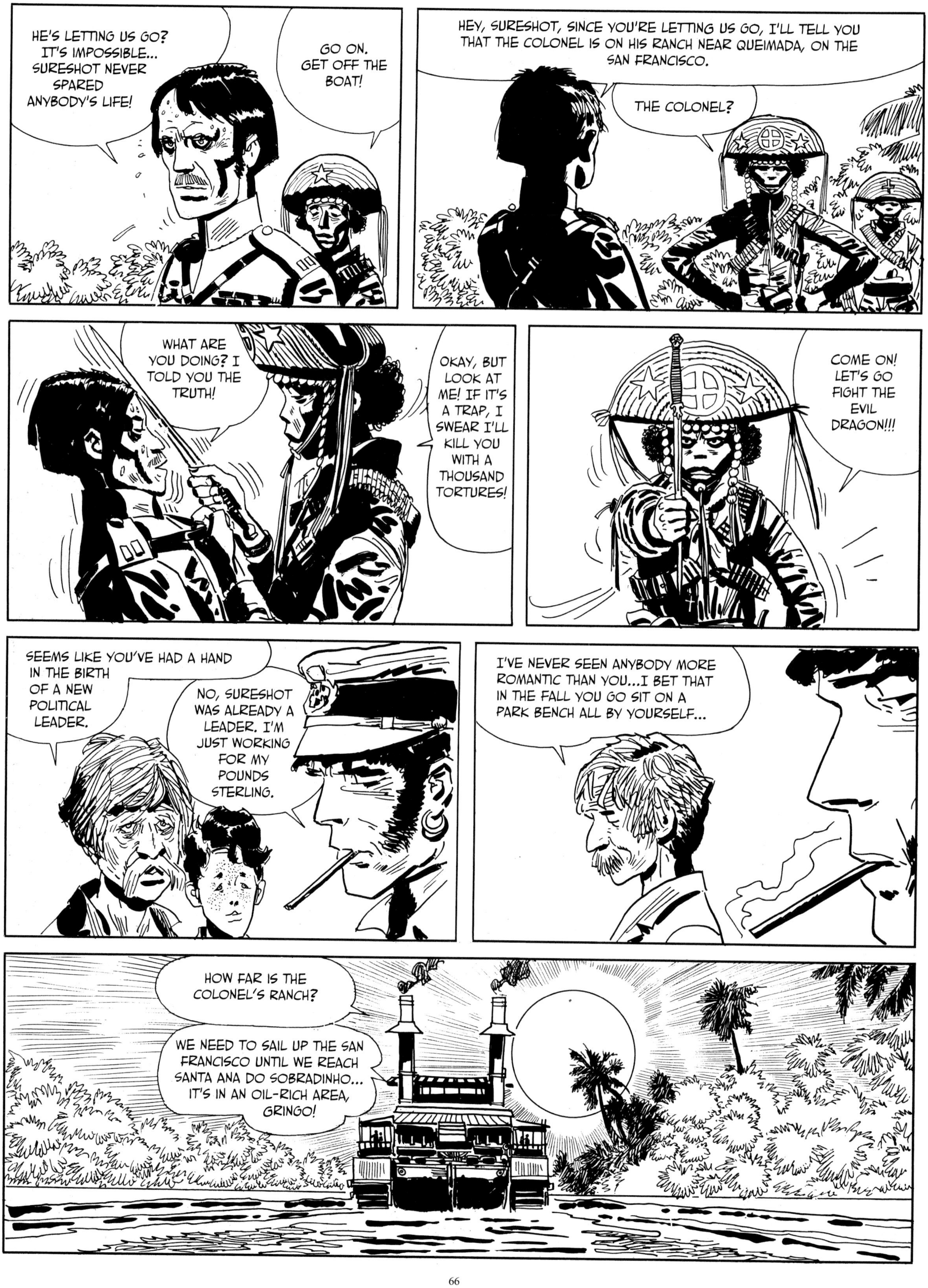
HE'S LETTING US GO? IT'S IMPOSSIBLE... SURESHOT NEVER SPARED ANYBODY'S LIFE!
GO ON. GET OFF THE BOAT!
HEY, SURESHOT, SINCE YOU'RE LETTING US GO, I'LL TELL YOU THAT THE COLONEL IS ON HIS RANCH NEAR QUEIMADA, ON THE SAN FRANCISCO.
THE COLONEL?
WHAT ARE YOU DOING? I TOLD YOU THE TRUTH!
OKAY, BUT LOOK AT ME! IF IT'S A TRAP, I SWEAR I'LL KILL YOU WITH A THOUSAND TORTURES!
COME ON! LET'S GO FIGHT THE EVIL DRAGON!!!
SEEMS LIKE YOU'VE HAD A HAND IN THE BIRTH OF A NEW POLITICAL LEADER.
NO, SURESHOT WAS ALREADY A LEADER. I'M JUST WORKING FOR MY POUNDS STERLING.
I'VE NEVER SEEN ANYBODY MORE ROMANTIC THAN YOU...I BET THAT IN THE FALL YOU GO SIT ON A PARK BENCH ALL BY YOURSELF...
HOW FAR IS THE COLONEL'S RANCH?
WE NEED TO SAIL UP THE SAN FRANCISCO UNTIL WE REACH SANTA ANA DO SOBRADINHO... IT'S IN AN OIL-RICH AREA, GRINGO!

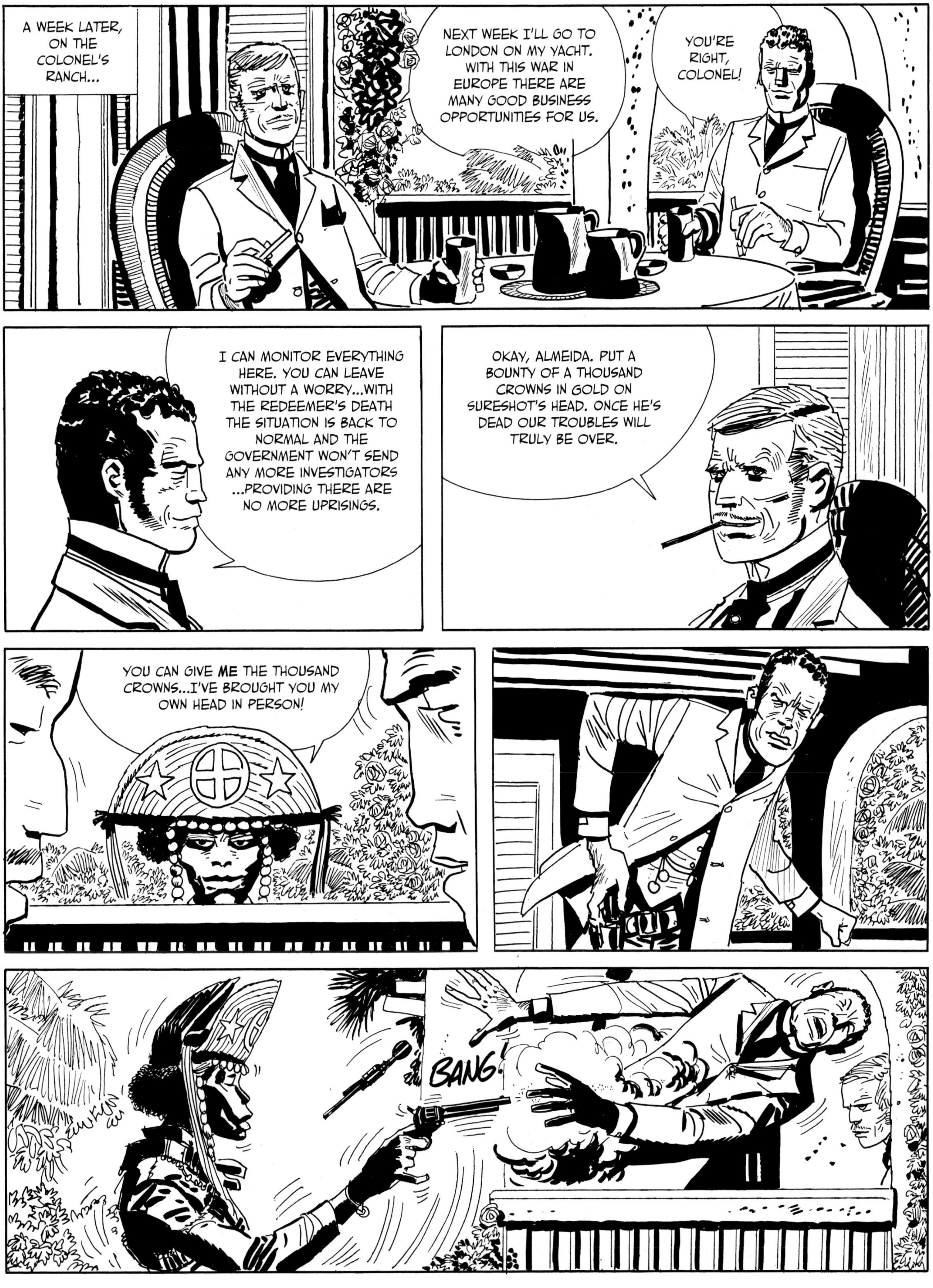
A WEEK LATER, ON THE COLONEL'S RANCH...
NEXT WEEK I'LL GO TO LONDON ON MY YACHT. WITH THIS WAR IN EUROPE THERE ARE MANY GOOD BUSINESS OPPORTUNITIES FOR US.
YOU'RE RIGHT, COLONEL!
I CAN MONITOR EVERYTHING HERE. YOU CAN LEAVE WITHOUT A WORRY...WITH THE REDEEMER'S DEATH THE SITUATION IS BACK TO NORMAL AND THE GOVERNMENT WON'T SEND ANY MORE INVESTIGATORS ...PROVIDING THERE ARE NO MORE UPRISINGS.
OKAY, ALMEIDA. PUT A BOUNTY OF A THOUSAND CROWNS IN GOLD ON SURESHOT'S HEAD. ONCE HE'S DEAD OUR TROUBLES WILL TRULY BE OVER.
YOU CAN GIVE **ME** THE THOUSAND CROWNS...I'VE BROUGHT YOU MY OWN HEAD IN PERSON!
BANG!

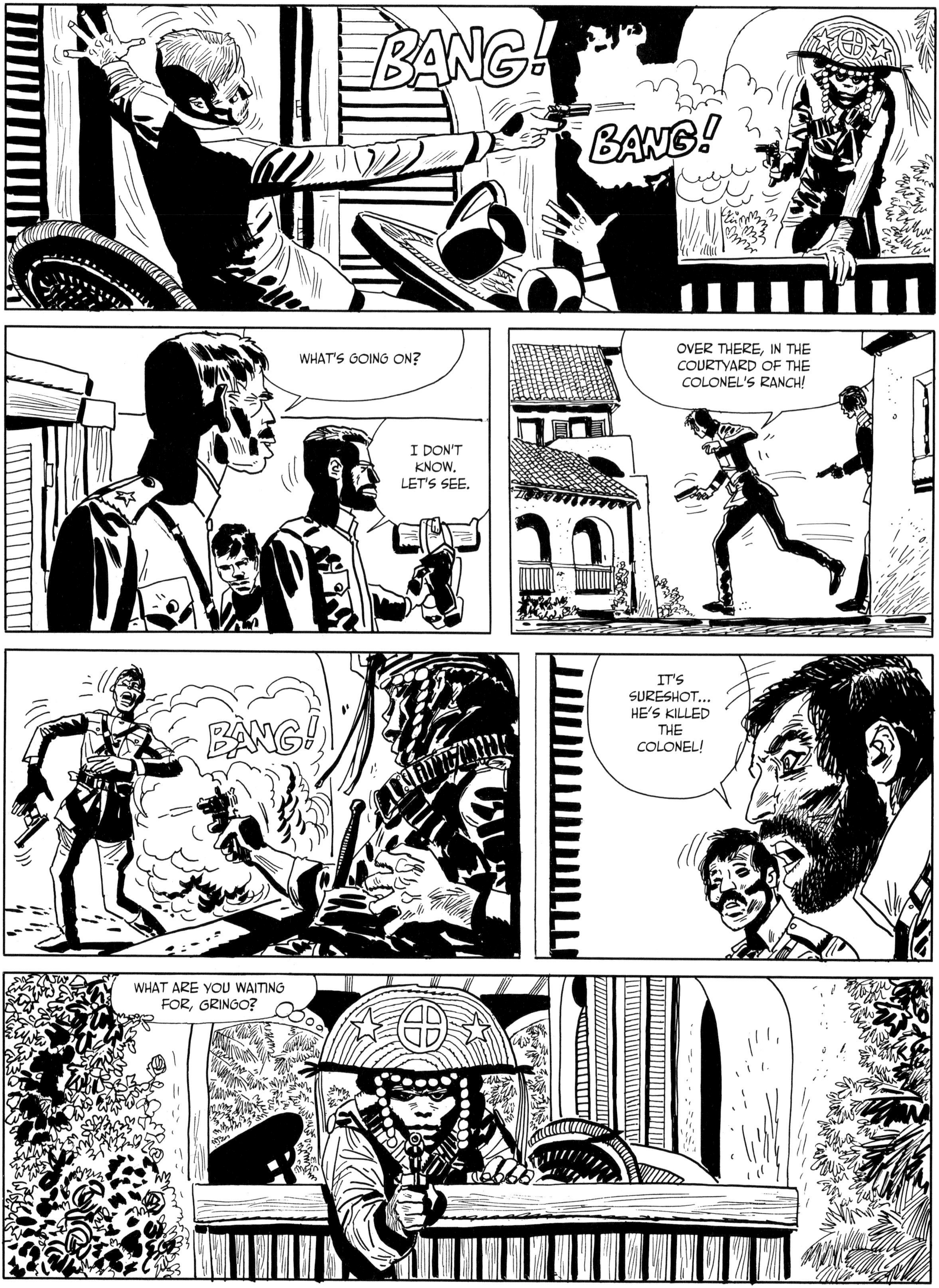
BANG!
BANG!
WHAT'S GOING ON?
I DON'T KNOW. LET'S SEE.
OVER THERE, IN THE COURTYARD OF THE COLONEL'S RANCH!
BANG!
IT'S SURESHOT... HE'S KILLED THE COLONEL!
WHAT ARE YOU WAITING FOR, GRINGO?

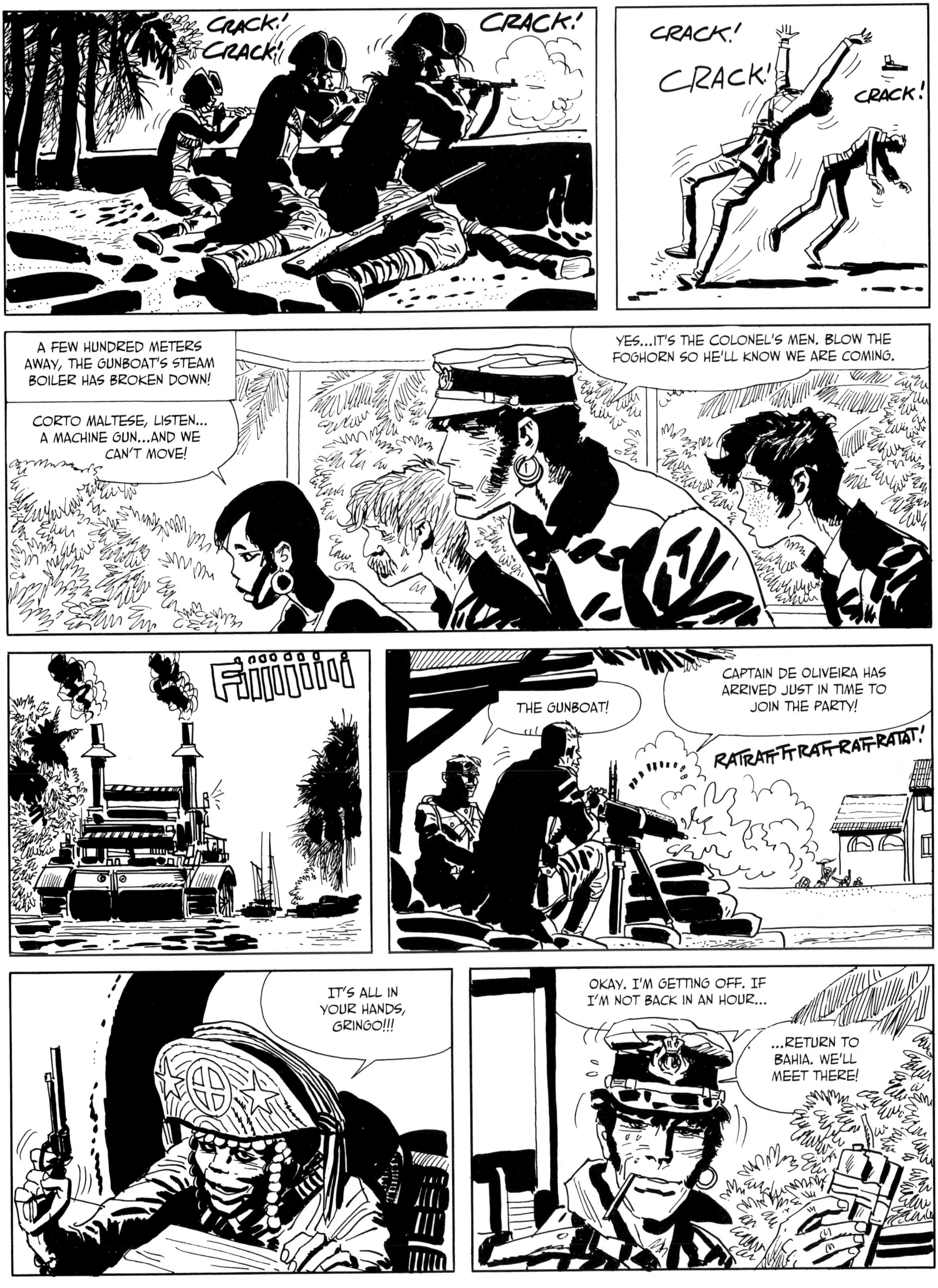
CRACK!
CRACK!
CRACK!
CRACK!
CRACK!
CRACK!
A FEW HUNDRED METERS AWAY, THE GUNBOAT'S STEAM BOILER HAS BROKEN DOWN!
CORTO MALTESE, LISTEN... A MACHINE GUN...AND WE CAN'T MOVE!
YES...IT'S THE COLONEL'S MEN. BLOW THE FOGHORN SO HE'LL KNOW WE ARE COMING.
FIIIIIII
THE GUNBOAT!
CAPTAIN DE OLIVEIRA HAS ARRIVED JUST IN TIME TO JOIN THE PARTY!
RATRATTTTRATTRATTRATAT!
IT'S ALL IN YOUR HANDS, GRINGO!!!
OKAY. I'M GETTING OFF. IF I'M NOT BACK IN AN HOUR...
...RETURN TO BAHIA. WE'LL MEET THERE!

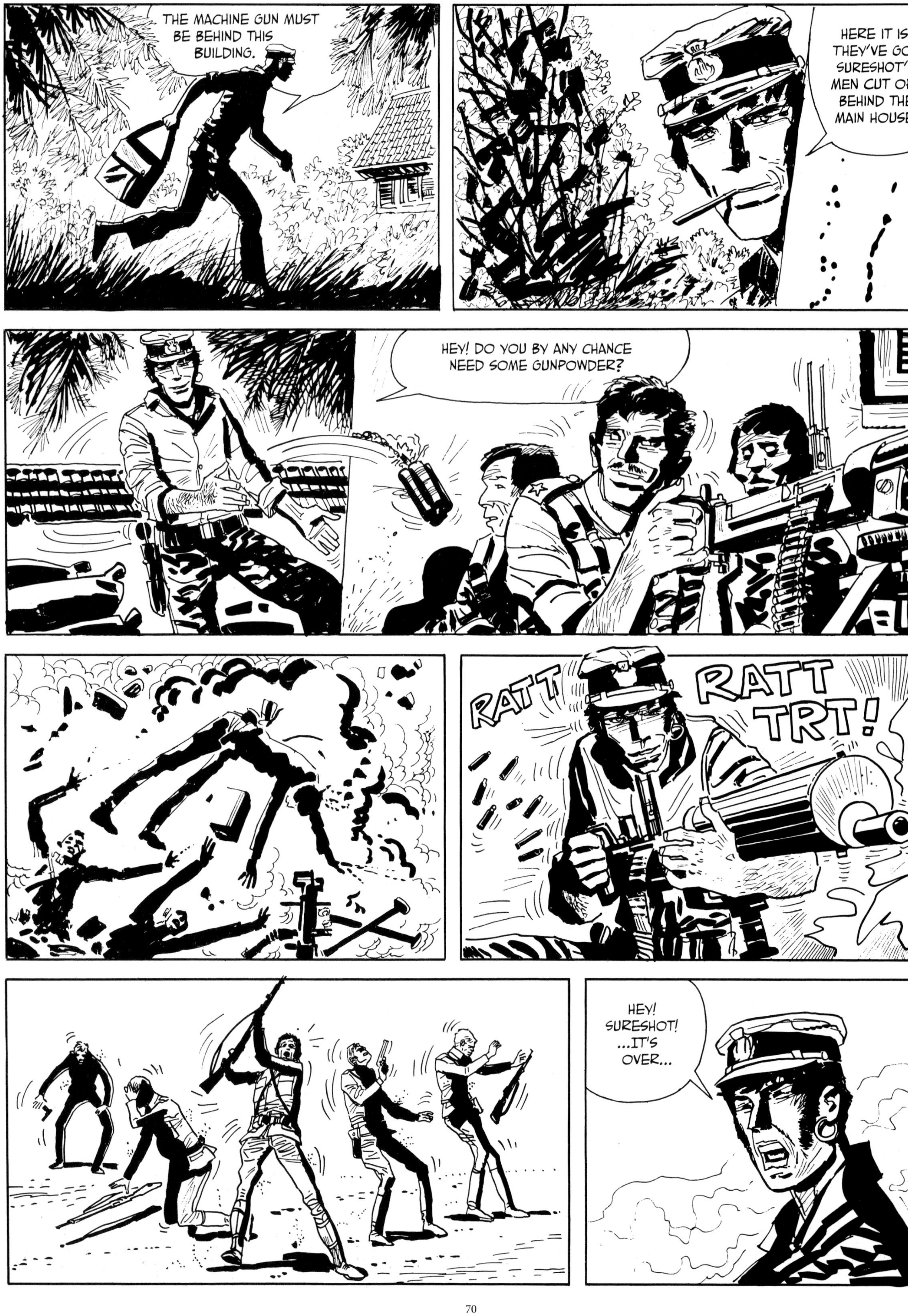
THE MACHINE GUN MUST BE BEHIND THIS BUILDING.
HERE IT IS! THEY'VE GOT SURESHOT'S MEN CUT OFF BEHIND THE MAIN HOUSE!
HEY! DO YOU BY ANY CHANCE NEED SOME GUNPOWDER?
RATT
RATT TRT!
HEY! SURESHOT! ...IT'S OVER...

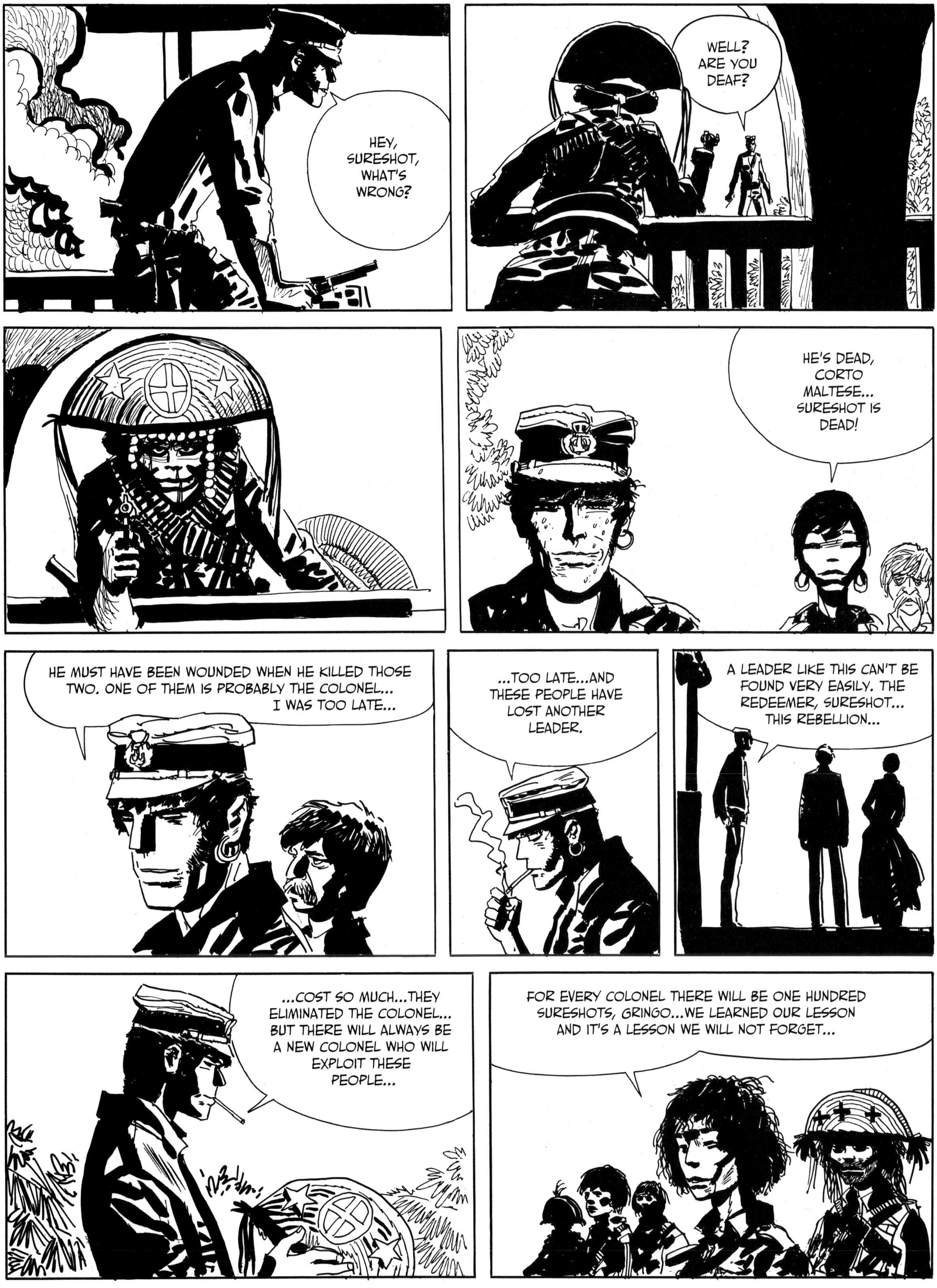
HEY, SURESHOT, WHAT'S WRONG?
WELL? ARE YOU DEAF?
HE'S DEAD, CORTO MALTESE... SURESHOT IS DEAD!
HE MUST HAVE BEEN WOUNDED WHEN HE KILLED THOSE TWO. ONE OF THEM IS PROBABLY THE COLONEL... I WAS TOO LATE...
...TOO LATE...AND THESE PEOPLE HAVE LOST ANOTHER LEADER.
A LEADER LIKE THIS CAN'T BE FOUND VERY EASILY. THE REDEEMER, SURESHOT... THIS REBELLION...
...COST SO MUCH...THEY ELIMINATED THE COLONEL... BUT THERE WILL ALWAYS BE A NEW COLONEL WHO WILL EXPLOIT THESE PEOPLE...
FOR EVERY COLONEL THERE WILL BE ONE HUNDRED SURESHOTS, GRINGO...WE LEARNED OUR LESSON AND IT'S A LESSON WE WILL NOT FORGET...

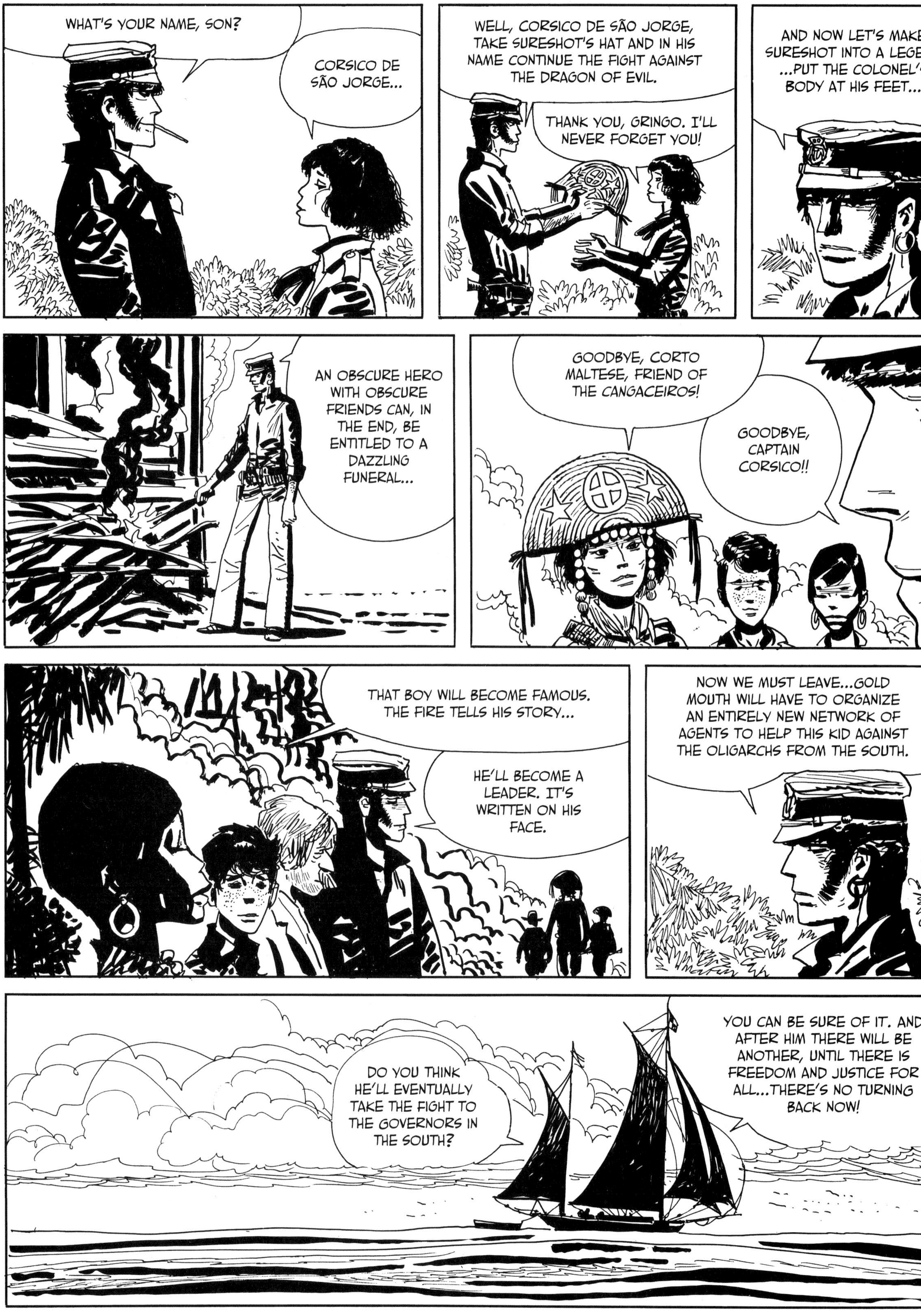
WHAT'S YOUR NAME, SON?
CORSICO DE SÃO JORGE...
WELL, CORSICO DE SÃO JORGE, TAKE SURESHOT'S HAT AND IN HIS NAME CONTINUE THE FIGHT AGAINST THE DRAGON OF EVIL.
THANK YOU, GRINGO. I'LL NEVER FORGET YOU!
AND NOW LET'S MAKE SURESHOT INTO A LEGEND ...PUT THE COLONEL'S BODY AT HIS FEET...
AN OBSCURE HERO WITH OBSCURE FRIENDS CAN, IN THE END, BE ENTITLED TO A DAZZLING FUNERAL...
GOODBYE, CORTO MALTESE, FRIEND OF THE *CANGACEIROS*!
GOODBYE, CAPTAIN CORSICO!!
THAT BOY WILL BECOME FAMOUS. THE FIRE TELLS HIS STORY...
HE'LL BECOME A LEADER. IT'S WRITTEN ON HIS FACE.
NOW WE MUST LEAVE...GOLD MOUTH WILL HAVE TO ORGANIZE AN ENTIRELY NEW NETWORK OF AGENTS TO HELP THIS KID AGAINST THE OLIGARCHS FROM THE SOUTH.
DO YOU THINK HE'LL EVENTUALLY TAKE THE FIGHT TO THE GOVERNORS IN THE SOUTH?
YOU CAN BE SURE OF IT. AND AFTER HIM THERE WILL BE ANOTHER, UNTIL THERE IS FREEDOM AND JUSTICE FOR ALL...THERE'S NO TURNING BACK NOW!

CHAPTER FOUR:
THE
BRAZILIAN EAGLE

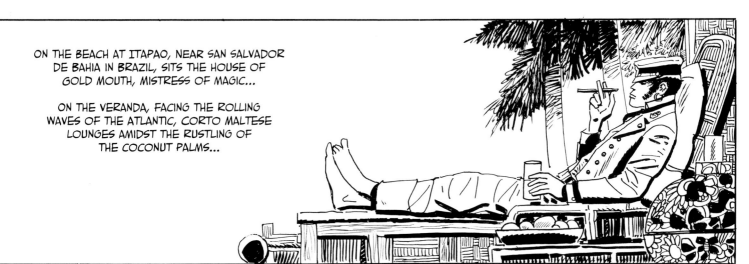

ON THE BEACH AT ITAPAO, NEAR SAN SALVADOR DE BAHIA IN BRAZIL, SITS THE HOUSE OF GOLD MOUTH, MISTRESS OF MAGIC...

ON THE VERANDA, FACING THE ROLLING WAVES OF THE ATLANTIC, CORTO MALTESE LOUNGES AMIDST THE RUSTLING OF THE COCONUT PALMS...

YOU DID A GREAT JOB IN THE SERTÃO... THAT BOY, CORSICO DO SÃO JORGE, HAS CONTINUED THE FIGHT AGAINST THE OTHER SLAVERS WITH SUCCESS! YES...YES... ...IT WAS A VERY GOOD JOB.

I KNOW. I ALREADY HEARD ABOUT IT.

AH, CORTO MALTESE! WHY DO YOU ALWAYS PRETEND TO BE INDIFFERENT TO WHAT GOES ON AROUND YOU?

YOUR MOTHER, LA NIÑA DE GIBRALTAR, HAD A MORE OUTGOING DISPOSITION.... OH, I NEARLY FORGOT...!

THESE GOLD COINS ARE FOR YOU, AS A PAYMENT FOR THE HELP YOU GAVE TO SURESHOT.

I DON'T WANT THEM. IT'S PARTLY MY FAULT THAT SURESHOT DIED... GIVE THEM TO HIS PEOPLE.

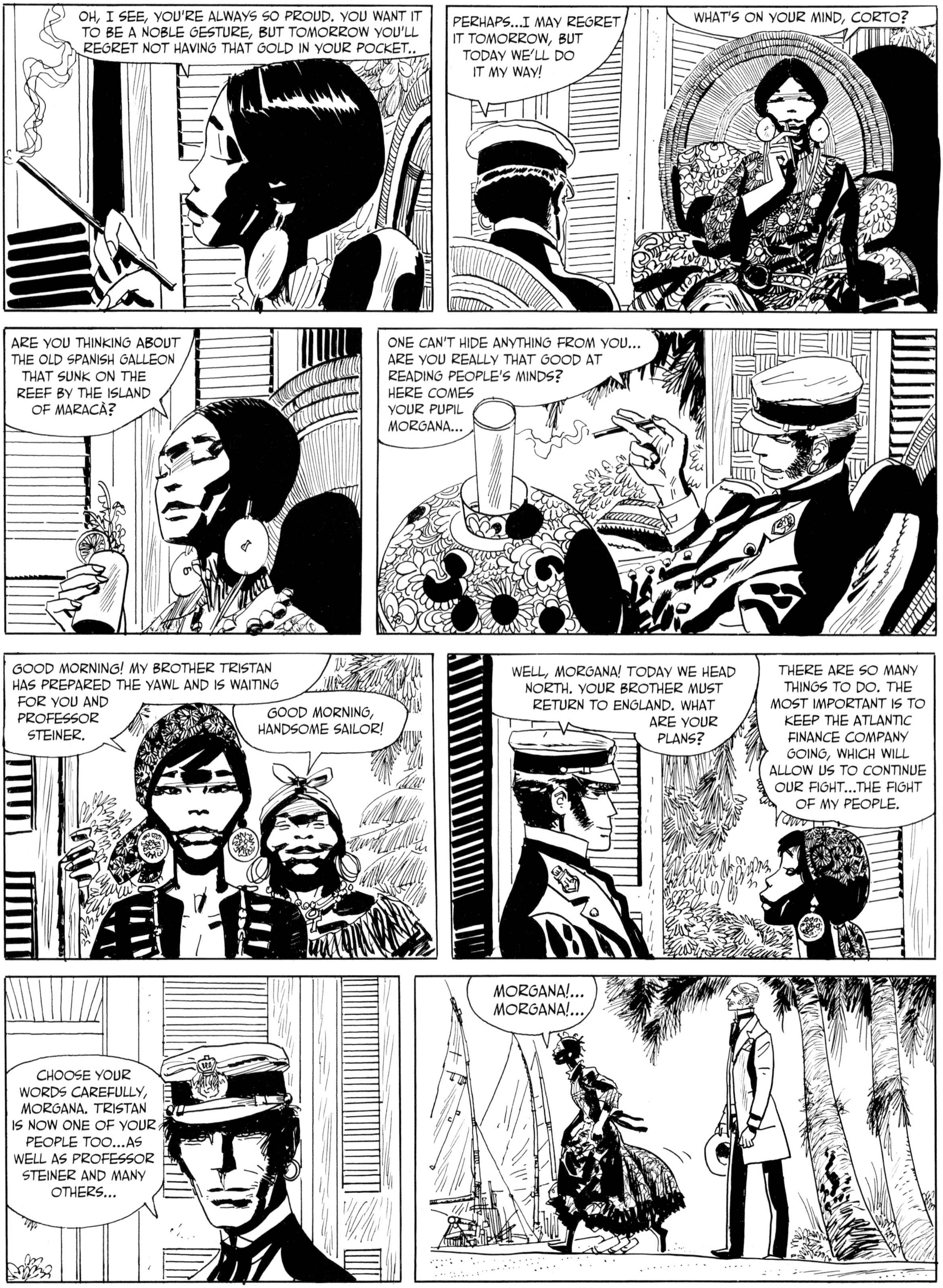
OH, I SEE, YOU'RE ALWAYS SO PROUD. YOU WANT IT TO BE A NOBLE GESTURE, BUT TOMORROW YOU'LL REGRET NOT HAVING THAT GOLD IN YOUR POCKET..
PERHAPS...I MAY REGRET IT TOMORROW, BUT TODAY WE'LL DO IT MY WAY!
WHAT'S ON YOUR MIND, CORTO?
ARE YOU THINKING ABOUT THE OLD SPANISH GALLEON THAT SUNK ON THE REEF BY THE ISLAND OF MARACÀ?
ONE CAN'T HIDE ANYTHING FROM YOU... ARE YOU REALLY THAT GOOD AT READING PEOPLE'S MINDS? HERE COMES YOUR PUPIL MORGANA...
GOOD MORNING! MY BROTHER TRISTAN HAS PREPARED THE YAWL AND IS WAITING FOR YOU AND PROFESSOR STEINER.
GOOD MORNING, HANDSOME SAILOR!
WELL, MORGANA! TODAY WE HEAD NORTH. YOUR BROTHER MUST RETURN TO ENGLAND. WHAT ARE YOUR PLANS?
THERE ARE SO MANY THINGS TO DO. THE MOST IMPORTANT IS TO KEEP THE ATLANTIC FINANCE COMPANY GOING, WHICH WILL ALLOW US TO CONTINUE OUR FIGHT...THE FIGHT OF MY PEOPLE.
CHOOSE YOUR WORDS CAREFULLY, MORGANA. TRISTAN IS NOW ONE OF YOUR PEOPLE TOO...AS WELL AS PROFESSOR STEINER AND MANY OTHERS...
MORGANA!... MORGANA!...

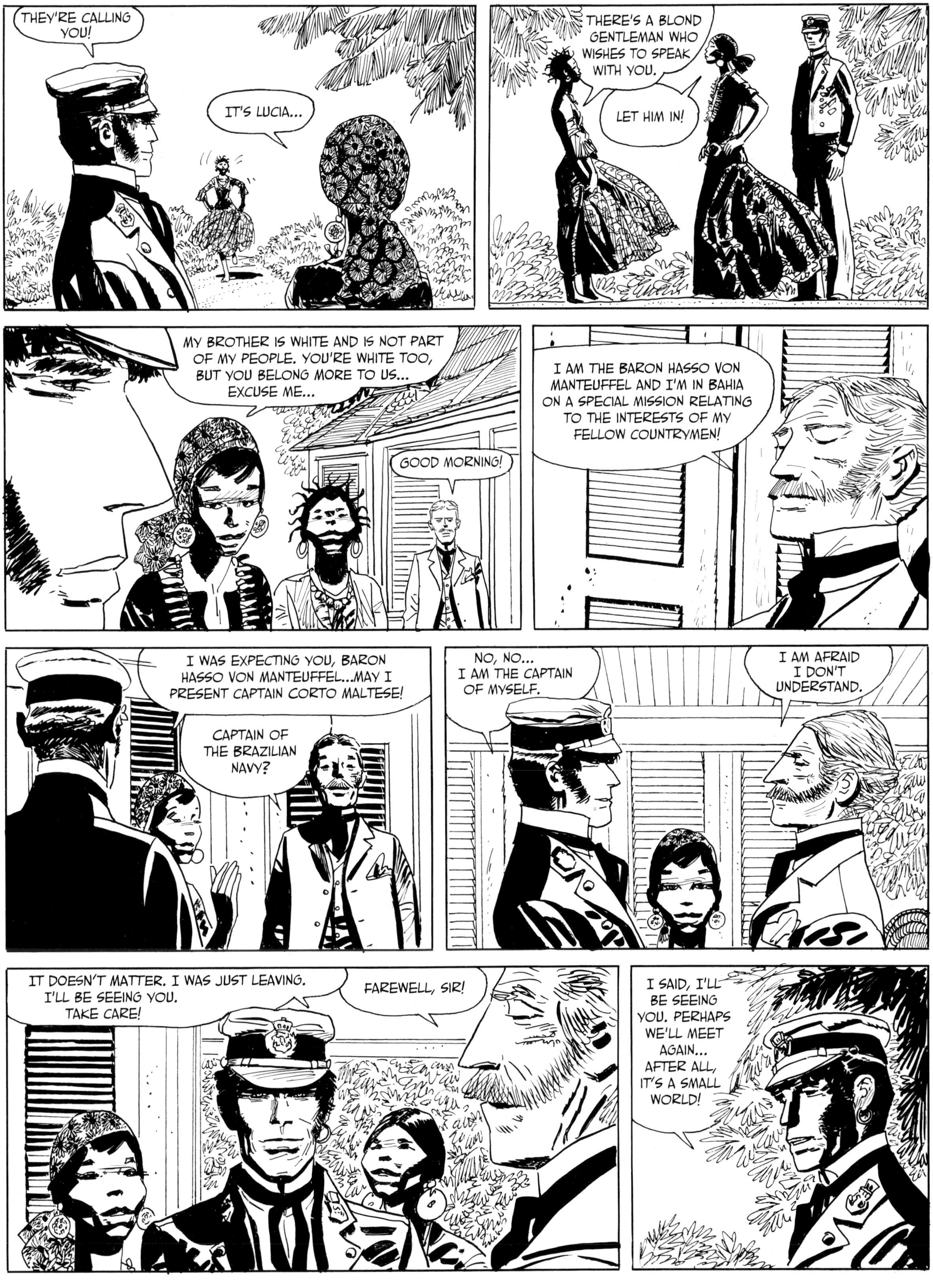
THEY'RE CALLING YOU!
IT'S LUCIA...
THERE'S A BLOND GENTLEMAN WHO WISHES TO SPEAK WITH YOU.
LET HIM IN!
MY BROTHER IS WHITE AND IS NOT PART OF MY PEOPLE. YOU'RE WHITE TOO, BUT YOU BELONG MORE TO US... EXCUSE ME...
GOOD MORNING!
I AM THE BARON HASSO VON MANTEUFFEL AND I'M IN BAHIA ON A SPECIAL MISSION RELATING TO THE INTERESTS OF MY FELLOW COUNTRYMEN!
I WAS EXPECTING YOU, BARON HASSO VON MANTEUFFEL...MAY I PRESENT CAPTAIN CORTO MALTESE!
CAPTAIN OF THE BRAZILIAN NAVY?
NO, NO... I AM THE CAPTAIN OF MYSELF.
I AM AFRAID I DON'T UNDERSTAND.
IT DOESN'T MATTER. I WAS JUST LEAVING. I'LL BE SEEING YOU. TAKE CARE!
FAREWELL, SIR!
I SAID, I'LL BE SEEING YOU. PERHAPS WE'LL MEET AGAIN... AFTER ALL, IT'S A SMALL WORLD!

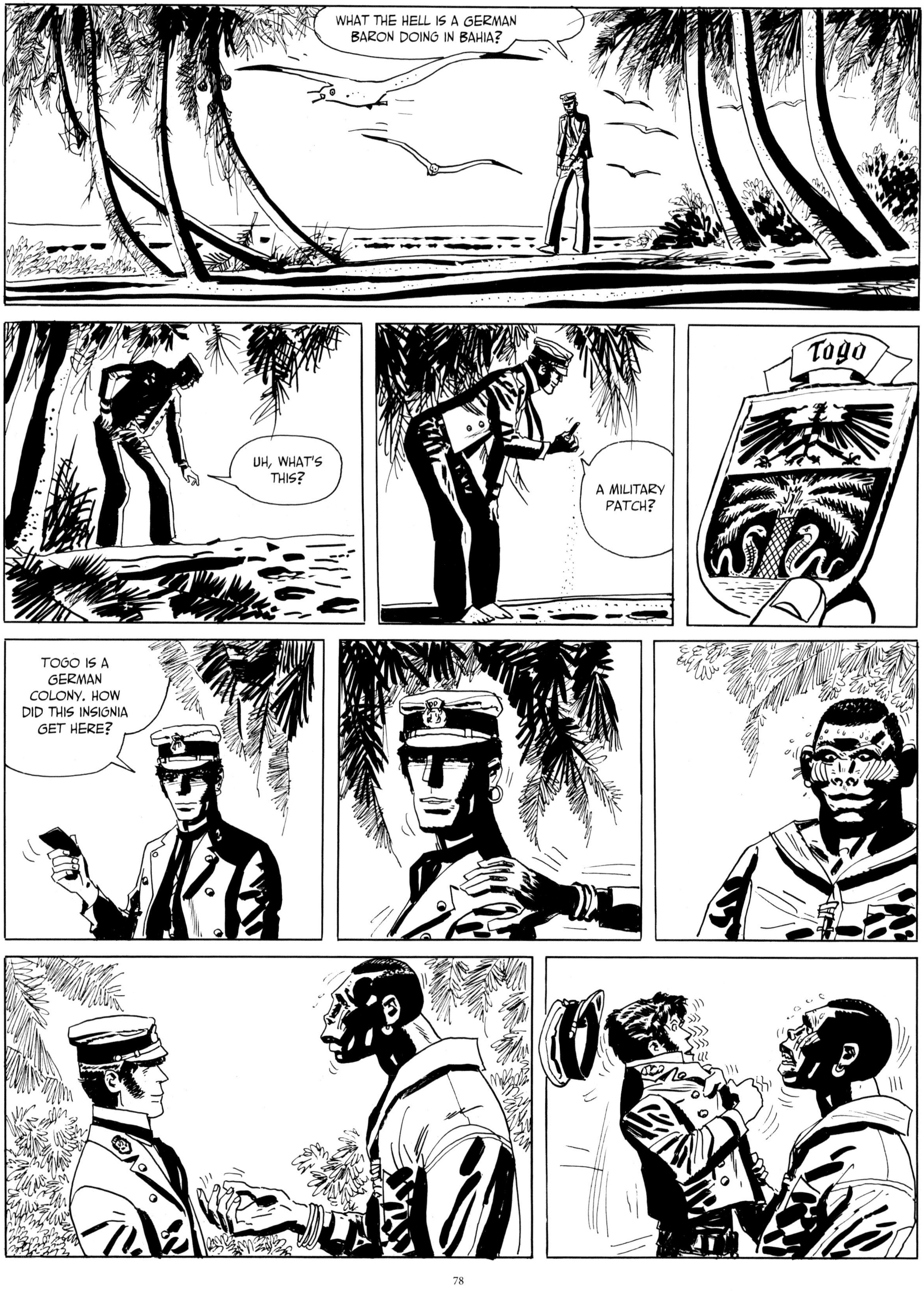
WHAT THE HELL IS A GERMAN BARON DOING IN BAHIA?
UH, WHAT'S THIS?
A MILITARY PATCH?
Togo
TOGO IS A GERMAN COLONY. HOW DID THIS INSIGNIA GET HERE?

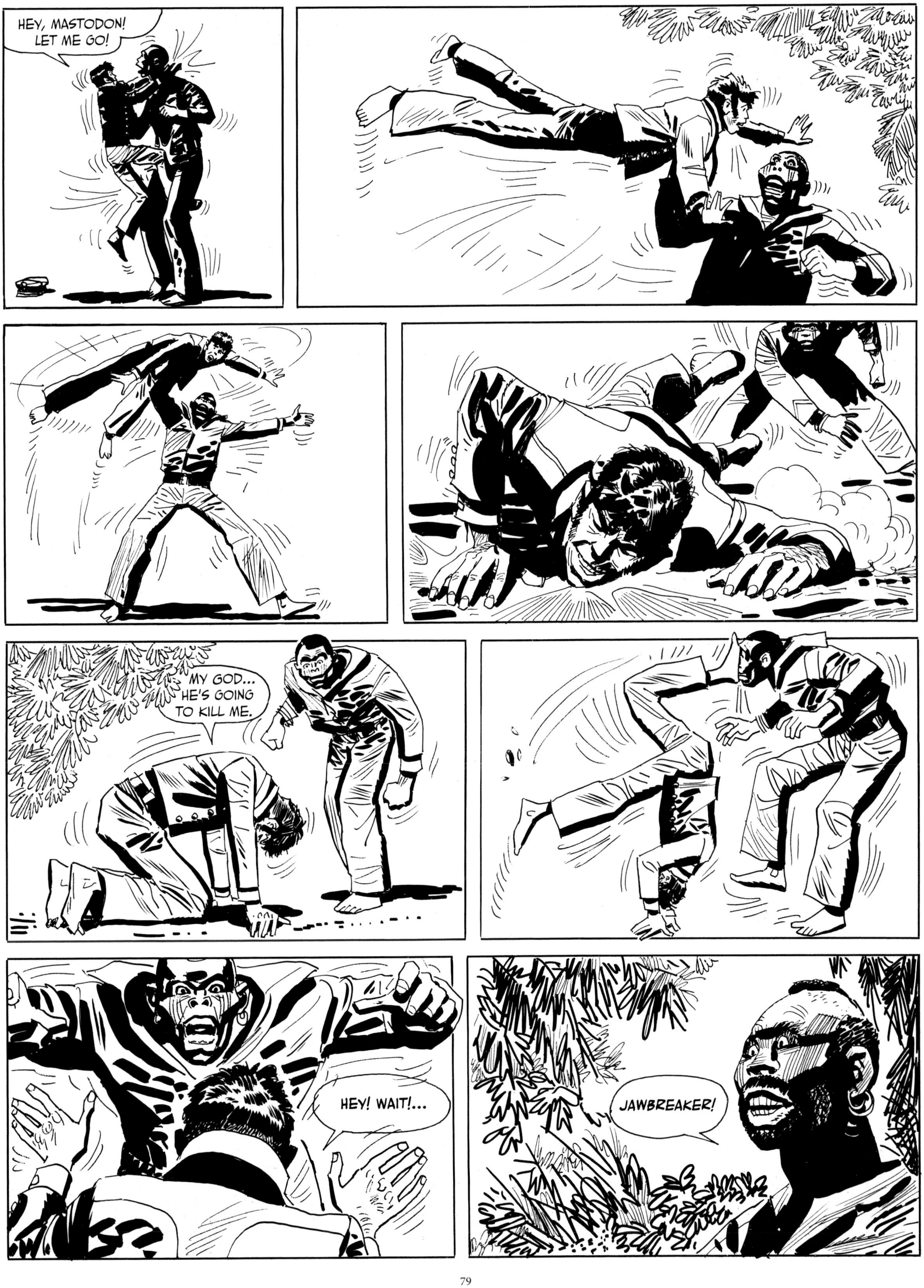
HEY, MASTODON! LET ME GO!
MY GOD... HE'S GOING TO KILL ME.
HEY! WAIT!...
JAWBREAKER!

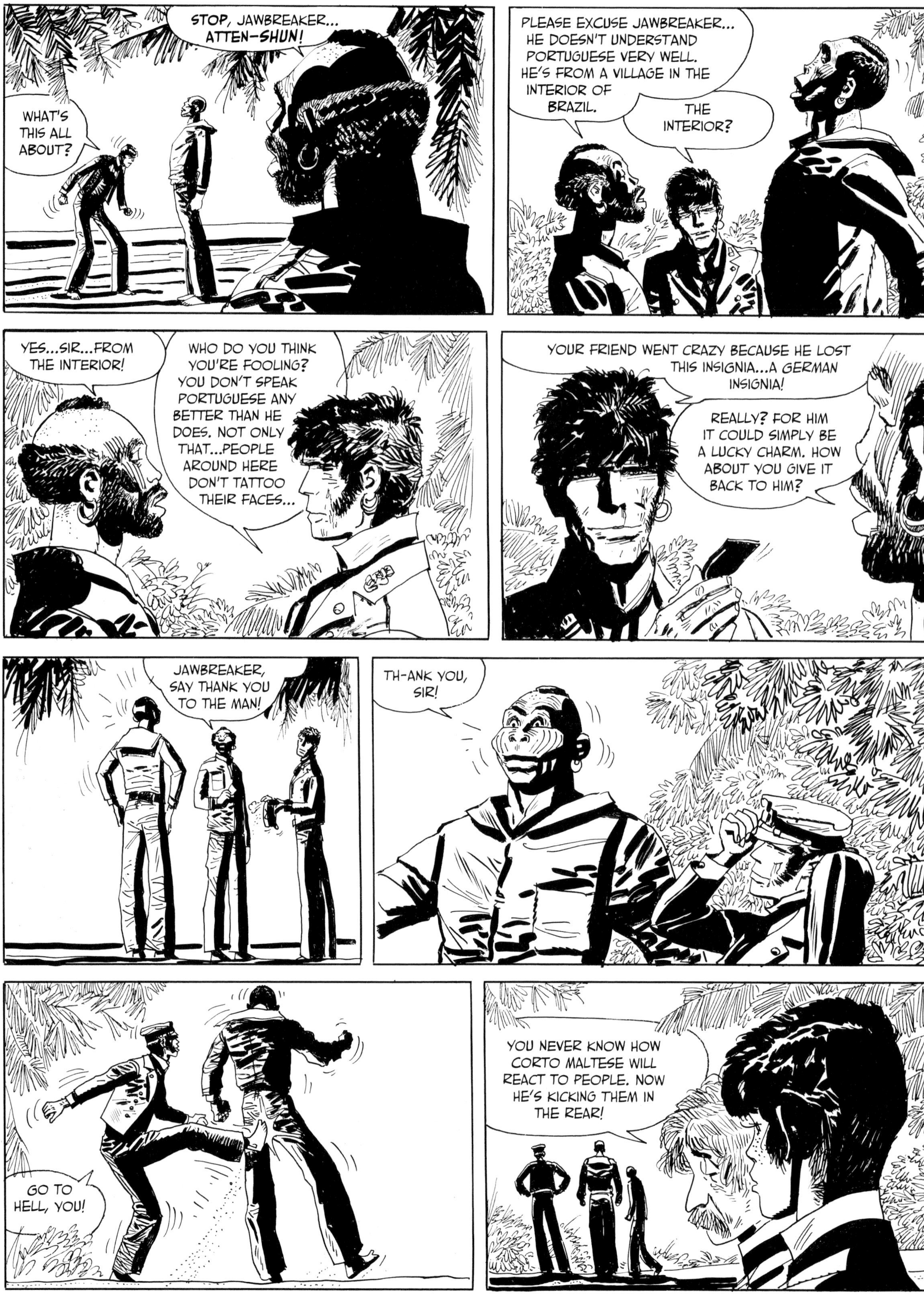
STOP, JAWBREAKER... ATTEN-SHUN!
WHAT'S THIS ALL ABOUT?
PLEASE EXCUSE JAWBREAKER... HE DOESN'T UNDERSTAND PORTUGUESE VERY WELL. HE'S FROM A VILLAGE IN THE INTERIOR OF BRAZIL.
THE INTERIOR?
YES...SIR...FROM THE INTERIOR!
WHO DO YOU THINK YOU'RE FOOLING? YOU DON'T SPEAK PORTUGUESE ANY BETTER THAN HE DOES. NOT ONLY THAT...PEOPLE AROUND HERE DON'T TATTOO THEIR FACES...
YOUR FRIEND WENT CRAZY BECAUSE HE LOST THIS INSIGNIA...A GERMAN INSIGNIA!
REALLY? FOR HIM IT COULD SIMPLY BE A LUCKY CHARM. HOW ABOUT YOU GIVE IT BACK TO HIM?
JAWBREAKER, SAY THANK YOU TO THE MAN!
TH-ANK YOU, SIR!
GO TO HELL, YOU!
YOU NEVER KNOW HOW CORTO MALTESE WILL REACT TO PEOPLE. NOW HE'S KICKING THEM IN THE REAR!

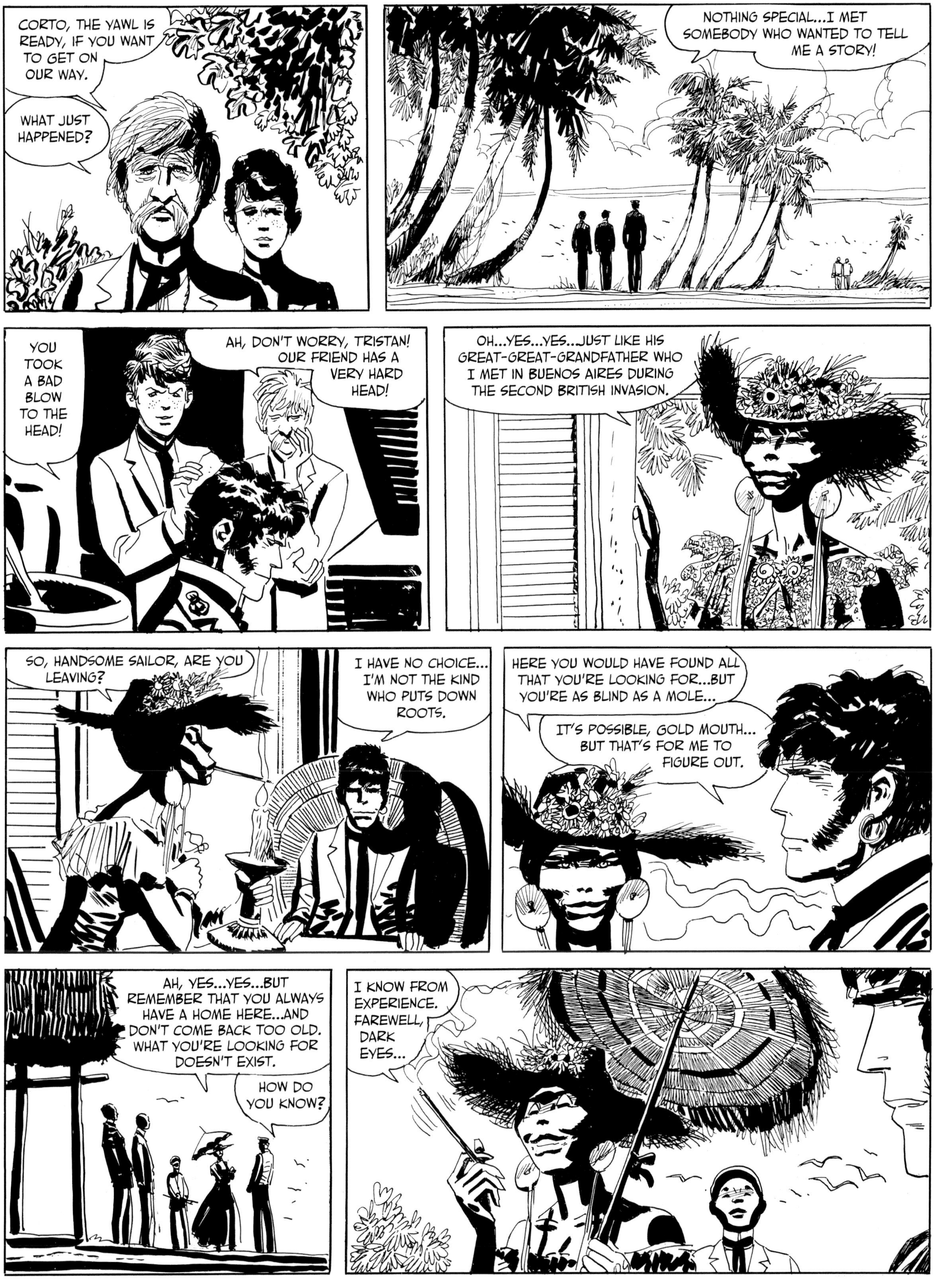
CORTO, THE YAWL IS READY, IF YOU WANT TO GET ON OUR WAY.
WHAT JUST HAPPENED?
NOTHING SPECIAL...I MET SOMEBODY WHO WANTED TO TELL ME A STORY!
YOU TOOK A BAD BLOW TO THE HEAD!
AH, DON'T WORRY, TRISTAN! OUR FRIEND HAS A VERY HARD HEAD!
OH...YES...YES...JUST LIKE HIS GREAT-GREAT-GRANDFATHER WHO I MET IN BUENOS AIRES DURING THE SECOND BRITISH INVASION.
SO, HANDSOME SAILOR, ARE YOU LEAVING?
I HAVE NO CHOICE... I'M NOT THE KIND WHO PUTS DOWN ROOTS.
HERE YOU WOULD HAVE FOUND ALL THAT YOU'RE LOOKING FOR...BUT YOU'RE AS BLIND AS A MOLE...
IT'S POSSIBLE, GOLD MOUTH... BUT THAT'S FOR ME TO FIGURE OUT.
AH, YES...YES...BUT REMEMBER THAT YOU ALWAYS HAVE A HOME HERE...AND DON'T COME BACK TOO OLD. WHAT YOU'RE LOOKING FOR DOESN'T EXIST.
HOW DO YOU KNOW?
I KNOW FROM EXPERIENCE. FAREWELL, DARK EYES...

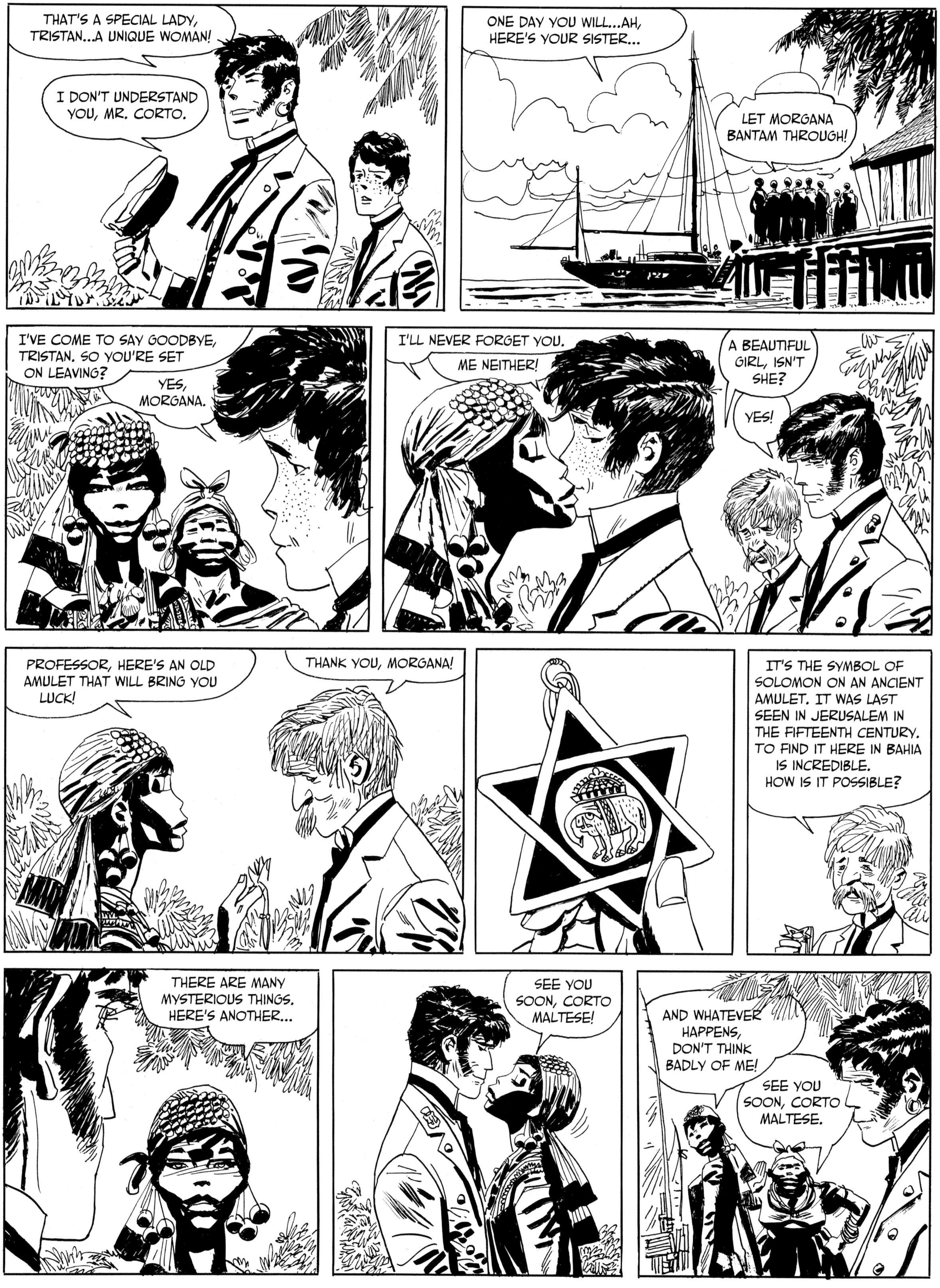
THAT'S A SPECIAL LADY, TRISTAN...A UNIQUE WOMAN!
I DON'T UNDERSTAND YOU, MR. CORTO.
ONE DAY YOU WILL...AH, HERE'S YOUR SISTER...
LET MORGANA BANTAM THROUGH!
I'VE COME TO SAY GOODBYE, TRISTAN. SO YOU'RE SET ON LEAVING?
YES, MORGANA.
I'LL NEVER FORGET YOU.
ME NEITHER!
A BEAUTIFUL GIRL, ISN'T SHE?
YES!
PROFESSOR, HERE'S AN OLD AMULET THAT WILL BRING YOU LUCK!
THANK YOU, MORGANA!
IT'S THE SYMBOL OF SOLOMON ON AN ANCIENT AMULET. IT WAS LAST SEEN IN JERUSALEM IN THE FIFTEENTH CENTURY. TO FIND IT HERE IN BAHIA IS INCREDIBLE. HOW IS IT POSSIBLE?
THERE ARE MANY MYSTERIOUS THINGS. HERE'S ANOTHER...
SEE YOU SOON, CORTO MALTESE!
AND WHATEVER HAPPENS, DON'T THINK BADLY OF ME!
SEE YOU SOON, CORTO MALTESE.

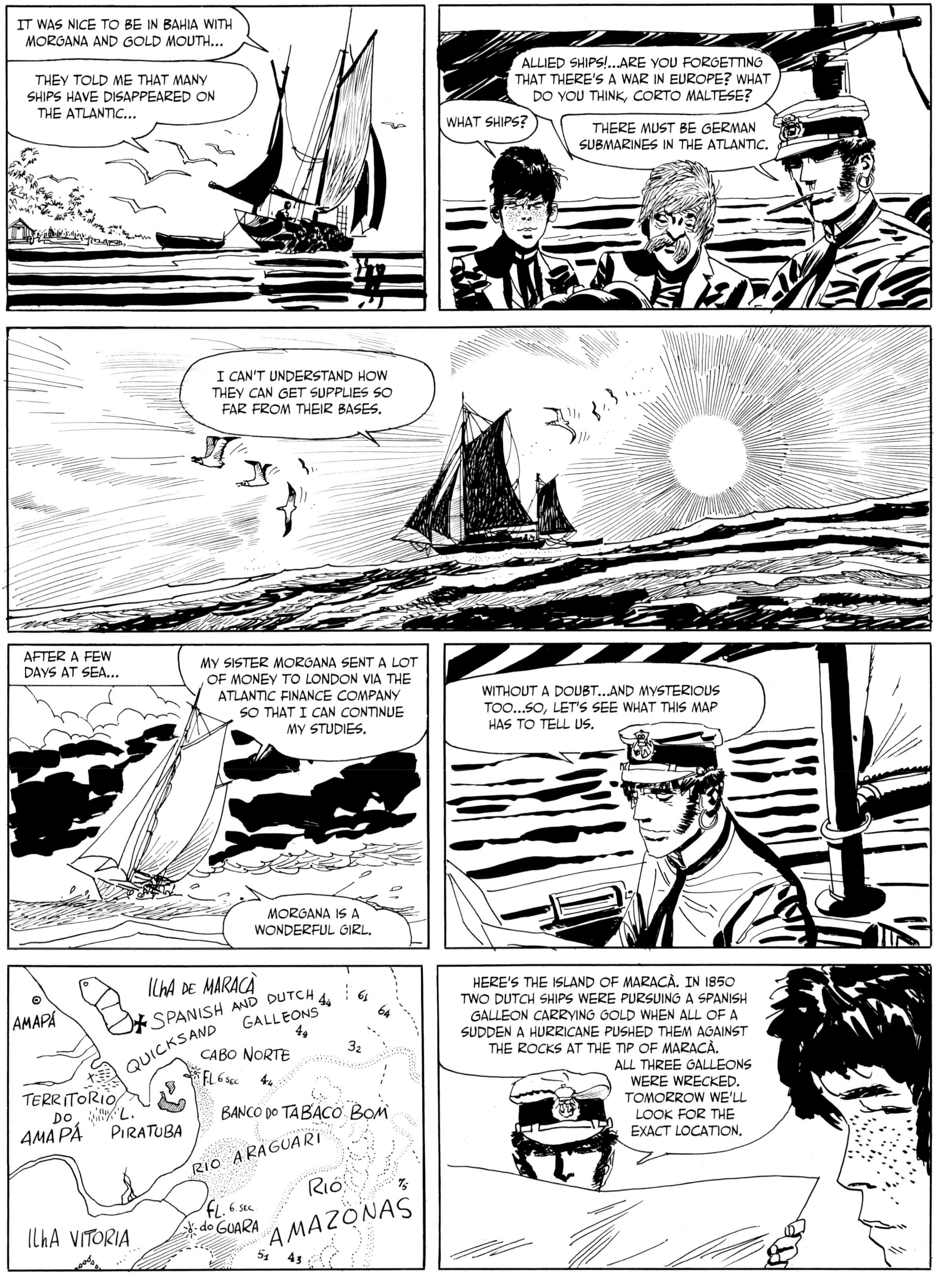

IT WAS NICE TO BE IN BAHIA WITH MORGANA AND GOLD MOUTH...
THEY TOLD ME THAT MANY SHIPS HAVE DISAPPEARED ON THE ATLANTIC...
WHAT SHIPS?
ALLIED SHIPS!...ARE YOU FORGETTING THAT THERE'S A WAR IN EUROPE? WHAT DO YOU THINK, CORTO MALTESE?
THERE MUST BE GERMAN SUBMARINES IN THE ATLANTIC.
I CAN'T UNDERSTAND HOW THEY CAN GET SUPPLIES SO FAR FROM THEIR BASES.
AFTER A FEW DAYS AT SEA...
MY SISTER MORGANA SENT A LOT OF MONEY TO LONDON VIA THE ATLANTIC FINANCE COMPANY SO THAT I CAN CONTINUE MY STUDIES.
MORGANA IS A WONDERFUL GIRL.
WITHOUT A DOUBT...AND MYSTERIOUS TOO...SO, LET'S SEE WHAT THIS MAP HAS TO TELL US.
IlhA DE MARACÀ
AMAPÁ
SPANISH AND DUTCH GALLEONS
QUICKSAND
CABO NORTE
F.L. 6 SEC
TERRITORIO DO AMAPÁ
L. PIRATUBA
BANCO DO TABACO BOM
RIO ARAGUARI
RIO AMAZONAS
FL. 6. SEC. do GUARA
IlhA VITORIA
HERE'S THE ISLAND OF MARACÀ. IN 1850 TWO DUTCH SHIPS WERE PURSUING A SPANISH GALLEON CARRYING GOLD WHEN ALL OF A SUDDEN A HURRICANE PUSHED THEM AGAINST THE ROCKS AT THE TIP OF MARACÀ.
ALL THREE GALLEONS WERE WRECKED. TOMORROW WE'LL LOOK FOR THE EXACT LOCATION.

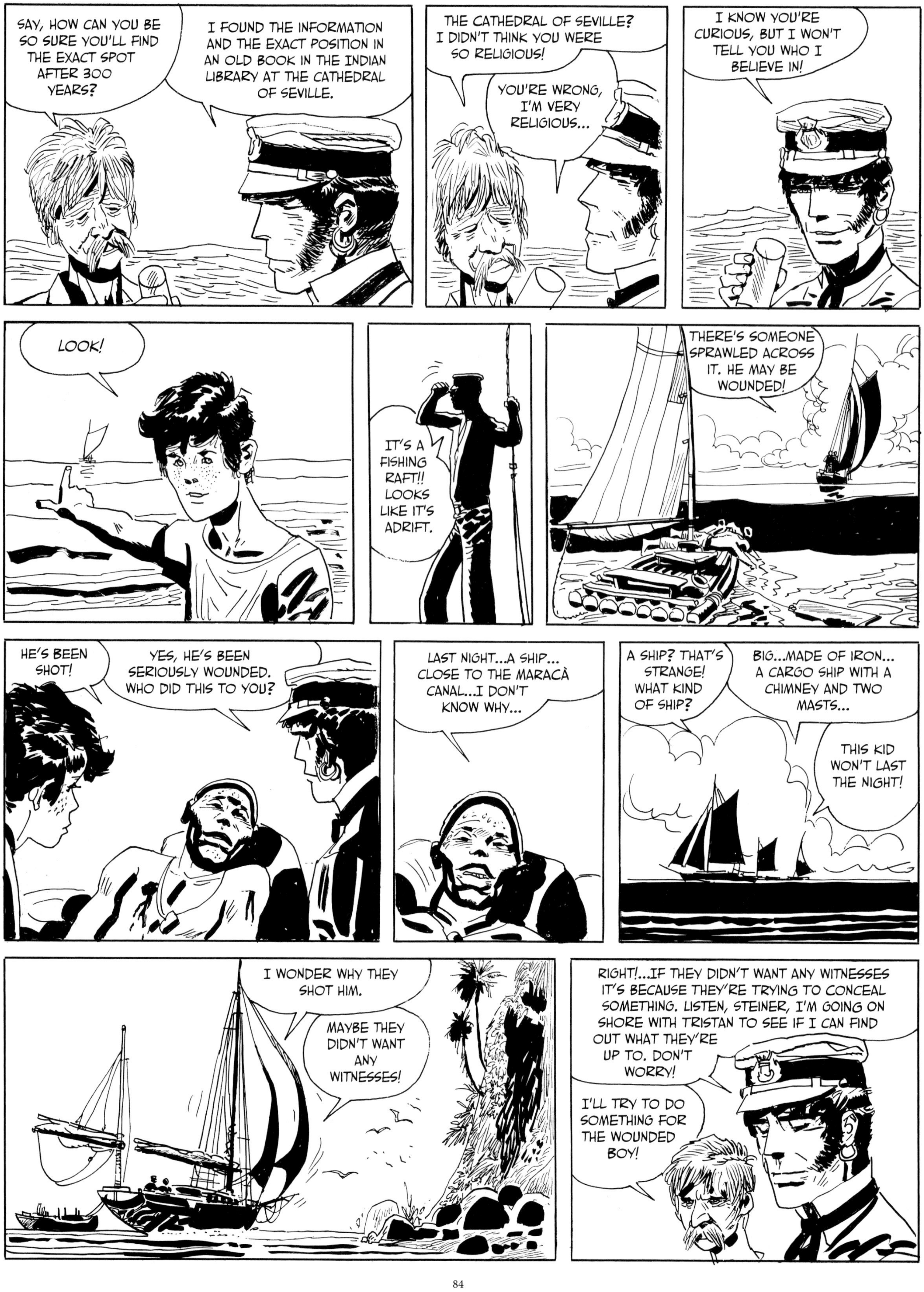

SAY, HOW CAN YOU BE SO SURE YOU'LL FIND THE EXACT SPOT AFTER 300 YEARS?
I FOUND THE INFORMATION AND THE EXACT POSITION IN AN OLD BOOK IN THE INDIAN LIBRARY AT THE CATHEDRAL OF SEVILLE.
THE CATHEDRAL OF SEVILLE? I DIDN'T THINK YOU WERE SO RELIGIOUS!
YOU'RE WRONG, I'M VERY RELIGIOUS...
I KNOW YOU'RE CURIOUS, BUT I WON'T TELL YOU WHO I BELIEVE IN!
LOOK!
IT'S A FISHING RAFT!! LOOKS LIKE IT'S ADRIFT.
THERE'S SOMEONE SPRAWLED ACROSS IT. HE MAY BE WOUNDED!
HE'S BEEN SHOT!
YES, HE'S BEEN SERIOUSLY WOUNDED. WHO DID THIS TO YOU?
LAST NIGHT...A SHIP... CLOSE TO THE MARACÀ CANAL...I DON'T KNOW WHY...
A SHIP? THAT'S STRANGE! WHAT KIND OF SHIP?
BIG...MADE OF IRON... A CARGO SHIP WITH A CHIMNEY AND TWO MASTS...
THIS KID WON'T LAST THE NIGHT!
I WONDER WHY THEY SHOT HIM.
MAYBE THEY DIDN'T WANT ANY WITNESSES!
RIGHT!...IF THEY DIDN'T WANT ANY WITNESSES IT'S BECAUSE THEY'RE TRYING TO CONCEAL SOMETHING. LISTEN, STEINER, I'M GOING ON SHORE WITH TRISTAN TO SEE IF I CAN FIND OUT WHAT THEY'RE UP TO. DON'T WORRY!
I'LL TRY TO DO SOMETHING FOR THE WOUNDED BOY!

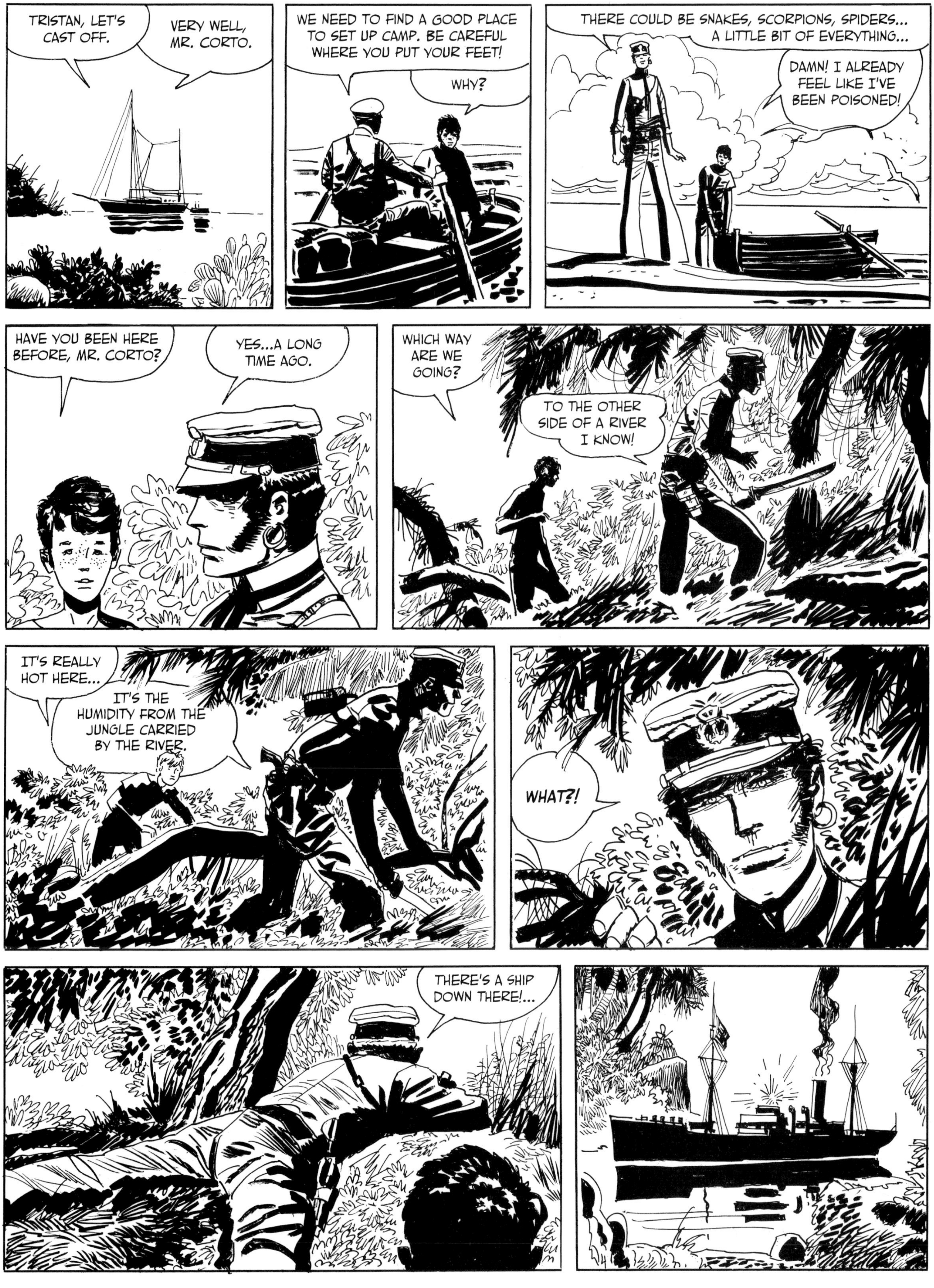
TRISTAN, LET'S CAST OFF.
VERY WELL, MR. CORTO.
WE NEED TO FIND A GOOD PLACE TO SET UP CAMP. BE CAREFUL WHERE YOU PUT YOUR FEET!
WHY?
THERE COULD BE SNAKES, SCORPIONS, SPIDERS... A LITTLE BIT OF EVERYTHING...
DAMN! I ALREADY FEEL LIKE I'VE BEEN POISONED!
HAVE YOU BEEN HERE BEFORE, MR. CORTO?
YES...A LONG TIME AGO.
WHICH WAY ARE WE GOING?
TO THE OTHER SIDE OF A RIVER I KNOW!
IT'S REALLY HOT HERE...
IT'S THE HUMIDITY FROM THE JUNGLE CARRIED BY THE RIVER.
WHAT?!
THERE'S A SHIP DOWN THERE!...

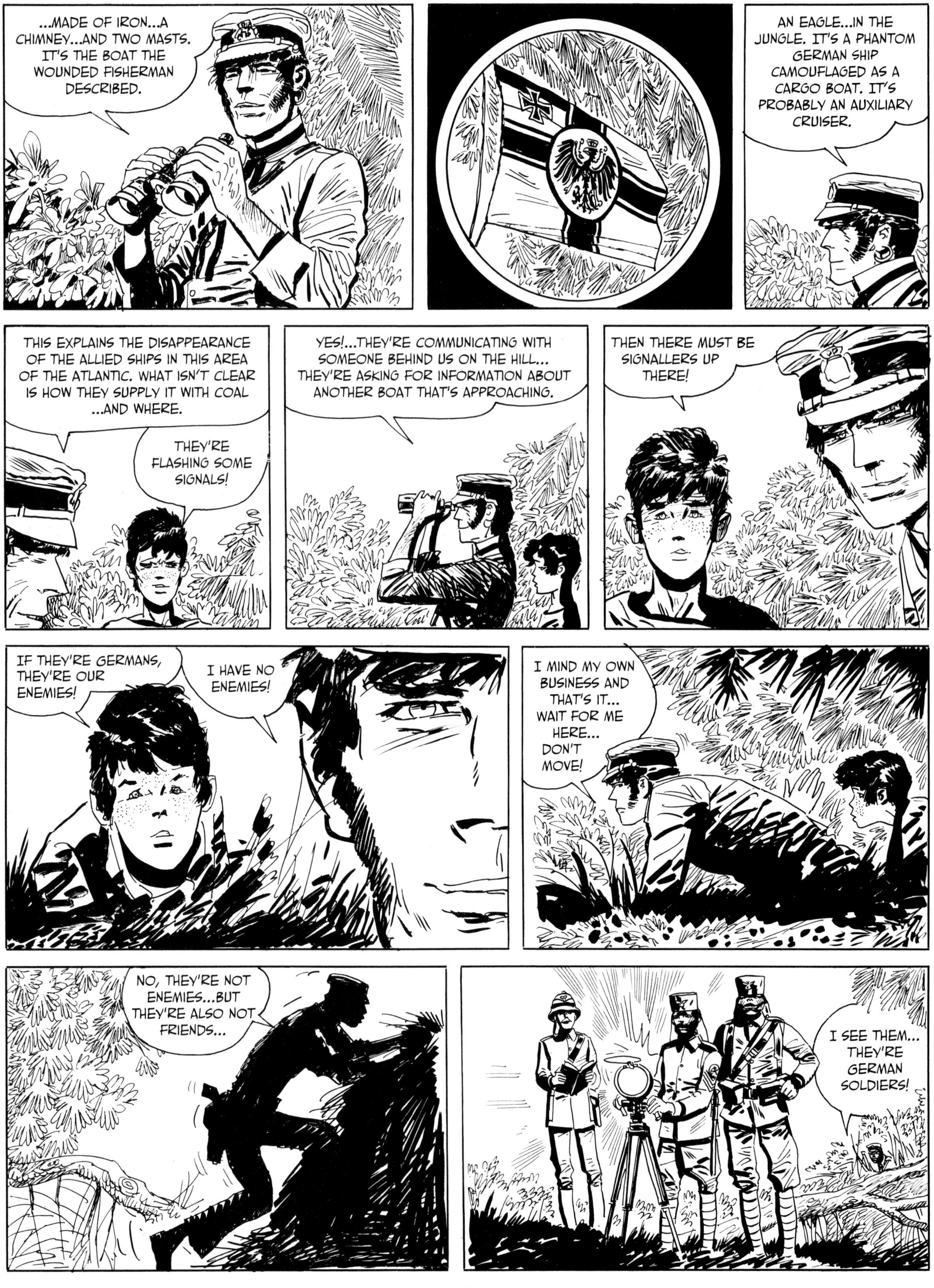
...MADE OF IRON...A CHIMNEY...AND TWO MASTS. IT'S THE BOAT THE WOUNDED FISHERMAN DESCRIBED.
AN EAGLE...IN THE JUNGLE. IT'S A PHANTOM GERMAN SHIP CAMOUFLAGED AS A CARGO BOAT. IT'S PROBABLY AN AUXILIARY CRUISER.
THIS EXPLAINS THE DISAPPEARANCE OF THE ALLIED SHIPS IN THIS AREA OF THE ATLANTIC. WHAT ISN'T CLEAR IS HOW THEY SUPPLY IT WITH COAL ...AND WHERE.
THEY'RE FLASHING SOME SIGNALS!
YES!...THEY'RE COMMUNICATING WITH SOMEONE BEHIND US ON THE HILL... THEY'RE ASKING FOR INFORMATION ABOUT ANOTHER BOAT THAT'S APPROACHING.
THEN THERE MUST BE SIGNALLERS UP THERE!
IF THEY'RE GERMANS, THEY'RE OUR ENEMIES!
I HAVE NO ENEMIES!
I MIND MY OWN BUSINESS AND THAT'S IT... WAIT FOR ME HERE... DON'T MOVE!
NO, THEY'RE NOT ENEMIES...BUT THEY'RE ALSO NOT FRIENDS...
I SEE THEM... THEY'RE GERMAN SOLDIERS!

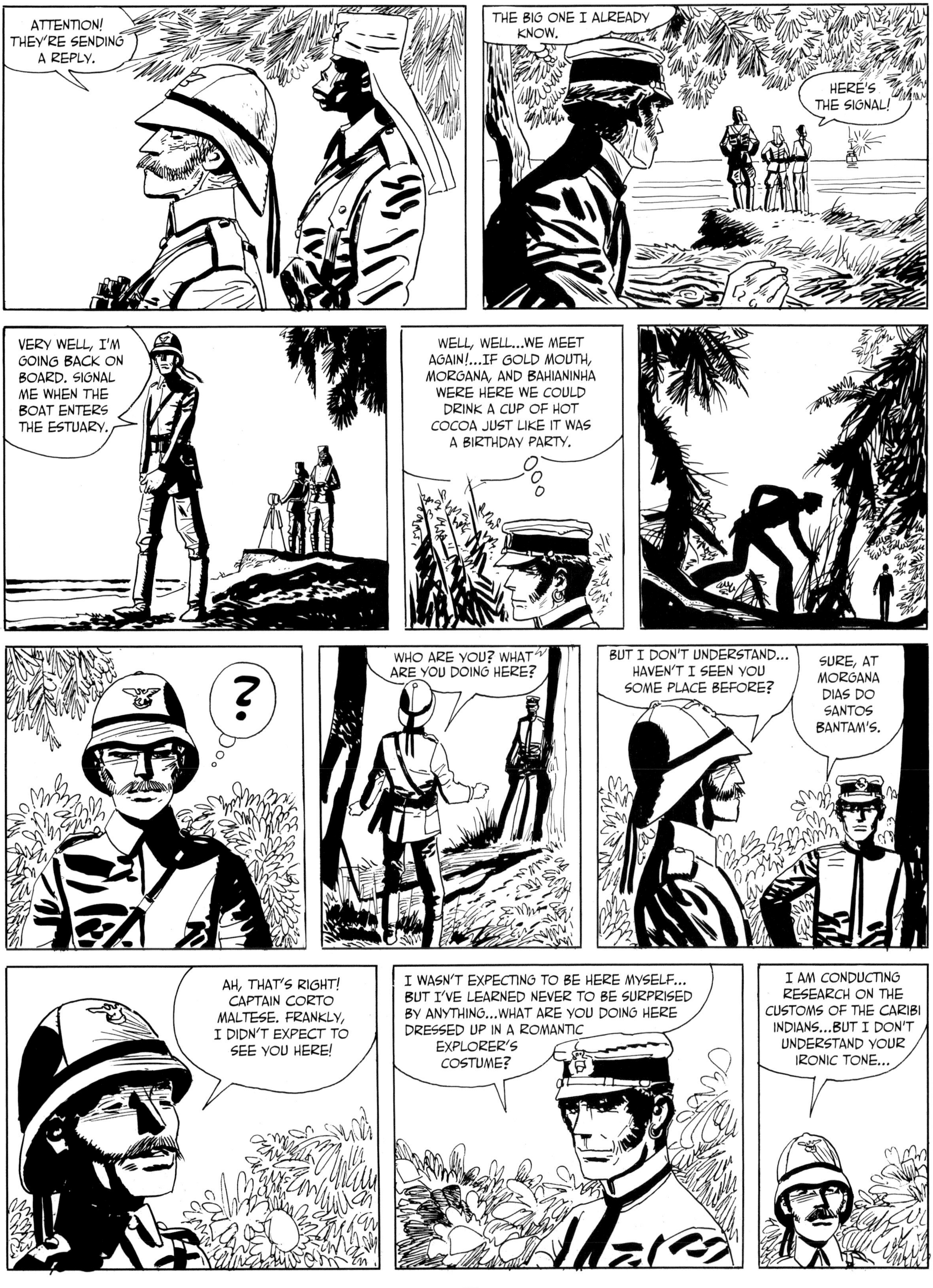
ATTENTION! THEY'RE SENDING A REPLY.
THE BIG ONE I ALREADY KNOW.
HERE'S THE SIGNAL!
VERY WELL, I'M GOING BACK ON BOARD. SIGNAL ME WHEN THE BOAT ENTERS THE ESTUARY.
WELL, WELL...WE MEET AGAIN!...IF GOLD MOUTH, MORGANA, AND BAHIANINHA WERE HERE WE COULD DRINK A CUP OF HOT COCOA JUST LIKE IT WAS A BIRTHDAY PARTY.
?
WHO ARE YOU? WHAT ARE YOU DOING HERE?
BUT I DON'T UNDERSTAND... HAVEN'T I SEEN YOU SOME PLACE BEFORE?
SURE, AT MORGANA DIAS DO SANTOS BANTAM'S.
AH, THAT'S RIGHT! CAPTAIN CORTO MALTESE. FRANKLY, I DIDN'T EXPECT TO SEE YOU HERE!
I WASN'T EXPECTING TO BE HERE MYSELF... BUT I'VE LEARNED NEVER TO BE SURPRISED BY ANYTHING...WHAT ARE YOU DOING HERE DRESSED UP IN A ROMANTIC EXPLORER'S COSTUME?
I AM CONDUCTING RESEARCH ON THE CUSTOMS OF THE CARIBI INDIANS...BUT I DON'T UNDERSTAND YOUR IRONIC TONE...

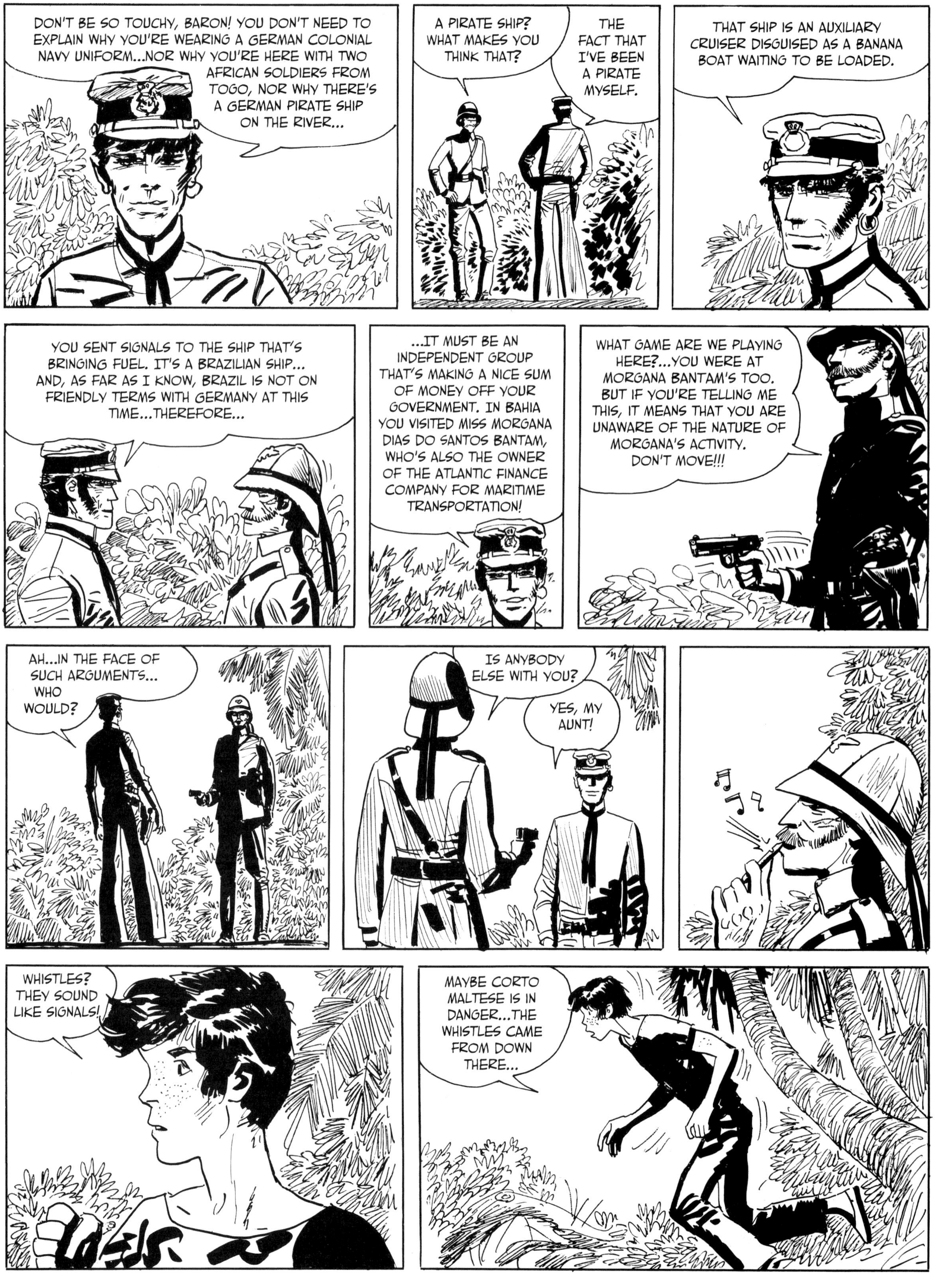
DON'T BE SO TOUCHY, BARON! YOU DON'T NEED TO EXPLAIN WHY YOU'RE WEARING A GERMAN COLONIAL NAVY UNIFORM...NOR WHY YOU'RE HERE WITH TWO AFRICAN SOLDIERS FROM TOGO, NOR WHY THERE'S A GERMAN PIRATE SHIP ON THE RIVER...
A PIRATE SHIP? WHAT MAKES YOU THINK THAT?
THE FACT THAT I'VE BEEN A PIRATE MYSELF.
THAT SHIP IS AN AUXILIARY CRUISER DISGUISED AS A BANANA BOAT WAITING TO BE LOADED.
YOU SENT SIGNALS TO THE SHIP THAT'S BRINGING FUEL. IT'S A BRAZILIAN SHIP... AND, AS FAR AS I KNOW, BRAZIL IS NOT ON FRIENDLY TERMS WITH GERMANY AT THIS TIME...THEREFORE...
...IT MUST BE AN INDEPENDENT GROUP THAT'S MAKING A NICE SUM OF MONEY OFF YOUR GOVERNMENT. IN BAHIA YOU VISITED MISS MORGANA DIAS DO SANTOS BANTAM, WHO'S ALSO THE OWNER OF THE ATLANTIC FINANCE COMPANY FOR MARITIME TRANSPORTATION!
WHAT GAME ARE WE PLAYING HERE?...YOU WERE AT MORGANA BANTAM'S TOO. BUT IF YOU'RE TELLING ME THIS, IT MEANS THAT YOU ARE UNAWARE OF THE NATURE OF MORGANA'S ACTIVITY. DON'T MOVE!!!
AH...IN THE FACE OF SUCH ARGUMENTS... WHO WOULD?
IS ANYBODY ELSE WITH YOU?
YES, MY AUNT!
WHISTLES? THEY SOUND LIKE SIGNALS!
MAYBE CORTO MALTESE IS IN DANGER...THE WHISTLES CAME FROM DOWN THERE...

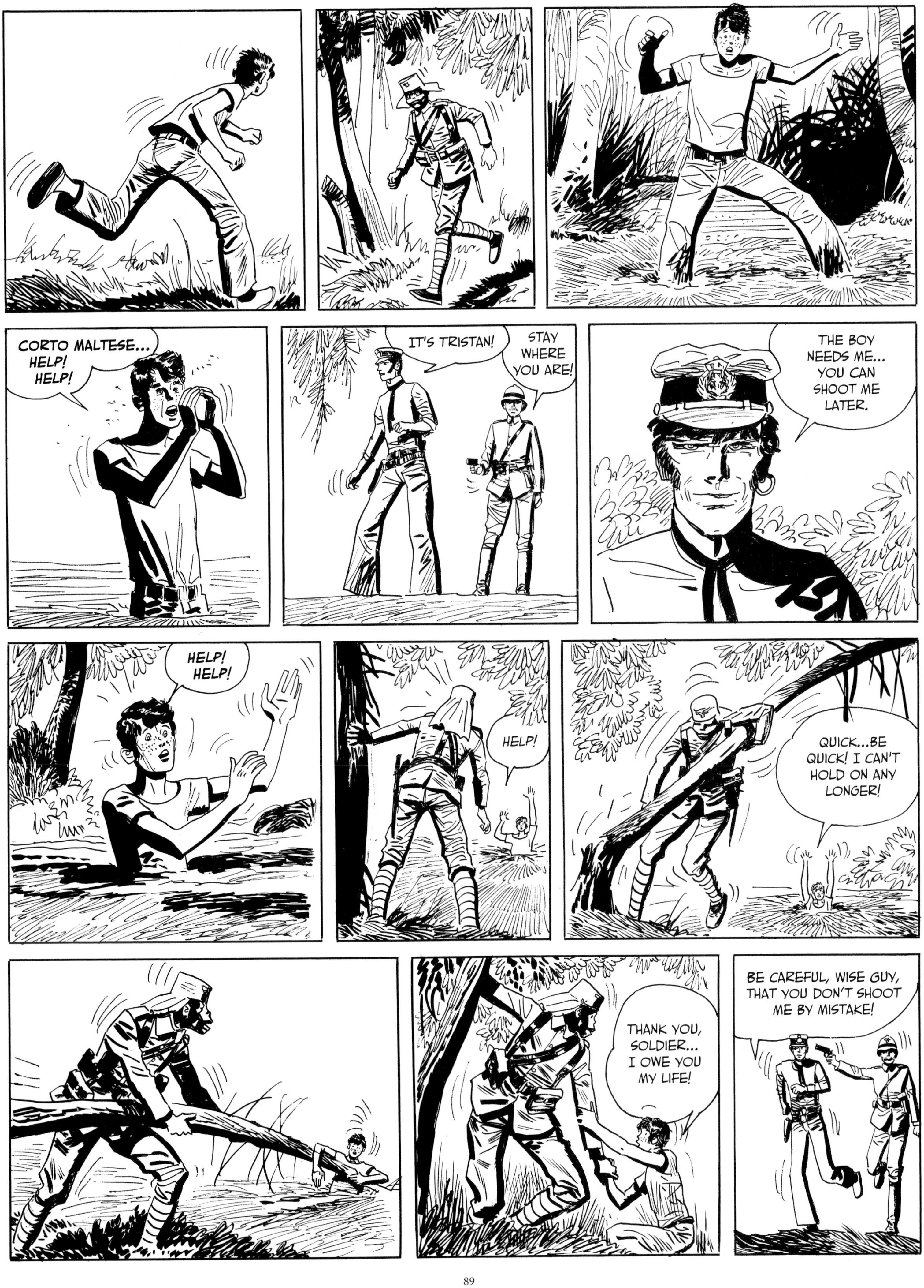
CORTO MALTESE... HELP! HELP!
IT'S TRISTAN!
STAY WHERE YOU ARE!
THE BOY NEEDS ME... YOU CAN SHOOT ME LATER.
HELP! HELP!
HELP!
QUICK...BE QUICK! I CAN'T HOLD ON ANY LONGER!
THANK YOU, SOLDIER... I OWE YOU MY LIFE!
BE CAREFUL, WISE GUY, THAT YOU DON'T SHOOT ME BY MISTAKE!

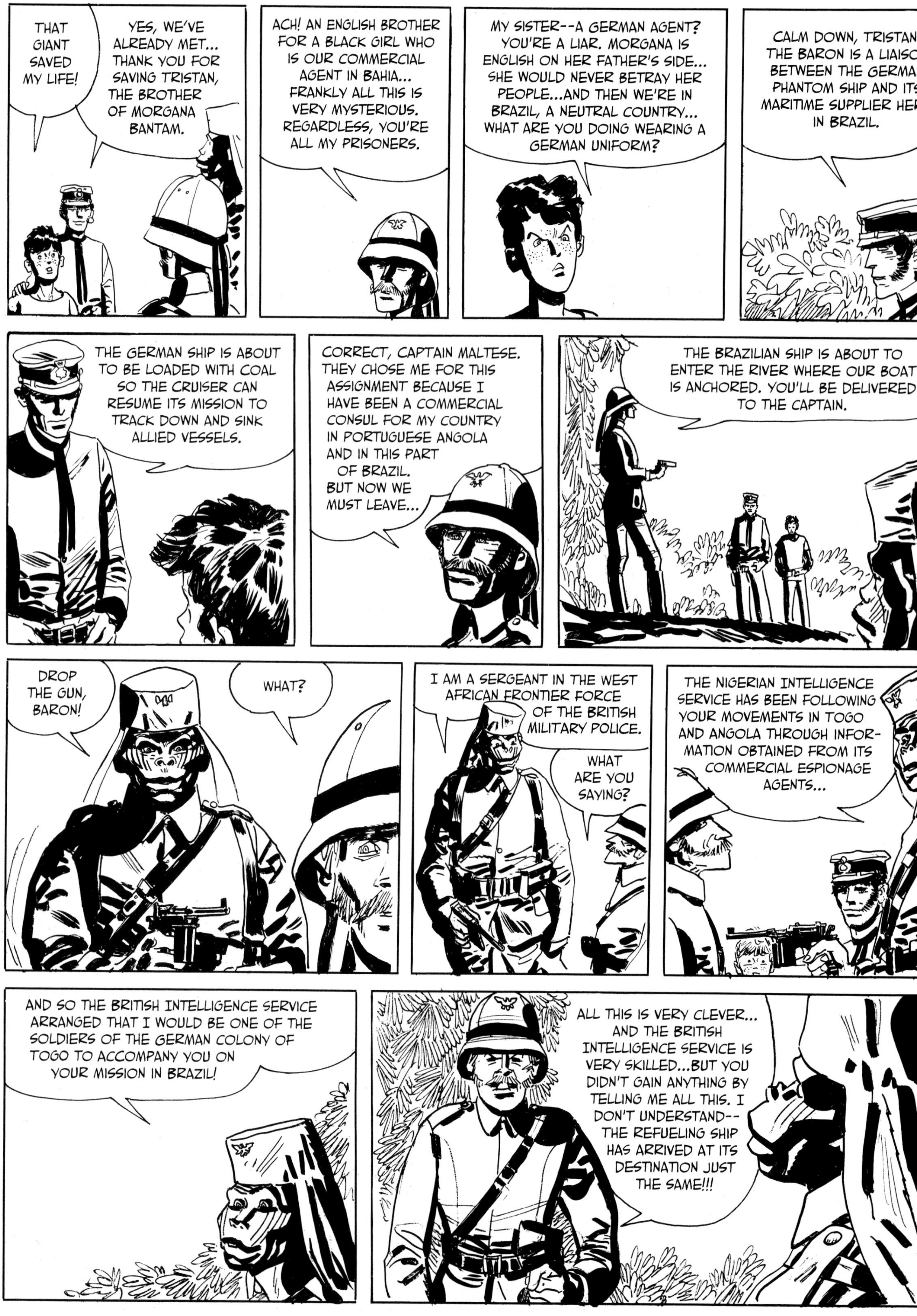
THAT GIANT SAVED MY LIFE!
YES, WE'VE ALREADY MET... THANK YOU FOR SAVING TRISTAN, THE BROTHER OF MORGANA BANTAM.
ACH! AN ENGLISH BROTHER FOR A BLACK GIRL WHO IS OUR COMMERCIAL AGENT IN BAHIA... FRANKLY ALL THIS IS VERY MYSTERIOUS. REGARDLESS, YOU'RE ALL MY PRISONERS.
MY SISTER--A GERMAN AGENT? YOU'RE A LIAR. MORGANA IS ENGLISH ON HER FATHER'S SIDE... SHE WOULD NEVER BETRAY HER PEOPLE...AND THEN WE'RE IN BRAZIL, A NEUTRAL COUNTRY... WHAT ARE YOU DOING WEARING A GERMAN UNIFORM?
CALM DOWN, TRISTAN. THE BARON IS A LIAISON BETWEEN THE GERMAN PHANTOM SHIP AND ITS MARITIME SUPPLIER HERE IN BRAZIL.
THE GERMAN SHIP IS ABOUT TO BE LOADED WITH COAL SO THE CRUISER CAN RESUME ITS MISSION TO TRACK DOWN AND SINK ALLIED VESSELS.
CORRECT, CAPTAIN MALTESE. THEY CHOSE ME FOR THIS ASSIGNMENT BECAUSE I HAVE BEEN A COMMERCIAL CONSUL FOR MY COUNTRY IN PORTUGUESE ANGOLA AND IN THIS PART OF BRAZIL. BUT NOW WE MUST LEAVE...
THE BRAZILIAN SHIP IS ABOUT TO ENTER THE RIVER WHERE OUR BOAT IS ANCHORED. YOU'LL BE DELIVERED TO THE CAPTAIN.
DROP THE GUN, BARON!
WHAT?
I AM A SERGEANT IN THE WEST AFRICAN FRONTIER FORCE OF THE BRITISH MILITARY POLICE.
WHAT ARE YOU SAYING?
THE NIGERIAN INTELLIGENCE SERVICE HAS BEEN FOLLOWING YOUR MOVEMENTS IN TOGO AND ANGOLA THROUGH INFORMATION OBTAINED FROM ITS COMMERCIAL ESPIONAGE AGENTS...
AND SO THE BRITISH INTELLIGENCE SERVICE ARRANGED THAT I WOULD BE ONE OF THE SOLDIERS OF THE GERMAN COLONY OF TOGO TO ACCOMPANY YOU ON YOUR MISSION IN BRAZIL!
ALL THIS IS VERY CLEVER... AND THE BRITISH INTELLIGENCE SERVICE IS VERY SKILLED...BUT YOU DIDN'T GAIN ANYTHING BY TELLING ME ALL THIS. I DON'T UNDERSTAND-- THE REFUELING SHIP HAS ARRIVED AT ITS DESTINATION JUST THE SAME!!!

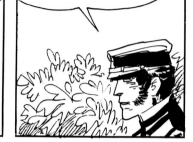

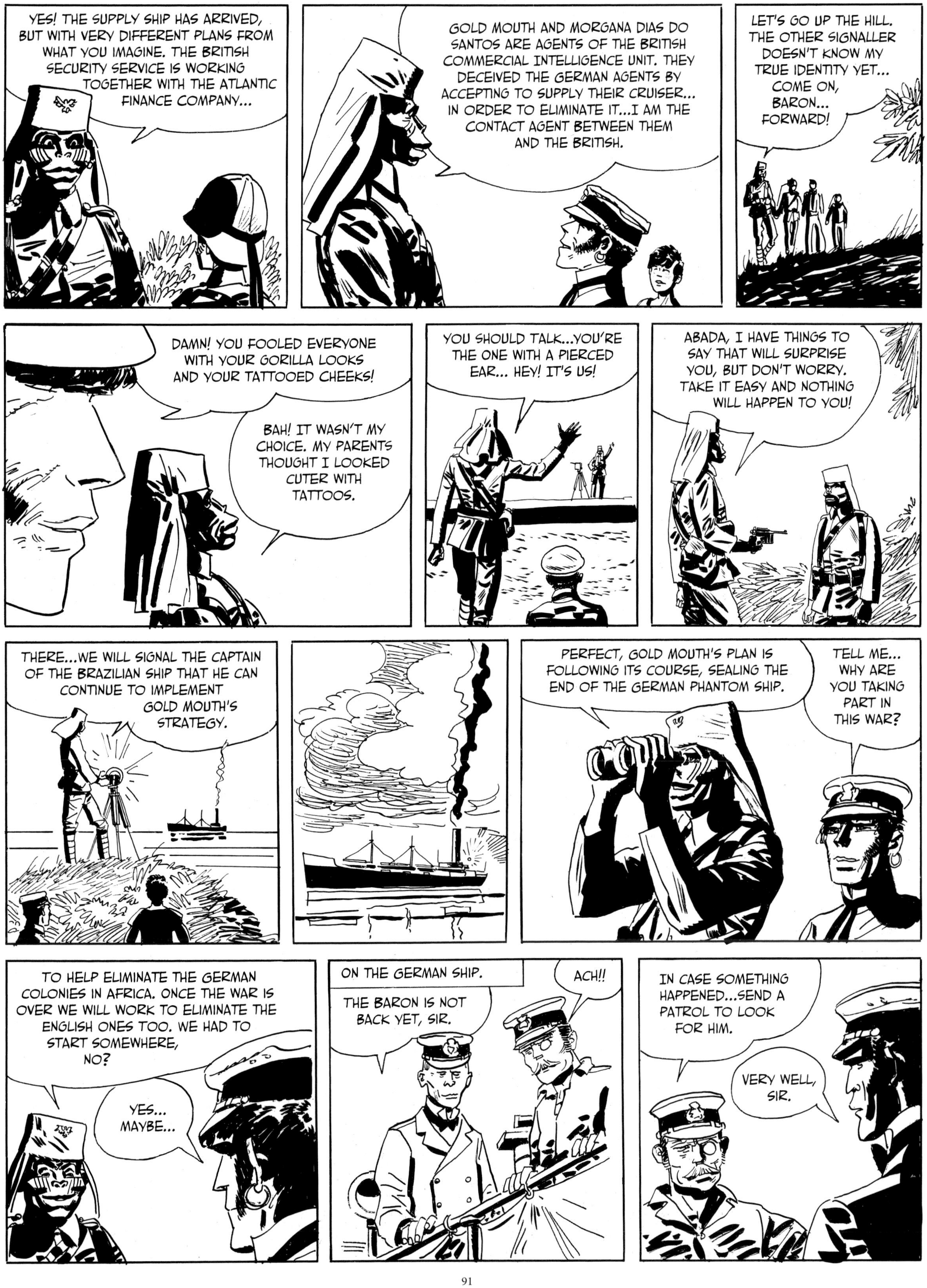

YES! THE SUPPLY SHIP HAS ARRIVED, BUT WITH VERY DIFFERENT PLANS FROM WHAT YOU IMAGINE. THE BRITISH SECURITY SERVICE IS WORKING TOGETHER WITH THE ATLANTIC FINANCE COMPANY...
GOLD MOUTH AND MORGANA DIAS DO SANTOS ARE AGENTS OF THE BRITISH COMMERCIAL INTELLIGENCE UNIT. THEY DECEIVED THE GERMAN AGENTS BY ACCEPTING TO SUPPLY THEIR CRUISER... IN ORDER TO ELIMINATE IT...I AM THE CONTACT AGENT BETWEEN THEM AND THE BRITISH.
LET'S GO UP THE HILL. THE OTHER SIGNALLER DOESN'T KNOW MY TRUE IDENTITY YET... COME ON, BARON... FORWARD!
DAMN! YOU FOOLED EVERYONE WITH YOUR GORILLA LOOKS AND YOUR TATTOOED CHEEKS!
BAH! IT WASN'T MY CHOICE. MY PARENTS THOUGHT I LOOKED CUTER WITH TATTOOS.
YOU SHOULD TALK...YOU'RE THE ONE WITH A PIERCED EAR... HEY! IT'S US!
ABADA, I HAVE THINGS TO SAY THAT WILL SURPRISE YOU, BUT DON'T WORRY. TAKE IT EASY AND NOTHING WILL HAPPEN TO YOU!
THERE...WE WILL SIGNAL THE CAPTAIN OF THE BRAZILIAN SHIP THAT HE CAN CONTINUE TO IMPLEMENT GOLD MOUTH'S STRATEGY.
PERFECT, GOLD MOUTH'S PLAN IS FOLLOWING ITS COURSE, SEALING THE END OF THE GERMAN PHANTOM SHIP.
TELL ME... WHY ARE YOU TAKING PART IN THIS WAR?
TO HELP ELIMINATE THE GERMAN COLONIES IN AFRICA. ONCE THE WAR IS OVER WE WILL WORK TO ELIMINATE THE ENGLISH ONES TOO. WE HAD TO START SOMEWHERE, NO?
YES... MAYBE...
ON THE GERMAN SHIP.
THE BARON IS NOT BACK YET, SIR.
ACH!!
IN CASE SOMETHING HAPPENED...SEND A PATROL TO LOOK FOR HIM.
VERY WELL, SIR.

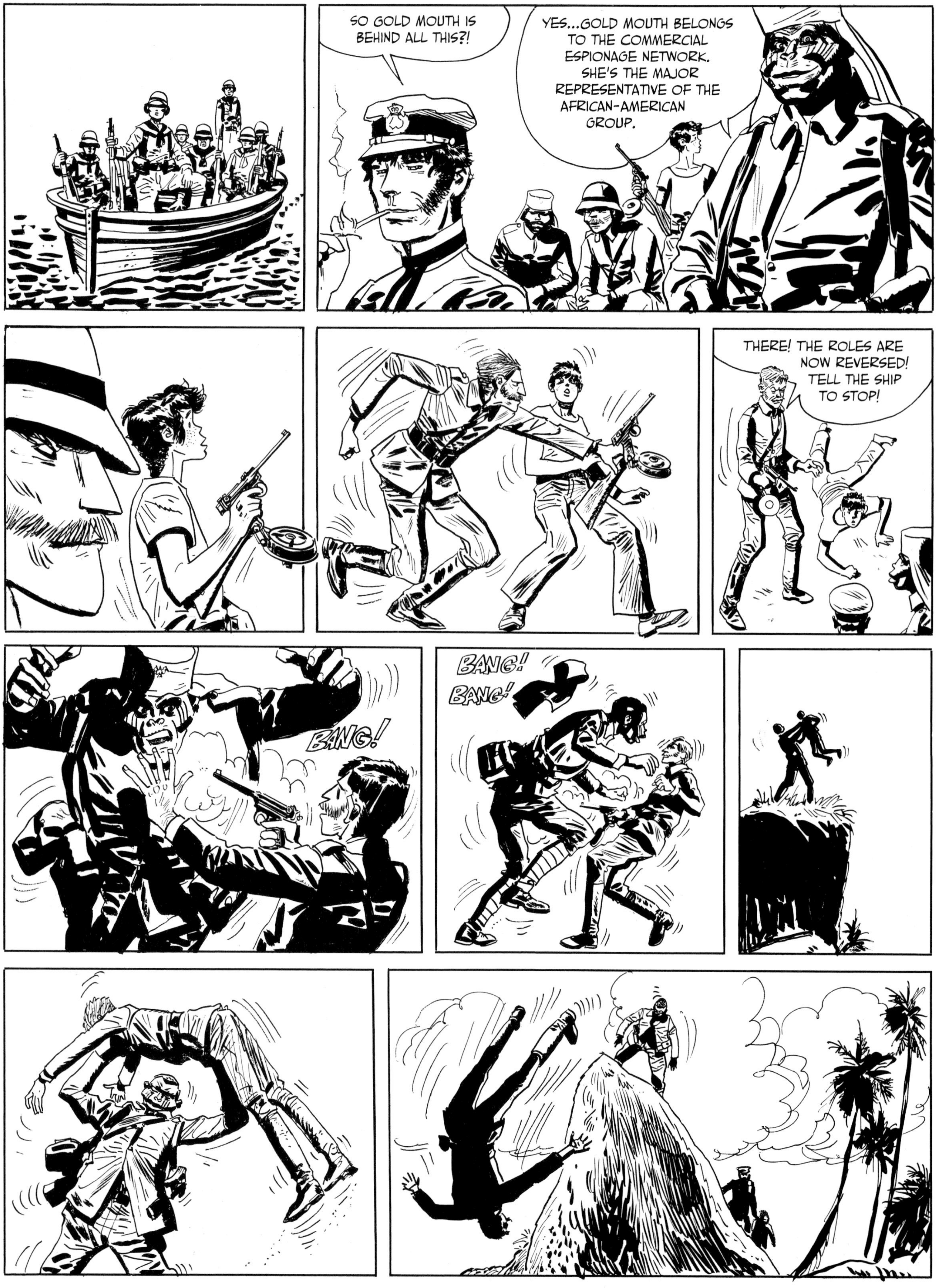

SO GOLD MOUTH IS BEHIND ALL THIS?!
YES...GOLD MOUTH BELONGS TO THE COMMERCIAL ESPIONAGE NETWORK. SHE'S THE MAJOR REPRESENTATIVE OF THE AFRICAN-AMERICAN GROUP.
THERE! THE ROLES ARE NOW REVERSED! TELL THE SHIP TO STOP!
BANG!
BANG!
BANG!

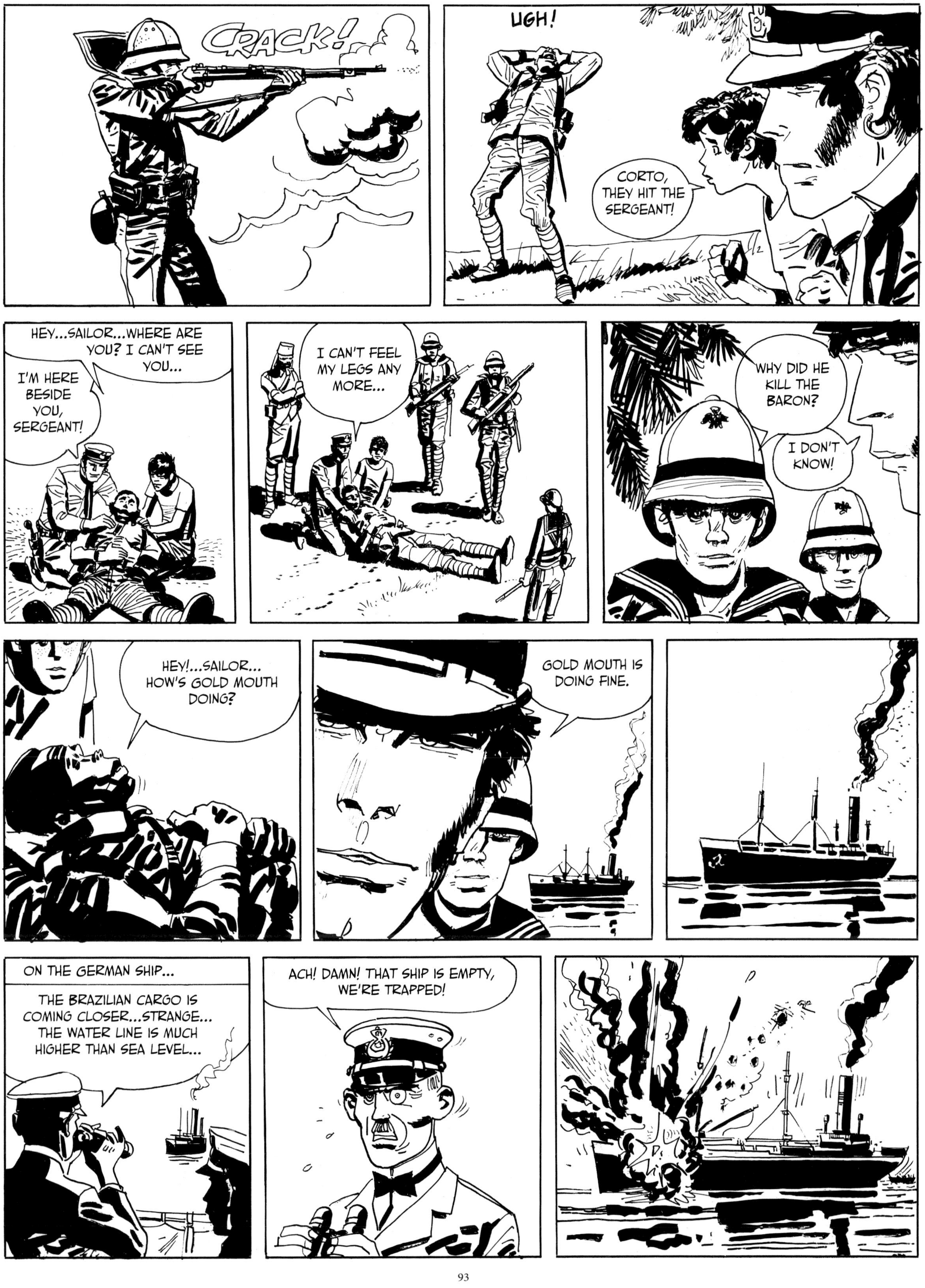
CRACK!
UGH!
CORTO, THEY HIT THE SERGEANT!
HEY...SAILOR...WHERE ARE YOU? I CAN'T SEE YOU...
I'M HERE BESIDE YOU, SERGEANT!
I CAN'T FEEL MY LEGS ANY MORE...
WHY DID HE KILL THE BARON?
I DON'T KNOW!
HEY!...SAILOR... HOW'S GOLD MOUTH DOING?
GOLD MOUTH IS DOING FINE.
ON THE GERMAN SHIP...
THE BRAZILIAN CARGO IS COMING CLOSER...STRANGE... THE WATER LINE IS MUCH HIGHER THAN SEA LEVEL...
ACH! DAMN! THAT SHIP IS EMPTY, WE'RE TRAPPED!

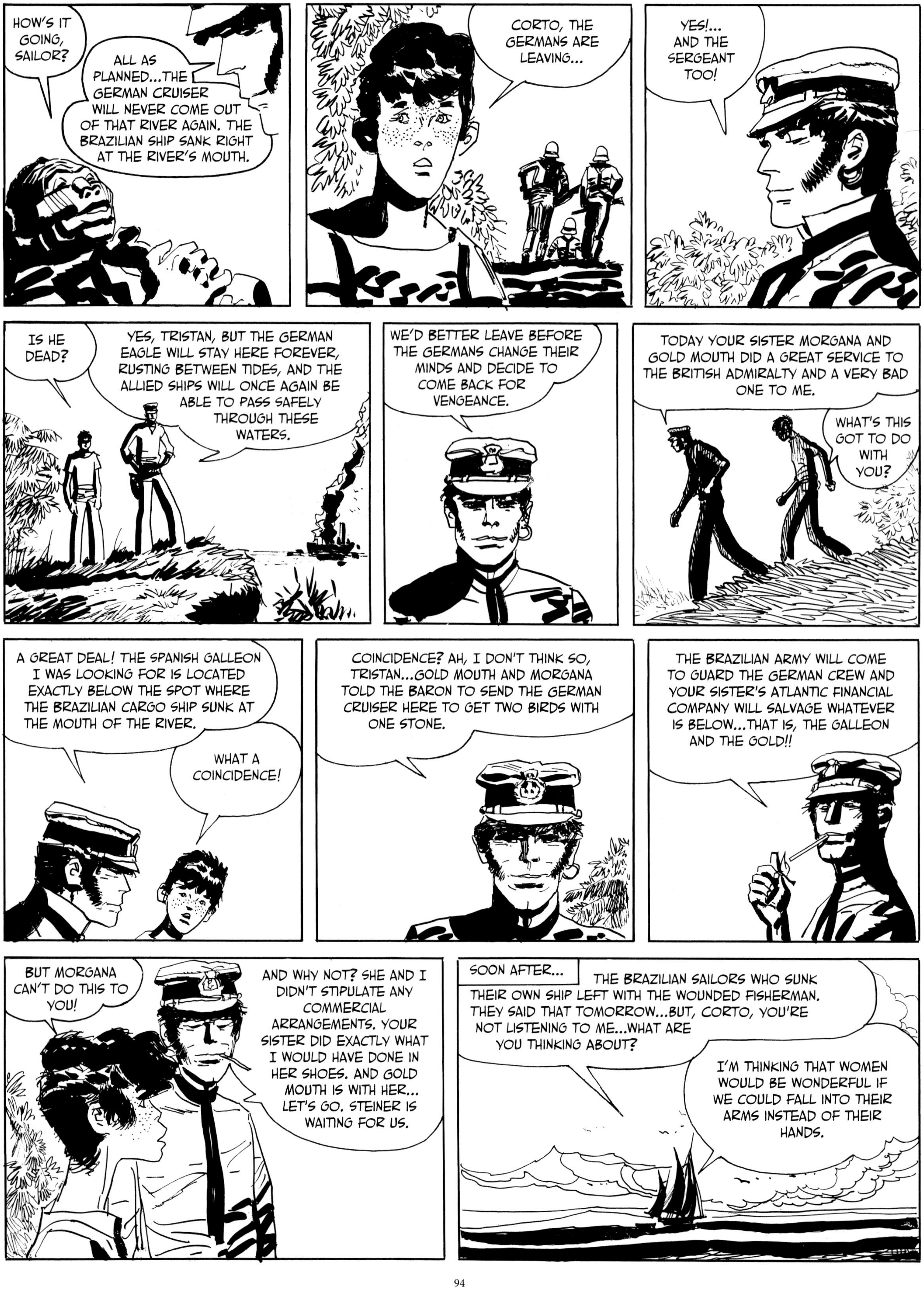

HOW'S IT GOING, SAILOR?
ALL AS PLANNED...THE GERMAN CRUISER WILL NEVER COME OUT OF THAT RIVER AGAIN. THE BRAZILIAN SHIP SANK RIGHT AT THE RIVER'S MOUTH.
CORTO, THE GERMANS ARE LEAVING...
YES!... AND THE SERGEANT TOO!
IS HE DEAD?
YES, TRISTAN, BUT THE GERMAN EAGLE WILL STAY HERE FOREVER, RUSTING BETWEEN TIDES, AND THE ALLIED SHIPS WILL ONCE AGAIN BE ABLE TO PASS SAFELY THROUGH THESE WATERS.
WE'D BETTER LEAVE BEFORE THE GERMANS CHANGE THEIR MINDS AND DECIDE TO COME BACK FOR VENGEANCE.
TODAY YOUR SISTER MORGANA AND GOLD MOUTH DID A GREAT SERVICE TO THE BRITISH ADMIRALTY AND A VERY BAD ONE TO ME.
WHAT'S THIS GOT TO DO WITH YOU?
A GREAT DEAL! THE SPANISH GALLEON I WAS LOOKING FOR IS LOCATED EXACTLY BELOW THE SPOT WHERE THE BRAZILIAN CARGO SHIP SUNK AT THE MOUTH OF THE RIVER.
WHAT A COINCIDENCE!
COINCIDENCE? AH, I DON'T THINK SO, TRISTAN...GOLD MOUTH AND MORGANA TOLD THE BARON TO SEND THE GERMAN CRUISER HERE TO GET TWO BIRDS WITH ONE STONE.
THE BRAZILIAN ARMY WILL COME TO GUARD THE GERMAN CREW AND YOUR SISTER'S ATLANTIC FINANCIAL COMPANY WILL SALVAGE WHATEVER IS BELOW...THAT IS, THE GALLEON AND THE GOLD!!
BUT MORGANA CAN'T DO THIS TO YOU!
AND WHY NOT? SHE AND I DIDN'T STIPULATE ANY COMMERCIAL ARRANGEMENTS. YOUR SISTER DID EXACTLY WHAT I WOULD HAVE DONE IN HER SHOES. AND GOLD MOUTH IS WITH HER... LET'S GO. STEINER IS WAITING FOR US.
SOON AFTER...
THE BRAZILIAN SAILORS WHO SUNK THEIR OWN SHIP LEFT WITH THE WOUNDED FISHERMAN. THEY SAID THAT TOMORROW...BUT, CORTO, YOU'RE NOT LISTENING TO ME...WHAT ARE YOU THINKING ABOUT?
I'M THINKING THAT WOMEN WOULD BE WONDERFUL IF WE COULD FALL INTO THEIR ARMS INSTEAD OF THEIR HANDS.

CHAPTER FIVE:

SO MUCH FOR GENTLEMEN OF FORTUNE

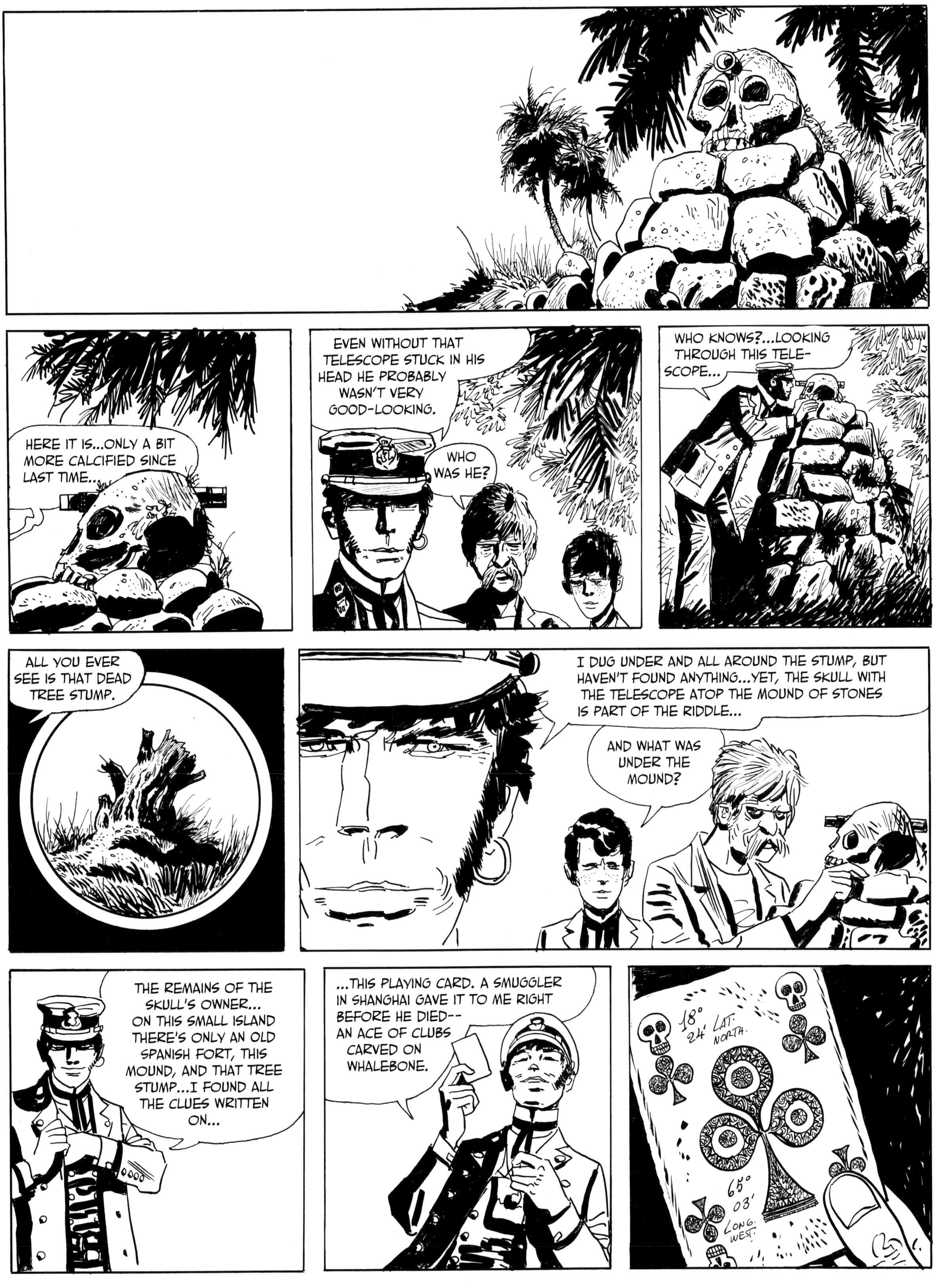
HERE IT IS...ONLY A BIT MORE CALCIFIED SINCE LAST TIME...
EVEN WITHOUT THAT TELESCOPE STUCK IN HIS HEAD HE PROBABLY WASN'T VERY GOOD-LOOKING.
WHO WAS HE?
WHO KNOWS?...LOOKING THROUGH THIS TELE-SCOPE...
ALL YOU EVER SEE IS THAT DEAD TREE STUMP.
I DUG UNDER AND ALL AROUND THE STUMP, BUT HAVEN'T FOUND ANYTHING...YET, THE SKULL WITH THE TELESCOPE ATOP THE MOUND OF STONES IS PART OF THE RIDDLE...
AND WHAT WAS UNDER THE MOUND?
THE REMAINS OF THE SKULL'S OWNER... ON THIS SMALL ISLAND THERE'S ONLY AN OLD SPANISH FORT, THIS MOUND, AND THAT TREE STUMP...I FOUND ALL THE CLUES WRITTEN ON...
...THIS PLAYING CARD. A SMUGGLER IN SHANGHAI GAVE IT TO ME RIGHT BEFORE HE DIED-- AN ACE OF CLUBS CARVED ON WHALEBONE.
18° 24' LAT. NORTH.
65° 03' LONG. WEST.

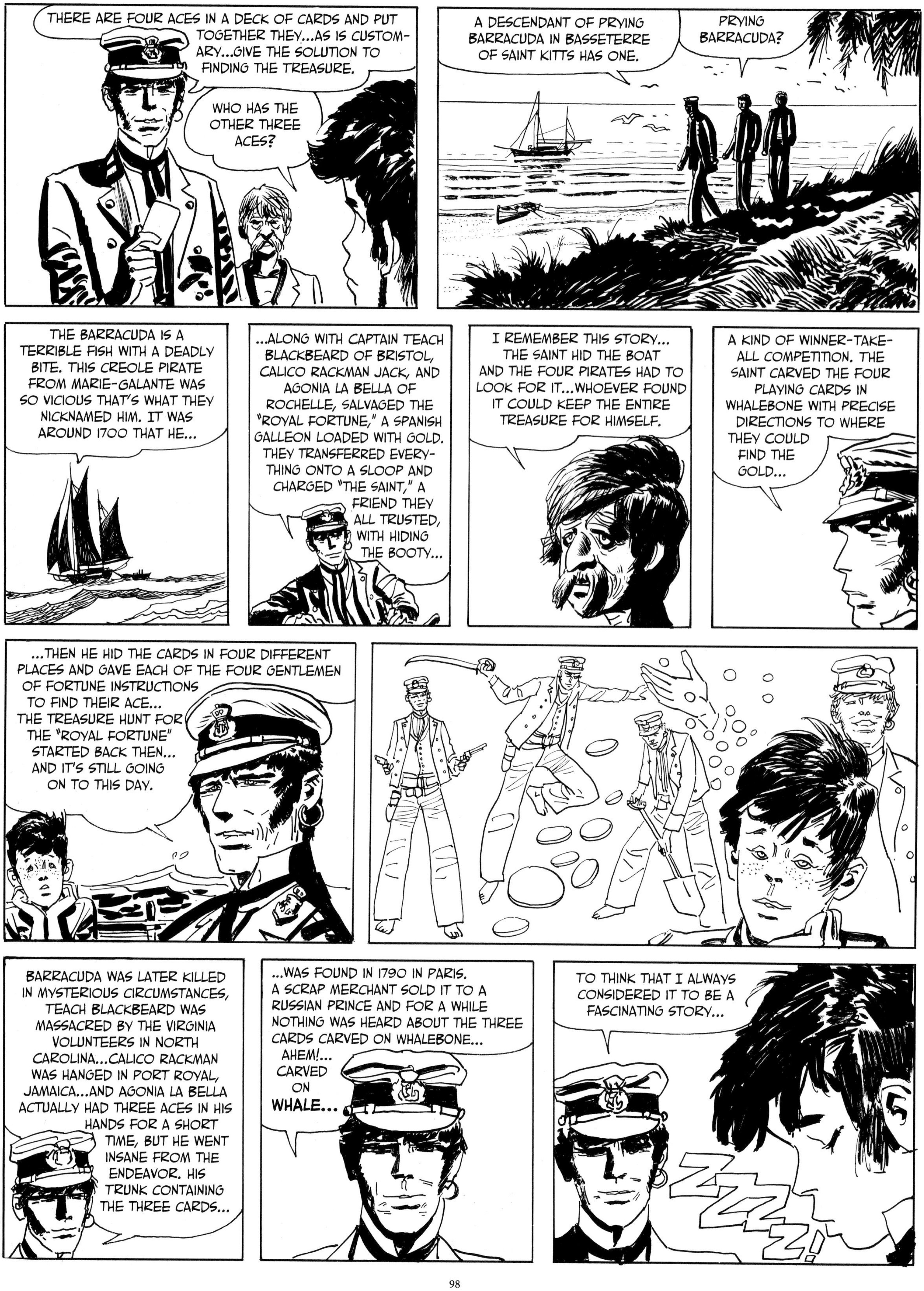

THERE ARE FOUR ACES IN A DECK OF CARDS AND PUT TOGETHER THEY...AS IS CUSTOMARY...GIVE THE SOLUTION TO FINDING THE TREASURE.
WHO HAS THE OTHER THREE ACES?
A DESCENDANT OF PRYING BARRACUDA IN BASSETERRE OF SAINT KITTS HAS ONE.
PRYING BARRACUDA?
THE BARRACUDA IS A TERRIBLE FISH WITH A DEADLY BITE. THIS CREOLE PIRATE FROM MARIE-GALANTE WAS SO VICIOUS THAT'S WHAT THEY NICKNAMED HIM. IT WAS AROUND 1700 THAT HE...
...ALONG WITH CAPTAIN TEACH BLACKBEARD OF BRISTOL, CALICO RACKMAN JACK, AND AGONIA LA BELLA OF ROCHELLE, SALVAGED THE "ROYAL FORTUNE," A SPANISH GALLEON LOADED WITH GOLD. THEY TRANSFERRED EVERYTHING ONTO A SLOOP AND CHARGED "THE SAINT," A FRIEND THEY ALL TRUSTED, WITH HIDING THE BOOTY...
I REMEMBER THIS STORY... THE SAINT HID THE BOAT AND THE FOUR PIRATES HAD TO LOOK FOR IT...WHOEVER FOUND IT COULD KEEP THE ENTIRE TREASURE FOR HIMSELF.
A KIND OF WINNER-TAKE-ALL COMPETITION. THE SAINT CARVED THE FOUR PLAYING CARDS IN WHALEBONE WITH PRECISE DIRECTIONS TO WHERE THEY COULD FIND THE GOLD...
...THEN HE HID THE CARDS IN FOUR DIFFERENT PLACES AND GAVE EACH OF THE FOUR GENTLEMEN OF FORTUNE INSTRUCTIONS TO FIND THEIR ACE... THE TREASURE HUNT FOR THE "ROYAL FORTUNE" STARTED BACK THEN... AND IT'S STILL GOING ON TO THIS DAY.
BARRACUDA WAS LATER KILLED IN MYSTERIOUS CIRCUMSTANCES, TEACH BLACKBEARD WAS MASSACRED BY THE VIRGINIA VOLUNTEERS IN NORTH CAROLINA...CALICO RACKMAN WAS HANGED IN PORT ROYAL, JAMAICA...AND AGONIA LA BELLA ACTUALLY HAD THREE ACES IN HIS HANDS FOR A SHORT TIME, BUT HE WENT INSANE FROM THE ENDEAVOR. HIS TRUNK CONTAINING THE THREE CARDS...
...WAS FOUND IN 1790 IN PARIS. A SCRAP MERCHANT SOLD IT TO A RUSSIAN PRINCE AND FOR A WHILE NOTHING WAS HEARD ABOUT THE THREE CARDS CARVED ON WHALEBONE...
AHEM!... CARVED ON WHALE...
TO THINK THAT I ALWAYS CONSIDERED IT TO BE A FASCINATING STORY...
ZZZZZ!

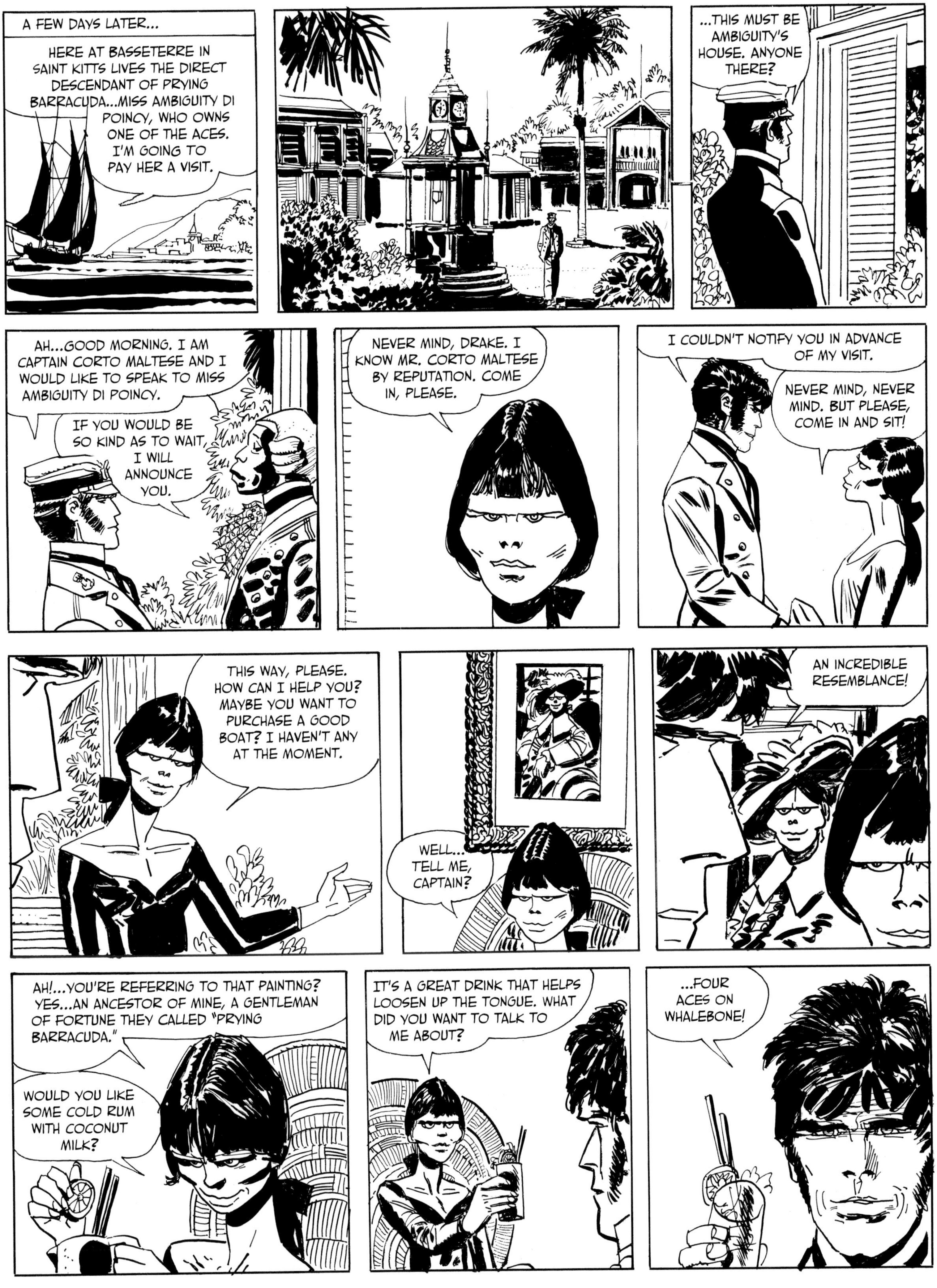
A FEW DAYS LATER...
HERE AT BASSETERRE IN SAINT KITTS LIVES THE DIRECT DESCENDANT OF PRYING BARRACUDA...MISS AMBIGUITY DI POINCY, WHO OWNS ONE OF THE ACES. I'M GOING TO PAY HER A VISIT.
...THIS MUST BE AMBIGUITY'S HOUSE. ANYONE THERE?
AH...GOOD MORNING. I AM CAPTAIN CORTO MALTESE AND I WOULD LIKE TO SPEAK TO MISS AMBIGUITY DI POINCY.
IF YOU WOULD BE SO KIND AS TO WAIT, I WILL ANNOUNCE YOU.
NEVER MIND, DRAKE. I KNOW MR. CORTO MALTESE BY REPUTATION. COME IN, PLEASE.
I COULDN'T NOTIFY YOU IN ADVANCE OF MY VISIT.
NEVER MIND, NEVER MIND. BUT PLEASE, COME IN AND SIT!
THIS WAY, PLEASE. HOW CAN I HELP YOU? MAYBE YOU WANT TO PURCHASE A GOOD BOAT? I HAVEN'T ANY AT THE MOMENT.
WELL... TELL ME, CAPTAIN?
AN INCREDIBLE RESEMBLANCE!
AH!...YOU'RE REFERRING TO THAT PAINTING? YES...AN ANCESTOR OF MINE, A GENTLEMAN OF FORTUNE THEY CALLED "PRYING BARRACUDA."
WOULD YOU LIKE SOME COLD RUM WITH COCONUT MILK?
IT'S A GREAT DRINK THAT HELPS LOOSEN UP THE TONGUE. WHAT DID YOU WANT TO TALK TO ME ABOUT?
...FOUR ACES ON WHALEBONE!

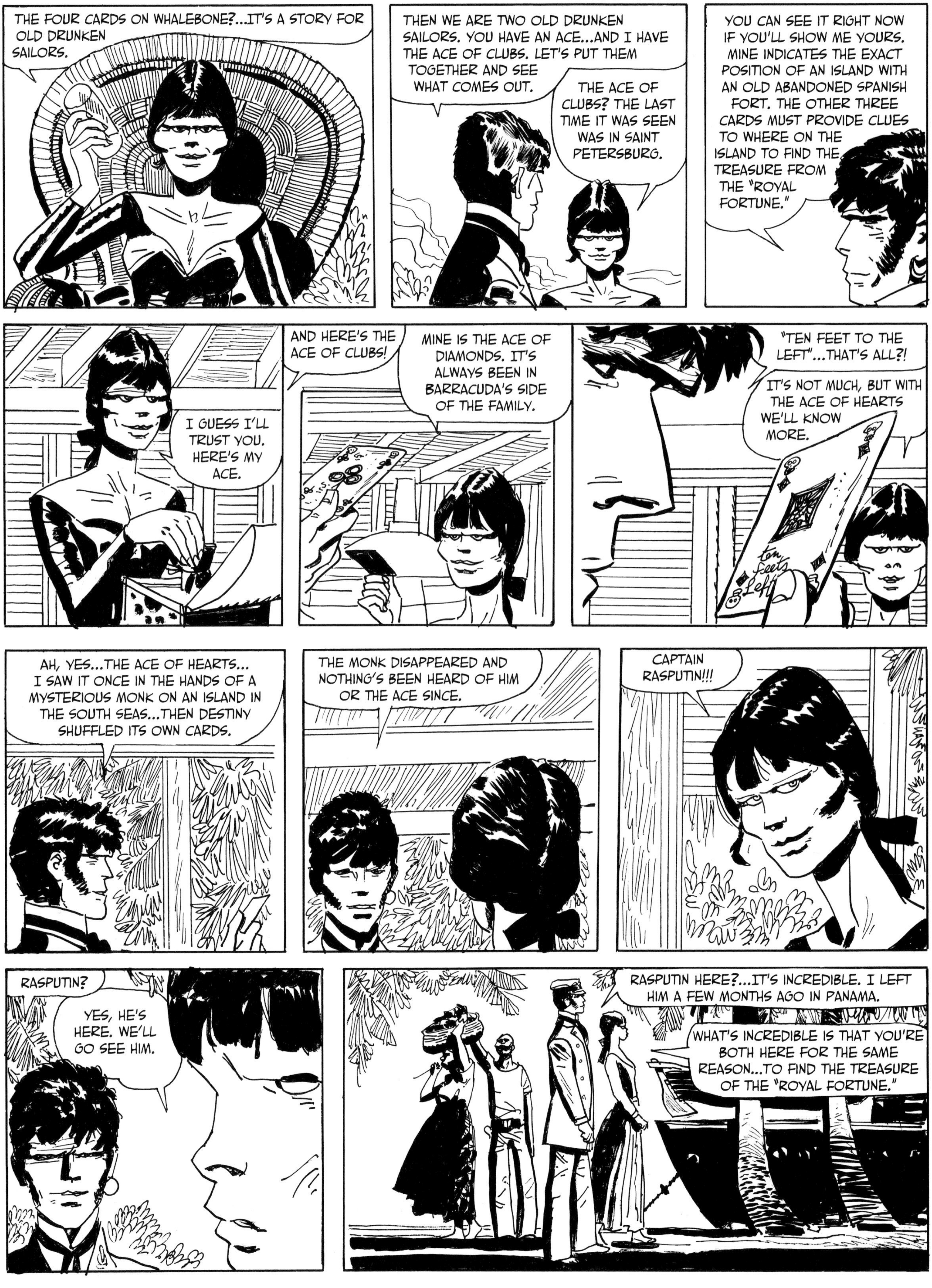

THE FOUR CARDS ON WHALEBONE?...IT'S A STORY FOR OLD DRUNKEN SAILORS.
THEN WE ARE TWO OLD DRUNKEN SAILORS. YOU HAVE AN ACE...AND I HAVE THE ACE OF CLUBS. LET'S PUT THEM TOGETHER AND SEE WHAT COMES OUT.
THE ACE OF CLUBS? THE LAST TIME IT WAS SEEN WAS IN SAINT PETERSBURG.
YOU CAN SEE IT RIGHT NOW IF YOU'LL SHOW ME YOURS. MINE INDICATES THE EXACT POSITION OF AN ISLAND WITH AN OLD ABANDONED SPANISH FORT. THE OTHER THREE CARDS MUST PROVIDE CLUES TO WHERE ON THE ISLAND TO FIND THE TREASURE FROM THE "ROYAL FORTUNE."
I GUESS I'LL TRUST YOU. HERE'S MY ACE.
AND HERE'S THE ACE OF CLUBS!
MINE IS THE ACE OF DIAMONDS. IT'S ALWAYS BEEN IN BARRACUDA'S SIDE OF THE FAMILY.
"TEN FEET TO THE LEFT"...THAT'S ALL?!
IT'S NOT MUCH, BUT WITH THE ACE OF HEARTS WE'LL KNOW MORE.
ten feets Left
AH, YES...THE ACE OF HEARTS... I SAW IT ONCE IN THE HANDS OF A MYSTERIOUS MONK ON AN ISLAND IN THE SOUTH SEAS...THEN DESTINY SHUFFLED ITS OWN CARDS.
THE MONK DISAPPEARED AND NOTHING'S BEEN HEARD OF HIM OR THE ACE SINCE.
CAPTAIN RASPUTIN!!!
RASPUTIN?
YES, HE'S HERE. WE'LL GO SEE HIM.
RASPUTIN HERE?...IT'S INCREDIBLE. I LEFT HIM A FEW MONTHS AGO IN PANAMA.
WHAT'S INCREDIBLE IS THAT YOU'RE BOTH HERE FOR THE SAME REASON...TO FIND THE TREASURE OF THE "ROYAL FORTUNE."

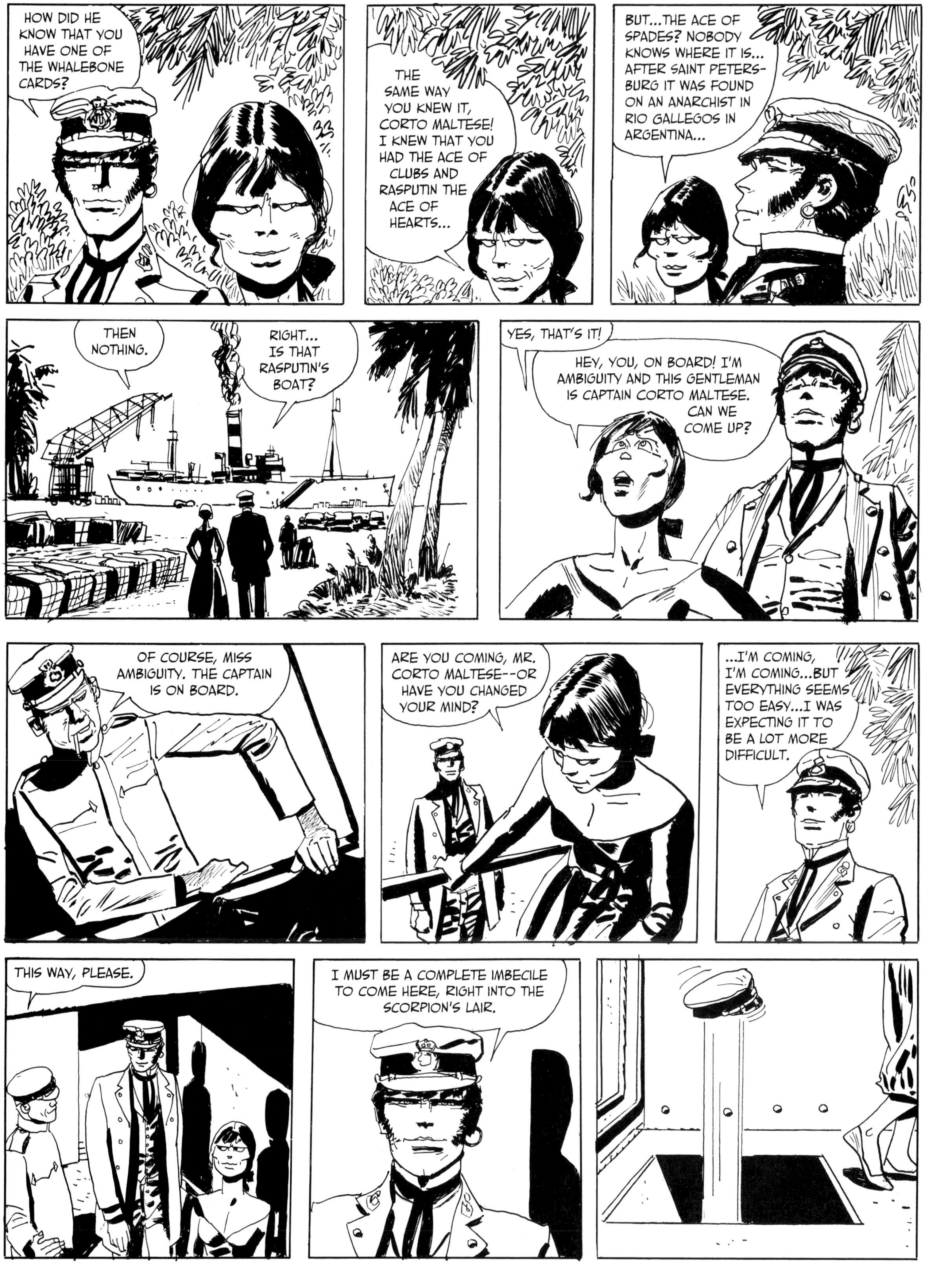
HOW DID HE KNOW THAT YOU HAVE ONE OF THE WHALEBONE CARDS?
THE SAME WAY YOU KNEW IT, CORTO MALTESE! I KNEW THAT YOU HAD THE ACE OF CLUBS AND RASPUTIN THE ACE OF HEARTS...
BUT...THE ACE OF SPADES? NOBODY KNOWS WHERE IT IS... AFTER SAINT PETERSBURG IT WAS FOUND ON AN ANARCHIST IN RIO GALLEGOS IN ARGENTINA...
THEN NOTHING.
RIGHT... IS THAT RASPUTIN'S BOAT?
YES, THAT'S IT!
HEY, YOU, ON BOARD! I'M AMBIGUITY AND THIS GENTLEMAN IS CAPTAIN CORTO MALTESE. CAN WE COME UP?
OF COURSE, MISS AMBIGUITY. THE CAPTAIN IS ON BOARD.
ARE YOU COMING, MR. CORTO MALTESE--OR HAVE YOU CHANGED YOUR MIND?
...I'M COMING, I'M COMING...BUT EVERYTHING SEEMS TOO EASY...I WAS EXPECTING IT TO BE A LOT MORE DIFFICULT.
THIS WAY, PLEASE.
I MUST BE A COMPLETE IMBECILE TO COME HERE, RIGHT INTO THE SCORPION'S LAIR.

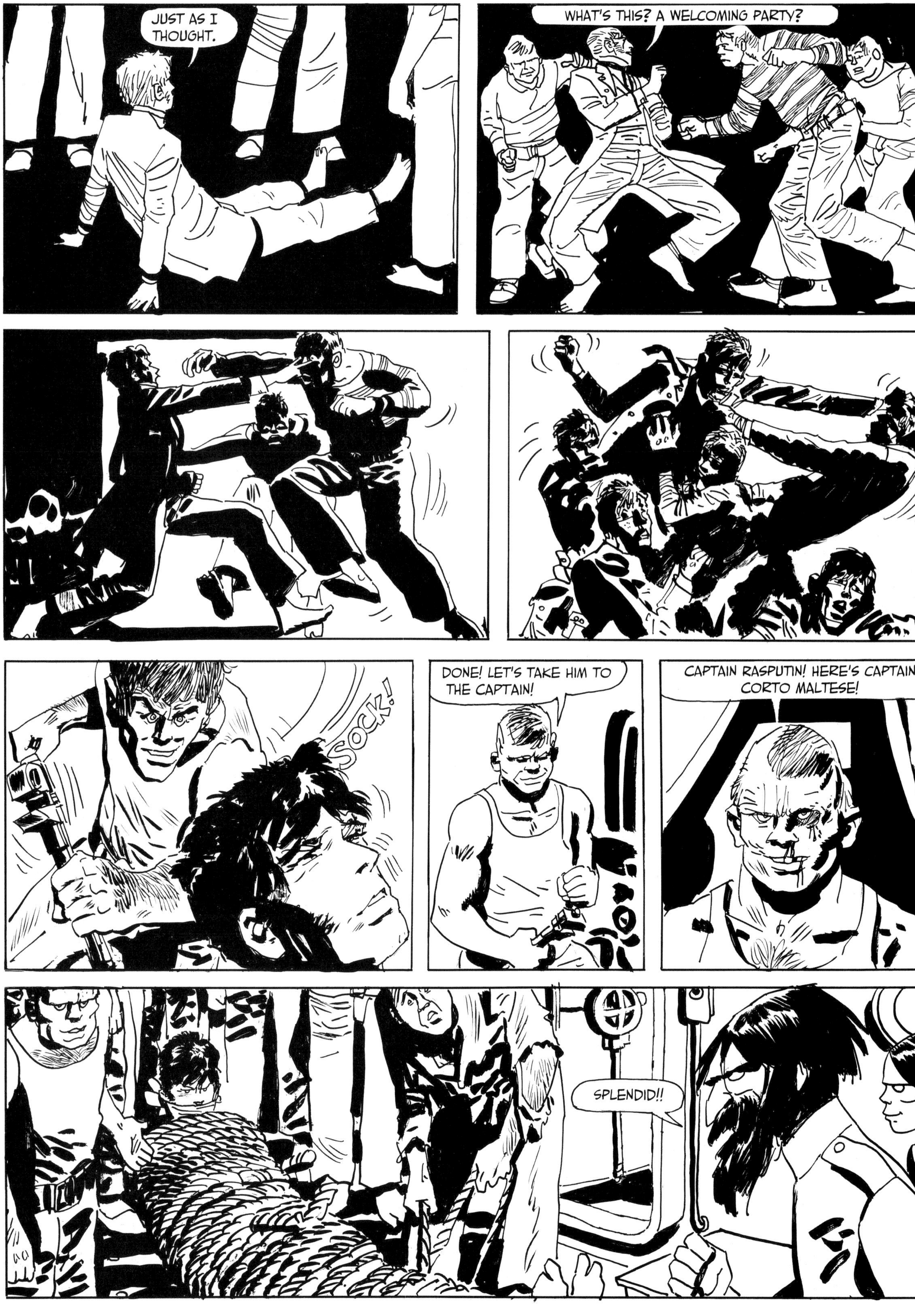
JUST AS I THOUGHT.
WHAT'S THIS? A WELCOMING PARTY?
SOCK!
DONE! LET'S TAKE HIM TO THE CAPTAIN!
CAPTAIN RASPUTIN! HERE'S CAPTAIN CORTO MALTESE!
SPLENDID!!

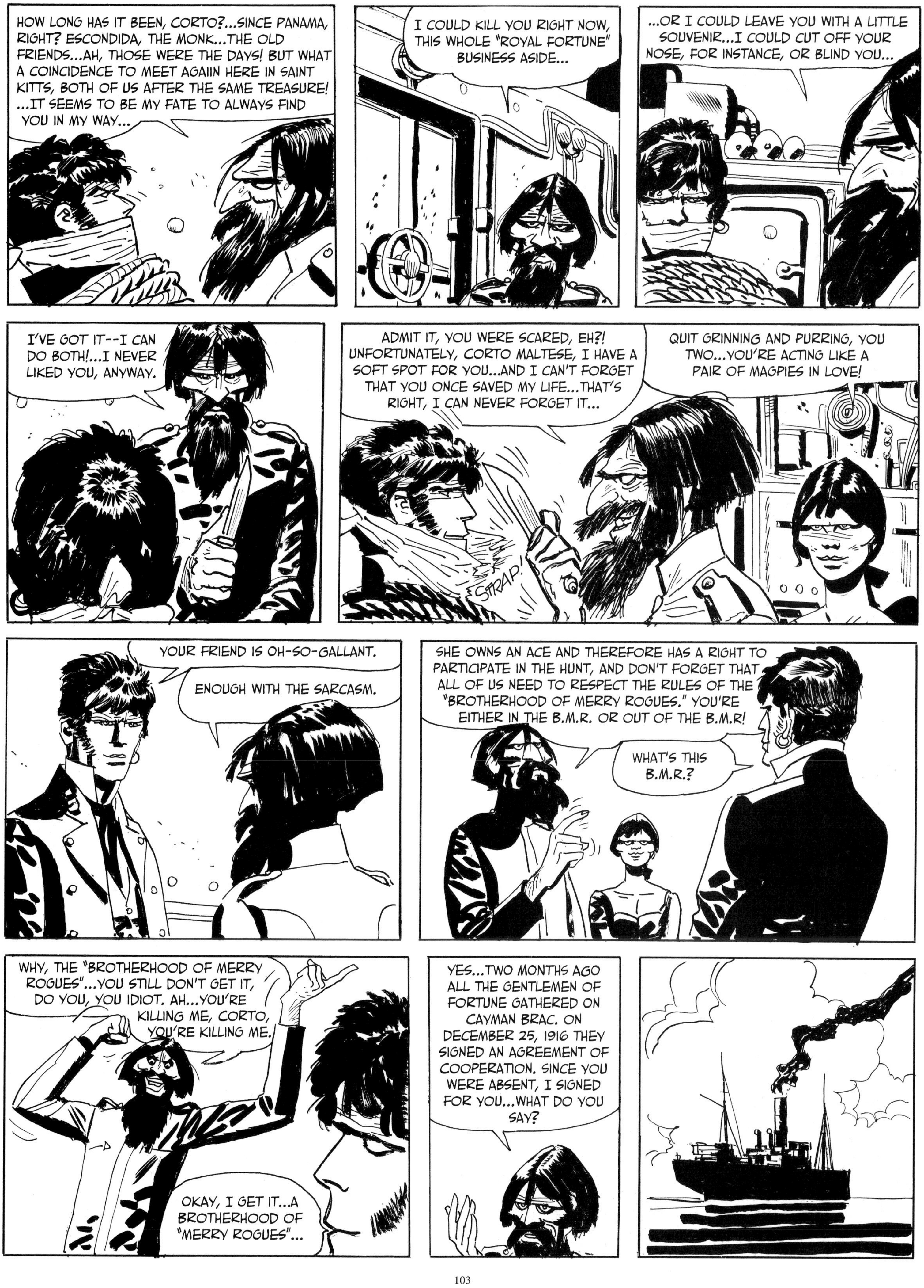

HOW LONG HAS IT BEEN, CORTO?...SINCE PANAMA, RIGHT? ESCONDIDA, THE MONK...THE OLD FRIENDS...AH, THOSE WERE THE DAYS! BUT WHAT A COINCIDENCE TO MEET AGAIIN HERE IN SAINT KITTS, BOTH OF US AFTER THE SAME TREASURE! ...IT SEEMS TO BE MY FATE TO ALWAYS FIND YOU IN MY WAY...
I COULD KILL YOU RIGHT NOW, THIS WHOLE "ROYAL FORTUNE" BUSINESS ASIDE...
...OR I COULD LEAVE YOU WITH A LITTLE SOUVENIR...I COULD CUT OFF YOUR NOSE, FOR INSTANCE, OR BLIND YOU...
I'VE GOT IT--I CAN DO BOTH!...I NEVER LIKED YOU, ANYWAY.
ADMIT IT, YOU WERE SCARED, EH?! UNFORTUNATELY, CORTO MALTESE, I HAVE A SOFT SPOT FOR YOU...AND I CAN'T FORGET THAT YOU ONCE SAVED MY LIFE...THAT'S RIGHT, I CAN NEVER FORGET IT...
QUIT GRINNING AND PURRING, YOU TWO...YOU'RE ACTING LIKE A PAIR OF MAGPIES IN LOVE!
STRAP!
YOUR FRIEND IS OH-SO-GALLANT.
ENOUGH WITH THE SARCASM.
SHE OWNS AN ACE AND THEREFORE HAS A RIGHT TO PARTICIPATE IN THE HUNT, AND DON'T FORGET THAT ALL OF US NEED TO RESPECT THE RULES OF THE "BROTHERHOOD OF MERRY ROGUES." YOU'RE EITHER IN THE B.M.R. OR OUT OF THE B.M.R!
WHAT'S THIS B.M.R.?
WHY, THE "BROTHERHOOD OF MERRY ROGUES"...YOU STILL DON'T GET IT, DO YOU, YOU IDIOT. AH...YOU'RE KILLING ME, CORTO, YOU'RE KILLING ME.
OKAY, I GET IT...A BROTHERHOOD OF "MERRY ROGUES"...
YES...TWO MONTHS AGO ALL THE GENTLEMEN OF FORTUNE GATHERED ON CAYMAN BRAC. ON DECEMBER 25, 1916 THEY SIGNED AN AGREEMENT OF COOPERATION. SINCE YOU WERE ABSENT, I SIGNED FOR YOU...WHAT DO YOU SAY?

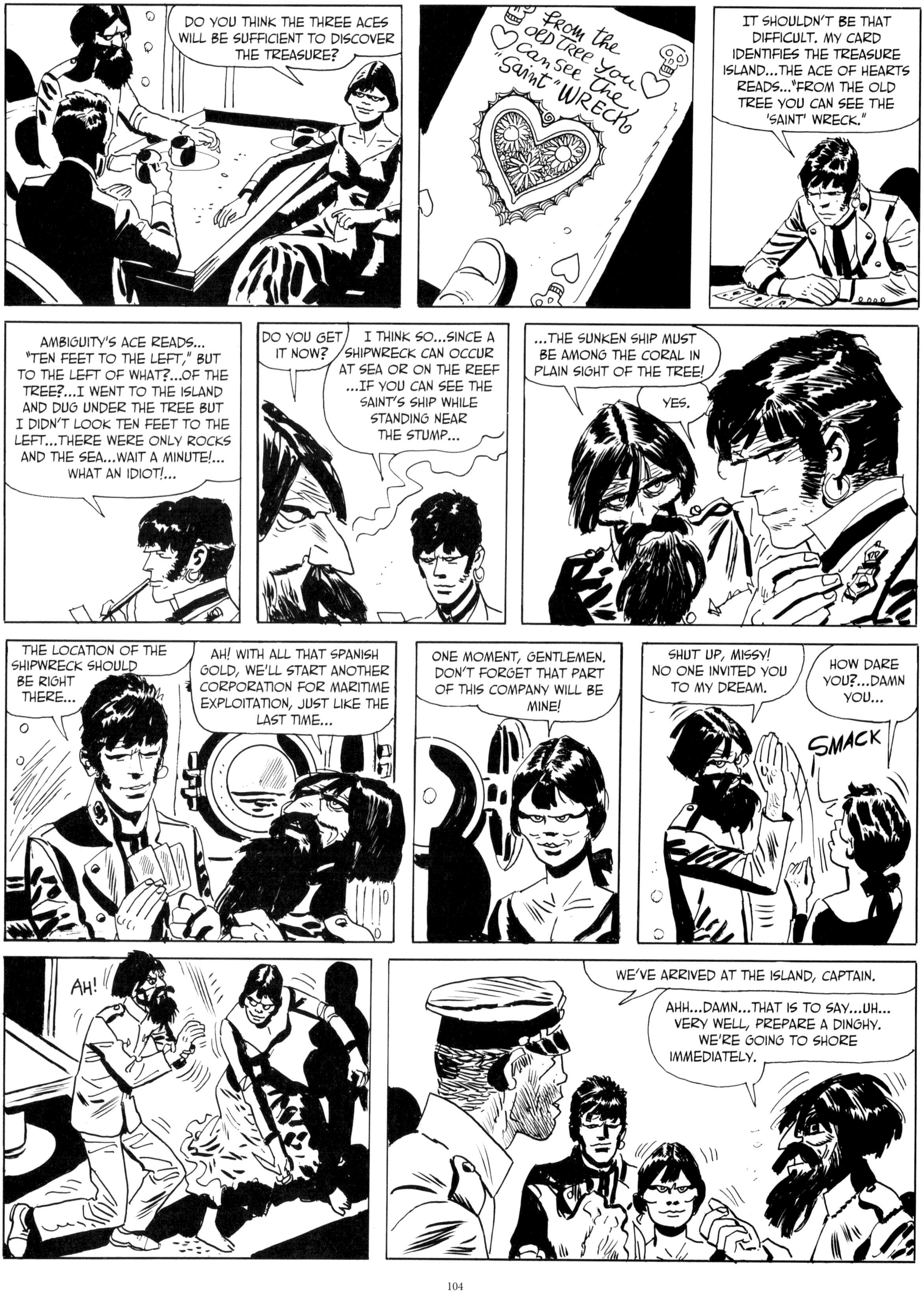
DO YOU THINK THE THREE ACES WILL BE SUFFICIENT TO DISCOVER THE TREASURE?
From the OLD TREE you can see the "Saint" WRECK
IT SHOULDN'T BE THAT DIFFICULT. MY CARD IDENTIFIES THE TREASURE ISLAND...THE ACE OF HEARTS READS..."FROM THE OLD TREE YOU CAN SEE THE 'SAINT' WRECK."
AMBIGUITY'S ACE READS... "TEN FEET TO THE LEFT," BUT TO THE LEFT OF WHAT?...OF THE TREE?...I WENT TO THE ISLAND AND DUG UNDER THE TREE BUT I DIDN'T LOOK TEN FEET TO THE LEFT...THERE WERE ONLY ROCKS AND THE SEA...WAIT A MINUTE!... WHAT AN IDIOT!...
DO YOU GET IT NOW?
I THINK SO...SINCE A SHIPWRECK CAN OCCUR AT SEA OR ON THE REEF ...IF YOU CAN SEE THE SAINT'S SHIP WHILE STANDING NEAR THE STUMP...
...THE SUNKEN SHIP MUST BE AMONG THE CORAL IN PLAIN SIGHT OF THE TREE!
YES.
THE LOCATION OF THE SHIPWRECK SHOULD BE RIGHT THERE...
AH! WITH ALL THAT SPANISH GOLD, WE'LL START ANOTHER CORPORATION FOR MARITIME EXPLOITATION, JUST LIKE THE LAST TIME...
ONE MOMENT, GENTLEMEN. DON'T FORGET THAT PART OF THIS COMPANY WILL BE MINE!
SHUT UP, MISSY! NO ONE INVITED YOU TO MY DREAM.
HOW DARE YOU?...DAMN YOU...
SMACK
AH!
WE'VE ARRIVED AT THE ISLAND, CAPTAIN.
AHH...DAMN...THAT IS TO SAY...UH... VERY WELL, PREPARE A DINGHY. WE'RE GOING TO SHORE IMMEDIATELY.

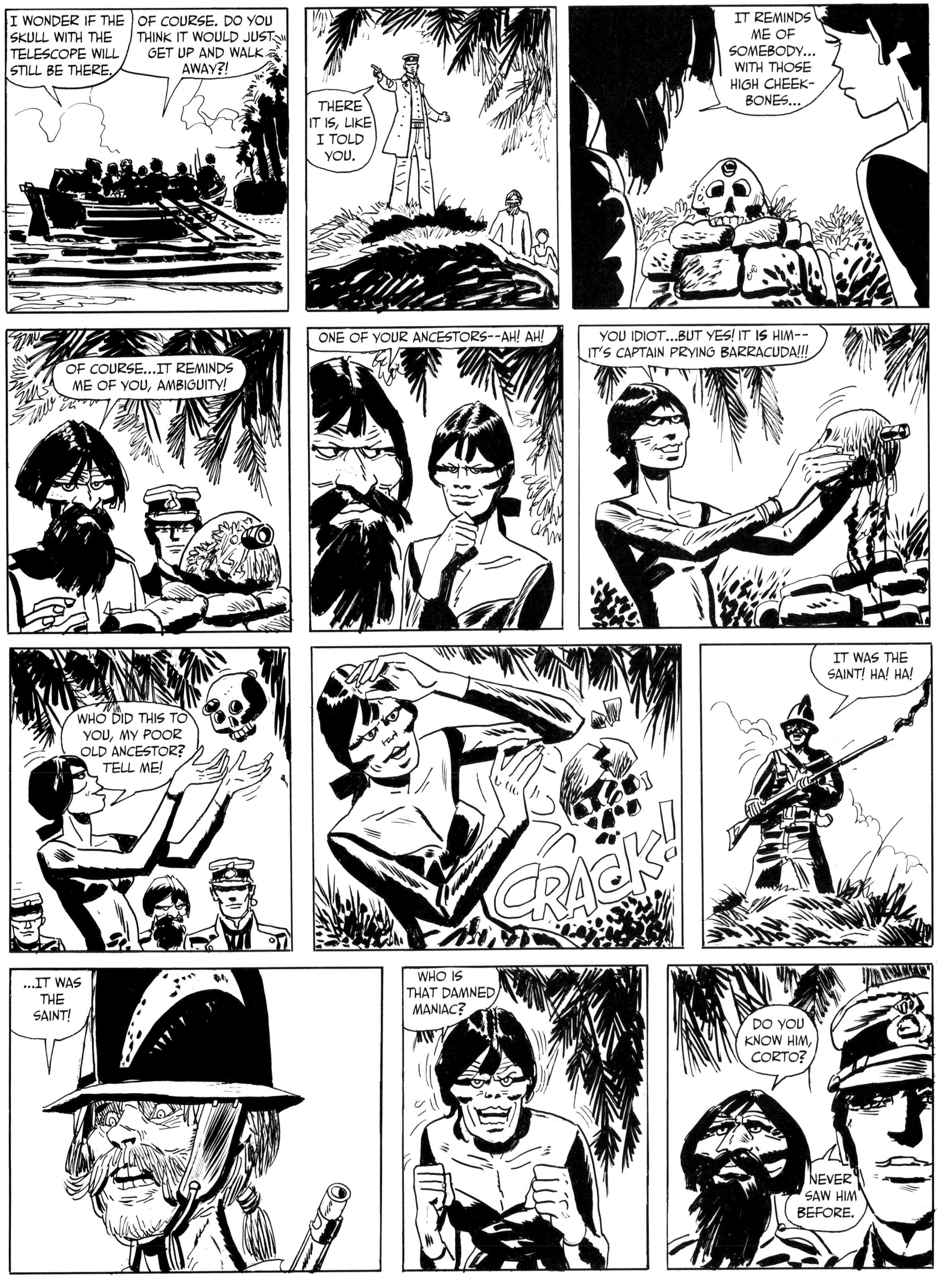
I WONDER IF THE SKULL WITH THE TELESCOPE WILL STILL BE THERE.
OF COURSE. DO YOU THINK IT WOULD JUST GET UP AND WALK AWAY?!
THERE IT IS, LIKE I TOLD YOU.
IT REMINDS ME OF SOMEBODY... WITH THOSE HIGH CHEEK-BONES...
OF COURSE...IT REMINDS ME OF YOU, AMBIGUITY!
ONE OF YOUR ANCESTORS--AH! AH!
YOU IDIOT...BUT YES! IT IS HIM--IT'S CAPTAIN PRYING BARRACUDA!!!
WHO DID THIS TO YOU, MY POOR OLD ANCESTOR? TELL ME!
CRACK!
IT WAS THE SAINT! HA! HA!
...IT WAS THE SAINT!
WHO IS THAT DAMNED MANIAC?
DO YOU KNOW HIM, CORTO?
NEVER SAW HIM BEFORE.

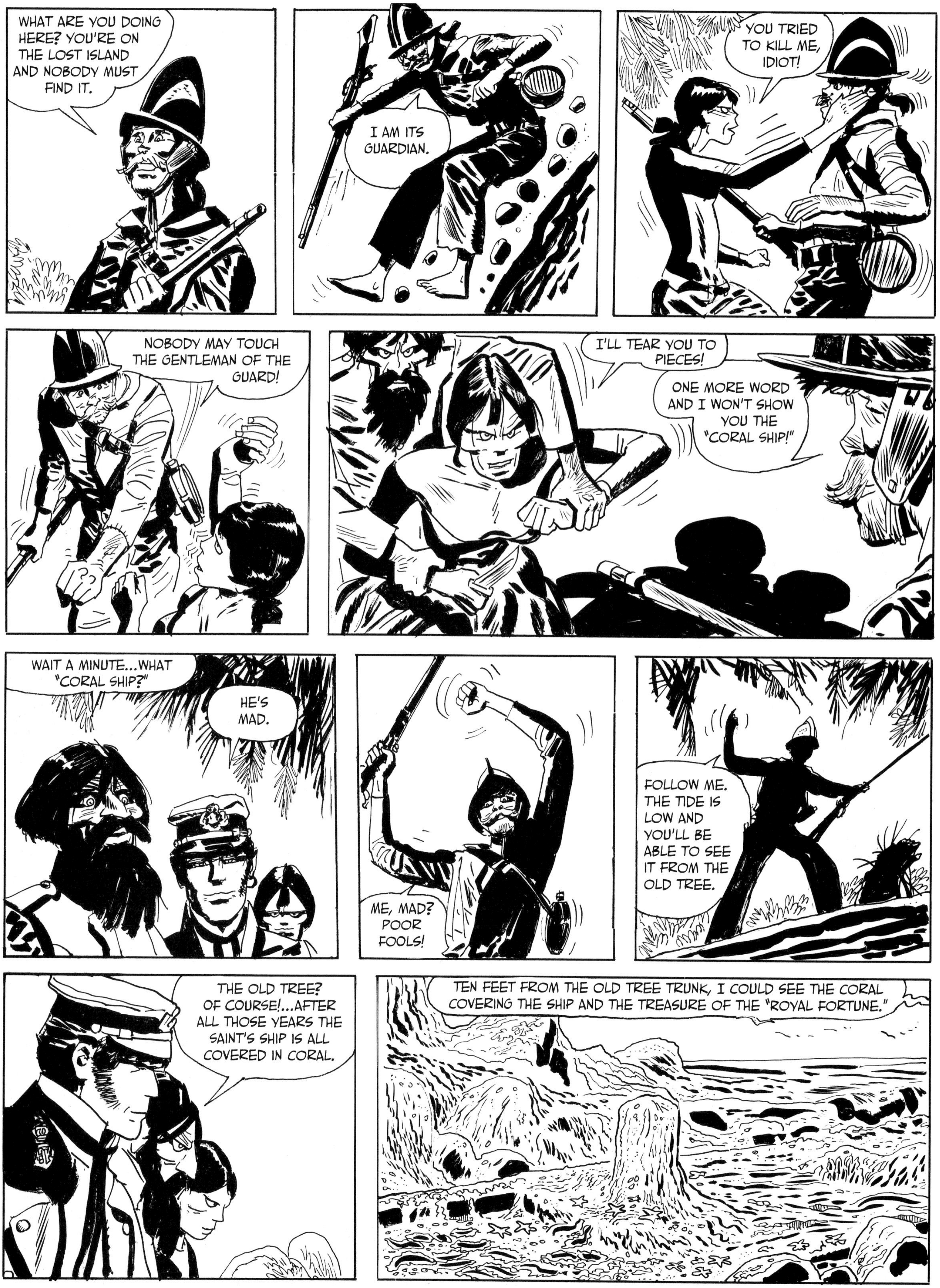

WHAT ARE YOU DOING HERE? YOU'RE ON THE LOST ISLAND AND NOBODY MUST FIND IT.
I AM ITS GUARDIAN.
YOU TRIED TO KILL ME, IDIOT!
NOBODY MAY TOUCH THE GENTLEMAN OF THE GUARD!
I'LL TEAR YOU TO PIECES!
ONE MORE WORD AND I WON'T SHOW YOU THE "CORAL SHIP!"
WAIT A MINUTE...WHAT "CORAL SHIP?"
HE'S MAD.
ME, MAD? POOR FOOLS!
FOLLOW ME. THE TIDE IS LOW AND YOU'LL BE ABLE TO SEE IT FROM THE OLD TREE.
THE OLD TREE? OF COURSE!...AFTER ALL THOSE YEARS THE SAINT'S SHIP IS ALL COVERED IN CORAL.
TEN FEET FROM THE OLD TREE TRUNK, I COULD SEE THE CORAL COVERING THE SHIP AND THE TREASURE OF THE "ROYAL FORTUNE."

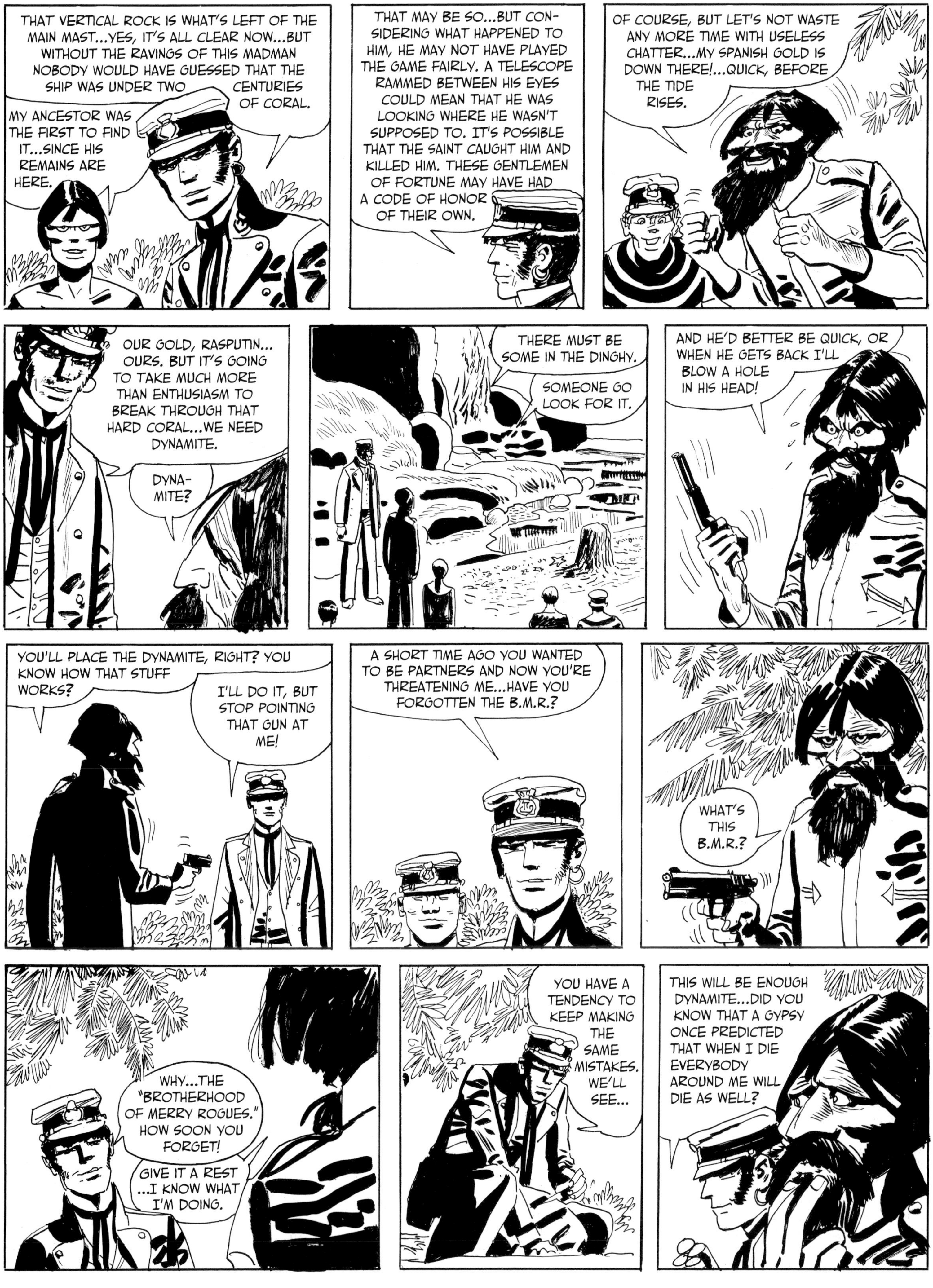
THAT VERTICAL ROCK IS WHAT'S LEFT OF THE MAIN MAST...YES, IT'S ALL CLEAR NOW...BUT WITHOUT THE RAVINGS OF THIS MADMAN NOBODY WOULD HAVE GUESSED THAT THE SHIP WAS UNDER TWO CENTURIES OF CORAL.
MY ANCESTOR WAS THE FIRST TO FIND IT...SINCE HIS REMAINS ARE HERE.
THAT MAY BE SO...BUT CONSIDERING WHAT HAPPENED TO HIM, HE MAY NOT HAVE PLAYED THE GAME FAIRLY. A TELESCOPE RAMMED BETWEEN HIS EYES COULD MEAN THAT HE WAS LOOKING WHERE HE WASN'T SUPPOSED TO. IT'S POSSIBLE THAT THE SAINT CAUGHT HIM AND KILLED HIM. THESE GENTLEMEN OF FORTUNE MAY HAVE HAD A CODE OF HONOR OF THEIR OWN.
OF COURSE, BUT LET'S NOT WASTE ANY MORE TIME WITH USELESS CHATTER...MY SPANISH GOLD IS DOWN THERE!...QUICK, BEFORE THE TIDE RISES.
OUR GOLD, RASPUTIN... OURS. BUT IT'S GOING TO TAKE MUCH MORE THAN ENTHUSIASM TO BREAK THROUGH THAT HARD CORAL...WE NEED DYNAMITE.
DYNAMITE?
THERE MUST BE SOME IN THE DINGHY.
SOMEONE GO LOOK FOR IT.
AND HE'D BETTER BE QUICK, OR WHEN HE GETS BACK I'LL BLOW A HOLE IN HIS HEAD!
YOU'LL PLACE THE DYNAMITE, RIGHT? YOU KNOW HOW THAT STUFF WORKS?
I'LL DO IT, BUT STOP POINTING THAT GUN AT ME!
A SHORT TIME AGO YOU WANTED TO BE PARTNERS AND NOW YOU'RE THREATENING ME...HAVE YOU FORGOTTEN THE B.M.R.?
WHAT'S THIS B.M.R.?
WHY...THE "BROTHERHOOD OF MERRY ROGUES." HOW SOON YOU FORGET!
GIVE IT A REST ...I KNOW WHAT I'M DOING.
YOU HAVE A TENDENCY TO KEEP MAKING THE SAME MISTAKES. WE'LL SEE...
THIS WILL BE ENOUGH DYNAMITE...DID YOU KNOW THAT A GYPSY ONCE PREDICTED THAT WHEN I DIE EVERYBODY AROUND ME WILL DIE AS WELL?

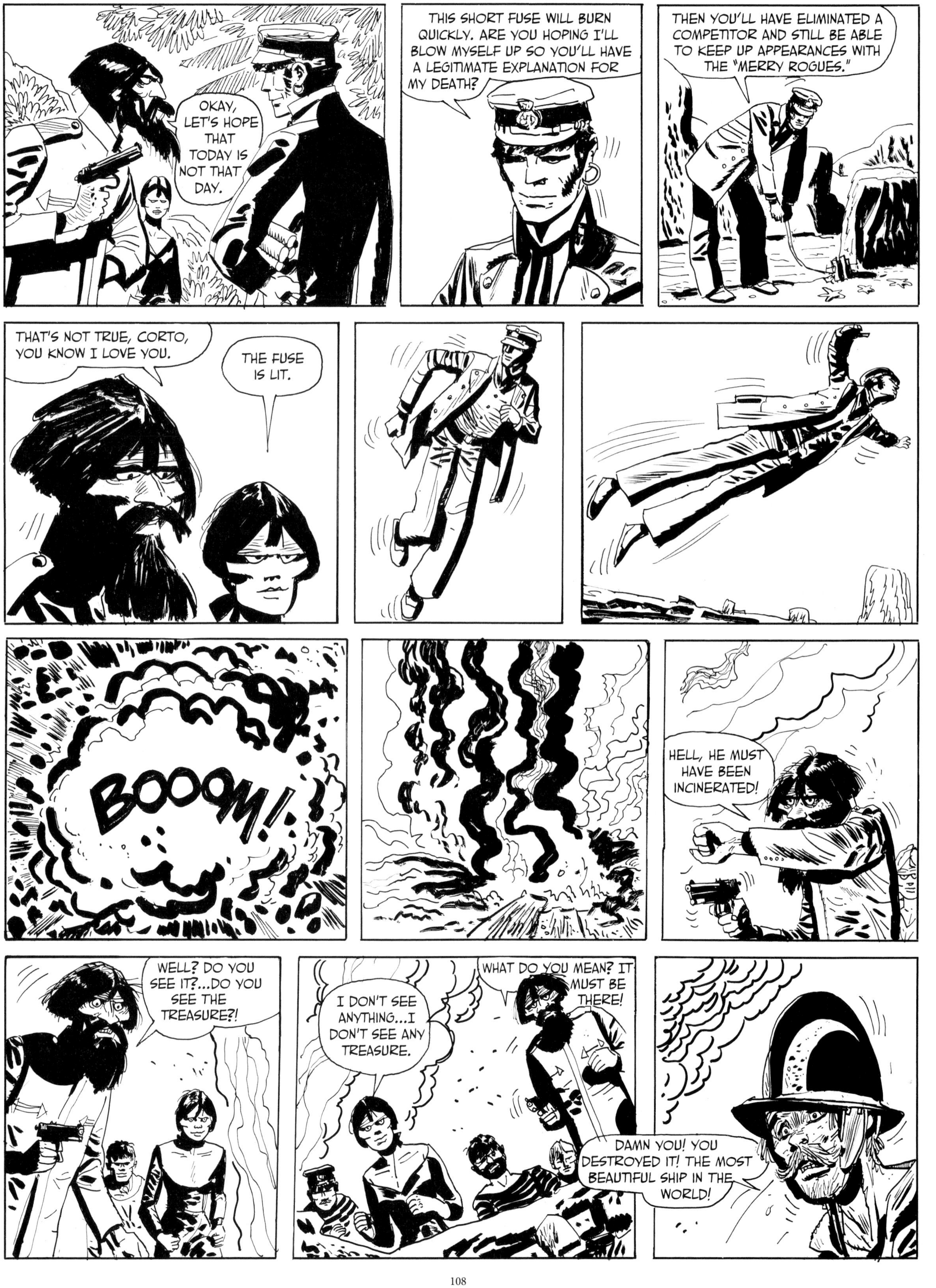
OKAY, LET'S HOPE THAT TODAY IS NOT THAT DAY.
THIS SHORT FUSE WILL BURN QUICKLY. ARE YOU HOPING I'LL BLOW MYSELF UP SO YOU'LL HAVE A LEGITIMATE EXPLANATION FOR MY DEATH?
THEN YOU'LL HAVE ELIMINATED A COMPETITOR AND STILL BE ABLE TO KEEP UP APPEARANCES WITH THE "MERRY ROGUES."
THAT'S NOT TRUE, CORTO, YOU KNOW I LOVE YOU.
THE FUSE IS LIT.
BOOOM!
HELL, HE MUST HAVE BEEN INCINERATED!
WELL? DO YOU SEE IT?...DO YOU SEE THE TREASURE?!
I DON'T SEE ANYTHING...I DON'T SEE ANY TREASURE.
WHAT DO YOU MEAN? IT MUST BE THERE!
DAMN YOU! YOU DESTROYED IT! THE MOST BEAUTIFUL SHIP IN THE WORLD!

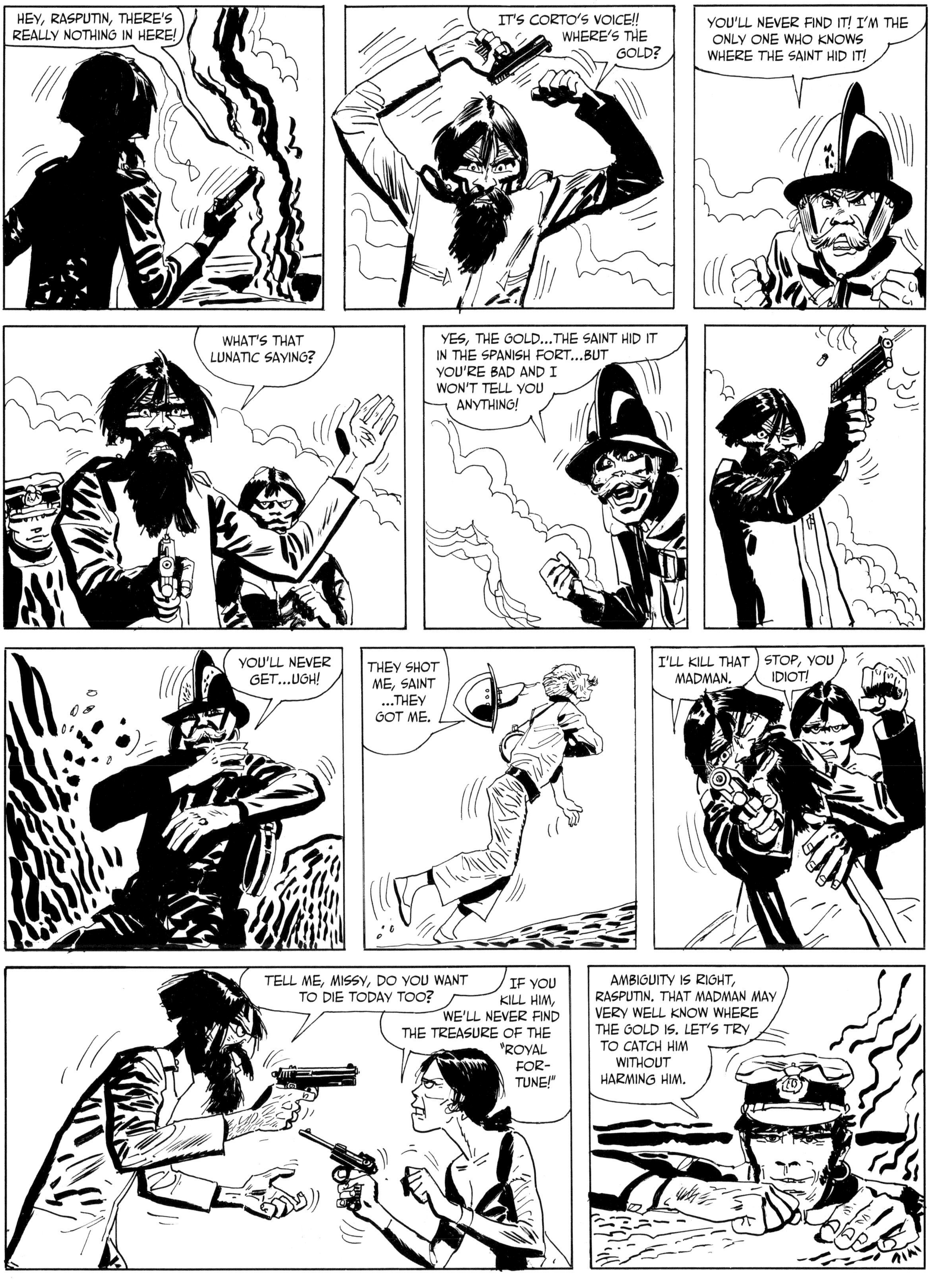
HEY, RASPUTIN, THERE'S REALLY NOTHING IN HERE!
IT'S CORTO'S VOICE!! WHERE'S THE GOLD?
YOU'LL NEVER FIND IT! I'M THE ONLY ONE WHO KNOWS WHERE THE SAINT HID IT!
WHAT'S THAT LUNATIC SAYING?
YES, THE GOLD...THE SAINT HID IT IN THE SPANISH FORT...BUT YOU'RE BAD AND I WON'T TELL YOU ANYTHING!
YOU'LL NEVER GET...UGH!
THEY SHOT ME, SAINT ...THEY GOT ME.
I'LL KILL THAT MADMAN.
STOP, YOU IDIOT!
TELL ME, MISSY, DO YOU WANT TO DIE TODAY TOO?
IF YOU KILL HIM, WE'LL NEVER FIND THE TREASURE OF THE "ROYAL FORTUNE!"
AMBIGUITY IS RIGHT, RASPUTIN. THAT MADMAN MAY VERY WELL KNOW WHERE THE GOLD IS. LET'S TRY TO CATCH HIM WITHOUT HARMING HIM.

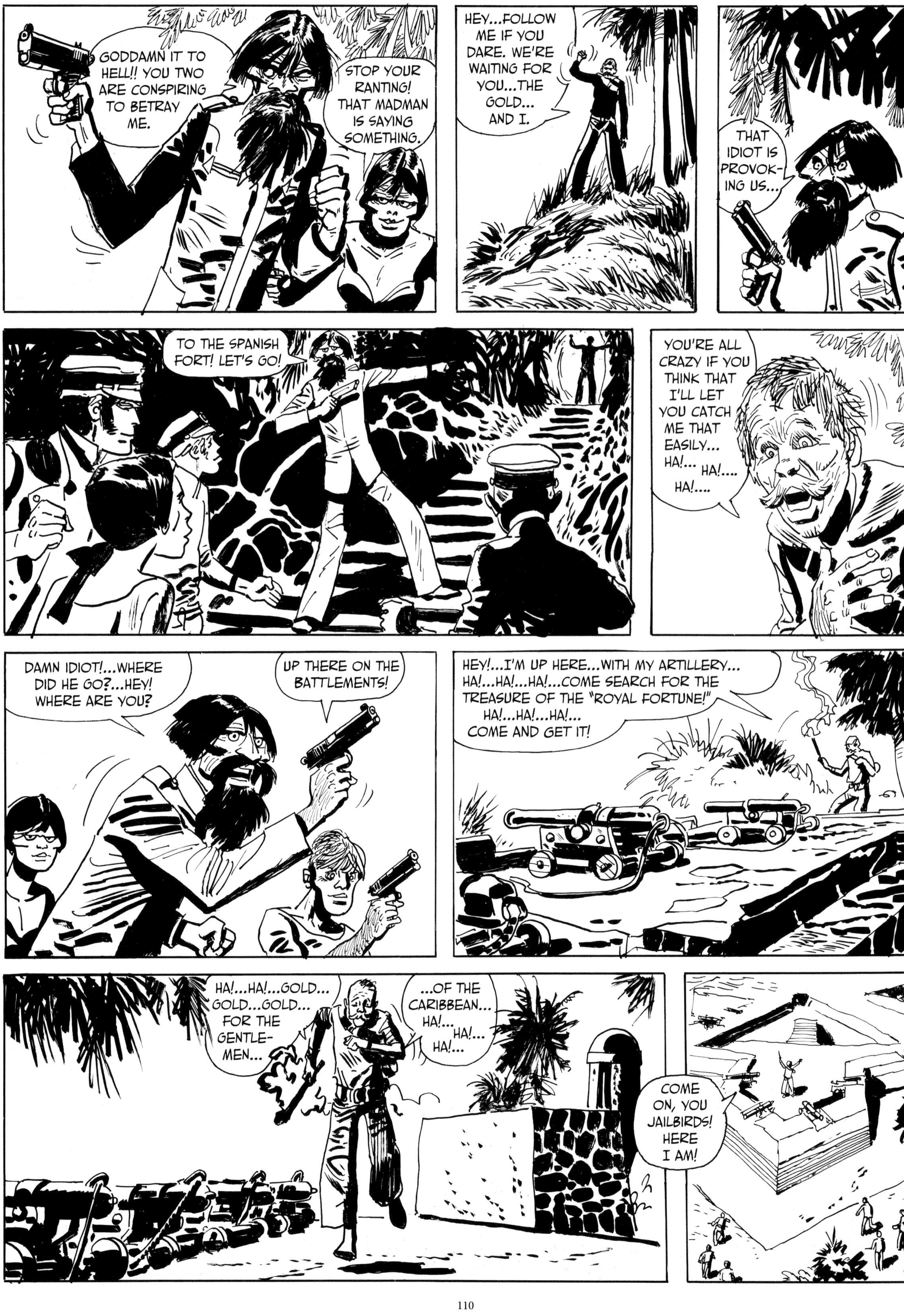

GODDAMN IT TO HELL!! YOU TWO ARE CONSPIRING TO BETRAY ME.
STOP YOUR RANTING! THAT MADMAN IS SAYING SOMETHING.
HEY...FOLLOW ME IF YOU DARE. WE'RE WAITING FOR YOU...THE GOLD... AND I.
THAT IDIOT IS PROVOK-ING US...
TO THE SPANISH FORT! LET'S GO!
YOU'RE ALL CRAZY IF YOU THINK THAT I'LL LET YOU CATCH ME THAT EASILY... HA!... HA!.... HA!....
DAMN IDIOT!...WHERE DID HE GO?...HEY! WHERE ARE YOU?
UP THERE ON THE BATTLEMENTS!
HEY!...I'M UP HERE...WITH MY ARTILLERY... HA!...HA!...HA!...COME SEARCH FOR THE TREASURE OF THE "ROYAL FORTUNE!" HA!...HA!...HA!... COME AND GET IT!
HA!...HA!...GOLD... GOLD...GOLD... FOR THE GENTLE-MEN...
...OF THE CARIBBEAN... HA!... HA!... HA!...
COME ON, YOU JAILBIRDS! HERE I AM!

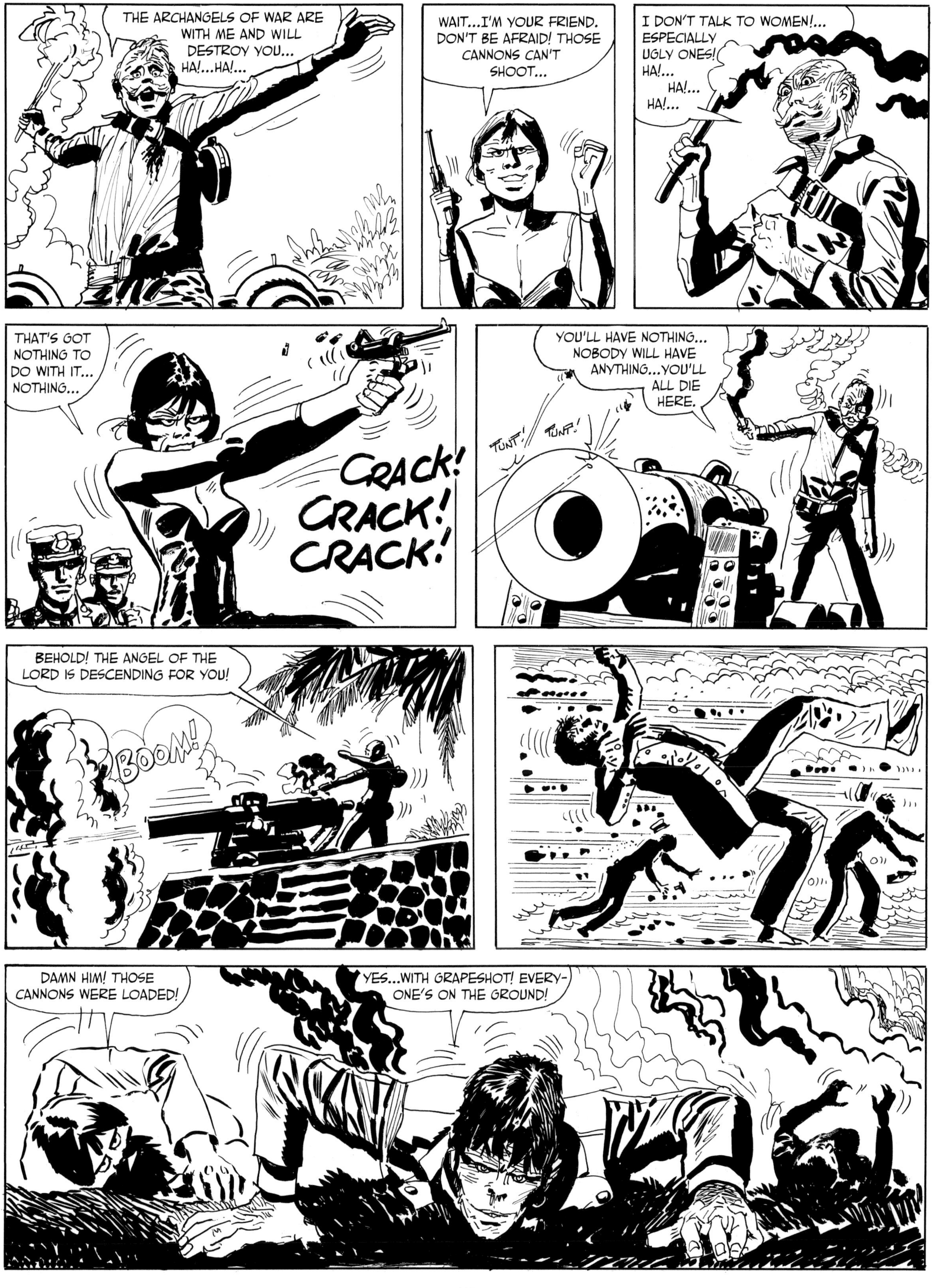
THE ARCHANGELS OF WAR ARE WITH ME AND WILL DESTROY YOU... HA!...HA!...
WAIT...I'M YOUR FRIEND. DON'T BE AFRAID! THOSE CANNONS CAN'T SHOOT...
I DON'T TALK TO WOMEN!... ESPECIALLY UGLY ONES! HA!... HA!... HA!...
THAT'S GOT NOTHING TO DO WITH IT... NOTHING...
CRACK! CRACK! CRACK!
YOU'LL HAVE NOTHING... NOBODY WILL HAVE ANYTHING...YOU'LL ALL DIE HERE.
TUNT! TUNT!
BEHOLD! THE ANGEL OF THE LORD IS DESCENDING FOR YOU!
BOOM!
DAMN HIM! THOSE CANNONS WERE LOADED!
YES...WITH GRAPESHOT! EVERY-ONE'S ON THE GROUND!

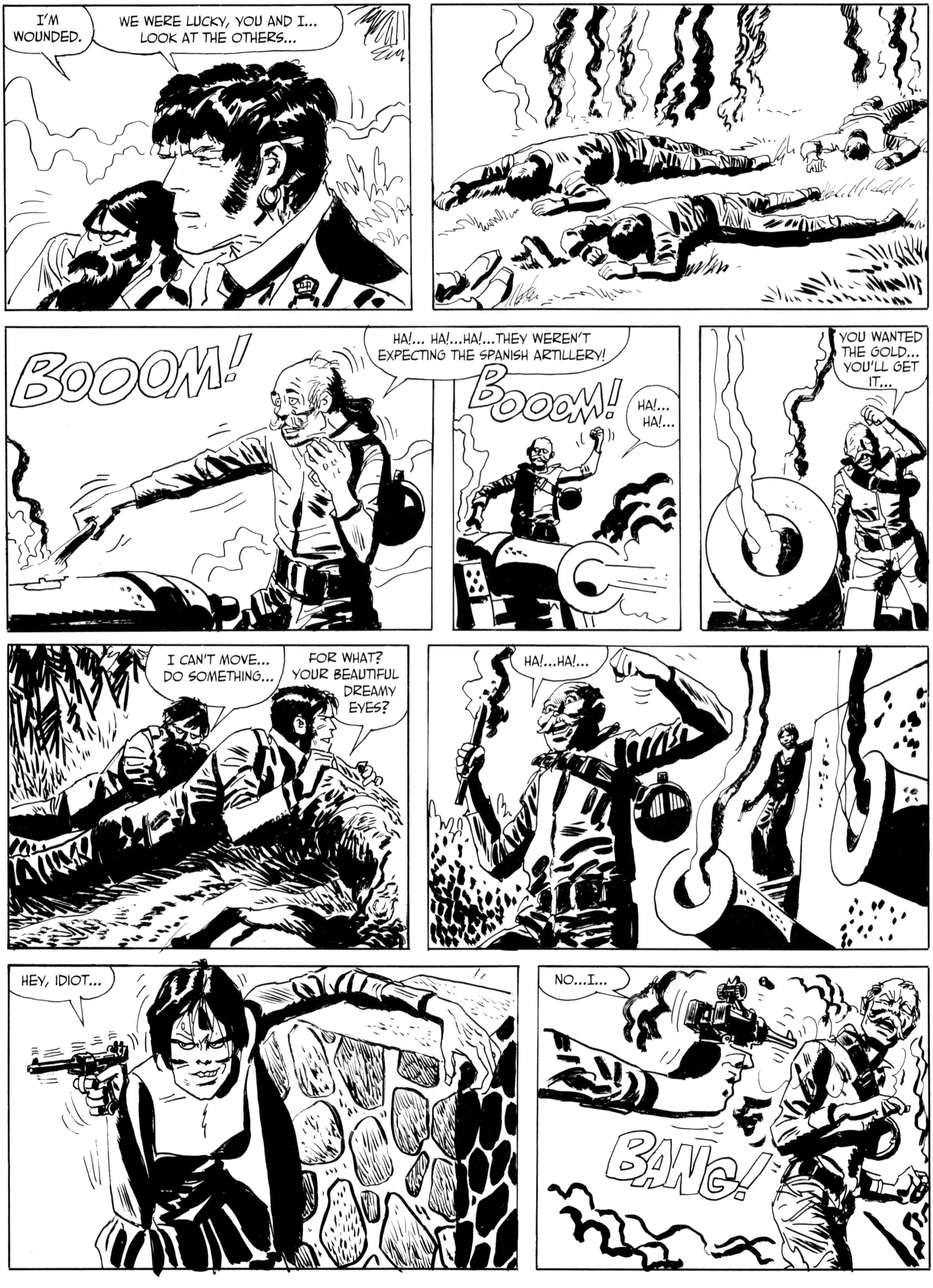

I'M WOUNDED.
WE WERE LUCKY, YOU AND I... LOOK AT THE OTHERS...
BOOOM!
HA!... HA!...HA!...THEY WEREN'T EXPECTING THE SPANISH ARTILLERY!
BOOOM!
HA!... HA!...
YOU WANTED THE GOLD... YOU'LL GET IT...
I CAN'T MOVE... DO SOMETHING...
FOR WHAT? YOUR BEAUTIFUL DREAMY EYES?
HA!...HA!...
HEY, IDIOT...
NO...I...
BANG!

AMBIGUITY!

THEY'VE KILLED EACH OTHER, THOSE TWO LUNATICS!

WAIT, CORTO... I'M WOUNDED AND CAN'T MOVE.

YOU'RE NOT GOING ANYWHERE WITHOUT ME. COME AND HELP ME...THIS HURTS LIKE HELL WHEN I MOVE.

YOU HAVE A BIG PIECE STUCK BETWEEN YOUR RIBS. WE NEED TO TAKE IT OUT.

HMM! WHAT ARE YOU WAITING FOR?

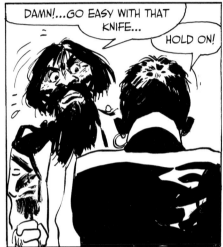

DAMN!...GO EASY WITH THAT KNIFE...

HOLD ON!

THERE YOU GO, DREAMY EYES...A VERY PRECIOUS SPLINTER!...HA!...HA!...

WHAT ARE YOU LAUGHING ABOUT?

I'M LAUGHING ABOUT YOUR FACE...AND ALSO FOR ANOTHER REASON!...LOOK!...

BAH...I HAVE NO TIME...LET'S GO LOOK FOR MY...OUR GOLD.

OUR GOLD?...HERE IT IS...I EXTRACTED IT FROM YOUR SIDE. THE TREASURE WAS HIDDEN IN THE FORT'S CANNONS.

THAT MADMAN FIRED THE MOST EXPENSIVE CANNON SHOT IN HISTORY. HE MOWED US DOWN WITH THE SPANISH DOUBLOONS THAT THE SAINT HAD HIDDEN IN THE CANNONS... HERE'S WHAT'S LEFT...

WHAT DO YOU MEAN?... WHAT ARE YOU TALKING ABOUT?!

YOU UNDER-STOOD PER-FECTLY!

NO, IT'S NOT POSSIBLE. YOU WANT TO STEAL MY GOLD...CORTO...HEY, CORTO!...

AMBIGUITY!

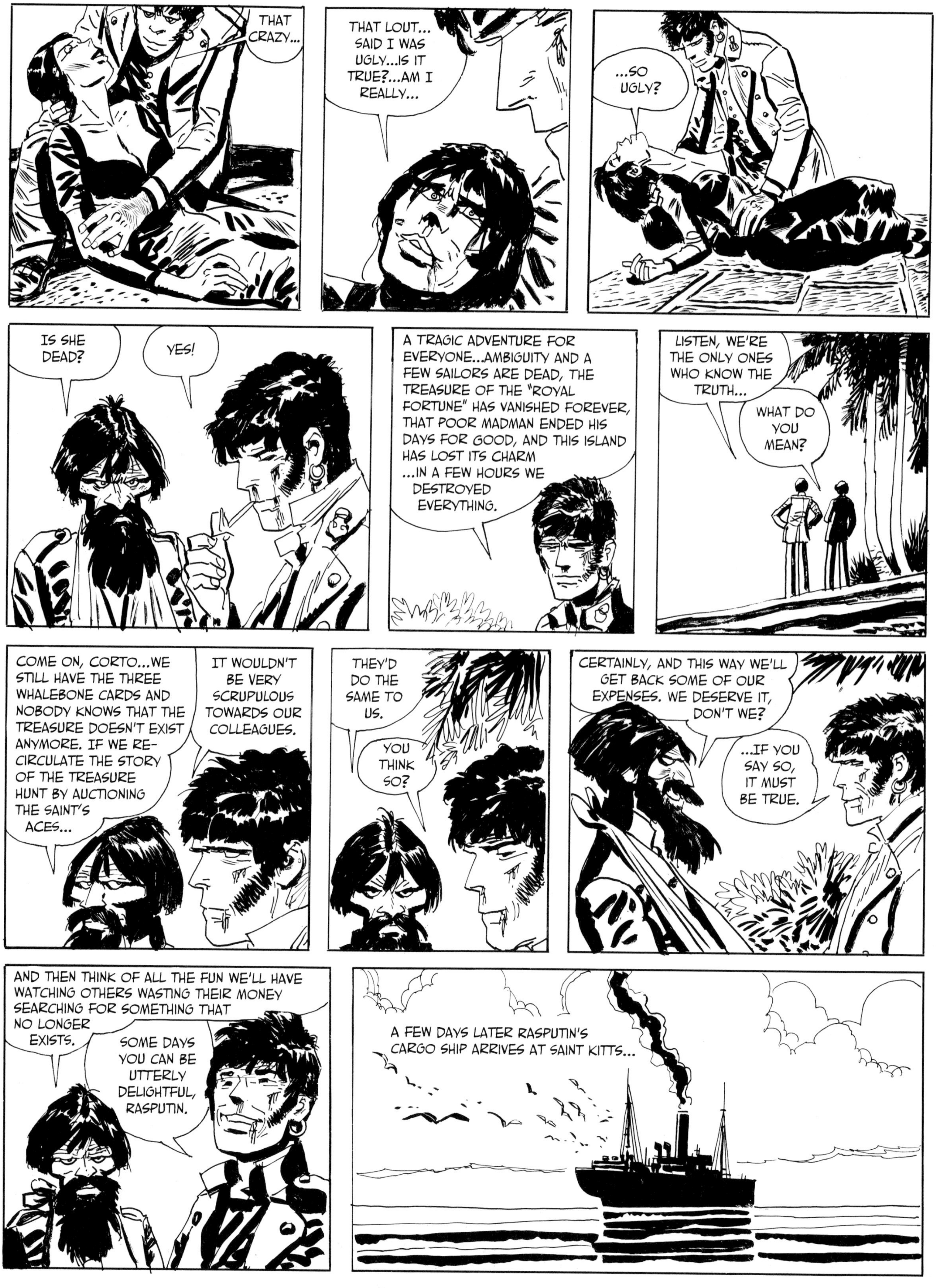
THAT CRAZY...
THAT LOUT... SAID I WAS UGLY...IS IT TRUE?...AM I REALLY...
...SO UGLY?
IS SHE DEAD?
YES!
A TRAGIC ADVENTURE FOR EVERYONE...AMBIGUITY AND A FEW SAILORS ARE DEAD, THE TREASURE OF THE "ROYAL FORTUNE" HAS VANISHED FOREVER, THAT POOR MADMAN ENDED HIS DAYS FOR GOOD, AND THIS ISLAND HAS LOST ITS CHARM ...IN A FEW HOURS WE DESTROYED EVERYTHING.
LISTEN, WE'RE THE ONLY ONES WHO KNOW THE TRUTH...
WHAT DO YOU MEAN?
COME ON, CORTO...WE STILL HAVE THE THREE WHALEBONE CARDS AND NOBODY KNOWS THAT THE TREASURE DOESN'T EXIST ANYMORE. IF WE RE-CIRCULATE THE STORY OF THE TREASURE HUNT BY AUCTIONING THE SAINT'S ACES...
IT WOULDN'T BE VERY SCRUPULOUS TOWARDS OUR COLLEAGUES.
THEY'D DO THE SAME TO US.
YOU THINK SO?
CERTAINLY, AND THIS WAY WE'LL GET BACK SOME OF OUR EXPENSES. WE DESERVE IT, DON'T WE?
...IF YOU SAY SO, IT MUST BE TRUE.
AND THEN THINK OF ALL THE FUN WE'LL HAVE WATCHING OTHERS WASTING THEIR MONEY SEARCHING FOR SOMETHING THAT NO LONGER EXISTS.
SOME DAYS YOU CAN BE UTTERLY DELIGHTFUL, RASPUTIN.
A FEW DAYS LATER RASPUTIN'S CARGO SHIP ARRIVES AT SAINT KITTS...

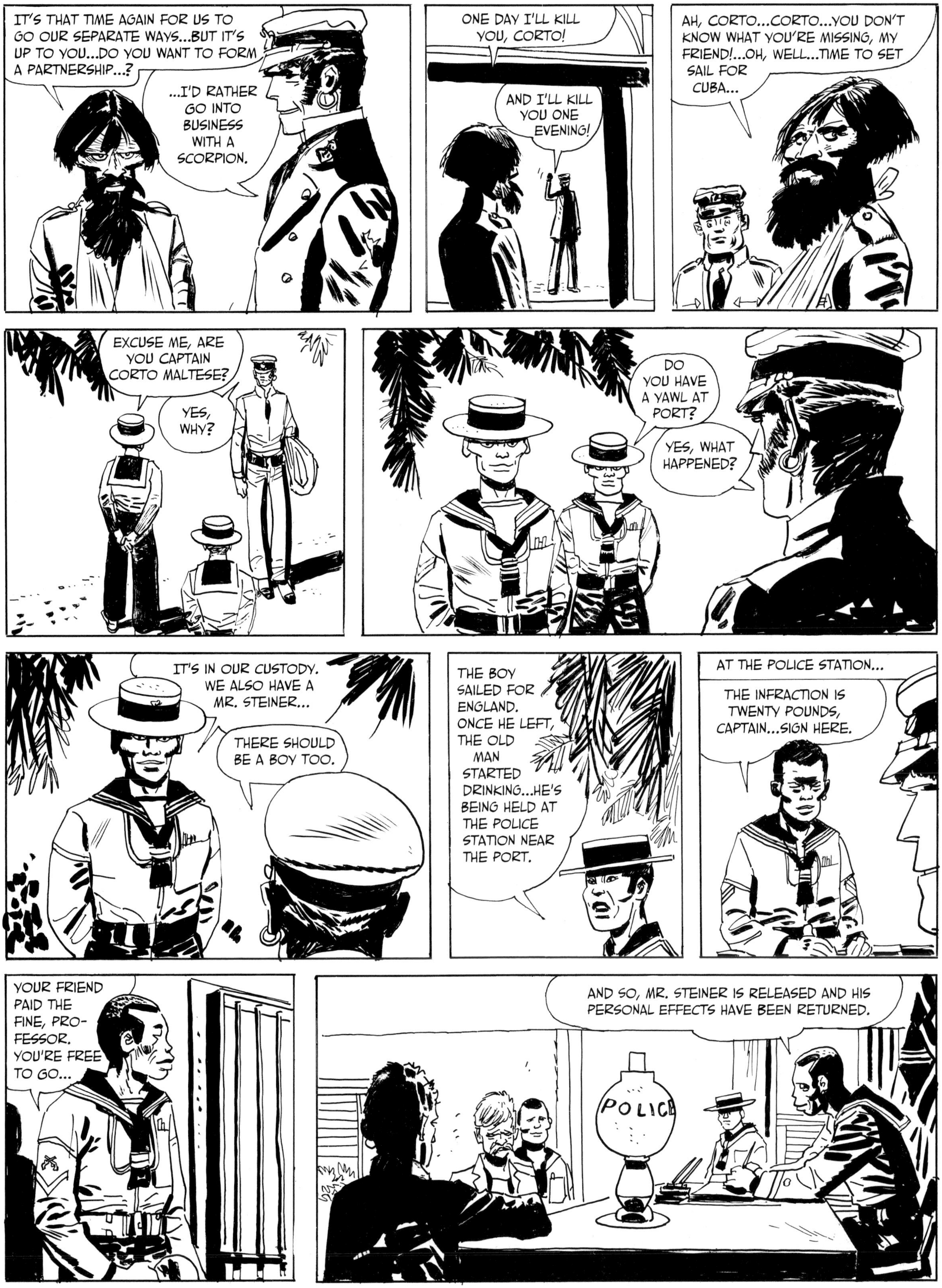

IT'S THAT TIME AGAIN FOR US TO GO OUR SEPARATE WAYS...BUT IT'S UP TO YOU...DO YOU WANT TO FORM A PARTNERSHIP...?
...I'D RATHER GO INTO BUSINESS WITH A SCORPION.
ONE DAY I'LL KILL YOU, CORTO!
AND I'LL KILL YOU ONE EVENING!
AH, CORTO...CORTO...YOU DON'T KNOW WHAT YOU'RE MISSING, MY FRIEND!...OH, WELL...TIME TO SET SAIL FOR CUBA...
EXCUSE ME, ARE YOU CAPTAIN CORTO MALTESE?
YES, WHY?
DO YOU HAVE A YAWL AT PORT?
YES, WHAT HAPPENED?
IT'S IN OUR CUSTODY. WE ALSO HAVE A MR. STEINER...
THERE SHOULD BE A BOY TOO.
THE BOY SAILED FOR ENGLAND. ONCE HE LEFT, THE OLD MAN STARTED DRINKING...HE'S BEING HELD AT THE POLICE STATION NEAR THE PORT.
AT THE POLICE STATION...
THE INFRACTION IS TWENTY POUNDS, CAPTAIN...SIGN HERE.
YOUR FRIEND PAID THE FINE, PROFESSOR. YOU'RE FREE TO GO...
AND SO, MR. STEINER IS RELEASED AND HIS PERSONAL EFFECTS HAVE BEEN RETURNED.
POLICE

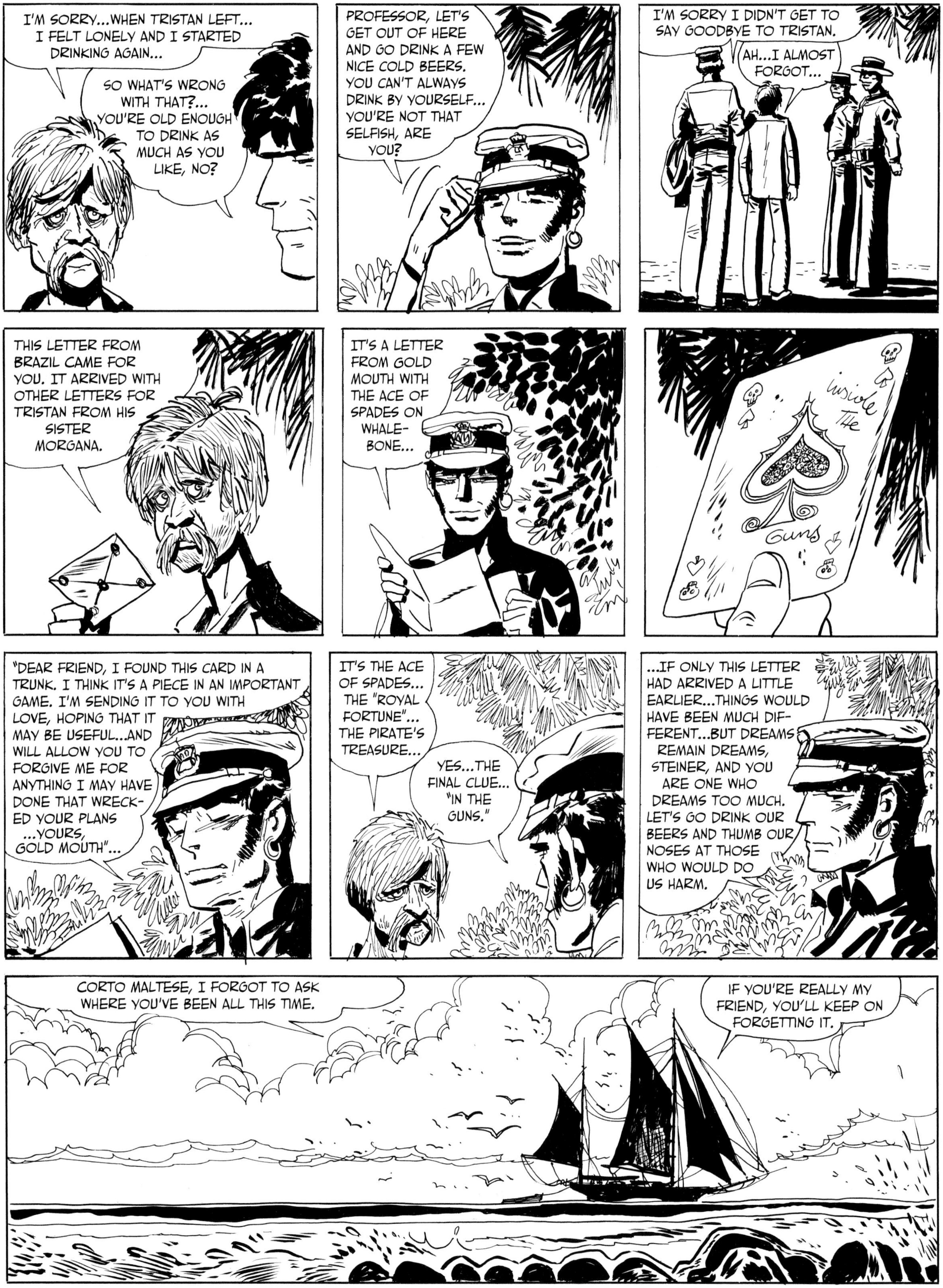

I'M SORRY...WHEN TRISTAN LEFT... I FELT LONELY AND I STARTED DRINKING AGAIN...
SO WHAT'S WRONG WITH THAT?... YOU'RE OLD ENOUGH TO DRINK AS MUCH AS YOU LIKE, NO?
PROFESSOR, LET'S GET OUT OF HERE AND GO DRINK A FEW NICE COLD BEERS. YOU CAN'T ALWAYS DRINK BY YOURSELF... YOU'RE NOT THAT SELFISH, ARE YOU?
I'M SORRY I DIDN'T GET TO SAY GOODBYE TO TRISTAN.
AH...I ALMOST FORGOT...
THIS LETTER FROM BRAZIL CAME FOR YOU. IT ARRIVED WITH OTHER LETTERS FOR TRISTAN FROM HIS SISTER MORGANA.
IT'S A LETTER FROM GOLD MOUTH WITH THE ACE OF SPADES ON WHALE-BONE...
"DEAR FRIEND, I FOUND THIS CARD IN A TRUNK. I THINK IT'S A PIECE IN AN IMPORTANT GAME. I'M SENDING IT TO YOU WITH LOVE, HOPING THAT IT MAY BE USEFUL...AND WILL ALLOW YOU TO FORGIVE ME FOR ANYTHING I MAY HAVE DONE THAT WRECKED YOUR PLANS ...YOURS, GOLD MOUTH"...
IT'S THE ACE OF SPADES... THE "ROYAL FORTUNE"... THE PIRATE'S TREASURE...
YES...THE FINAL CLUE... "IN THE GUNS."
...IF ONLY THIS LETTER HAD ARRIVED A LITTLE EARLIER...THINGS WOULD HAVE BEEN MUCH DIFFERENT...BUT DREAMS REMAIN DREAMS, STEINER, AND YOU ARE ONE WHO DREAMS TOO MUCH. LET'S GO DRINK OUR BEERS AND THUMB OUR NOSES AT THOSE WHO WOULD DO US HARM.
CORTO MALTESE, I FORGOT TO ASK WHERE YOU'VE BEEN ALL THIS TIME.
IF YOU'RE REALLY MY FRIEND, YOU'LL KEEP ON FORGETTING IT.

CHAPTER SIX:
THE
SEAGULL'S FAULT

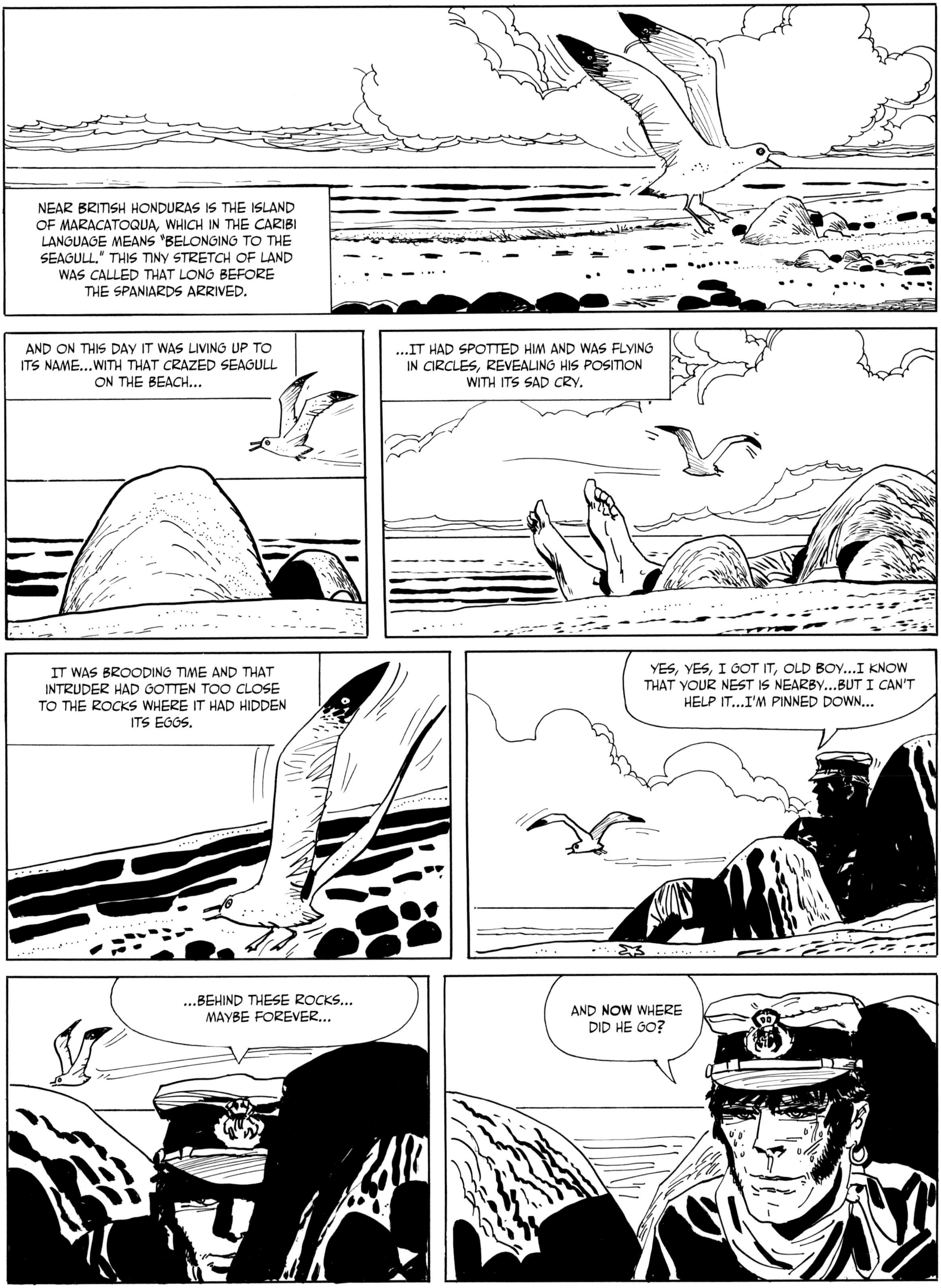

NEAR BRITISH HONDURAS IS THE ISLAND OF MARACATOQUA, WHICH IN THE CARIBI LANGUAGE MEANS "BELONGING TO THE SEAGULL." THIS TINY STRETCH OF LAND WAS CALLED THAT LONG BEFORE THE SPANIARDS ARRIVED.
AND ON THIS DAY IT WAS LIVING UP TO ITS NAME...WITH THAT CRAZED SEAGULL ON THE BEACH...
...IT HAD SPOTTED HIM AND WAS FLYING IN CIRCLES, REVEALING HIS POSITION WITH ITS SAD CRY.
IT WAS BROODING TIME AND THAT INTRUDER HAD GOTTEN TOO CLOSE TO THE ROCKS WHERE IT HAD HIDDEN ITS EGGS.
YES, YES, I GOT IT, OLD BOY...I KNOW THAT YOUR NEST IS NEARBY...BUT I CAN'T HELP IT...I'M PINNED DOWN...
...BEHIND THESE ROCKS... MAYBE FOREVER...
AND NOW WHERE DID HE GO?

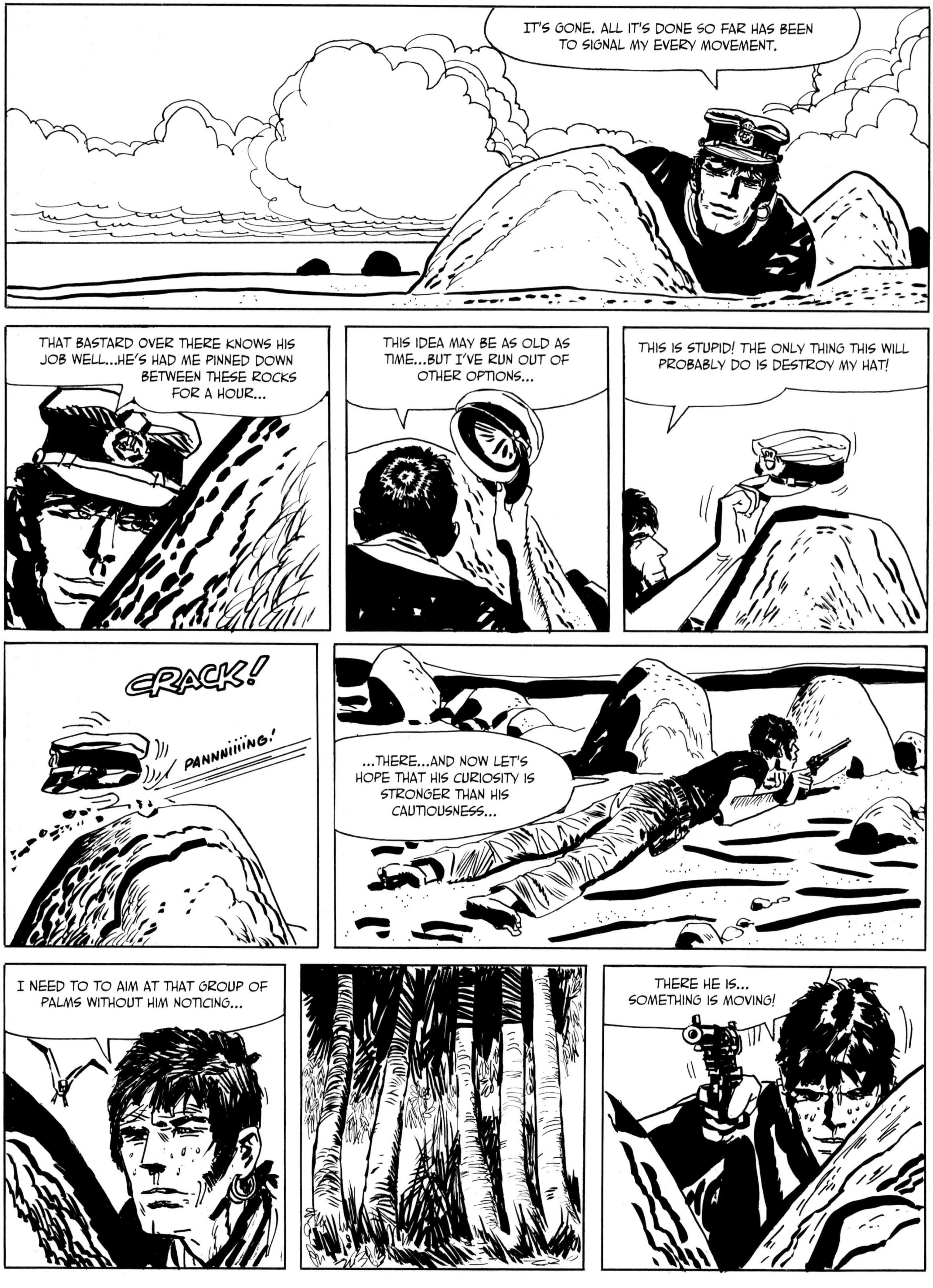

IT'S GONE. ALL IT'S DONE SO FAR HAS BEEN TO SIGNAL MY EVERY MOVEMENT.
THAT BASTARD OVER THERE KNOWS HIS JOB WELL...HE'S HAD ME PINNED DOWN BETWEEN THESE ROCKS FOR A HOUR...
THIS IDEA MAY BE AS OLD AS TIME...BUT I'VE RUN OUT OF OTHER OPTIONS...
THIS IS STUPID! THE ONLY THING THIS WILL PROBABLY DO IS DESTROY MY HAT!
CRACK!
PANNNIIIING!
...THERE...AND NOW LET'S HOPE THAT HIS CURIOSITY IS STRONGER THAN HIS CAUTIOUSNESS...
I NEED TO TO AIM AT THAT GROUP OF PALMS WITHOUT HIM NOTICING...
THERE HE IS... SOMETHING IS MOVING!

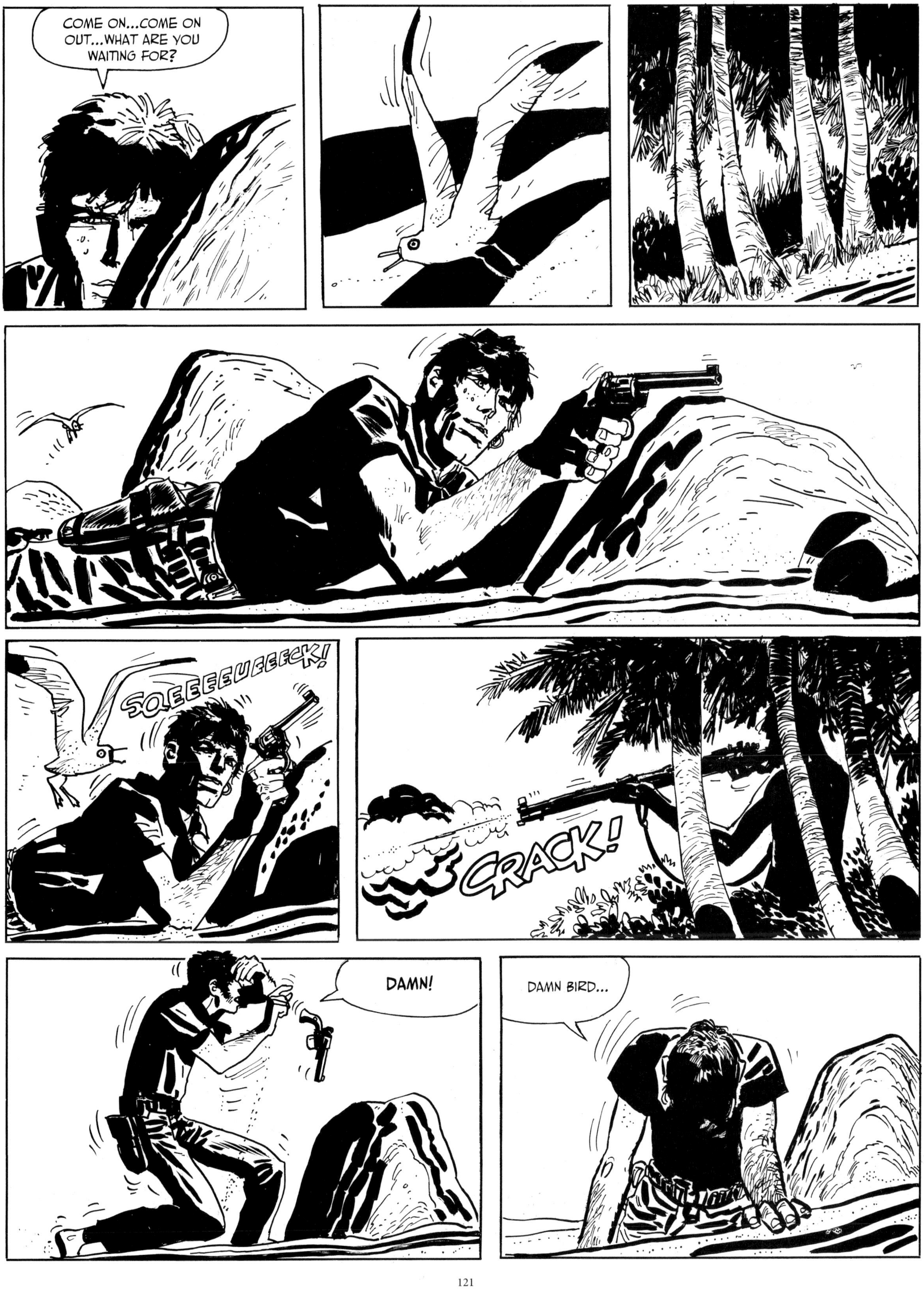
COME ON...COME ON OUT...WHAT ARE YOU WAITING FOR?
SQEEEEEUEEECK!
CRACK!
DAMN!
DAMN BIRD...

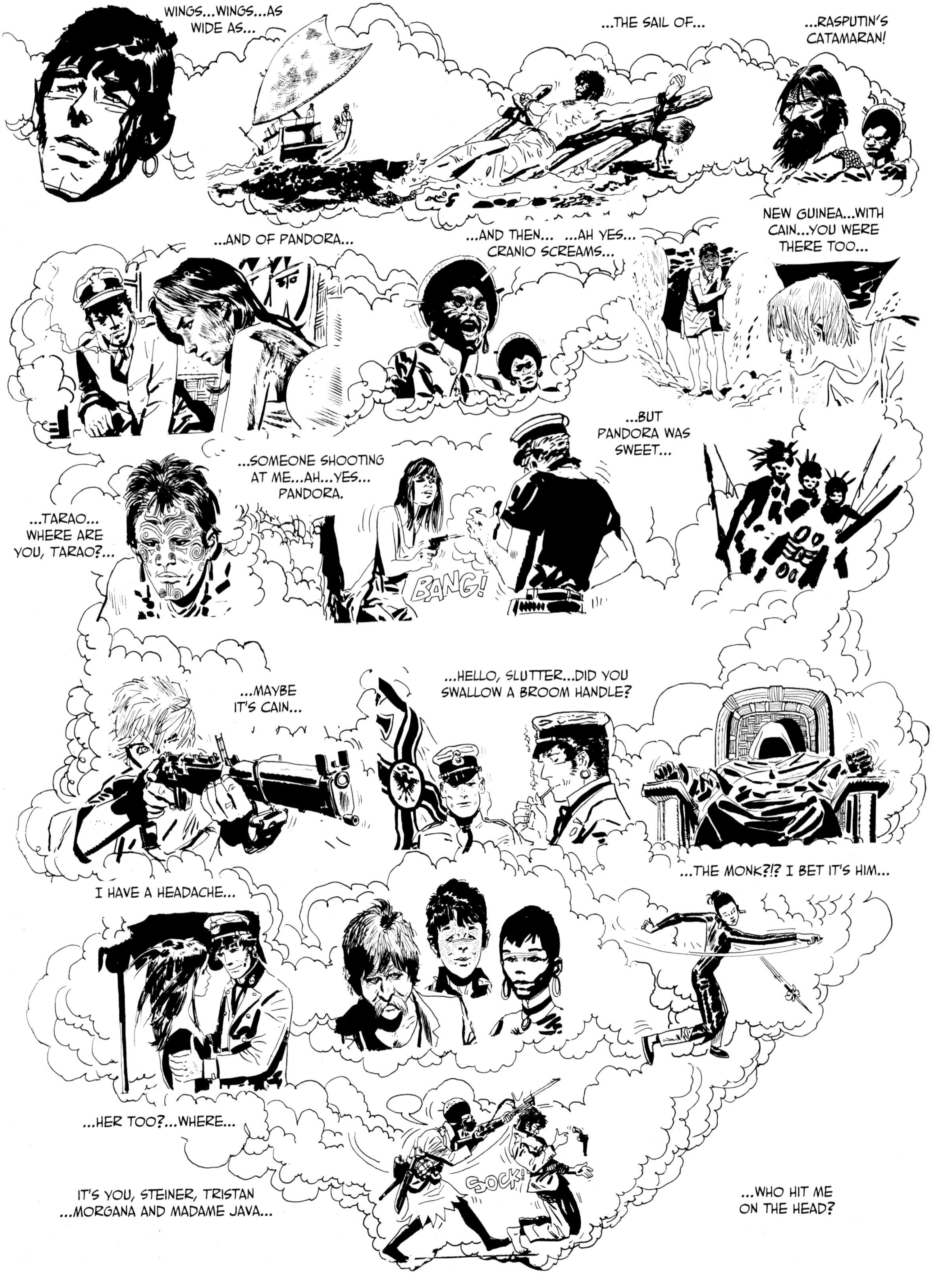
WINGS...WINGS...AS WIDE AS...
...THE SAIL OF...
...RASPUTIN'S CATAMARAN!
...AND OF PANDORA...
...AND THEN... ...AH YES... CRANIO SCREAMS...
NEW GUINEA...WITH CAIN...YOU WERE THERE TOO...
...TARAO... WHERE ARE YOU, TARAO?...
...SOMEONE SHOOTING AT ME...AH...YES... PANDORA.
BANG!
...BUT PANDORA WAS SWEET...
...MAYBE IT'S CAIN...
...HELLO, SLUTTER...DID YOU SWALLOW A BROOM HANDLE?
...THE MONK?!? I BET IT'S HIM...
I HAVE A HEADACHE...
...HER TOO?...WHERE...
IT'S YOU, STEINER, TRISTAN ...MORGANA AND MADAME JAVA...
SOCK!
...WHO HIT ME ON THE HEAD?

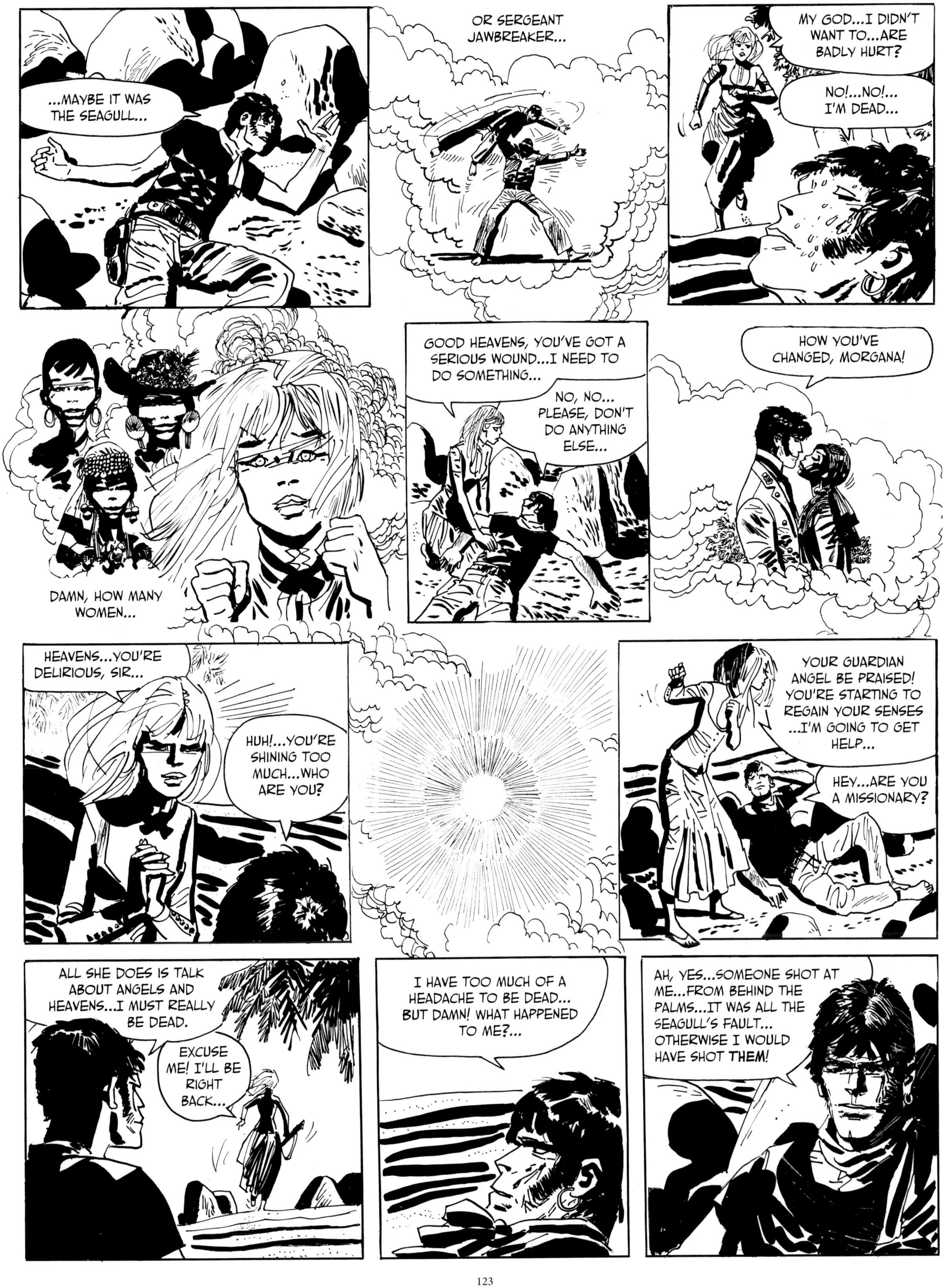
...MAYBE IT WAS THE SEAGULL...
OR SERGEANT JAWBREAKER...
MY GOD...I DIDN'T WANT TO...ARE BADLY HURT?
NO!...NO!... I'M DEAD...
DAMN, HOW MANY WOMEN...
GOOD HEAVENS, YOU'VE GOT A SERIOUS WOUND...I NEED TO DO SOMETHING...
NO, NO... PLEASE, DON'T DO ANYTHING ELSE...
HOW YOU'VE CHANGED, MORGANA!
HEAVENS...YOU'RE DELIRIOUS, SIR...
HUH!...YOU'RE SHINING TOO MUCH...WHO ARE YOU?
YOUR GUARDIAN ANGEL BE PRAISED! YOU'RE STARTING TO REGAIN YOUR SENSES ...I'M GOING TO GET HELP...
HEY...ARE YOU A MISSIONARY?
ALL SHE DOES IS TALK ABOUT ANGELS AND HEAVENS...I MUST REALLY BE DEAD.
EXCUSE ME! I'LL BE RIGHT BACK...
I HAVE TOO MUCH OF A HEADACHE TO BE DEAD... BUT DAMN! WHAT HAPPENED TO ME?...
AH, YES...SOMEONE SHOT AT ME...FROM BEHIND THE PALMS...IT WAS ALL THE SEAGULL'S FAULT... OTHERWISE I WOULD HAVE SHOT **THEM**!

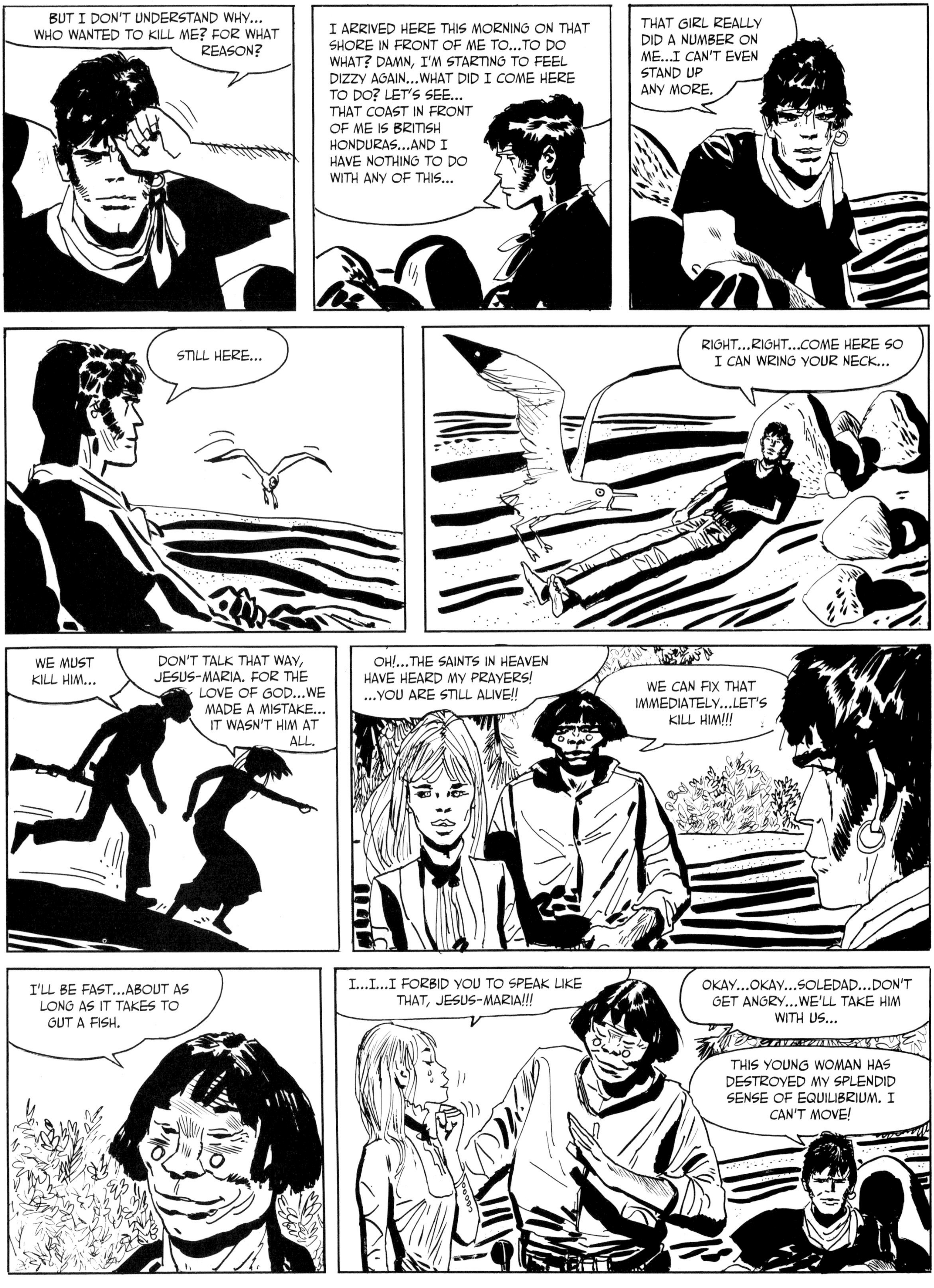
BUT I DON'T UNDERSTAND WHY... WHO WANTED TO KILL ME? FOR WHAT REASON?
I ARRIVED HERE THIS MORNING ON THAT SHORE IN FRONT OF ME TO...TO DO WHAT? DAMN, I'M STARTING TO FEEL DIZZY AGAIN...WHAT DID I COME HERE TO DO? LET'S SEE... THAT COAST IN FRONT OF ME IS BRITISH HONDURAS...AND I HAVE NOTHING TO DO WITH ANY OF THIS...
THAT GIRL REALLY DID A NUMBER ON ME...I CAN'T EVEN STAND UP ANY MORE.
STILL HERE...
RIGHT...RIGHT...COME HERE SO I CAN WRING YOUR NECK...
WE MUST KILL HIM...
DON'T TALK THAT WAY, JESUS-MARIA. FOR THE LOVE OF GOD...WE MADE A MISTAKE... IT WASN'T HIM AT ALL.
OH!...THE SAINTS IN HEAVEN HAVE HEARD MY PRAYERS! ...YOU ARE STILL ALIVE!!
WE CAN FIX THAT IMMEDIATELY...LET'S KILL HIM!!!
I'LL BE FAST...ABOUT AS LONG AS IT TAKES TO GUT A FISH.
I...I...I FORBID YOU TO SPEAK LIKE THAT, JESUS-MARIA!!!
OKAY...OKAY...SOLEDAD...DON'T GET ANGRY...WE'LL TAKE HIM WITH US...
THIS YOUNG WOMAN HAS DESTROYED MY SPLENDID SENSE OF EQUILIBRIUM. I CAN'T MOVE!

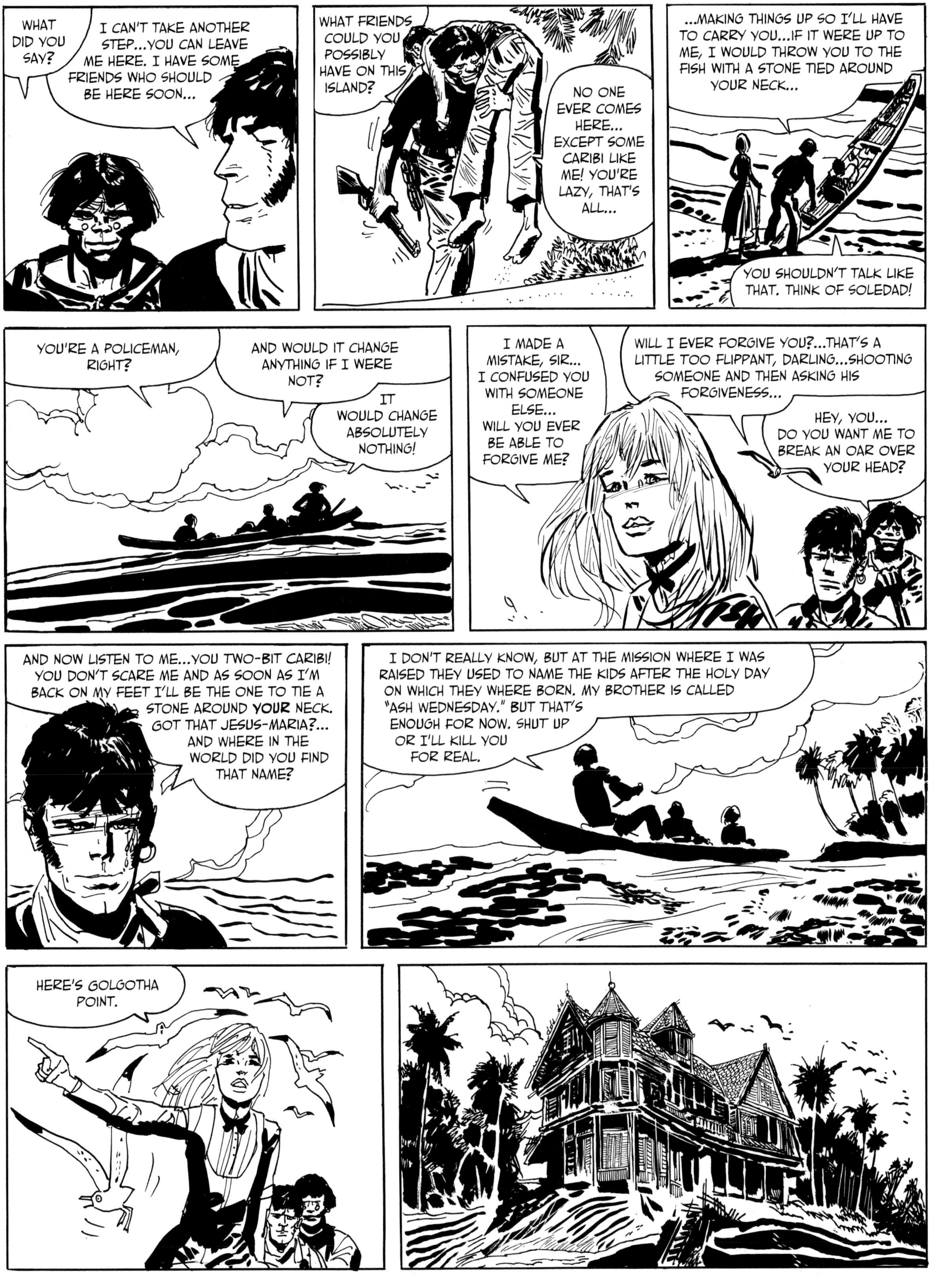

WHAT DID YOU SAY?
I CAN'T TAKE ANOTHER STEP...YOU CAN LEAVE ME HERE. I HAVE SOME FRIENDS WHO SHOULD BE HERE SOON...
WHAT FRIENDS COULD YOU POSSIBLY HAVE ON THIS ISLAND?
NO ONE EVER COMES HERE... EXCEPT SOME CARIBI LIKE ME! YOU'RE LAZY, THAT'S ALL...
...MAKING THINGS UP SO I'LL HAVE TO CARRY YOU...IF IT WERE UP TO ME, I WOULD THROW YOU TO THE FISH WITH A STONE TIED AROUND YOUR NECK...
YOU SHOULDN'T TALK LIKE THAT. THINK OF SOLEDAD!
YOU'RE A POLICEMAN, RIGHT?
AND WOULD IT CHANGE ANYTHING IF I WERE NOT?
IT WOULD CHANGE ABSOLUTELY NOTHING!
I MADE A MISTAKE, SIR... I CONFUSED YOU WITH SOMEONE ELSE... WILL YOU EVER BE ABLE TO FORGIVE ME?
WILL I EVER FORGIVE YOU?...THAT'S A LITTLE TOO FLIPPANT, DARLING...SHOOTING SOMEONE AND THEN ASKING HIS FORGIVENESS...
HEY, YOU... DO YOU WANT ME TO BREAK AN OAR OVER YOUR HEAD?
TSH
AND NOW LISTEN TO ME...YOU TWO-BIT CARIBI! YOU DON'T SCARE ME AND AS SOON AS I'M BACK ON MY FEET I'LL BE THE ONE TO TIE A STONE AROUND YOUR NECK. GOT THAT JESUS-MARIA?... AND WHERE IN THE WORLD DID YOU FIND THAT NAME?
I DON'T REALLY KNOW, BUT AT THE MISSION WHERE I WAS RAISED THEY USED TO NAME THE KIDS AFTER THE HOLY DAY ON WHICH THEY WHERE BORN. MY BROTHER IS CALLED "ASH WEDNESDAY." BUT THAT'S ENOUGH FOR NOW. SHUT UP OR I'LL KILL YOU FOR REAL.
HERE'S GOLGOTHA POINT.

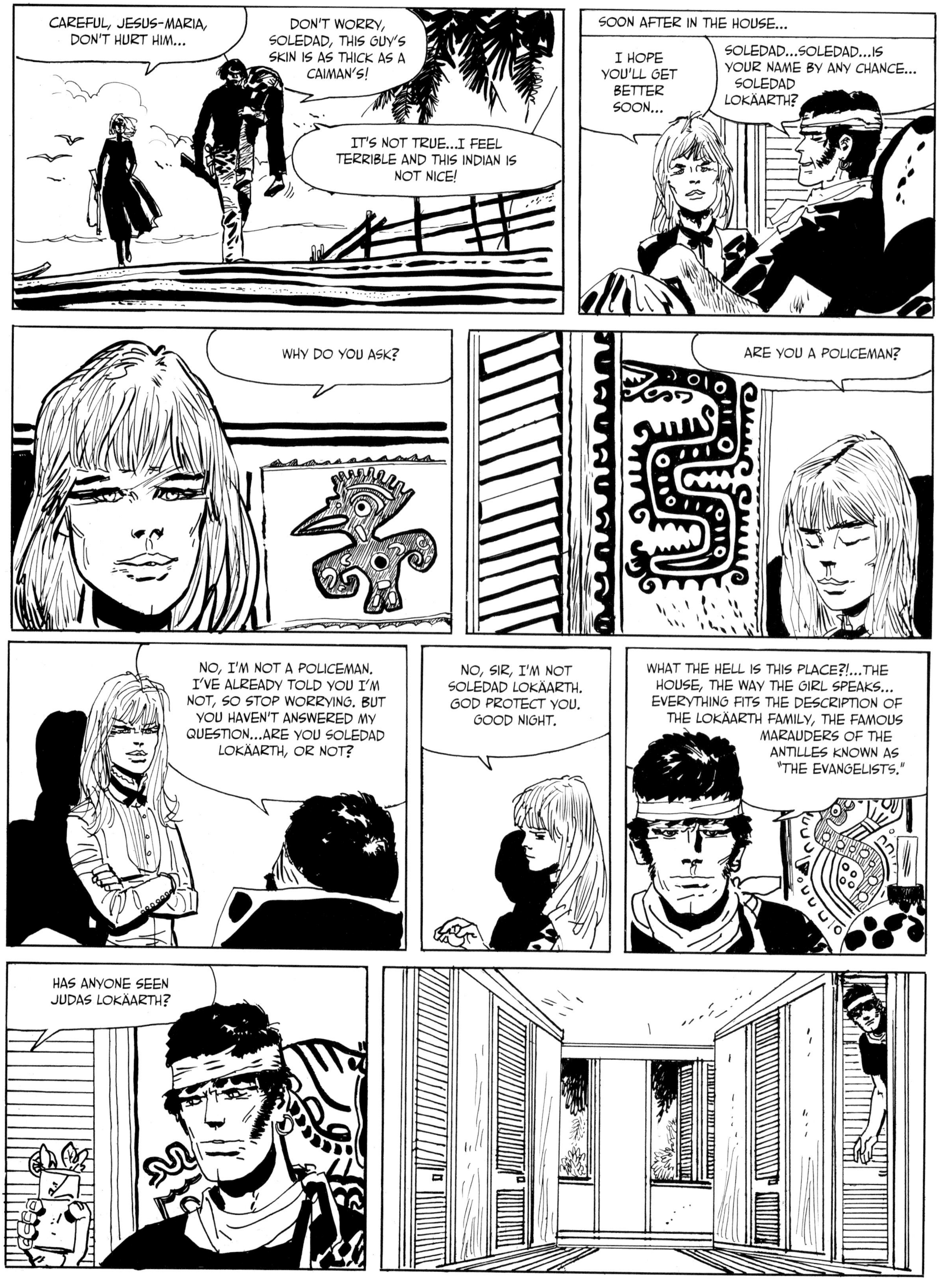

CAREFUL, JESUS-MARIA, DON'T HURT HIM...
DON'T WORRY, SOLEDAD, THIS GUY'S SKIN IS AS THICK AS A CAIMAN'S!
IT'S NOT TRUE...I FEEL TERRIBLE AND THIS INDIAN IS NOT NICE!
SOON AFTER IN THE HOUSE...
I HOPE YOU'LL GET BETTER SOON...
SOLEDAD...SOLEDAD...IS YOUR NAME BY ANY CHANCE... SOLEDAD LOKÄARTH?
WHY DO YOU ASK?
ARE YOU A POLICEMAN?
NO, I'M NOT A POLICEMAN. I'VE ALREADY TOLD YOU I'M NOT, SO STOP WORRYING. BUT YOU HAVEN'T ANSWERED MY QUESTION...ARE YOU SOLEDAD LOKÄARTH, OR NOT?
NO, SIR, I'M NOT SOLEDAD LOKÄARTH. GOD PROTECT YOU. GOOD NIGHT.
WHAT THE HELL IS THIS PLACE?!...THE HOUSE, THE WAY THE GIRL SPEAKS... EVERYTHING FITS THE DESCRIPTION OF THE LOKÄARTH FAMILY, THE FAMOUS MARAUDERS OF THE ANTILLES KNOWN AS "THE EVANGELISTS."
HAS ANYONE SEEN JUDAS LOKÄARTH?

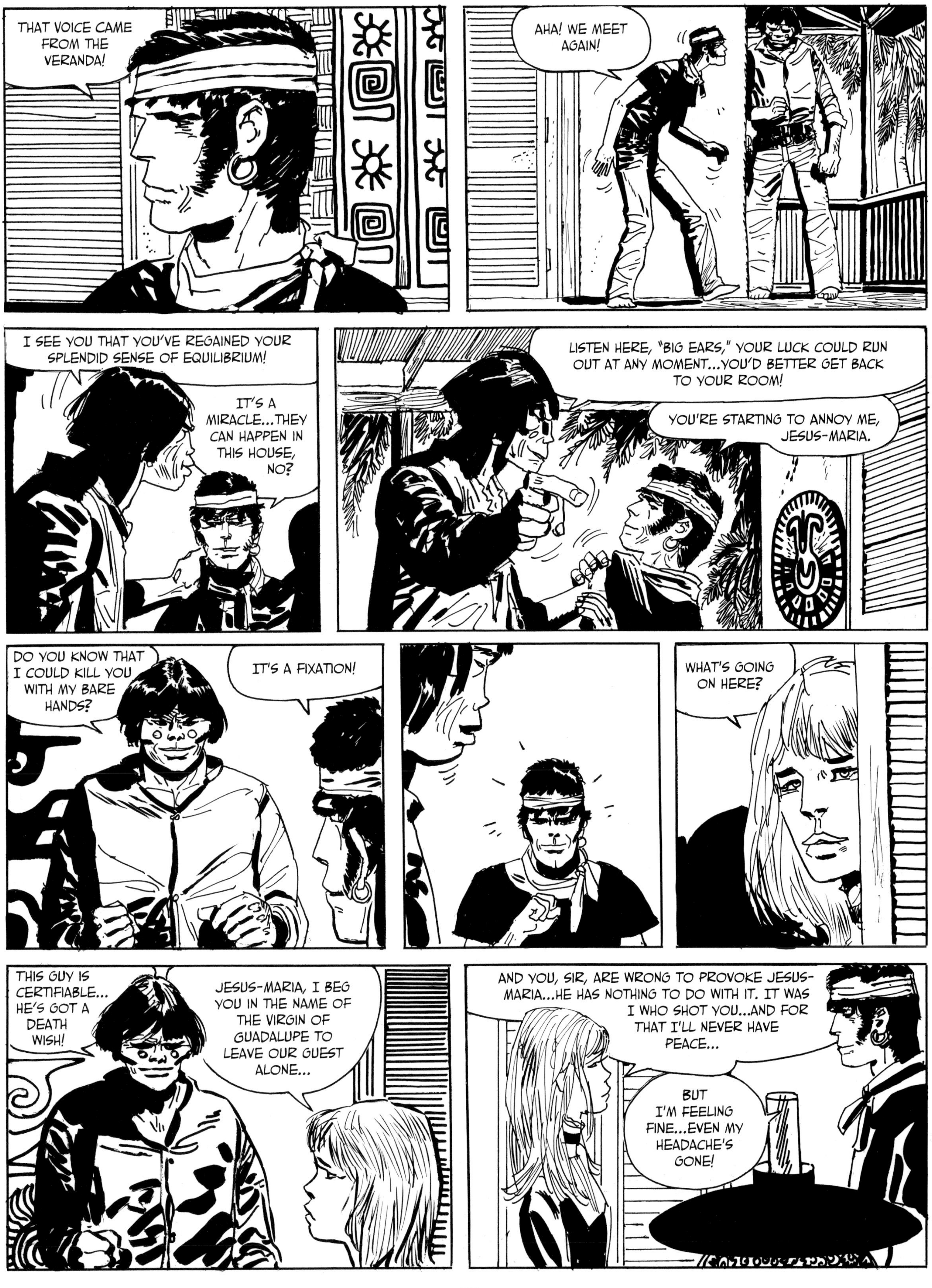
THAT VOICE CAME FROM THE VERANDA!
AHA! WE MEET AGAIN!
I SEE YOU THAT YOU'VE REGAINED YOUR SPLENDID SENSE OF EQUILIBRIUM!
IT'S A MIRACLE...THEY CAN HAPPEN IN THIS HOUSE, NO?
LISTEN HERE, "BIG EARS," YOUR LUCK COULD RUN OUT AT ANY MOMENT...YOU'D BETTER GET BACK TO YOUR ROOM!
YOU'RE STARTING TO ANNOY ME, JESUS-MARIA.
DO YOU KNOW THAT I COULD KILL YOU WITH MY BARE HANDS?
IT'S A FIXATION!
WHAT'S GOING ON HERE?
THIS GUY IS CERTIFIABLE... HE'S GOT A DEATH WISH!
JESUS-MARIA, I BEG YOU IN THE NAME OF THE VIRGIN OF GUADALUPE TO LEAVE OUR GUEST ALONE...
AND YOU, SIR, ARE WRONG TO PROVOKE JESUS-MARIA...HE HAS NOTHING TO DO WITH IT. IT WAS I WHO SHOT YOU...AND FOR THAT I'LL NEVER HAVE PEACE...
BUT I'M FEELING FINE...EVEN MY HEADACHE'S GONE!

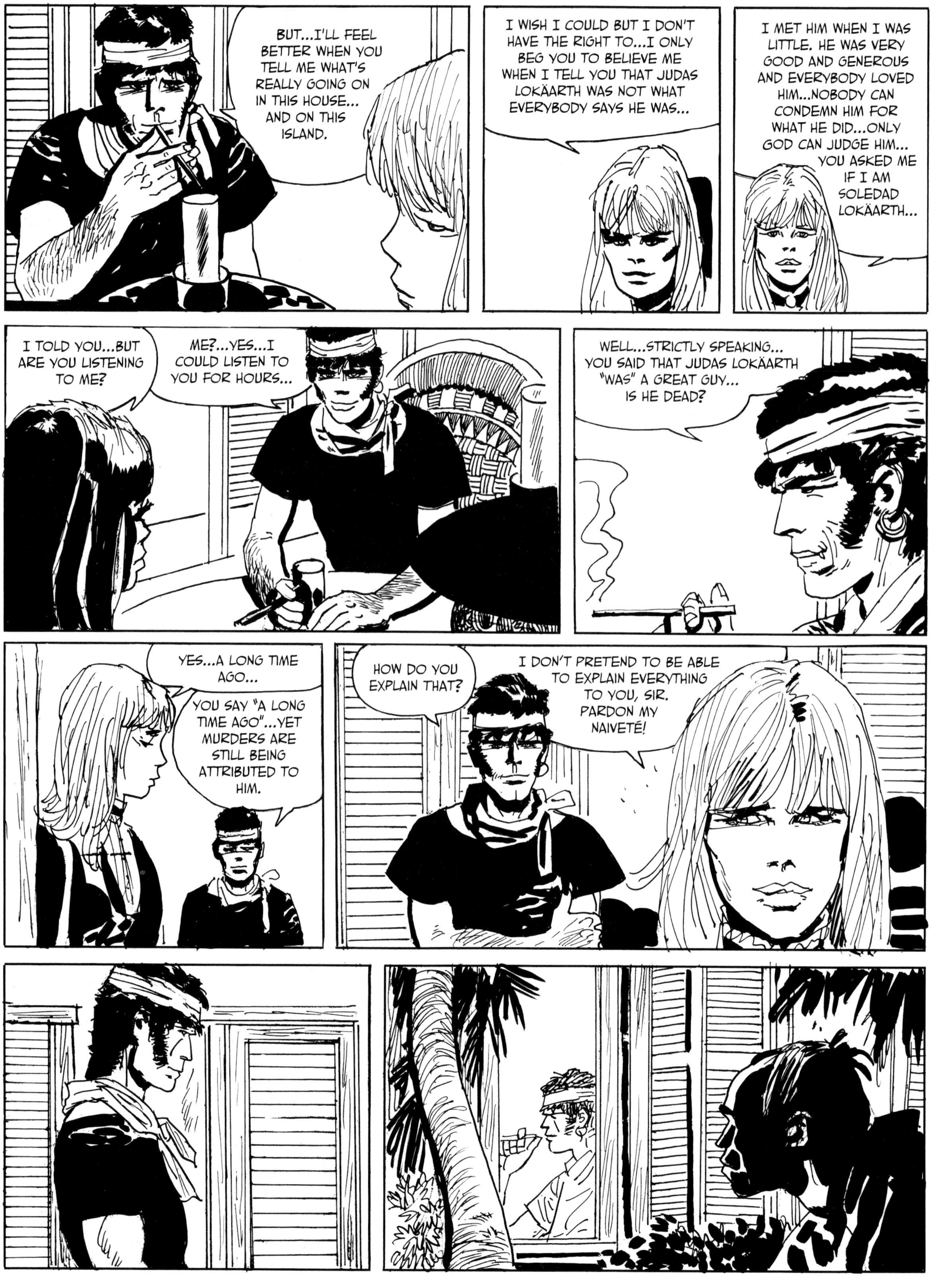

BUT...I'LL FEEL BETTER WHEN YOU TELL ME WHAT'S REALLY GOING ON IN THIS HOUSE... AND ON THIS ISLAND.
I WISH I COULD BUT I DON'T HAVE THE RIGHT TO...I ONLY BEG YOU TO BELIEVE ME WHEN I TELL YOU THAT JUDAS LOKÄARTH WAS NOT WHAT EVERYBODY SAYS HE WAS...
I MET HIM WHEN I WAS LITTLE. HE WAS VERY GOOD AND GENEROUS AND EVERYBODY LOVED HIM...NOBODY CAN CONDEMN HIM FOR WHAT HE DID...ONLY GOD CAN JUDGE HIM... YOU ASKED ME IF I AM SOLEDAD LOKÄARTH...
I TOLD YOU...BUT ARE YOU LISTENING TO ME?
ME?...YES...I COULD LISTEN TO YOU FOR HOURS...
WELL...STRICTLY SPEAKING... YOU SAID THAT JUDAS LOKÄARTH "WAS" A GREAT GUY... IS HE DEAD?
YES...A LONG TIME AGO...
YOU SAY "A LONG TIME AGO"...YET MURDERS ARE STILL BEING ATTRIBUTED TO HIM.
HOW DO YOU EXPLAIN THAT?
I DON'T PRETEND TO BE ABLE TO EXPLAIN EVERYTHING TO YOU, SIR. PARDON MY NAIVETÉ!

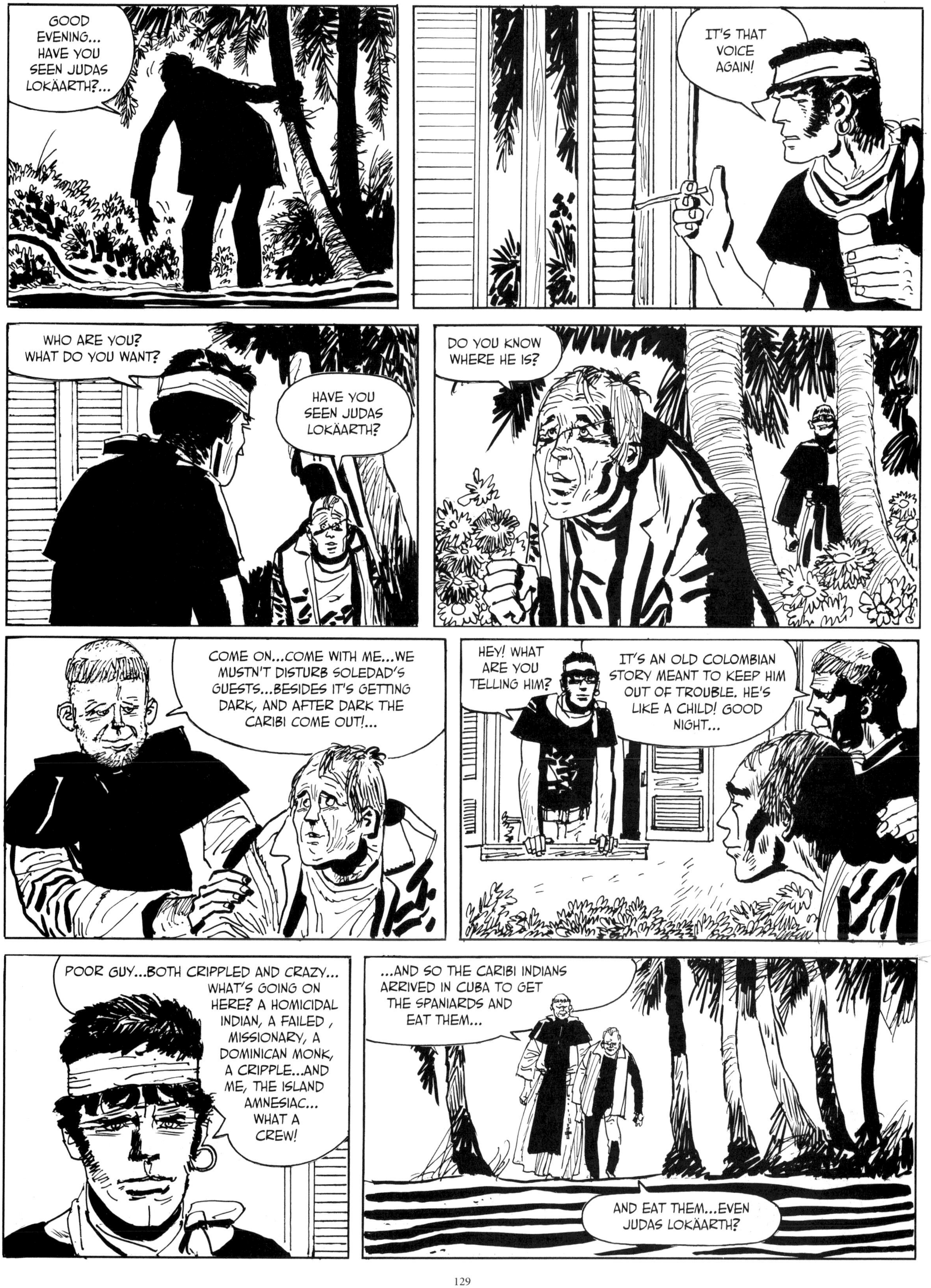
GOOD EVENING... HAVE YOU SEEN JUDAS LOKÄARTH?...
IT'S THAT VOICE AGAIN!
WHO ARE YOU? WHAT DO YOU WANT?
HAVE YOU SEEN JUDAS LOKÄARTH?
DO YOU KNOW WHERE HE IS?
COME ON...COME WITH ME...WE MUSTN'T DISTURB SOLEDAD'S GUESTS...BESIDES IT'S GETTING DARK, AND AFTER DARK THE CARIBI COME OUT!...
HEY! WHAT ARE YOU TELLING HIM?
IT'S AN OLD COLOMBIAN STORY MEANT TO KEEP HIM OUT OF TROUBLE. HE'S LIKE A CHILD! GOOD NIGHT...
POOR GUY...BOTH CRIPPLED AND CRAZY... WHAT'S GOING ON HERE? A HOMICIDAL INDIAN, A FAILED , MISSIONARY, A DOMINICAN MONK, A CRIPPLE...AND ME, THE ISLAND AMNESIAC... WHAT A CREW!
...AND SO THE CARIBI INDIANS ARRIVED IN CUBA TO GET THE SPANIARDS AND EAT THEM...
AND EAT THEM...EVEN JUDAS LOKÄARTH?

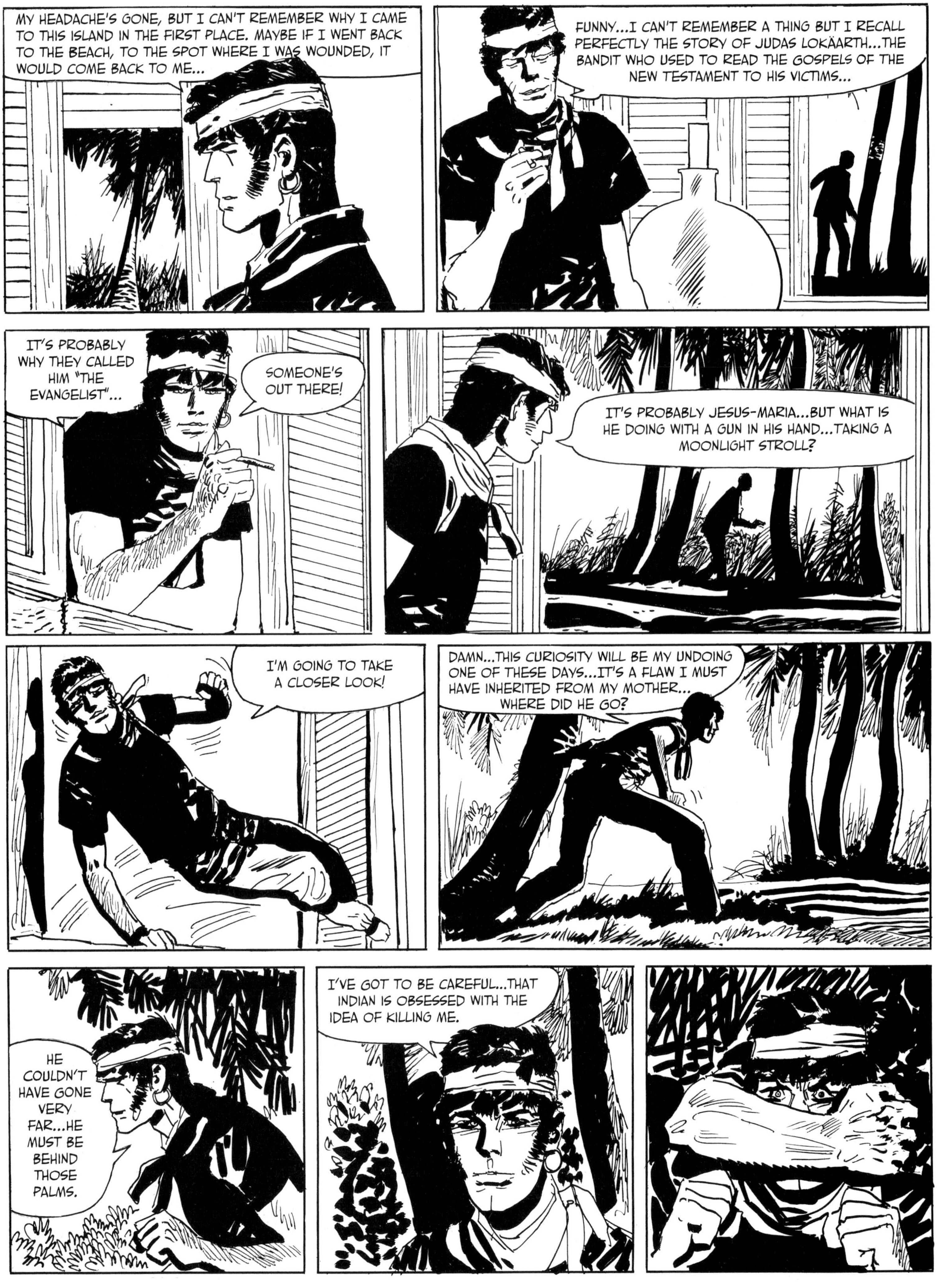
MY HEADACHE'S GONE, BUT I CAN'T REMEMBER WHY I CAME TO THIS ISLAND IN THE FIRST PLACE. MAYBE IF I WENT BACK TO THE BEACH, TO THE SPOT WHERE I WAS WOUNDED, IT WOULD COME BACK TO ME...
FUNNY...I CAN'T REMEMBER A THING BUT I RECALL PERFECTLY THE STORY OF JUDAS LOKÄARTH...THE BANDIT WHO USED TO READ THE GOSPELS OF THE NEW TESTAMENT TO HIS VICTIMS...
IT'S PROBABLY WHY THEY CALLED HIM "THE EVANGELIST"...
SOMEONE'S OUT THERE!
IT'S PROBABLY JESUS-MARIA...BUT WHAT IS HE DOING WITH A GUN IN HIS HAND...TAKING A MOONLIGHT STROLL?
I'M GOING TO TAKE A CLOSER LOOK!
DAMN...THIS CURIOSITY WILL BE MY UNDOING ONE OF THESE DAYS...IT'S A FLAW I MUST HAVE INHERITED FROM MY MOTHER... WHERE DID HE GO?
HE COULDN'T HAVE GONE VERY FAR...HE MUST BE BEHIND THOSE PALMS.
I'VE GOT TO BE CAREFUL...THAT INDIAN IS OBSESSED WITH THE IDEA OF KILLING ME.

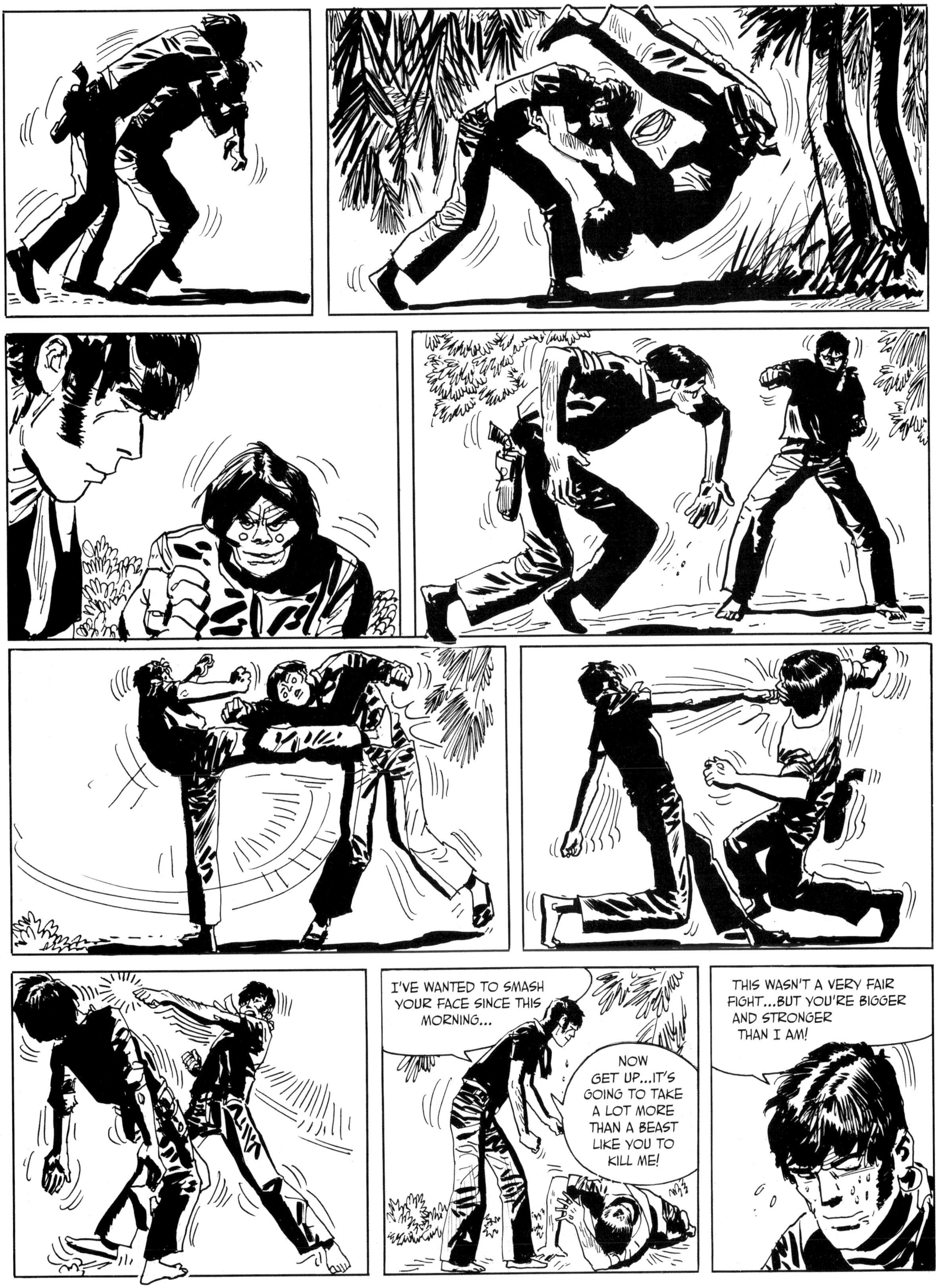
I'VE WANTED TO SMASH YOUR FACE SINCE THIS MORNING...
NOW GET UP...IT'S GOING TO TAKE A LOT MORE THAN A BEAST LIKE YOU TO KILL ME!
THIS WASN'T A VERY FAIR FIGHT...BUT YOU'RE BIGGER AND STRONGER THAN I AM!

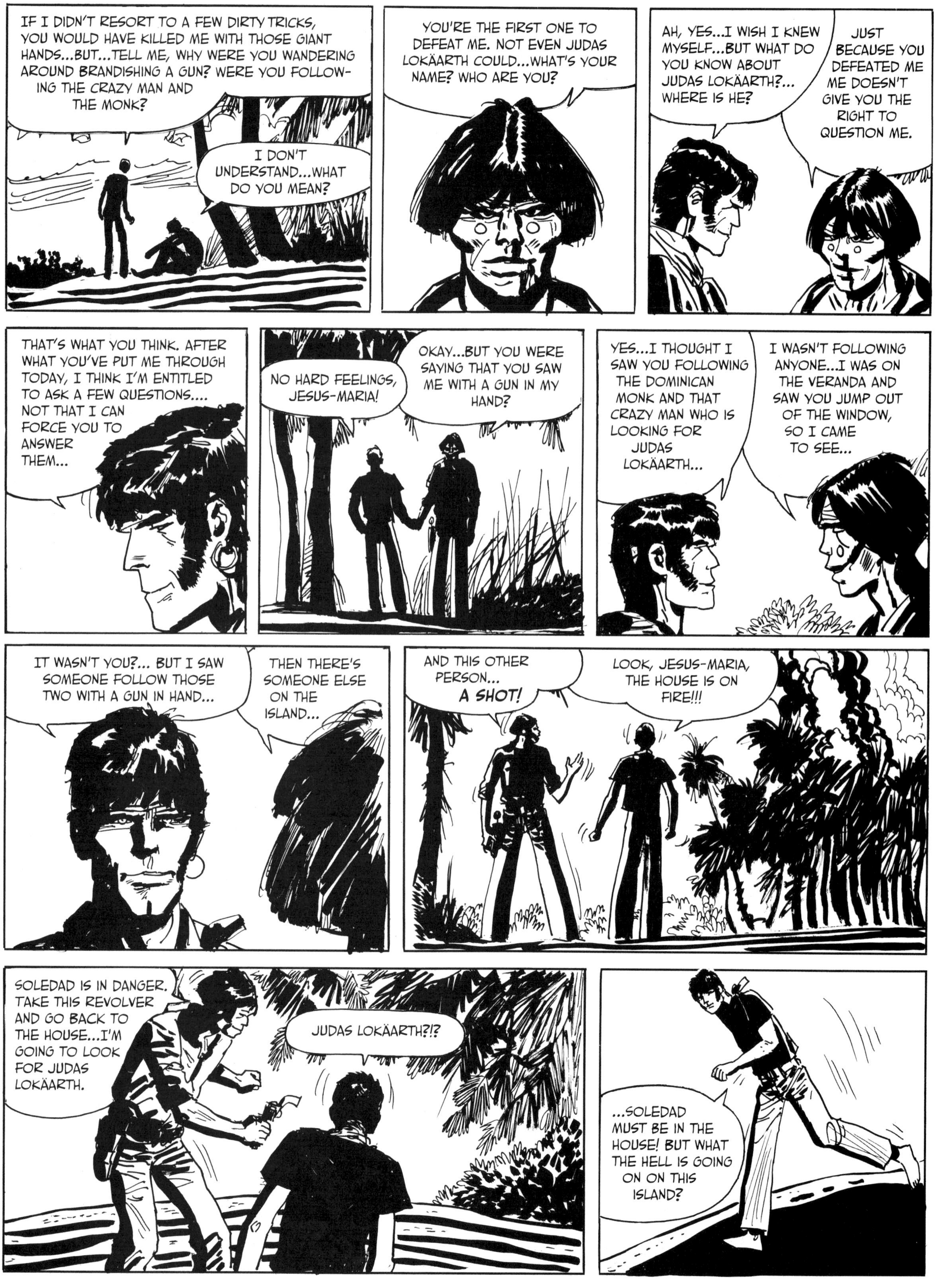

IF I DIDN'T RESORT TO A FEW DIRTY TRICKS, YOU WOULD HAVE KILLED ME WITH THOSE GIANT HANDS...BUT...TELL ME, WHY WERE YOU WANDERING AROUND BRANDISHING A GUN? WERE YOU FOLLOWING THE CRAZY MAN AND THE MONK?
I DON'T UNDERSTAND...WHAT DO YOU MEAN?
YOU'RE THE FIRST ONE TO DEFEAT ME. NOT EVEN JUDAS LOKÄARTH COULD...WHAT'S YOUR NAME? WHO ARE YOU?
AH, YES...I WISH I KNEW MYSELF...BUT WHAT DO YOU KNOW ABOUT JUDAS LOKÄARTH?... WHERE IS HE?
JUST BECAUSE YOU DEFEATED ME ME DOESN'T GIVE YOU THE RIGHT TO QUESTION ME.
THAT'S WHAT YOU THINK. AFTER WHAT YOU'VE PUT ME THROUGH TODAY, I THINK I'M ENTITLED TO ASK A FEW QUESTIONS.... NOT THAT I CAN FORCE YOU TO ANSWER THEM...
NO HARD FEELINGS, JESUS-MARIA!
OKAY...BUT YOU WERE SAYING THAT YOU SAW ME WITH A GUN IN MY HAND?
YES...I THOUGHT I SAW YOU FOLLOWING THE DOMINICAN MONK AND THAT CRAZY MAN WHO IS LOOKING FOR JUDAS LOKÄARTH...
I WASN'T FOLLOWING ANYONE...I WAS ON THE VERANDA AND SAW YOU JUMP OUT OF THE WINDOW, SO I CAME TO SEE...
IT WASN'T YOU?... BUT I SAW SOMEONE FOLLOW THOSE TWO WITH A GUN IN HAND...
THEN THERE'S SOMEONE ELSE ON THE ISLAND...
AND THIS OTHER PERSON... A SHOT!
LOOK, JESUS-MARIA, THE HOUSE IS ON FIRE!!!
SOLEDAD IS IN DANGER. TAKE THIS REVOLVER AND GO BACK TO THE HOUSE...I'M GOING TO LOOK FOR JUDAS LOKÄARTH.
JUDAS LOKÄARTH?!?
...SOLEDAD MUST BE IN THE HOUSE! BUT WHAT THE HELL IS GOING ON ON THIS ISLAND?

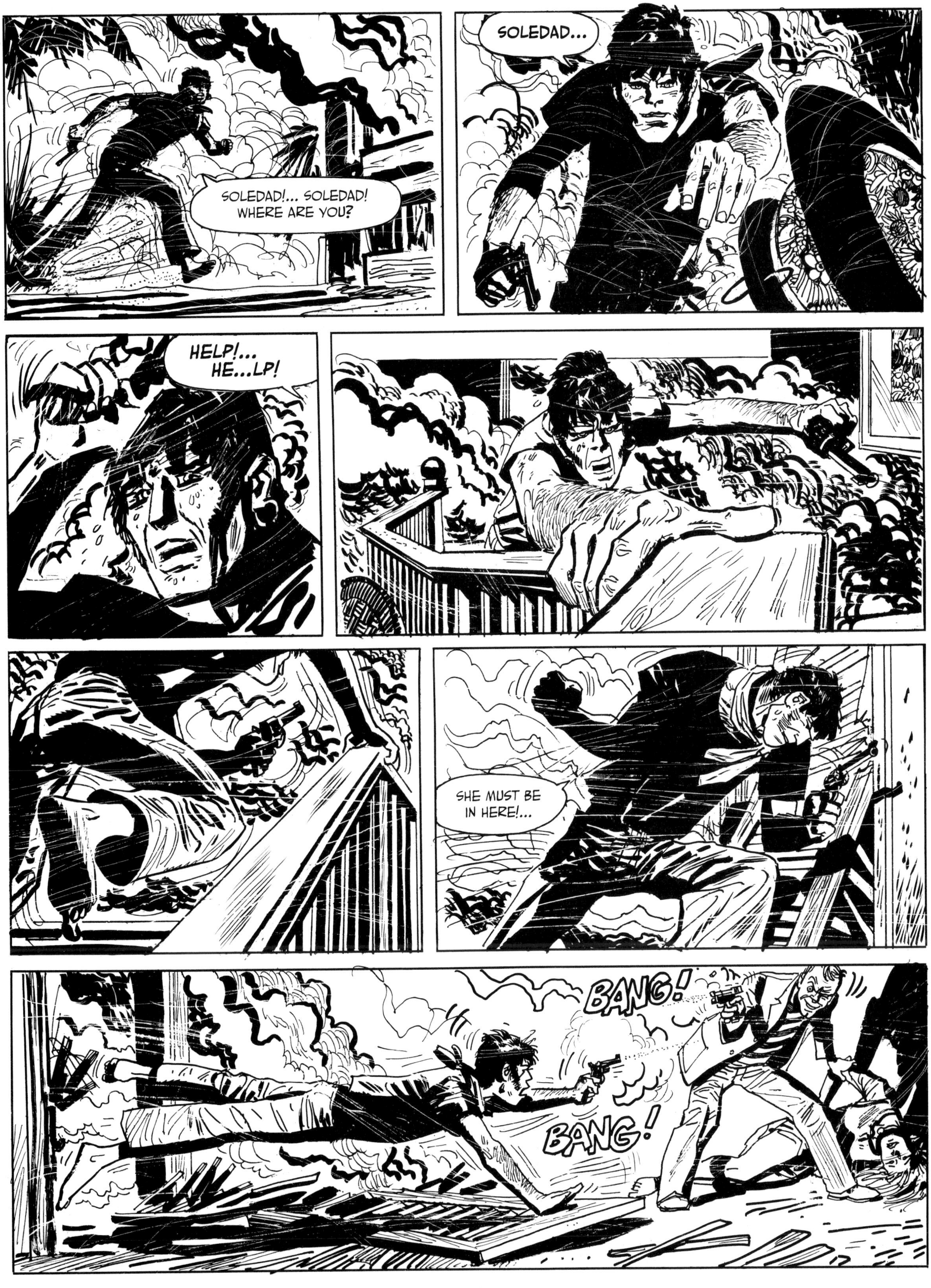
SOLEDAD!... SOLEDAD! WHERE ARE YOU?
SOLEDAD...
HELP!... HE...LP!
SHE MUST BE IN HERE!...
BANG!
BANG!

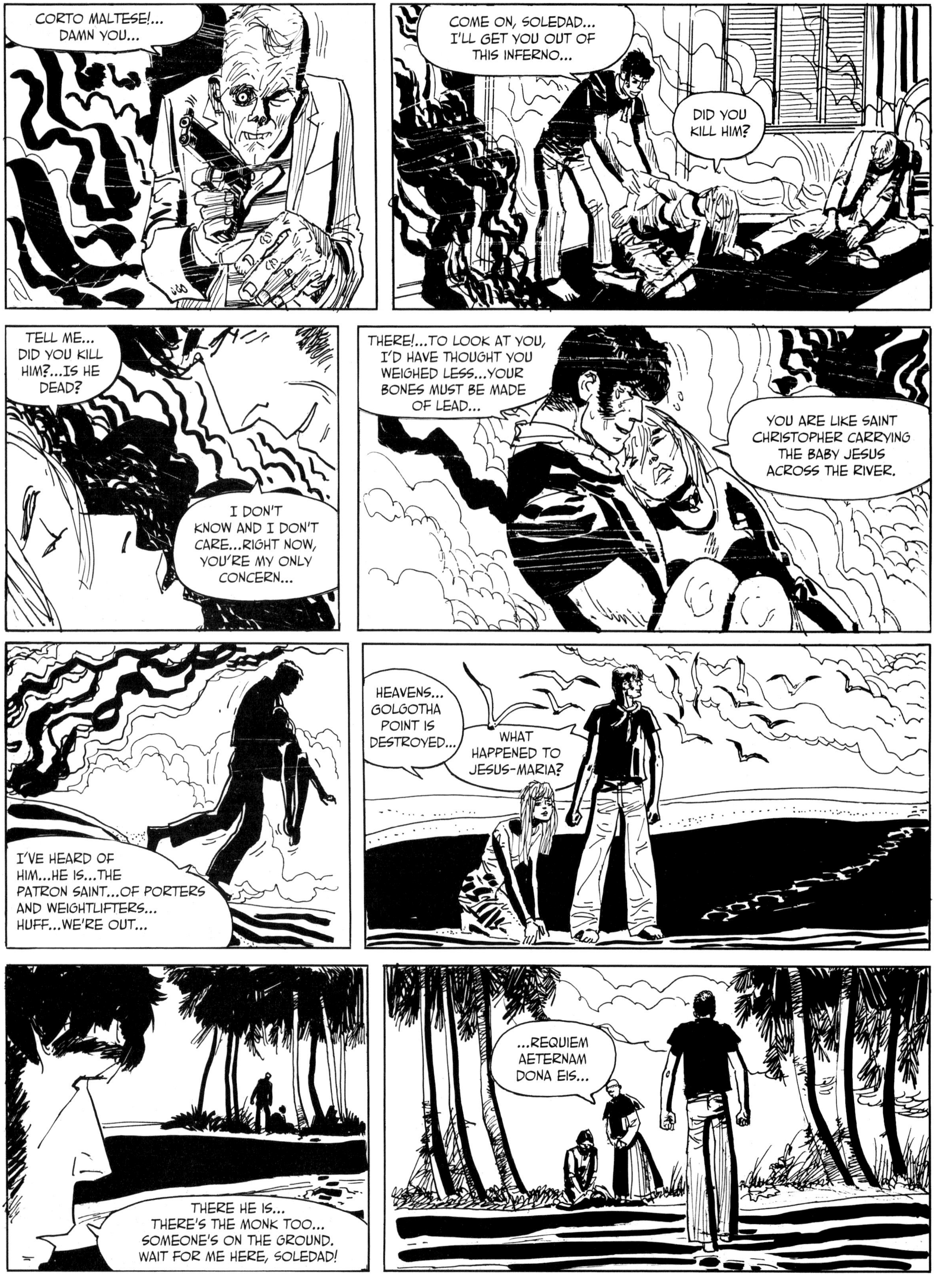
CORTO MALTESE!... DAMN YOU...
COME ON, SOLEDAD... I'LL GET YOU OUT OF THIS INFERNO...
DID YOU KILL HIM?
TELL ME... DID YOU KILL HIM?...IS HE DEAD?
I DON'T KNOW AND I DON'T CARE...RIGHT NOW, YOU'RE MY ONLY CONCERN...
THERE!...TO LOOK AT YOU, I'D HAVE THOUGHT YOU WEIGHED LESS...YOUR BONES MUST BE MADE OF LEAD...
YOU ARE LIKE SAINT CHRISTOPHER CARRYING THE BABY JESUS ACROSS THE RIVER.
I'VE HEARD OF HIM...HE IS...THE PATRON SAINT...OF PORTERS AND WEIGHTLIFTERS... HUFF...WE'RE OUT...
HEAVENS... GOLGOTHA POINT IS DESTROYED...
WHAT HAPPENED TO JESUS-MARIA?
THERE HE IS... THERE'S THE MONK TOO... SOMEONE'S ON THE GROUND. WAIT FOR ME HERE, SOLEDAD!
...REQUIEM AETERNAM DONA EIS...

THE CRAZY MAN? POOR GUY... HE MUST HAVE BEEN KILLED BY WHOEVER SET FIRE TO THE HOUSE. IT WAS PROBABLY THAT SHOT WE HEARD...

YES!!!

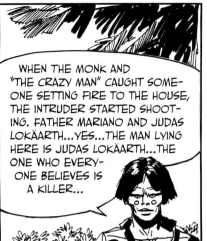

WHEN THE MONK AND "THE CRAZY MAN" CAUGHT SOMEONE SETTING FIRE TO THE HOUSE, THE INTRUDER STARTED SHOOTING. FATHER MARIANO AND JUDAS LOKÄARTH...YES...THE MAN LYING HERE IS JUDAS LOKÄARTH...THE ONE WHO EVERYONE BELIEVES IS A KILLER...

JUDAS LOKÄARTH?...

YES... THE GREATEST MAN IN THE WORLD, SAILOR. ...A LONG TIME AGO...HE WAS A WONDERFUL MAN...WHAT HE DID WAS RIGHTEOUS AND JUST. HE WAS THE ELDEST OF FOUR BROTHERS...

...HE WAS SIXTEEN WHEN A WEALTHY LANDOWNER KILLED HIS MOTHER AND FATHER!

HE ONLY TOLD HIS BROTHERS MANY YEARS LATER WHEN HIS REVENGE WAS COMPLETE. YOU SEE, HE WORKED ALONE TO TRACK DOWN THOSE RESPONSIBLE. HE EVENTUALLY KILLED THE MURDERER OF HIS MOTHER AND FATHER... AND THEN CAME HERE TO HIDE.

JESUS-MARIA...

IS MY BROTHER DEAD?...

YES, SOLEDAD... I FAILED TO PROTECT HIM...

DON'T SAY THAT, JESUS-MARIA. POOR JUDAS LOKÄARTH WOULDN'T WANT TO HEAR YOU TALK THIS WAY. WE NEED TO LEAVE THIS PLACE...THERE'S NO MORE REASON TO STAY.

YES...THE MONK IS RIGHT...THE POLICE BOAT IS COMING THIS WAY...

THEY MUST HAVE SEEN THE FIRE FROM THE COAST!

YOU'LL BE ABLE TO EXPLAIN EVERYTHING TO THE GOVERNOR...

THE TRUMPED-UP PIRACY CHARGES AGAINST US ARE AIRTIGHT...THE SON OF THE MAN WHO WAS RESPONSIBLE FOR KILLING JUDAS'S PARENTS IS A CERTAIN CRESTER, A CONTEMPTIBLE LAWYER FROM BRITISH GUIANA...

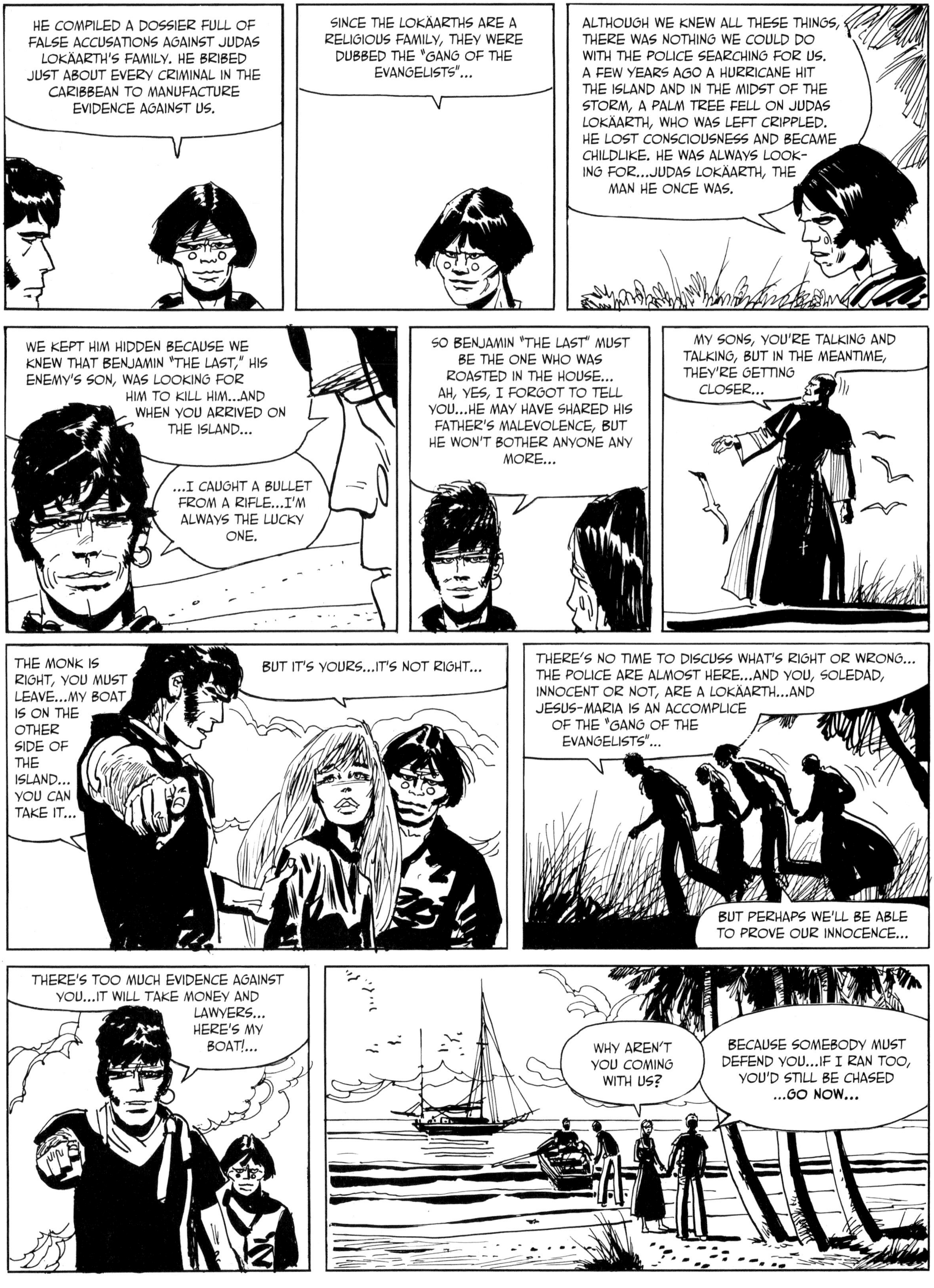
HE COMPILED A DOSSIER FULL OF FALSE ACCUSATIONS AGAINST JUDAS LOKÄARTH'S FAMILY. HE BRIBED JUST ABOUT EVERY CRIMINAL IN THE CARIBBEAN TO MANUFACTURE EVIDENCE AGAINST US.
SINCE THE LOKÄARTHS ARE A RELIGIOUS FAMILY, THEY WERE DUBBED THE "GANG OF THE EVANGELISTS"...
ALTHOUGH WE KNEW ALL THESE THINGS, THERE WAS NOTHING WE COULD DO WITH THE POLICE SEARCHING FOR US. A FEW YEARS AGO A HURRICANE HIT THE ISLAND AND IN THE MIDST OF THE STORM, A PALM TREE FELL ON JUDAS LOKÄARTH, WHO WAS LEFT CRIPPLED. HE LOST CONSCIOUSNESS AND BECAME CHILDLIKE. HE WAS ALWAYS LOOKING FOR...JUDAS LOKÄARTH, THE MAN HE ONCE WAS.
WE KEPT HIM HIDDEN BECAUSE WE KNEW THAT BENJAMIN "THE LAST," HIS ENEMY'S SON, WAS LOOKING FOR HIM TO KILL HIM...AND WHEN YOU ARRIVED ON THE ISLAND...
...I CAUGHT A BULLET FROM A RIFLE...I'M ALWAYS THE LUCKY ONE.
SO BENJAMIN "THE LAST" MUST BE THE ONE WHO WAS ROASTED IN THE HOUSE... AH, YES, I FORGOT TO TELL YOU...HE MAY HAVE SHARED HIS FATHER'S MALEVOLENCE, BUT HE WON'T BOTHER ANYONE ANY MORE...
MY SONS, YOU'RE TALKING AND TALKING, BUT IN THE MEANTIME, THEY'RE GETTING CLOSER...
THE MONK IS RIGHT, YOU MUST LEAVE...MY BOAT IS ON THE OTHER SIDE OF THE ISLAND... YOU CAN TAKE IT...
BUT IT'S YOURS...IT'S NOT RIGHT...
THERE'S NO TIME TO DISCUSS WHAT'S RIGHT OR WRONG... THE POLICE ARE ALMOST HERE...AND YOU, SOLEDAD, INNOCENT OR NOT, ARE A LOKÄARTH...AND JESUS-MARIA IS AN ACCOMPLICE OF THE "GANG OF THE EVANGELISTS"...
BUT PERHAPS WE'LL BE ABLE TO PROVE OUR INNOCENCE...
THERE'S TOO MUCH EVIDENCE AGAINST YOU...IT WILL TAKE MONEY AND LAWYERS... HERE'S MY BOAT!...
WHY AREN'T YOU COMING WITH US?
BECAUSE SOMEBODY MUST DEFEND YOU...IF I RAN TOO, YOU'D STILL BE CHASED ...GO NOW...

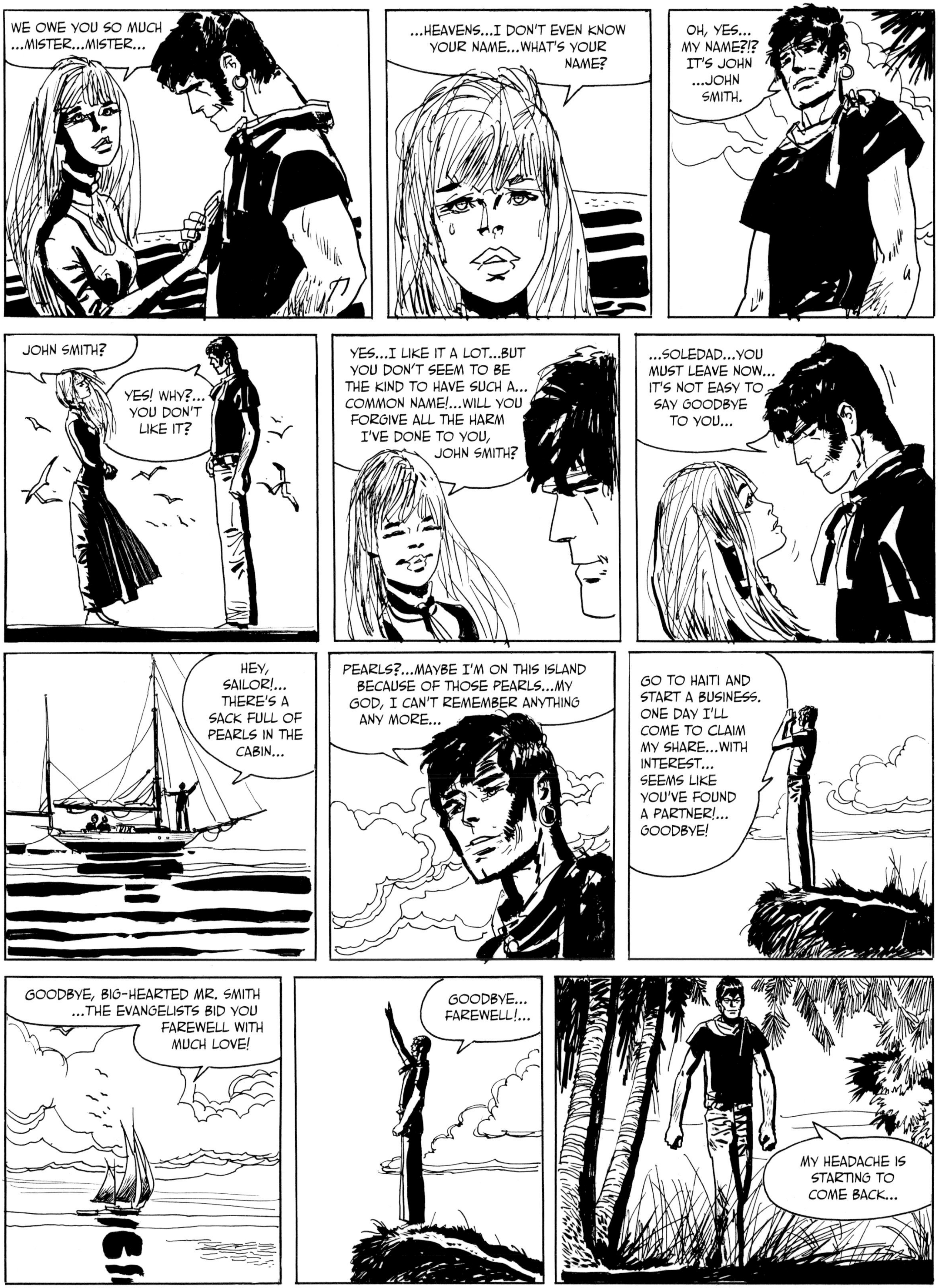
WE OWE YOU SO MUCH ...MISTER...MISTER...
...HEAVENS...I DON'T EVEN KNOW YOUR NAME...WHAT'S YOUR NAME?
OH, YES... MY NAME?!? IT'S JOHN ...JOHN ...JOHN SMITH.
JOHN SMITH?
YES! WHY?... YOU DON'T LIKE IT?
YES...I LIKE IT A LOT...BUT YOU DON'T SEEM TO BE THE KIND TO HAVE SUCH A... COMMON NAME!...WILL YOU FORGIVE ALL THE HARM I'VE DONE TO YOU, JOHN SMITH?
...SOLEDAD...YOU MUST LEAVE NOW... IT'S NOT EASY TO SAY GOODBYE TO YOU...
HEY, SAILOR!... THERE'S A SACK FULL OF PEARLS IN THE CABIN...
PEARLS?...MAYBE I'M ON THIS ISLAND BECAUSE OF THOSE PEARLS...MY GOD, I CAN'T REMEMBER ANYTHING ANY MORE...
GO TO HAITI AND START A BUSINESS. ONE DAY I'LL COME TO CLAIM MY SHARE...WITH INTEREST... SEEMS LIKE YOU'VE FOUND A PARTNER!... GOODBYE!
GOODBYE, BIG-HEARTED MR. SMITH ...THE EVANGELISTS BID YOU FAREWELL WITH MUCH LOVE!
GOODBYE... FAREWELL!...
MY HEADACHE IS STARTING TO COME BACK...

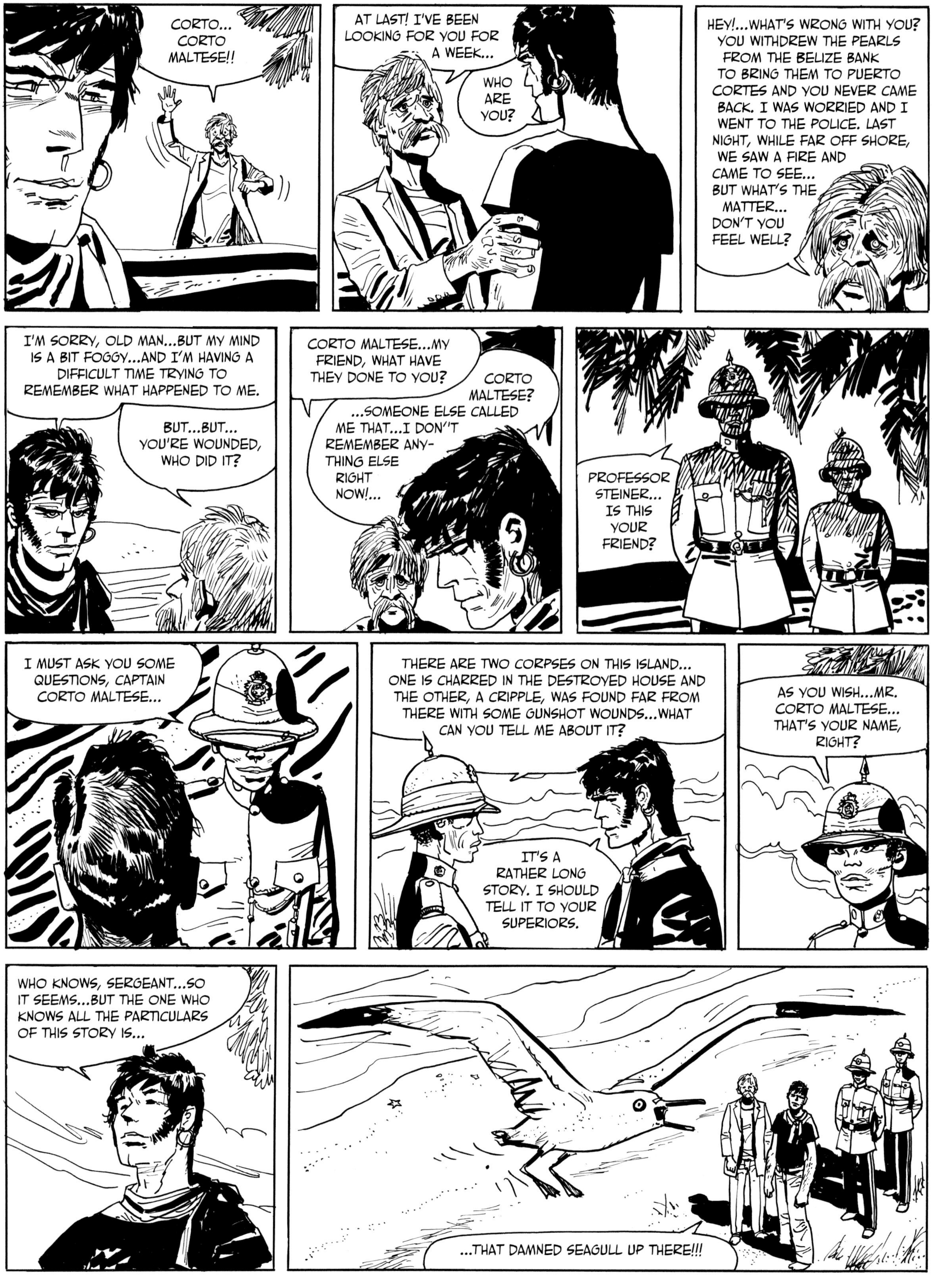
CORTO... CORTO MALTESE!!
AT LAST! I'VE BEEN LOOKING FOR YOU FOR A WEEK...
WHO ARE YOU?
HEY!...WHAT'S WRONG WITH YOU? YOU WITHDREW THE PEARLS FROM THE BELIZE BANK TO BRING THEM TO PUERTO CORTES AND YOU NEVER CAME BACK. I WAS WORRIED AND I WENT TO THE POLICE. LAST NIGHT, WHILE FAR OFF SHORE, WE SAW A FIRE AND CAME TO SEE... BUT WHAT'S THE MATTER... DON'T YOU FEEL WELL?
I'M SORRY, OLD MAN...BUT MY MIND IS A BIT FOGGY...AND I'M HAVING A DIFFICULT TIME TRYING TO REMEMBER WHAT HAPPENED TO ME.
BUT...BUT... YOU'RE WOUNDED, WHO DID IT?
CORTO MALTESE...MY FRIEND, WHAT HAVE THEY DONE TO YOU?
CORTO MALTESE?
...SOMEONE ELSE CALLED ME THAT...I DON'T REMEMBER ANY-THING ELSE RIGHT NOW!...
PROFESSOR STEINER... IS THIS YOUR FRIEND?
I MUST ASK YOU SOME QUESTIONS, CAPTAIN CORTO MALTESE...
THERE ARE TWO CORPSES ON THIS ISLAND... ONE IS CHARRED IN THE DESTROYED HOUSE AND THE OTHER, A CRIPPLE, WAS FOUND FAR FROM THERE WITH SOME GUNSHOT WOUNDS...WHAT CAN YOU TELL ME ABOUT IT?
IT'S A RATHER LONG STORY. I SHOULD TELL IT TO YOUR SUPERIORS.
AS YOU WISH...MR. CORTO MALTESE... THAT'S YOUR NAME, RIGHT?
WHO KNOWS, SERGEANT...SO IT SEEMS...BUT THE ONE WHO KNOWS ALL THE PARTICULARS OF THIS STORY IS...
...THAT DAMNED SEAGULL UP THERE!!!

The CORTO MALTESE Series

The Early Years
The Ballad of the Salty Sea
Under the Sign of Capricorn
Beyond the Windy Isles
Celtic Tales
The Ethiopian
In Siberia
Fable of Venice
The Golden House of Samarkand
Tango
The Secret Rose
Mu

Caniff, Sickles, Toth, and ...

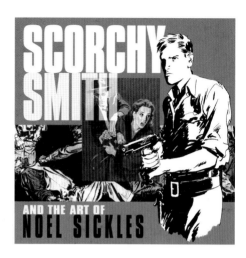

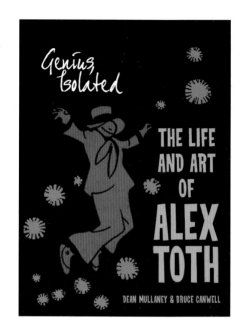

The Library of American Comics is dedicated to preserving, in definitive editions, the long and jubilantly creative history of the American newspaper comic strip, as well as publishing monographs featuring the leading and most influential cartoonists of all time. The Library was created in 2007 and ushered in a new Golden Age of strip collections. While our production values are archival, the material we present is fresh and exciting. Each Library release frames the comics so readers can start turning pages and immediately begin to enjoy strips that may be decades ir even a century old.

We invite you to visit us online at
LibraryofAmericanComics.com

THE LIBRARY OF AMERICAN COMICS